Genetics
may be the core of our existence,
but communication
is the key to our legacy.

—S. A. Hysen

A VERY DAIRY
CHRISTMAS

A NOVEL BY
SYLVIA HYSEN

1ST IMPRESSION PUBLISHING
LOS ANGELES

1ST IMPRESSION PUBLISHING
P.O. Box 10339
Burbank, CA 91510-0339
http://www.1stimpressionpublishing.com

For information regarding bulk purchases,
please contact 1st Impression Publishing at (818) 843-1300
or visit our website.

Jacket and Title page designed by Petrol Advertising, Los Angeles
Interior design and typography by Sylvia Hysen
Cover and Title page photo by Imke Schulze

10 9 8 7 6 5 4 3 2 1 0

Publisher's Cataloging-in-Publication Data available

Library of Congress Control Number: 2005933960

ISBN: 0-9763365-6-1

Manufactured in the United States of America

To Horst and Anna-Luise,
may you rest in peace
knowing that your legacy
touched so many hearts.

Contents

1

It's not pizza if it's not Patsy's

Callie Michaels shook her head in amusement as she watched her friends scatter to the different racks of clothing. Individually, they were unique. But as a group, they were extraordinary. Alexia Grant, Bianca Bertoli, and Danielle Hamilton—their backgrounds were as varied as their personal tastes. And yet, they were the glue that held Callie's dysfunctional life together. Her eyes glanced at her Tag Heuer watch, marking the time. They had a date for lunch and she refused to be late.

Fashion was Callie's forte, and if there really was a *fashion police*, she would be the head of the precinct. So when she found Alexia admiring herself in the mirror, she immediately came to her rescue. Animal prints were one thing, but looking like Jane of the Jungle was quite another. And when Danielle made the mistake of strutting past her in an extreme mini skirt, she questioned her motives, stating that perhaps a thong would be less revealing. Reluctantly, Danielle added a couple of inches to her hemline. But the kicker was when Bianca showed up in army fatigues and combat boots. Callie dragged her to the Baby Phat rack and insisted she drop the Destiny's Child survivor-look because yesterday's fashion was such a faux pas!

She felt like a sheepdog, rounding up her friends and herding them to the cash register.

And what a spectacle! Their purchases were extravagant, and the salesclerk's eyes widened in delight as he swiped their American Express cards and mentally tallied his commission.

On their way down the escalator, they stood frozen on the steps in exaggerated poses, much like the women that Callie's mother photographed would do. They looked liked models—tall and leggy—with long, perfectly styled hair, and they were dressed in the latest designer fashions.

When the escalator reached the bottom level, they broke their poses and rushed to the department store exit, attempting to squeeze all their purchases through the swinging doors. And they burst outside laughing—their arms loaded with more bags than even the savviest of shoppers could carry.

Jolted by the cool, brisk air of New York City in the fall, the girls were reminded that Christmas was just around the corner. Shoppers were everywhere and it was a miracle they avoided a fatal collision with all the foot traffic.

Alexia was immediately mesmerized by the gorgeous window display—and like a zombie, she burrowed her way through the crowds. Bloomingdale's did a great job of decorating for Christmas and they certainly knew how to attract teenage girls.

Callie breathed a sigh of relief as she hailed a cab. Noticing her missing friend, she yelled out, "Alex, get your butt over here or we're leaving without you!"

Alexia knew all too well that Callie meant what she said. And since she was from Los Angeles, she couldn't risk being left alone in the city. So she marched to the beat of Callie's drum and obediently delivered her bags to the back of the cab.

It took some effort to fit all their packages into the trunk, but with Callie's German ingenuity, she managed to do just that with a little room to spare. Then Alexia, Bianca, and Danielle jostled one another over the window seats. The only spot relinquished without argument was the front passenger side, which was Callie's. It was hers by right as unnamed, but acknowledged, leader of the group.

"I need to make a stop before we go to the restaurant," she said to the girls. "I have to pick up Zoey's Christmas present." Then she proceeded to give the driver specific directions to Tiffany's.

Her friends readily approved, knowing how much Callie was looking forward to spending time with her mother—something she didn't get to do very often.

The cab pulled up in front of the famous jewelry store and Callie jumped out. "I'll be back in a sec," she announced. And just as Alexia was about to unbuckle her seatbelt, she popped back in as if she were a mind reader. "Stay in the car, Alex. This isn't about *you*."

Disappointed, Alexia sat back in her seat, rolled down her window, and took in all the unfamiliar sights and sounds of the city.

Callie's face was well known to the staff at Tiffany's since her mother was the preferred photographer for their jewelry line. They could tell by her demeanor that she wasn't there to browse or chat, but rather to pick up the package that had been set aside for her in the back. She returned to the cab swiftly and immediately resumed barking orders.

She checked her watch again. "There's a $20.00 tip in it for you if you get us to the restaurant by noon," she informed the driver. It was going to be close, but Callie knew money was a universal language and that even a magic carpet couldn't have moved them through the streets any faster. The swarthy immigrant happily put the pedal to the metal.

In one of the speediest cab rides she had ever taken, Callie and her friends arrived on time and in one piece. She sorted their purchases and shepherded the girls into the restaurant. The maitre de knew her by name and led the group to a table where Callie's mother was waiting, looking as usual—gorgeous, casual, and elegant, all at the same time.

Her daughter first, and then the other girls, greeted Zoey with international hellos and European kisses, which just missed her cheek. With a nod, she indicated that the maitre de should use an empty table as a storage area for the packages, and the girls chaotically arranged themselves in their seats.

Callie—usually the one with the most to say—was silent as she watched her mother ask how everyone was and about their families. Her friends, because they knew her so well, could see a wistful look flit across her face. But when her mother finally addressed her, it had vanished—replaced by an air of defiance.

Zoey took a good, long look at her daughter. Behind that tough exterior, hid a sensitive and vulnerable little girl. And though she would never openly admit it, she realized the chip on Callie's shoulder was a direct result of the neglect and empty promises she was forced to endure over the years.

Zoey's career came first, and when other mothers were playing *make believe* and reading bedtime stories, she was out clawing her way to the top. And it paid off. She achieved world renowned celebrity status in high fashion photography. Her calendar was booked months in advance and she made more money than most CEOs of Fortune 500 companies. Life was good. Now, if *only* she could get past the guilt that consumed her each time she looked into the eyes of her neglected child.

"What's wrong—why are you staring? Did you forget who I am?" Callie taunted. If the truth were known, she would have given up every ounce of privilege for just one uninterrupted weekend with her mother. And while she loved her independence, she would have gladly traded it for even the slightest amount of parental supervision.

"No, just thinking how grown up you are. Seems like only yesterday you were toddling around, taking the film out of my camera."

Callie rolled her eyes. "I'm sure that went over well!"

Zoey continued, "I remember one Christmas—you were about two. You gathered all the film in the house and used it as tinsel for the tree. You were so proud of your work."

The girls laughed and Callie had to smile, too. "I don't remember doing that."

"Well you weren't very old, and we didn't have any film left to capture the moment. The only record is in my memory."

"I can't even remember being at home for Christmas—let alone having our own tree," Callie divulged. "You sure it wasn't somebody else's kid?"

"Real funny," Zoey replied, accustomed to her daughter's subtle digs. "This was at your grandparents' in Wisconsin. But it's not like you've ever suffered at Christmas."

"No, you're right. I have everything *money* can buy."

Zoey was about to argue the point when the waiter arrived and asked if they were ready to order. He clearly recognized her by now and appeared a little star struck, which only managed to frustrate Callie even more.

"I'll have the organic veggie pita with low fat Swiss and a cucumber salad—DRESSING ON THE SIDE—and a diet Coke with lemon," Callie said emphatically.

Danielle politely asked for the same, and Alexia made it a trio.

The waiter looked to Bianca who was still browsing the menu. "I'll have the medallions of beef in béarnaise sauce, red potatoes, sautéed mushrooms, and..." was all she got out before Callie interrupted.

"BIANCA!"

"Oh Callie, stop being such a drag. We're in the city now. We're supposed to be having fun." But Bianca saw the look of horror on Callie's face and relented. "Oh fine...just give me what *she's* having!"

Zoey objected. "Bianca, get what you want."

"That's okay, Zoey. We wouldn't want to upset the nutrition Nazi."

The waiter stood dumbfounded, not knowing which order to write.

"You heard her," Callie snapped, "she wants what I want."

Zoey felt badly for the flustered young man and quickly interjected, "Make it easy on yourself. I'll have the same thing."

Unfortunately, he made the mistake of asking for an autograph and was forced to suffer Callie's wrath. She slapped the menus into his stomach. "Sure, dude—right after you bring us our lunch. I'm starving!"

Embarrassed by her daughter's behavior, Zoey flashed a smile and graciously added, "I'd be happy to."

As soon as the waiter was out of sight, she turned to her daughter with exasperation. "Grow up, Callie! You're getting too old for this."

"I will, if *you* will," she responded in a contentious manner.

Danielle, having the utmost respect for adults, came to Zoey's rescue. "You shouldn't speak to your mother like that, Callie."

"Well if she ever acted like a mother, Dani, I wouldn't."

Zoey had enough of her daughter's insolence. "Okay, knock it off!"

Realizing she crossed the line, Callie felt the need to further express her feelings. "I'm sorry—I'm just not as impressed with you as everyone else seems to be."

"And I'm sorry you feel that way."

Callie's friends knew better than to get involved in a mother-daughter cat fight, so the table remained uncomfortably silent for what seemed like an eternity. Finally, Zoey broke the tension by asking the girls about their plans for the Christmas holiday.

Alexia's extended family—meaning hordes of stepbrothers and sisters—were gathering in Malibu. Some years she wondered exactly who her stepparents were as they seemed to change as often as the daily news. Danielle's family would be having a traditional Hamptons holiday, which she found incredibly boring. And Bianca would spend most of the time playing hostess in her father's restaurant. Granted, it was an upscale restaurant, but Bianca was the only one in the group whose family actually expected her to do work. Most of the girls at Ridgecrest Prep didn't even have to do the dishes! They had maids for that. But Bianca's was a rather old-fashioned Italian family, and the only way to get out of doing chores was to either blackmail one of her older brothers or beat them to a pulp, which didn't happen very often.

Danielle finally asked, "So what are you two doing?"

Zoey answered before Callie could make another snide remark. "We're going skiing…in Aspen. Our reservations were confirmed this morning."

"What? Really?" Callie asked in a rush, both delighted and apprehensive at the same time.

"Yep, Roxanne called me with the confirmation number while I was waiting for you."

"And what are the odds this time, *Mother*?"

"I'll cover any bets you place," Zoey answered smugly, knowing her daughter was *way* too good a poker player for a young debutante. "My agent cleared the whole month, and we're going! I promise."

Callie's face broke into the first real smile they had seen since arriving at the restaurant, and the remainder of the meal passed in happy chatter. She even reminded her mother to sign an autograph for the waiter before they left.

After lunch, Zoey escorted the foursome to the limousine that was waiting to take them back to their exclusive boarding school. She hugged each of the girls and wished them well on their mid-terms.

When it came to Callie, she squeezed extra tight, whispering into her ear, "I love you, baby. Take care of yourself."

"I always do," she replied, breaking their embrace.

Callie felt pretty good by then, and once settled in the limousine, wrote a note to the driver and passed it through the window partition. She announced that they had one last stop to make before heading home.

The girls were used to Callie making plans without consulting them and they trusted her judgement, but they were a little shocked at the run down area they drove to. And it wasn't until they approached Patsy's—one of the most famous pizzerias in all of New York City—that Bianca's face lit up.

"Does this mean what I think it means?" she asked enthusiastically. "I haven't had pizza since summer."

"Yeah well…it is almost Christmas, and I was pretty rough on you back at the restaurant," Callie admitted, acting like an apologetic parent might.

But when the limousine pulled up to the curb, Bianca completely changed her mind. "On second thought, why don't we just head back to school. I have a paper due tomorrow."

This made Callie suspicious since Bianca never thought of homework before she thought of food—especially when it was this close. She quickly realized the problem. A familiar delivery van was parked directly in front of the limousine. On the back doors, in big bold letters, were the words *BERTOLI GOURMET MEATS*, and Callie knew from experience that it belonged to one of Bianca's many uncles.

"C'mon B, what are the odds?" Callie said, trying to remember exactly which uncle owned the meat business.

"Are you kidding? They're completely stacked against us!" she insisted.

Bianca loved the men in her family, but she was getting tired of being viewed as just another insignificant female. "Oh all right. It'll be worth it…" She paused before finishing her sentence. "…to watch *you* pig out on a big, fat, greasy piece of carb-filled dough!"

Callie cringed and smacked her best friend in the arm as Danielle responded with "Ew!" and Alexia added, "Gross!"

And sure enough, when Bianca and Callie entered Patsy's they were affectionately accosted by Uncle Vito who insisted on introducing them to everyone in the joint, including the customers.

Bianca was completely embarrassed by the time they got back to the limousine, but she did have good news. The pizza was free! And Uncle Vito—while making them very late—totally redeemed himself by presenting the girls with a huge gift basket of gourmet cheeses from his van. Callie didn't make the connection then, but the name on the gold cellophane wrapper read *MICHELSOHN & MEYERS GOURMET CHEESE.*

And the pizza? Well, it only lasted about six blocks.

2

Promises aren't meant to be broken

In a very different setting, Elsa and Johan Michelsohn were finishing their evening meal in the small dairy community of Deer Creek, Wisconsin. In the old German tradition, Elsa had prepared sauerbraten, fried potatoes, cheeses and bread. Their plates had already been cleared, and they were about to have a dessert of apple strudel with vanilla sauce.

The couple had been married for just over fifty years and had remained best friends as well as husband and wife since their immigration to the United States in the 1950s. Over the years, they had developed their own comfortable routines, and it was their custom at dinner to discuss the events of the day and the needs of their business.

"Any news on your order?" Elsa asked, knowing Johan was eagerly awaiting an acquisition to the farm.

"Only that it hasn't arrived yet!" he replied, frustrated by the situation. "They keep telling me to track it on the Internet, and I feel like a dinosaur when I tell them I don't have a computer."

Elsa knew that Johan had been anxiously awaiting his shipment, and that he was becoming more impatient by the day. "Well, it is being shipped from California."

Johan continued his rant. "Every time I call, I get this automated recording that routes me through four different messages before I finally get a human being who tells me exactly what I already know—that it hasn't arrived!" He shook his head in frustration. "I tell you Elsa, I never thought technology could be so useless."

"Ja well…you should've paid for overnight delivery," she insisted, implying his frugality finally got the best of him.

"And what, blow the deal of the century?"

A stranger would have thought Johan had purchased the Mona Lisa for five bucks, he looked so proud. And Elsa knew it wasn't a matter of being able to afford the purchase, but rather wasting money where it wasn't necessary.

Her eyes twinkled as she thought about the phone conversation she had overheard. "I'm surprised that poor man didn't offer to pay *you*, after what you put him through!"

Johan laughed at her observation.

"You know," Elsa said matter-of-factly, "I remember a time when you were willing to pay well above market price to own an original oil painting from an unknown artist."

"And I would have paid four times that amount to keep it out of the hands of Heinrich Putzkammer. He didn't appreciate your talents like I did."

Elsa blushed at the ancient rivalry, and her mind drifted to memories of their lives long ago in Dresden, Germany.

The Saxony region, where she and Johan were born, was famous for its music and fine art and was considered one of Europe's premiere cultural and transportation centers. Elsa reflected on her grandfather and the setback he suffered when his brother nearly lost the family fortune at the turn of the century. How he managed to rebuild a life of privilege and prominence during such an unstable period was a tribute to his German acumen and a mystery to many of his colleagues.

Elsa remembered her childhood vividly. She thought about her nanny, her private tutors, and all the luxuries she enjoyed, and how her parents—God rest their souls—recognized early on that she was unusually talented at painting. They provided her with both exposure to works of art and training to encourage her gift. Memories of the family art collection swelled in her mind as she envisioned the Renoir hanging above the mantel and the Faberge egg sitting on the piano like a shimmering star.

Her mother's salon was a gathering place for the artistic and intellectual minds of their region, and the family dinner parties were always elegant, formal affairs with stimulating conversation. She was allowed to attend as long as she behaved, and her parents eagerly displayed her canvases to their friends.

"Putzkammer," she reflected, "now there's a name I haven't heard in years."

Elsa didn't like thinking about the war, as was common with most Germans who had lived through that period. But hearing the name Putzkammer took her back to a time she would rather forget altogether. He was the son of a Nazi official who frequently visited her family, and just the mention of his name brought back images of horror and devastation that plagued her beloved city and forever changed the course of her life.

She remembered how the Nazi regime started as a slow spread across Germany, with only a few uniforms here and there. But then like a swarm of greedy locusts, they were suddenly everywhere. Elsa's family had ties with both the art world and German society, and the Nazis sought to establish their authority in both. Her parents were forced by necessity to tolerate their presence while not welcoming it.

But in an effort to minimize Elsa's contact with the war, she was sent to live with her cousins in Austria. They were farmers who produced cheeses and other marketable goods, and it was there that she learned how to cook and clean and the basics of making cheese. She laughed to herself, remembering the first time she had milked a cow, and not very successfully either. But it didn't take her long to set aside her lace-trimmed dresses in exchange for hard work and more practical clothing.

"Ach! Putzkammer. That shmuck!" Johan protested. "He rode the coattail of his father's rank...always trying to profit from his connections. I doubt he would have known a Picasso from a kindergartner's finger painting."

Elsa laughed. "And you would have?"

"Humph!" Johan scoffed, having spent much of his savings making sure that Elsa's paintings didn't fall into the wrong hands. And Heinrich Putzkammer's were *definitely* the wrong hands!

"Well he did admire my work, so he couldn't have been that bad," Elsa offered in his defense.

"No, Elsa, he admired *you*. You were just too naive to recognize it."

Johan was a couple of years older than his wife and came from a family of scholars. He decided early on to become an engineer and despite the difficulties of continuing his education during the war, managed to keep his focus. Because his early performance in that field was so promising, and because the Third Reich desperately wanted to maintain an edge over the countries it fought, he was allowed to continue his studies and was not forced to enlist. But his hatred toward the regime was so strong that even now the memories of his youth turned his face red with anger, and Elsa could see that it was time to change the subject.

"Did I mention my dishwasher is making that noise again?" She knew she could always distract him with practical matters.

Johan paused before answering, trying to recall the last time he had worked on it. He started thinking out loud, and Elsa only half paid attention. She had managed to calm him down, but her thoughts were still in the past.

By the time the war ended, Germany was in shambles and much of its industry would be regulated by the Allies. Johan's colleagues scattered to various countries and would never come together again to rebuild their own nation. There would have been plenty of work for Johan as Germany rebuilt, but he realized this would put him in close contact with those people who had collaborated with the Nazis, and for him to do so would mean compromising his personal beliefs. He loved Germany, but as he saw it his only option was to leave his homeland and pursue opportunities overseas.

Elsa's dreams of a career in art also dimmed during the years following the war. The balls and the elegant dinners were a thing of the past, and life—as she had known it—ceased to exist. For the first time, her future was uncertain. "How ironic," she thought to herself, that her cousin's farm would be the foundation of her destiny.

As they finished dessert, her mind returned to the present and to her favorite topic—their granddaughter, Callie.

Elsa began the conversation timidly, almost as if she were afraid of the answer. "Did Zoey call you back, Johan?" She had asked this question so many times before with the same results.

Johan knew how much the matter pained Elsa, and aside from missing his granddaughter, he was becoming quite angry with Zoey for ignoring their requests to see her.

"No liebchen, she didn't." He was overwhelmed by the sadness in her eyes. "Don't worry…I'll get through. And this time, I won't give up. If she doesn't call back by the end of next week, I'll get Klaus to take care of it. He'll know what to do. He *does* administer Callie's trust fund."

"Oh Johan, do we really need to involve an attorney?"

"Klaus is a good man. He's handled our business for years. I'll just explain the situation and tell him to be fair. I'm sure he can convince Zoey to see things our way," he said confidently. "Eleven years without our granddaughter is far too long." Johan spoke firmly as he reached for Elsa's hand. "Callie *will* be here for Christmas—I promise."

Now Johan was a man of his word, and he wasn't in the habit of making commitments he couldn't keep. He was tired of seeing his beloved wife in such agony. After all, they weren't asking for much—just a week or two of Callie's time. He knew what he had to do to get his granddaughter back, and he was prepared to launch a full scale attack if necessary.

ZOEY WAS IN THE DARKROOM of her studio, analyzing the last roll of film she had shot. There were only a few days left to complete the Victoria's Secret spring catalogue, and there wasn't any room for error.

Victoria's Secret was one of her most enjoyable accounts as well as one of the *bread and butter* basics for which the name Zoey Michaels was known. Not only had it helped her gain her reputation in a very competitive business that was usually male dominated, but it also rewarded her with life-long friendships with top models like Tyra Banks,

Claudia Schiffer, and Heidi Klum. Zoey knew how to wear clothes with style and she knew how to show them off to maximize their potential. Designers and models, alike, insisted on her for their portfolios. And she gladly accommodated them in between agency assignments—it kept her calendar booked, her bank account filled, and her mind occupied.

Her hectic schedule also gave her an excuse to avoid personal relationships. Oh, she was asked out often and by attractive and desirable men, but she only accepted when there was an event she wanted to attend. And when they would call back to ask for another date, she always managed to be out of town or working on a long project. Her heart had been broken once, and she promised *never* to let it happen again.

Zoey heard a tap on the door followed by her assistant's voice. "Is it safe?"

"Yeah, come in Roxy."

"I finished the breakdown for tomorrow's shoot, made all the confirmations, and gathered the lenses you requested. They're over there by the front door." Roxanne pointed to a large black bag across the room. "Don't forget, Diego said he would be a little late. So we'll have to rearrange the hair and makeup list in the morning."

"Damn him, why does he always have to pick the critical days to be late?" Zoey blurted in anguish.

"Well he did tell you this before he committed to taking the job, so you had the option of hiring someone else." Roxanne was far from the normal assistant. She was young and aggressive, overly pierced and heavily tattooed—and Zoey was lucky to have her!

"Why don't you tell me how you really feel, Roxy!" Zoey cracked a smile then continued, "You're right—I'm wrong. So what else is new? But I'm still allowed to vent, aren't I?"

"Absolutely. That's why I'm leaving now," Roxanne announced with certainty. "Oh, and you might want to check your message machine. It's blinking."

"Yeah…so? When isn't it?" Zoey replied. "Now go home and feed your cat!"

Roxanne grabbed her coat from the sofa and walked to the door. She turned back to Zoey and confessed, "You know I don't *really* have a cat."

Zoey squinted her eyes before whispering, "Yeah, Roxy. I figured that out a long time ago."

Once Roxanne cleared the doorway, Zoey engaged the series of deadbolts one would expect to find in a New York loft. The apartment was moderately furnished and far too clean to be lived in regularly. As she made her way to the kitchen, she noticed the red indicator light flashing on her answering machine and remembered Roxanne's words. Hardly in the mood for added stress, Zoey reluctantly hit the play button.

"You have twelve messages," a generic voice announced.

She reacted with frustration, shaking her head and lashing out. "Leave me alone!"

BEEP.

"Zoey, Darling." She recognized the deep, raspy Italian voice. "It's Donatella. I'm lining up my schedule, and I need you at the end of January. Have your agent call my assistant. I'm counting on you. *Don't disappoint me!*"

Donatella, or more commonly known by her last name, Versace, was a long-time client and dear friend of Zoey's. She rarely scheduled her own bookings, so it was an honor to receive her call.

Zoey realized at that moment that any message, regardless of her mood, was worth listening to. So she stopped the machine, grabbed a diet soda from the refrigerator, took out a notepad from the counter drawer, and hit the play button again.

BEEP.

The messages rolled off one by one, from a diverse group of callers, all equally important and by most standards, very impressive. And finally, a message that had her frozen in her seat. She knew the voice all too well. It was her father-in-law.

"Zoey?" A thick, German accent resonated through her soul. "It's Johan. I want to talk to you about sending Callie for Christmas. Please return my call as soon as you get this message." Johan cleared his throat and continued speaking, "And if this is Zoey's helper, please have her call her father-in-law as soon as possible." He paused for a split second then concluded, "Thank you."

BEEP.

Zoey took a deep breath and hit the stop button on the machine. Then speaking out loud as if he could hear her, she responded, "Sorry Johan…I just can't help you."

She loved her daughter more than anything, and though it often appeared they didn't get along, Zoey knew in her heart it was due to her unconventional lifestyle. She had committed to taking Callie to Aspen for Christmas, and there was no way in hell she was going to break her promise.

Not this time.

3

Acceptance isn't always for sale

Ridgecrest Prep was old—ancient in the girls' opinion. It held an air of elegance and dignity and looked as though it had been built to last for centuries. Constructed of stone and brick, with steep gables and high chimneys, it bore a distinct resemblance to castles and European manor houses.

The lawns were as exquisitely maintained as the buildings themselves—to the extent that Callie and her friends frequently joked about planting Dixie cups and using the grass as a putting green. They mentioned it once in front of the groundskeeper, and he nearly died of a heart attack. Of course, that was the reaction they had hoped to achieve.

Inside, the individual rooms were as impressive as the exterior and similar to what most of the students were accustomed to in their own homes. The common areas and the library had ornate furnishings carved by master carpenters, and the lavish window treatments and custom upholstery added sophistication to the decor.

Quiet elegance was the overwhelming impression one had upon entering the massive double doors to Waldorf Hall. However, *quiet*, was not the keyword as one approached the gymnasium.

The voices of girls as they yelled and cheered, the sound of a bouncing ball, the coach's whistle, and the squeak of sneakers bellowed from the windows. Anyone not used to the school would have expected to see a whole squadron inside. But that wasn't the case.

It was early afternoon, and P.E. was nearly over. The girls in the class had divided themselves as they usually did—Callie's group against the snobbiest, and least athletic, girls in the school.

With about thirty seconds remaining, Bianca passed the ball to Callie at the top of the circle where she took it in for a lay up. Kaitlin Marriott, who had appointed herself as Callie's main rival, moved in front of her just as she jumped into the air and took the shot.

Without hesitating, Callie lifted her arm and watched the ball graze the backboard before falling neatly through the net. At the same time, her body—still moving with the momentum it carried down the court—crashed into her opponent who had attempted *the block*. Kaitlin landed hard on the floor.

"Great shot, Callie!" Danielle cheered.

"I've seen better," Kaitlin whined, as she stood and dusted off her backside.

"Yeah, but from the floor? Great view from down there!" Alexia observed.

"Callie fouled me."

"Hate to tell you Kaitlin, but your feet weren't set. You would've been called for a foul in the game. And the way Callie shoots free throws, your team would be down another couple of points!" Coach Humphries interjected.

Kaitlin's frown deepened. She would have argued the point, but class was over and it was time to head for the showers.

The locker room retained much of the same decor as the rest of the school, with the exception of a slight odor of sweaty socks, which was covered to some extent by strategically placed air fresheners. It looked similar to an upscale country club and was fully carpeted, with oak woodwork and benches. Even the lockers were designed of wood and large enough that a dress could be hung up without gathering wrinkles. The counters were made of marble, the sinks of porcelain, and there was a myriad of blow dryers and curling irons lining the walls. The towels were large and plush, with the school emblem embroidered in gold; and shampoo, hair spray, and shower caps were readily available. The school even provided an attendant—just in case the students ran low on anything. Ridgecrest Prep was a school, but it catered to its students like a five-star hotel.

The girls took everything for granted. They were used to a life of privilege. Anything else would have been a shock to their system, so the room didn't impress them much. But as nonchalant as they were to their surroundings, Callie's group was very cognizant of the enemy—Kaitlin and her coterie of pretentious snobs. They were positioned in their own area of the locker room, which they liked to pretend was a better location than the corner that Callie and her friends had staked out. Even here, the lines were drawn.

Callie, Danielle, and Alexia were dressing at their lockers when Bianca—fresh from the shower—started collecting money from Kaitlin's team, who in spite of a lousy record, still thought they were better at basketball. Of course, in *their* minds, they were better at almost everything else, too.

Bianca snapped towels, slammed lockers, and stole talcum powder from the unfortunate souls who owed her money. Most of the girls were more than happy to part with their cash because they believed she had mob connections—a never-ending source of amusement to her friends who were not above exploiting the clout it gave them. But if the truth were known, the closest Bianca's family came to the mafia was sharing a distinct love for the tiramisu from Little Italy. Just the thought of that heavenly pastry was enough to make Bianca drool and long for home.

As Callie put on her school uniform—pleated skirt, white blouse, knee highs, penny loafers, tie, and blazer—she thought about the incident on the basketball court and how it was likely to affect her. All the girls at Ridgecrest came from wealthy families—they had to, tuition was over $30,000.00 a year. Not to mention the other things that were required to fit in like designer clothing, expensive jewelry and of course, a personal trainer. Some of the girls even had plastic surgeons! And if you didn't have the right street address and traceable family lineage—forget it, you didn't stand a chance.

Callie's mother had to work, and her family didn't come from *old money*. Still, she spent the same way and bought the same things. But in the eyes of some of the parents and their daughters, Callie would never quite belong. Considering that most of them acted like Kaitlin, she really didn't mind, but sometimes it made things tense. Like at that moment when Danielle pulled the invitation for the annual Christmas Social from her locker and asked if Callie was going.

"No, way. Those things are so gay," Callie answered as firmly as she could. "Besides, Zoey is out of town all next week."

"Like that's a surprise!" Kaitlin remarked, hoping to dig the knife a little deeper.

Alexia immediately consoled Callie. "Who cares, we'll be there. Besides, *we're* your family."

Bianca was just about finished with her collections and caught the tail end of Alexia's comment. "Where? Where are we going to be?"

Danielle answered, "The Christmas party. Callie doesn't want to go without her mom."

Kaitlin piped in again, "Can you blame her? I'd feel like crap if my mother made a habit of ditching me during the holidays, and besides it's for families. She'd look like an idiot."

"Well if my family looked like yours, Kaitlin, I'd rather show up with the Sopranos," Alexia blurted with her face buried in her locker.

Bianca, hearing what sounded like an ethnic slur, peered around to Alexia. "Hey, what's wrong with the Sopranos?" then turned to Kaitlin, "And you still owe me money…and for the record, Callie is part of my family."

Kaitlin, having some misguided idea of what *family* meant to Bianca, immediately started hemming and hawing her way out of that part of the discussion and instead started to point out that gambling was illegal.

"Then stop making bets!" Callie demanded, shaking her head in disgust.

While Kaitlin searched her locker for money, Bianca nonchalantly spit her gum onto the bench where she had been sitting. Callie's group watched out of the corner of their eyes as Kaitlin sat back down directly upon it. "Sorry, no cash. You'll just have to accept an IOU."

The girls tried to suppress their laughter without success.

"What?" Kaitlin blurted defensively. "You don't think I'm good for it?" She cringed at the thought of being in debt to losers!

But it wasn't until Callie and her friends left the locker room that they felt truly vindicated. An angry scream—followed by a lot of bad language—echoed through the halls when Kaitlin realized she had gum stuck to her butt!

Later that night, Bianca knocked on Callie's door. She could see the light shining from underneath and figured it was still safe. Upon hearing a response, she entered the room.

Callie was under her covers reading Albert Einstein's *Evolution of Physics* with an old, tattered rag doll by her side. A framed picture of her as an infant with her parents was displayed on the nightstand next to her bed.

The girls were allowed to decorate their rooms as they chose, with only a few overriding censorships in place—all in the name of good taste, of course. Callie's room was feminine but modern. She incorporated antique brass lamps with the most up-to-date computers and peripherals. And the draperies would have been strangely out of place, made from moss green velvet and chartreuse silk, except for the way Callie had tied them into the rest of the room. Only Bianca and a few of her close friends knew that they were reproductions of the curtains from her favorite movie.

An authentic poster from *Gone with the Wind* was hung on the wall; and surrounding it were black and white photos of Vivien Leigh and Clark Gable. Callie had liked that movie for as long as she could remember. The idea of a dashing Rhett coming to her rescue was irresistible. And in all honesty, she loved how Scarlett was afraid of nothing and no one, and she found it easy to relate to her character. She hoped, however, that if and when she ever did meet her Rhett, his ears would be just a little bit smaller!

And of course, being a teenage girl, there was a dressing table—a replica of Scarlett's, covered with more cosmetics than Scarlett would have dreamt of owning, and certainly more than any female needed.

A comfortable armchair in the corner of the room was half burried with clothes that Callie hadn't quite gotten around to putting away. But that was okay because a maid came in every other day and did it for her, for a small out-of-pocket fee. Callie hated anything as mundane as chores, learning early on that most of the staff was eager to do a little more work for a few extra bucks, and she gladly took advantage of their services.

"You awake?" Bianca asked unnecessarily. "I couldn't sleep."

"Yep—what's up?"

Bianca dashed across the room with a package tucked under her arm and grabbed the book from Callie's hands. "*This* is not required reading for the semester, or for that matter, this school. Are you turning *geek* on me or something?"

"If being smart makes me a geek, then I guess I am," Callie laughed, knowing Bianca didn't mean it that way. "Zoey told me my dad was into this kind of stuff. So I guess I got it from him."

"I thought he was a war photographer?" Bianca asked, knowing very little about Callie's father.

"It's called a photojournalist, but that doesn't mean he didn't like science."

"Yeah right. Well if you ask me, I think you should be reading classic authors instead like Stephen King and Jackie Collins, but not something this heavy. It'll weigh down your brain and you won't be able to think about boys or Christmas, or clothes, or boys. You know—the important things!"

Having presented her theory, Bianca offered Callie a sample of the cheese Uncle Vito had given them and said with her mouth full, "This stuff is scrumpt-u-lescent! Got any crackers?" But she changed the subject before Callie could answer. "You know, you never talk about him—your dad I mean. How come?"

"I don't remember him. He was killed when I was four. They left me with his parents on some stinking farm in the middle of nowhere while they were off exploiting the injustices of war." Callie picked up the picture from her nightstand and examined it as if it were a piece of evidence.

"Doesn't your mom talk about him?" Bianca couldn't fathom such a concept. It was impossible to keep anything quiet in her family.

"No. When I was young, I would ask. But she'd just cry, so eventually I stopped asking. She did mention though, that his parents have our photo albums and that I could visit their farm some day. But that sounds like an awful lot of torture just to see some lousy pictures. Ycch!" she said with emphasis. Callie set the frame back on the nightstand. "Sometimes it seems as if my life began after my father died, at least the life I remember. All I have from him is that old picture and Mandy."

"Who's Mandy?" Bianca asked.

Callie grabbed the rag doll and waved it in front of her friend. "Mandy?"

"Oh—you mean the mop," Bianca teased.

"She's not a mop, Bianca!"

"Nope you're right. Most mops don't sleep in beds, most of them have handles, and most people don't put faces on them." Bianca continued to tease Callie until she lightened up and they both had tears of laughter streaming down their faces.

"Okay! That's it! Get out! You broke your diet and talked me into breaking mine. You made fun of Mandy…" Callie sniffed, as though her feelings were hurt. "…and you interrupted my reading."

"Sure! Eat my food and laugh at my jokes then throw me out into the cold, cruel hallways of Ridgecrest—I'll remember that!" and Bianca hugged her friend good night before heading off to bed.

4

What goes around comes around

The cafeteria was noisy—silverware clicking on plates, trays sliding across counters, and the high-pitched chattering of a hundred or so teenage girls. But the energy in the room hadn't affected Callie and her friends just yet, as their eyes were still foggy with sleep.

They weren't morning people. Instead, they preferred to stay up late gabbing away or even doing homework, and it was their firm belief that the world would be a much better place if the day started at noon. So the last person they wanted to see was Kaitlin Marriott, but that didn't prevent her and her clique from stopping by their table.

The girls looked up, knowing full well that Kaitlin was on a mission. But no matter how fatigued and lethargic they felt, they were always prepared to give back whatever she dished out.

Bianca decided that going on the attack was the best defense, so she spoke up first. "I trust you have our money?"

"Gambling is illegal," Kaitlin argued. She *was* on a mission and intended to put Callie and her band of undesirables—with the exception of Danielle—firmly in their places once and for all.

"Tell *that* to the Headmistress," Alexia chimed, annoyed by the whole thing and tired of Kaitlin's double standards.

Kaitlin threw the ten dollars she owed at Bianca who happily accepted the bill and said, "You can leave now. Thank you." Bianca had her mouth full of a bagel with a mere smidgen of cream cheese on it and waved her dismissal to Kaitlin. She had no intention of letting this parasite disrupt the miniscule meal Callie had allowed her.

But Kaitlin remained in her place and spoke again. "By the way, someone here didn't make the DAR list."

"The what?" Callie asked, giving Kaitlin more time than she deserved.

"Bingo, that would answer the question of who," she gloated.

Danielle whispered into Callie's ear, "The Daughters of the American Republic. It has to do with lineage." And then she impassively recited, "The DAR, founded in 1890, is a volunteer women's service organization dedicated to promoting patriotism, preserving American history, and securing America's future through better education for children."

Her friends looked at her like an alien had just invaded her body. "Whoa! What are you, possessed or something?" Bianca questioned.

"Is that right, Kaitlin?" Danielle said with a look of superiority. "But the one thing they don't mention in the brochures is that the organization is exclusive and snobbish!"

Danielle knew that Kaitlin's mother was trying to curry favor with her family, and had been attempting to wheedle invitations to the Hamilton home for as long as she could remember. But Mrs. Hamilton seemed to have a photographic memory for the family trees of all the Ridgecrest DAR members, and the Marriott's were on the fringe themselves, as their connection was distant. And though they had been accepted by the organization, they weren't the class of people the Hamiltons cared to socialize with.

Kaitlin stared at Callie with intensity. "Why do you hang out with these losers, Danielle? Your ancestors would *not* approve!"

Danielle tried to act nonchalant as she whispered into Callie's ear, "I told you, remember? My great, great something or other was Alexander Hamilton."

Callie remained dazed and confused. She wasn't able to process this much information so early in the day.

Danielle continued, "You know, the dude on the ten dollar bill?"

Callie still didn't get it.

"Like this!" Danielle grabbed the currency from Bianca's hand and thrust it into Callie's face.

"You were serious about that?" Callie knew that Danielle tended to exaggerate.

"God Callie, you're *so* out of your league." Kaitlin's words were fierce.

"You suck, Marriott!" Bianca was getting pissed by now, and her Italian temper was beginning to rise like the lava in Mt. Vesuvius.

"And you have poor English Bianca, but then again, Italians were never known for their class." Kaitlin was pushing her luck with this one.

"Like you would know a thing about class?"

"I wouldn't be so smug Bertoli, you barely made the list yourself. It's a good thing your dad decided to marry outside his neighborhood." Kaitlin just didn't know when to quit.

"Yeah right—it's just that your stupid DAR book doesn't go back far enough to trace the Romans. We had civilizations when your ancestors were still living in caves and wearing furs."

Bianca was about ready to blow, and she had good reason. Of all the girls in Callie's group, she was the closest to knowing her true identity. Her father was one hundred percent Italian, and if men were gorgeous, he was. Her mother was half Italian and the other half was directly connected to John Hancock, the only Catholic to sign the *Declaration of Independence*. The trust fund her mother controlled was four times that of the Marriott's. But when her parents met and fell in love, her father insisted the fund be set aside for future generations. His Italian pride demanded that *he* provide for his family.

Bianca's biggest pet peeve, however, was being treated like a second class citizen by the males in her family and her crusade carried over into her dislike of Kaitlin's discrimination of people from lower social classes. Bianca had no intentions of letting Kaitlin have the final say, and in large part it was her pranks that kept the intense dislike between the two groups at a constant peak.

Danielle felt compelled to interject one more tidbit of information that would get even Kaitlin's friends thinking. "You know Kaitlin, if your mother hadn't dug up that old Town Clerk, you wouldn't be a member either! And don't you think the descendant of a bookkeeper should know how to manage her money a little better?"

Danielle made yet another reference to the bet Kaitlin had lost and the fact that Kaitlin's parents' inclusion in the DAR was at best, very weak. It also made her perfectly aware that Mrs. Hamilton knew exactly what her mother's ancestry was—a fact that would *not* please Mrs. Marriott, and one that had now been shared with the entire cafeteria because of *her* big mouth.

Kaitlin fumed with anger and stormed off; and as she exited the cafeteria, she spiked a full carton of milk into the trash bag that Walter, the school janitor, was replacing. It exploded into his face upon impact.

The bell *rang*, and one by one, the girls all callously added their trash to the bag—milk still dripping from Walter's face.

Science was the first class of the day, so Callie and her friends headed toward the lab. Regular desks, arranged in a semicircle, surrounded the white board at the front of the room. In the back were lab tables, Bunsen burners with microscopes, and all the usual supplies of a laboratory. It was a very modern room and one of the few the school had. To the left was a life-sized skeleton they used for anatomy lessons; and to the right was a ten-foot boa constrictor in a terrarium that spent most of his days hungrily eying the mice that were there for his dinner.

A hand-written sign that read *DO NOT REMOVE* was taped to the outside of the mice cage because for some reason the little creatures kept mysteriously disappearing. Mr. Ripkin, the science teacher, assumed it was due to the efforts of an anonymous animal activist, but in fact, it was Bianca using them to torment some unsuspecting victims.

Callie was eager to get to class this morning, anticipating the results of her most recent work. Science was her favorite subject and she had been getting straight A's for as long as she could remember. Not to mention Mr. Ripkin had an inherent way of making everything seem so interesting. It wasn't easy retaining the attention of twenty-four prima donnas, let alone getting them to focus on science when they would rather be discussing fashion trends. But Mr. Ripkin was a master at enticing young minds to explore new ideas, and he found gratification from reaching youngsters—especially kids that showed as much promise as Callie.

As he began the daily lesson he handed out papers with the grades marked in red at the top. He paused as he handed Callie hers. "Well done," he said quietly.

Callie never had a grade lower than a B+ in any science class, and she only got that one because she had the flu on the day of the final. But that didn't stop her from giving it her all. The effort she put out, plus her natural aptitude, made for a winning combination. The more difficult the course, the better Callie seemed to do.

Kaitlin was full of jealousy and whispered to her friend. They were overheard giggling.

"Kaitlin, would you like to share the joke?" Mr. Ripkin asked.

Most of the teachers were aware of the ongoing rivalry between the two groups of girls, and he felt the need to remind everyone of that.

Kaitlin knew she was busted and did her best to cover up. "Sure, Ripkin! I was just corroborating your opinion of Callie's work."

"How so?" he asked, knowing full well that she would have to choose her words wisely.

Kaitlin rolled her eyes and said grudgingly—not meaning a word of it, "Just that Callie is really good in science."

"You're right, she takes it seriously," he concurred, placing Kaitlin's paper marked with a D on her desk. "Perhaps you could learn a thing or two from her."

Kaitlin grimaced and quickly turned the report over; and as she slumped in her chair, her pony tail landed on Bianca's desk.

Bianca watched as Mr. Ripkin moved to the back of the room. And seeing Callie nod her approval, tipped over a bottle of quick-drying nail glue she had been holding. The liquid spilled out—right over the middle of Kaitlin's ponytail!

Mr. Ripkin figured he had negated any damage Kaitlin had attempted and started explaining the Alcott Science Fair to the class. He knew he would not be allowed to actually interfere in the rivalry between these groups—not with the money and power the girls' parents possessed. At times, he had to walk a tightrope just to diplomatically give one of them the grade they actually deserved. Even the D he had given Kaitlin was quite likely to come back in his face, but she had put forth almost no effort, and he knew her mother could have arranged for someone to help or even write the paper for her as she usually did.

"The theme of this year's fair is conservation. All projects must pertain to the environment. It's a class project so your research and presentation must be done as a group. You may have some assistance with building any equipment, but it must be documented—as must your research," he read from the brochure. Then looking up from the paper Mr. Ripkin continued, "I want each of you to submit a recommendation with a basic blueprint. The girl whose project is chosen will be the team leader."

Alexia raised her hand in protest. "Is this mandatory? Do we have to do it?"

"No," he answered, knowing full well that Alexia only gave the bare minimum effort to anything other than her looks. "But it's worth an extra fifty points, which in some cases would raise you a full letter grade," and he looked directly at *her* as he said it.

"So then—what's in it for the winner?" Alexia pushed.

"How about the thrill of victory?" was Mr. Ripkin's reply, but he could see that wasn't enough to persuade the class. "Okay, if our team wins the science fair, I'll add fifty points to everyone's semester grade. And submitting the winning design is worth an extra hundred points for the quarter. Some of you could seriously use the boost to your grade."

The class still wasn't fully satisfied with Mr. Ripkin's reward system, but could tell his generosity had reached its max.

"Now open your books to page 262," he instructed.

As Kaitlin attempted to sit up, she *shrieked*! Her ponytail was firmly attached to Bianca's desk.

"Oh, Kaitlin, I'm so sorry. This must have tipped over by accident," Bianca said with fake sincerity. Callie, Alexia, and even Danielle snickered in the background. "Wow, and the stuff claims to be permanent." She looked at the bottle with complete innocence, in one of the best acting jobs Mr. Ripkin had ever seen, and the girls burst out laughing.

"That's enough!" he said firmly, as he contemplated calling the Headmistress or simply submitting his resignation. "Does anyone have any nail polish remover with acetone or *Glue be Gone*?"

"I've got scissors!" Callie offered, as the class frantically searched their bags.

Kaitlin freaked at the thought of Callie chopping off her hair and reacted like an animal trapped in a cage—flailing her arms wildly and trying to stand up. The weight of the desk, however, didn't let her go too far. She started screaming and calling for the Headmistress, the police, and the final motivator—her MOTHER!

At that point, Mr. Ripkin realized he had a potential crisis on his hands, and he would have rather faced Genghis Khan than an angry Mrs. Marriott. He immediately paged the office as teachers and other staff members ran into the room from nearby classrooms.

Chaos was erupting by the minute. Kaitlin's friends flocked around her desk offering moral support while the rest of the class was either traumatized by the sight or laughing themselves silly.

"That's enough! Everyone go to the library!" Mr. Ripkin said firmly. "The show is over!"

"Don't let Bianca leave—not until the police come!" Kaitlin insisted. Her face was flushed, and her head was bent back at an uncomfortable looking angle, so as not to put anymore strain on her already tender scalp.

"Oh, yeah? What are you gonna tell them? That I assaulted you with a bottle of nail glue? Give it up Kaitlin—it was an accident." Bianca still maintained her innocence. "You can't have me arrested for being clumsy!"

"Hey Ripkin, you want me to call the papers? This would make a killer front page story!" Alexia added.

The noise coming from Kaitlin's mouth at that point was best described as a howl. And it was a good thing that Mr. Ripkin was holding the desk in place because it prevented her from lunging at Alexia's throat.

"NOW...TO THE LIBRARY!" he shouted, and his voice left no room for further comment. "You too, Bianca. I'll talk to you later."

The girls gathered up their books, none too quickly. This was just beginning to get interesting and they hated to miss the finale.

"Nice job, Bianca. Too bad she didn't stand up a little faster," Callie laughed, as they strolled down the hallway to the library.

"I would've loved to have seen her with a bald spot on the back of her head!" Danielle admitted. She spoke quietly so no teachers would hear, although most of them were standing around Kaitlin trying to figure out how to release her.

"Wait a minute. It was an accident!" Bianca proclaimed in her most convincing voice. "At least that's my story and I'm sticking to it! Besides, you know I just think the world of her."

"Yeah, the underworld!" Alexia added. "Kaitlin fits right in with the Devil."

"Naw, too mean. She'd kill his business," Callie insisted, making them laugh even harder.

The girls checked the hallway to make sure there were no eyes observing them, formed a circle, and high-fived Bianca before joining the rest of the class in the library.

5

ne man's loss is another woman's nightmare

I t was December 7th, and Callie felt like hiding under a rock. She could see the entrance to Waldorf Hall from her dormitory window and painfully watched as parents, staff, and the other students trickled in for the Christmas extravaganza.

The energy at Ridgecrest seemed to be contagious. Even the weather seemed affected. It was cool, crisp, and overcast; and the vaguest scent of snow permeated the breeze. Cars were lined up as far as the eyes could see, and family members were disembarking at record speeds. Rolls-Royce, Bentley, Porsche, Mercedes and Jaguar were all represented, and only God could count how many limos were arriving by the minute. The valets were being run ragged just trying to keep up.

Everyone was dressed to the hilt. The men were in tuxedos and a few were in tails. The women were elegantly coiffed, wearing gowns with furs, and they flaunted jewels on their necks and ears that glittered like stars.

The commotion outside Callie's room echoed with the same excitement. She could hear the girls in their high heels clattering up and down the hall and the rustle of their gowns brushing against the floor. It was enough to make her puke!

Danielle, Alexia, and Bianca burst into Callie's room without knocking. They were dressed festively and looked stunning as only young, fresh beauty truly can.

Bianca wore Dolce and Gabbana. The cut was sleek and sophisticated with narrow straps and a slightly flared hemline. The gown draped her figure with absolutely no room to spare.

Alexia was sporting Gucci, and in a break from traditional formals, had chosen a velvet jacket with embroidered tulle pants. Her high heels even had real diamond straps! Chic and dramatic was the best way to describe her.

Danielle—whose parents even chose her toothpaste—was fashioned in a Christian Dior. This year's haute couture found her escaping into a world of color seldom matched at Ridgecrest. The iridescent fuchsia organza skirt with an oversized jacket of the same color would make her stand out in any crowd. And the Dior label added instant acceptance and would please even the most discriminating of tastes—though few of the women present would have the guts to wear the outfit.

Callie mentally calculated the combined value of their apparel and figured it was equal to the per capita income of some entire third world nations.

She, on the other hand, was still at her desk fashioning her Sponge Bob Square Pants pajama bottoms and a tank top, hammering away at the schematics of her science project. She already had an A in the class, but figured that another award would be good for her resume.

The girls were anxious to get to the party to see their parents, and of course, to show off their impressive clothing. Bianca, one of Callie's most serious scholastic competitors, eagerly eyed her blueprints and dashed across the room.

Concerned with her beauty, Alexia ran to the mirror and checked an imaginary blemish, prompting Callie to warn, "Don 't touch it! You'll only make it worse," and Alexia dropped her hand. The mere suggestion that she might have a pimple was enough to throw her into a panic and make her call a dermatologist. Callie wasn't above using Alexia's vanity to get her to conform to her diet or bend to her will in some other way, but she used that power discreetly, knowing it stemmed from Alexia's insecurities.

Danielle, conscious of the time, and truly concerned that Callie wasn't dressed, charged to her closet and started searching for an appropriate gown. "You haven't worn this Marc Jacobs yet, have you?"

she said with haste.

Callie rolled her blueprint and placed it gently into the top drawer of her desk. She knew Bianca had more integrity than to copy her work, but she was protective of her ideas and didn't quite have it pulled together just yet.

"No, but it doesn't matter anyway because I'm not going."

None of them had really believed her in the locker room when she said she wouldn't be attending the party. Alexia turned away from the mirror, startled. Danielle placed the dress back in the closet slowly and turned around. And even Bianca stopped spying for notes long enough to look up.

Callie could see the disappointment and concern in their faces. "It's for families, and mine couldn't be bothered to come."

"That's not fair, Callie. Your mom had to work," Bianca said. "And besides we're your family and we'll be there."

"And if you really need a parent, you can have one of mine," Alexia added. "I'll get out the scrapbook and you can take your pick. Blond, brunette, redhead—they're all there. They come in every size and shape and just about any profession. And most importantly, they all love to stick their nose in your business and tell you what you're doing wrong with your life!" She shuddered at the thought.

Alexia was an exotic beauty. But at Ridgecrest, she was referred to as the *Hollywood Heinz 57*. She was one quarter black, one quarter native American Indian, and one half French, and that was just on her mother's side. Her father was one hundred percent proper British.

Her mother was a socialite who tended to marry one wealthy man after the next. And her father was a successful Hollywood director who changed wives as often as leading ladies in his films. She had one natural brother—three years younger—whom she adored more than life itself, and numerous step brothers and sisters who after each ensuing divorce still hung around because of her father's popularity. Even those from her mother's side! Luckily, her parents got along well—that is, so long as neither one required anything from the other.

The girls laughed with Alexia, although they realized there was an element of truth in the fact that of all her stepparents, not one had been interested in her—let alone cared.

"Besides Callie, you know how much my mother loves you," Danielle offered proudly. Callie looked at her in denial. "Well, okay—my father anyway!" Now *that* was more accurate.

"I really appreciate all your support, but I'm not in the mood to face Mrs. Marriott. After what Bianca did to Kaitlin, I just know she's going to use me for target practice."

"Forget about it," Bianca said in her most impressive *good guy* imitation. "If she gives you trouble, I'll take care of her."

"That's okay, B. You've done enough. Besides, you're officially off-duty tonight." Callie said with sincere appreciation.

Meanwhile, Danielle was still going through Callie's closet as if finding more options would increase the chances of Callie going to the party.

"Hey, no peeking, I have Christmas presents in there," and with that one slip of the tongue, she realized she would now have to spend the next day wrapping gifts because her friends were prone to snooping.

Callie gathered the girls and shoved them through the door. "Now get out of here, you're interrupting my creative flow," she said firmly in a tone they always obeyed.

"But if you change your mind…" Alexia was still saying as Callie pushed her into the hallway.

"Yeah, yeah—I know where to find you." And before she slammed the door in their faces, she added, "By the way, *You look marvelous!*"

The girls stood in the hallway for a moment before realizing that Callie was serious. They looked to Bianca who shrugged her shoulders and said, "I guess that's our cue!" and off they went.

Callie turned and rested her back on the door, revealing her true disappointment for a brief moment. Then she walked back to her desk, retrieved her plans from the drawer, and continued mulling over her project.

AT THAT PRECISE MOMENT in Deer Creek, Johan was mulling over a project of his own—a stubborn piece of equipment that refused to work properly. It was December 7th—D-day, and Zoey had not yet responded to their requests for Callie's presence over the holidays.

Johan was tired of seeing Elsa disappointed and remembered his promise to get Callie there somehow. He lashed out at JR, a young farmhand, for being too slow in returning with a wrench.

Roy, the farm foreman, who had worked with Johan for quite a long time, was not used to seeing his employer so edgy.

"Something bothering you, boss?" he asked.

Through the years, a friendship and mutual respect had developed between the two men, allowing Roy the freedom to question his moods.

Johan stood up and sighed, "Ja, it's my granddaughter, Callie. We're trying to get her back for a visit, but her mother won't answer our calls. Elsa is counting on her coming this year, and I promised I would arrange it."

"Been a long time, huh?" Roy responded with a question. He figured talking about it might release some of the stress.

"Ja, she was just…"

"…Hell on wheels!"

Casey Meyers, a dreamy-eyed seventeen-year-old boy, interrupted Johan's answer. "I was always bailing her out of some disaster or another," he said, coming up from behind. "But she was the only girl I ever knew that wasn't afraid of spiders and snakes!"

"Ja, she was quite a handful," Johan laughed, remembering some of the trouble she had gotten herself into—and how Casey would always come to her rescue.

"Is she still living in New York?" Casey asked. He had heard periodic updates, but not a whole lot. The subject usually came up around the holidays when Elsa and Johan were hoping for a visit that never came.

"Ja, but mostly in that fancy boarding school."

Casey found it odd that Callie never visited, and he was curious to see what she looked like these days. His memories were of a pigtailed tomboy who followed him around with a bad case of hero worship—especially after he saved her from drowning!

"Probably turned into one of those city girls who don't know the front side of a cow from the rear," Roy commented.

"Yeah, and I bet she's afraid of snakes now, too. Then again, so are you, Roy!" Casey poked fun at Roy's only known weakness—that, and his propensity for gambling whenever the chance arose.

"I suspect the Callie we used to know is still alive and thriving, regardless of where her life has taken her, Casey! After all, she is a Michelsohn." Johan was not going to let them poke too much fun at his granddaughter.

"Yeah, hard headed and stubborn!" Casey teased. In spite of the age difference between them, they were very close and even considered each other family.

"And those are my good traits!" Johan joked back. "And on that note, she's ready to roll. We should replace the rest of the gaskets soon, and I'm sure we'll need to order a few other parts as well." Johan placed his hand on Casey's shoulder. "It's time for you, young man, to get on with the milking, and for us, Roy, to get back to the farm. I have an important phone call to make."

Johan picked up his tools and headed for his truck, knowing exactly what he had to do. The issue of Callie's visit had gone beyond appealing to Zoey's consideration, and her grace period had officially expired.

THE BIG MOMENT HAD arrived, and Callie's friends were about to make their grand entrance. They straightened their gowns and made last minute adjustments to each other's hair before pausing just inside the double-wide doorway.

Waldorf Hall was exquisitely decorated, with the grand ball room being opened for this occasion. There was a fifteen-foot Christmas tree elegantly trimmed in white and silver in the center of the room. And a buffet—covered with traditional holiday fare as well as more exotic dishes like escargot, caviar, prawns and lobster—was set up in the corner. Waiters circulated with trays of appetizers and others kept drinks refreshed. And in the back of the immense room, a small chamber orchestra played a mix of classical music and Christmas carols while a few older couples danced.

One group of ladies, congregating in the corner, could be overheard dishing out gossip that would put the cast of *Desperate Housewives* to shame. Kaitlin's mother led the conversation and quickly turned it to her favorite subject—the nouveau riche and their main representative in the school. In her eyes that was Callie. Kathryn Marriott came from old money, and for some reason seemed to think that it didn't spend the same way as that which was earned in more recent centuries.

As the discussion evolved, the topic switched to the elusive Zoey Michaels. Not only did her daughter's performance in school outshine most of theirs, but on the rare occasion when Zoey had made an appearance at one of these functions, all eyes were drawn to her. She was gorgeous, intense, and vivacious; and the experiences she had were amusing and sometimes outrageous, so people were automatically drawn to her like moths to a flame.

If the truth were told, however, these women were actually jealous of her. They frequently used their money and positions to buy the attention that Zoey seemed to attain without effort, and it irritated them to no end that she could care less who they were.

Rosalyn Hamilton, Danielle's mother, whose husband traced his lineage back to Alexander Hamilton—and if the truth were openly known, could trace hers to Catherine the Great and some other crowned heads of Europe—overheard the tail end of Mrs. Marriott's last sentence.

"Frankly, I think Callie is a bad influence. And her mother has absolutely no traceable lineage."

"Did she tell you that, Kathryn?" Rosalyn asked, as she joined the group. "I know the school would certainly not release that information." Rosalyn also knew that Kathryn was not above sneaking through file drawers if she saw a need. "I could hear you talking from across the room." She really hadn't, but she wanted to see if any of them had the grace to be embarrassed. A couple of them did, and blushed.

"Won't you join us, Rosalyn?" Kathryn asked, just a tinge grudgingly. Compared to the Hamiltons, she was nouveau riche and had no desire to have that point brought up.

Suddenly, Mrs. Marriott's attention was distracted and within seconds the other women's eyes drifted to the exact location. Even their posture seemed to mimic hers as they became aware of Callie pausing in the massive entrance to the ballroom. One could almost detect their collective noses moving higher into the air as they became aware of her presence.

Callie looked rather like Cinderella at the ball making a grand entrance, but was just stopping to locate her friends before beginning the long trek across the room. She saw Bianca and her mother first, but failed to identify the rather dowdy shape of Mrs. Marriott from the backside. And it wasn't until she neared that she recognized Kaitlin's new hairstyle. But by then, it was too late to escape.

"Callie, dear, where's you mother? I haven't seen her yet this evening," Mrs. Marriott asked in an attempt to make obvious what they already knew and to put Callie in her place. The group eagerly awaited her answer.

"She's in San Francisco working on a spread for *Vanity Fair*. They're doing an exclusive with Robin Williams—you know, the actor? It was arranged months ago before the date for the social was set. And you know the rich and famous…they just can't stand to be put off," Callie answered in an affected voice.

"Oh, I'm sorry, dear. It must be terrible to always be alone," Mrs. Marriott said with fake concern. "I just can't imagine missing one of Kaitlin's special moments. Poor girl, I'm sure you feel out of place with all the families here." Which is exactly what she was hoping for.

Callie was hurt as much by the remark as the cruel intentions behind it and rudely answered, "You know Mrs. Marriott, some women *do* have to work for a living."

Mrs. Marriott was about to take exception to her tone when Mrs. Hamilton laughed quietly and said, "How true Callie, and how delightful to see you." She gave her a hug. "You look stunning as usual."

Just then, Bianca arrived and tugged at Callie's arm. "There you are... my parents have been asking about you all night." She had heard Mrs. Marriott's insults as she approached the group of women, and opted to take her anger out on Kaitlin by drawing attention to her totally unplanned and unflattering haircut. "Kaitlin, I just love what you've done to your hair. Though it's a lot shorter than the last time I saw it."

It would seem the episode with the super glue had succeeded beyond their wildest dreams, and Bianca's reference to it was a deliberate effort to hit the Marriotts below the belt.

And it worked like a charm!

Both Kaitlin and her mother grimaced, but they didn't want to explain Bianca's comment to the rest of the ladies, so they let it pass. Kaitlin was seething, however, and plots of revenge fermented in her mind.

"Let it go. We'll deal with her later!" Mrs. Marriott whispered under her breath.

After Bianca and Callie escaped the ladies—using that term was like attributing decency and manners to a school of piranhas who lay in wait for unsuspecting victims—Mrs. Hamilton turned and said to the group, "I think it's time to expose Danielle to European society. Perhaps she will find some friends there with whom she will have more in common," making a direct reference to Callie and Bianca, but at the same time letting the other women know that their daughters were not acceptable either.

Rosalyn was not the snob that Kathryn was, in her case it was unnecessary, as she had nothing to prove. But the society in which her family lived had certain expectations, and while it was nice that Danielle had loyal friends, Callie and her mother would never quite be acceptable at one of their dinner parties.

As soon as they were out of hearing distance, Callie thanked Bianca and vented her true feelings. "That BEEOCH!"

Of all Callie's friends, Bianca was the one who most understood the snobbish behavior of some of the parents and other students in the school.

The girls rushed to the comforting arms of Bianca's mother, Ysabelle Bertoli, who could have easily fit in with the Marriotts and Hamiltons, but had no use for their pretentiousness. She had come to be with her daughter and even enjoyed the company of Bianca's friends. So the hug *she* gave Callie was sincere.

The rest of the evening was spent gossiping about certain girls and mocking the other Ridgecrest families, and Mrs. Bertoli only pretended to frown when she heard the reason for Kaitlin's new haircut. She had enough of an Italian temper herself, and over the years had restrained from making derogatory comments and taking inappropriate actions. But these young girls were a new breed. They weren't afraid to do or say exactly what they meant. And they were bright, so she suspected they would eventually learn that some of the things they did were outside the realm of proper behavior. But then again, times were changing, and maybe society would have to change to fit them.

Bianca's parents had to leave earlier than most. Her dad was responsible for the daily operations of his restaurants, and Sunday was his busiest day. Bianca eagerly escorted her parents to their car, almost as if she was happy to get rid of them, which made Mrs. Bertoli suspicious. Of all her siblings—brothers to be exact—Bianca was the only one who was forced to go to boarding school. She loathed the double standard and always played the *guilt card* when her parents visited Ridgecrest. But for some strange reason, this time it was different. She lovingly kissed her parents goodbye, tucking them safely into their car.

As they pulled away from the school, Mr. Bertoli had a smug look on his face. "I told you this overly priced school would make a lady out of her, Issy. You can thank me anytime."

Mrs. Bertoli watched her daughter's actions through her rear view mirror and witnessed her consorting with the valet attendants. She had a feeling Bianca was up to no good and nearly asked her husband to turn the car around. But then with some trepidation, she decided she would rather not know.

"Oh yeah," she mocked. "You're a real case cracker!"

When Bianca returned to the party, about thirty minutes later, she looked like a cat that had just swallowed a mouse.

"B? What have you done?" Callie asked, knowing the look all too well.

The girls quickly gathered around.

"Let's just say Mrs. Marriott won't be traveling home alone tonight, and that Mr. Ripkin is going to have to buy some more food for that disgusting snake of his," Bianca divulged.

"You didn't." Alexia said in her most theatrical rendition.

"Oh yes I did," Bianca gloated. "I just wish I could be there to see one of those furry little creatures scurrying up her leg."

The girls reveled in the imagery.

"Well Mrs. Marriott is a stuck up old bat that wouldn't know good stock if it bit her in the ass!" Danielle declared.

"Dani, you're scaring me!" Callie was completely shocked by her bold statement.

"Well, that's what my mother said."

"Really?" She couldn't imagine the word *ass* coming from Mrs. Hamilton's lips.

"No…but I'm sure she'd agree," Danielle replied with a straight face.

Callie had a susceptibility to fall for Danielle's stories. Something about that sweet, innocent look and apparent naiveté fooled her every time.

Alexia changed the subject to Kaitlin. "I gotta admit Bianca, that *glue over the hair* thing was one of your best pranks yet. I would've loved to have seen her dragging that desk behind her!"

The girls laughed so hard that the room fell silent and the Headmistress looked at them disapprovingly. She moved to their group and suggested they head back to the dormitory, as the party had drawn to a conclusion—a subtle reminder that they were stepping over the lines.

By now the room was beginning to clear out, and Callie still had work to do on her project. She planned to immerse herself in books and research over the weekend and have it completed by Sunday afternoon. So she grabbed Bianca and headed back to their dormitory while Alexia and Danielle stayed behind to say goodbye to their families.

6

Silence can be deafening

Z oey's world was a study in apparent chaos—at least to the uninformed. Techno music blared as chic models recycled in front of the backdrops. And clothing draped over the top of portable screens in disarray as the young gods and goddesses quickly changed for the next set of photos. Makeup artists were set up just outside the dressing area, and one stood beside Zoey to instantly remove any blotches that showed under the intense lighting. Roxanne actually had the situation well under control as she staggered the different groups—enabling Zoey to concentrate on the shots, the lighting, and the overall ambiance of the session.

Roxanne surveyed everything with an eagle eye, catching and stopping any potential problems before they occurred. She was excellent at her job, and for that, Zoey paid her extremely well.

The fashion industry was funny. Here it was December and they were doing an underwear ad scheduled for a summer release. The models were used to parading about in next to nothing in an industry where bodies were arranged to fit the clothing. But it was a good thing that this shoot was indoors and not outside where anatomy parts may have frozen and fallen off!

The next set up was so ridiculous that even Zoey found it difficult to keep a straight face. The idea was to recreate an Uncle Sam *I want you* image with vivid patriotic colors set against a stark white backdrop. Zoey didn't create the campaigns, but it was her job to deliver what the advertising agency envisioned—regardless of the concept.

A male model, portraying Uncle Sam, was slender but muscular. He was scantily clad in Calvin Klein briefs with a patriotic top hat and a red, white, and blue tuxedo jacket spread open to reveal sleek and well-defined abdomen muscles. His features were young and chiseled—almost pretty, but still masculine.

The women, by the same token, were sexy, gorgeous, and noticeably underfed. They were poised on either side of Uncle Sam in matching solid-colored bras and panties. The clothes were revealing enough, but under Zoey's direction their poses became alluring and seductive.

Her instructions were brief and to the point, "Look intense! Touch his chest! Give me more attitude!" and the models instantly obeyed. They were trained for this, and it was amazing how effortlessly they seemed to mold themselves into whatever she demanded of them.

The session was moving quickly and Zoey was feeling pretty good. Actually, she was feeling great! Her work load had been intense this year and her portfolio had grown even stronger—if that were possible. She was eagerly anticipating the three weeks off she had scheduled over Christmas and had no intentions of letting anything interfere with her plans.

She brushed a strand of hair from her eyes as she finished the last of a series of photos. Her camera was nearly out of film, so she told the models to take a break while she reloaded.

But when Roxanne had the next scene set up and everyone in place, an ominous man in a black suit appeared in the doorway. He spoke to one of the models who pointed toward Zoey. Roxanne spotted him immediately and intercepted his path, but he pulled an envelope from his pocket, forcing her to pause and flag down her boss.

Zoey wasn't pleased at the interruption, but she knew Roxanne wouldn't disturb her work unless it was important. Nonetheless, her tone was impatient as she greeted the intruder.

"What can I do for you? As you can see, I'm very busy!"

"Are you Zoey Michaels?" he questioned.

"Yes, I am. What is this about?" Her tone was becoming less agreeable by the second.

"You're being served. Sign here, please." He handed her a legal document and instructed her where to put her signature.

Zoey struggled to retain her composure as she saw the names Johan and Elsa Michelson at the top. It was now clear that they were prepared to go to court to gain visitation rights to Callie.

Her shoulders sagged for a moment as she signed the papers. Court appearances were one thing she could *not* fit into her schedule. The man said "thank you," but she didn't acknowledge his manners—her eyes were too busy scanning the papers he had presented.

"Damn it!" she mumbled under her breath.

Zoey was used to having the unexpected happen, and in the end she had to maintain her equilibrium. If she didn't, the photographs would never get taken. But this was a personal matter and it disrupted all her plans. Even more than that, it revealed that there was a facet of her life over which she didn't have total control, and *that* went against the image she cultivated.

She was flustered for a moment and embarrassed, but that one brief lapse was all anyone was going to see. Zoey cleared all traces of irritation from her face and resumed her professional attitude.

"Are we ready?" she asked Roxanne who was still standing nearby.

"All set to go," she replied.

The models had been watching the action by the doorway and turned away seeing Zoey's attention once again focused on them. Everyone was curious about what had just happened, but it was none of their business and they had no intentions of butting in.

"Let's get things rolling then," Zoey said firmly. "I want this wrapped up as soon as possible." And she handed the envelope to Roxanne and moved back into her zone as if nothing had happened.

Roxanne's eyes opened wide as she skimmed the documents. She knew Zoey's mind must be in turmoil, so she kicked into overdrive and prompted, pushed, and nagged the models with resolve. Organization was her forte and no one did it better. Give her a clipboard and a cell phone and she could have the MTV video award ceremony set up within a day. But for now, her efforts were completely focused on making this shoot run like clockwork.

"That's a wrap," Zoey announced, as the afternoon waned. She put the lens cap on her camera and thanked all the models. They immediately dashed to change, leaving amid wishes for happy holidays.

Zoey turned to Roxanne. "Get my agent on the line. Tell her I'll do the London shoot after all."

Roxanne didn't say a word, but rather, questioned with her eyes.

Zoey continued, "I know you've already made plans Roxy, so I don't expect you to change them."

"Excuse me?" Roxanne's voice expressed her indignation. "Who do you think sets all this up for you?" She waved at the remnants of the shoot, looking at Zoey with conviction. "I go where you go!" And she began making the call.

WEDNESDAY HAD BEEN SET as the day Mr. Ripkin would announce the team leader for the Alcott science fair. It was also the last day of class before semester break. As the girls waited impatiently for the news, he finished writing *SENSE OF HIGHER PURPOSE* on the whiteboard—for *this* is what all great inventors possess. He underlined the words then turned and stalled, knowing the suspense was killing them.

"Let's all congratulate Callie Michaels! She'll be our team leader this year at Alcott."

The class reacted with mixed emotions. Callie beamed and her friends cheered. Kaitlin glared and her friends moaned, knowing they would soon be at Callie's beck and call.

"All of you will be expected to assist her in every possible way. And remember, this award is a credit to the school and not just to you as individuals." Mr. Ripkin handed out sheets of paper to the class that explained the project. "Look these over during the holiday. We'll start work when we return."

"Oh, and whoever freed the little *Willys*—it was a nice gesture, but the snake has to eat, too!" Mr. Ripkin had no idea that Bianca was the person deserving full credit.

Kaitlin focused her attention on the empty mice cage as the wheels clicked within her brain then whipped around to the culprit who smiled sweetly at her. Realizing that the mice in her mother's limo were deliberately planted made her temper boil, and if she were anywhere else, Bianca would have been in grave danger.

"That's it—you're free to go. Have a Merry Christmas, ladies," Mr. Ripkin said, as he gathered his papers.

The girls lunged from their seats as if Orlando Bloom was waiting in the foyer and was taking the first girl to arrive on a world tour with Gwen Stefani. They tripped, stumbled, and clogged the doorway in their urgency to be the first to exit.

Ridgecrest girls were sheltered, nurtured, and spoiled, and in spite of their wealth, freedom was only a dream for most of them. Christmas vacation at least released them from the confines of the school, and Ripkin's remark was like a parole to an inmate on death row. At least, that's how they saw it.

In the log jam at the door, friends and enemies were packed together. And once again, Bianca had planned for such a contingency. As she passed Kaitlin, she smacked her on the back and whispered, "Better luck next time, Leona."

Danielle followed closely behind and could barely suppress her laughter when she noticed a sign firmly taped between Kaitlin's shoulder blades. It read *LOSER*.

A voice in the distance added insult to injury. "Hey Kaitlin, didn't your mother buy your blueprints?"

At any other time Kaitlin would have immediately responded, but in her mind she was already far away from Ridgecrest. And nothing was going to break the thread of her daydreams. A few more hours there at school was not going to ruin her freedom. So she let it pass—this time—and moved with the rest of the girls back to their rooms.

MORNING COULDN'T HAVE ARRIVED any sooner. The girls were busy packing last minute items and spending the early hours chatting with friends before their departure. Normally after a late night, they would awaken bleary eyed and lethargic, but this morning they were excited and eager to get moving. The sun was barely up, but the activity inside and outside of the dorms was chaotic as one by one the students were picked up.

The staff was just as antsy because they couldn't leave until all the students had left in the manner dictated by their parents. Even the janitors had spent a restless night anticipating the messes they were going to have to clean up before they could get home to their own families.

Bianca burst into the room as Callie slipped her laptop into its case. Not only was her computer a necessity for the research she often did online, but it also served as her most reliable method of contact. Cell phones had a remarkable capacity for hitting a *dead zone* just as the conversation became interesting, so Callie never left school for more than twelve hours without her laptop ready to operate.

"My ride's here," Bianca said with unusual apathy.

"Your dad?" Callie asked. He was one of the few parents that actually came in person.

"I wish," Bianca admitted. "He sent Uncle Vito with the meat wagon!"

The concept didn't completely disgust Bianca because Kaitlin's group of ghouls was already intimidated by her family reputation, and she used it to her advantage. In the past, it helped expedite payment of delinquent debts, and it usually kept comments about the Bertolis to a minimum.

"My dad thinks he's making a point. Says I have way too much stuff, but he obviously hasn't seen yours! I don't even come close," Bianca added, as she analyzed the pile of Louis Vuitton luggage Callie had amassed in the center of her room.

"You're dad's a funny guy."

"Yeah, a regular Jim Carrey—and you're going to be gone for how long, six months? Bianca joked.

"You know me—I'm nothing without options!" Callie defended her need to be excessive. "Besides, you never want to run out of clothes!"

"Rigggght," Bianca replied, downplaying her friend's quirky habit. "And when are these bags being picked up?"

"Hopefully soon, but you know how Zoey hates crowds," Callie said with resentment. It annoyed the hell out of her that she was always the last one to leave.

As expected, Alexia and Danielle bounced into the room, too. As leader of the group, the girls had designated Callie's room as their meeting place, though nothing was ever formally stated. They just knew that if one of them were missing, *that* is where they could be found. Besides, Callie tended to be more organized, and they could usually all find a place to sit!

"Come on guys, Alex's limo is waiting," Danielle blurted.

"I'm going to kill my dad," Bianca said, shaking her head in disgust.

Callie headed downstairs with her friends to see them off. And sure enough, there was Uncle Vito with the delivery van—front and center—loading the last of Bianca's luggage. A number of the other girls were looking at him suspiciously as he closed the cargo doors and climbed into the driver's seat.

Alexia was the first to leave. She blew kisses out of the limousine window and waved goodbye like a movie star bowing to the demands of her fans. Knowing her as well as they did, they were more than aware of her need to be the center of attention. But just as they started to mimic Alexia's most common traits—her searches for imaginary blemishes and stray hairs—the sound of a horn blasting behind them made them jump.

"Care for a ride little girl," Mr. Bertoli called from the driver's seat of his Viper.

"DADDY!" Bianca screamed with delight. "I knew you couldn't do that to me."

"No Bianca, I couldn't do that to your Uncle Vito," her father laughed, as he waved goodbye to his brother. It appeared that Bianca inherited her sense of humor through genetics.

"Hello, ladies," he said to Callie and Danielle who were always mesmerized by his exceptional good looks. "Have a Merry Christmas. And don't forget to help out around the house!"

Bianca cringed, "God Dad, you're so pathetic." And she gave Callie and Danielle one last hug before climbing into the car.

They watched together as Mr. Bertoli revved the engine and flew down the drive. Then turning to Callie, Danielle said sadly, "I'm going to miss you."

"Lighten up—it's not like I'm dying," she responded, but then recognized the pain associated with Danielle's words and quickly changed her attitude. "Besides, I have my cell phone and I'll check my email several times a day," she added with reassurance.

"I know," Danielle confided. "It's just that I get pretty lonely when I go home and when I'm here with you guys, I don't feel that way."

Callie didn't push the issue. She knew Danielle gave a whole new meaning to the phrase *lonely little rich girl*.

Danielle was an afterthought in her parent's life. Actually she was a mistake and an unplanned child in a world where everything was structured and organized. Her only siblings—a brother and sister—were ten and fourteen years older, respectively. Both of them were involved in the family's publishing empire, and rightfully, commanded her father's attention. And her mother's social status demanded her participation on a number of committees, leaving very little time or energy for her youngest. As a result, Danielle did whatever she could to try to get noticed, frequently making up exaggerated stories to gain attention and for her own amusement. Without them she felt unimportant and overlooked. The only area where she truly gained recognition on her own was as an equestrian. And her bond with her horse was far closer than the one she had with her family.

"Mom says you can visit me anytime," Danielle offered optimistically.

"Yeah right, when hell freezes over!" Callie retorted. It was obvious that she was not acceptable to Mrs. Hamilton, no matter how graciously she was received in public. And an offer like that was even too far-fetched for Callie to believe.

"Now you'd better get going," she insisted, noticing Danielle's family Bentley in the background. "You know how she hates to wait."

"Yeah," Danielle said with a sigh. "I know." She gave Callie a big hug then dashed toward the car. The day's events had already been scheduled, and in her mother's agenda, being late was unacceptable.

Callie waved goodbye to the last of her friends then looked up at the facade of her dorm. It appeared formal and aloof to her and she expected that it would be nearly empty by then. She made her way through the maze of cars, luggage, and people as she headed back into the massive building and up to her room to wait for her mother.

The emptiness in the halls seemed to mirror her sense of isolation as if she had suddenly found herself adrift at sea—alone in a boat with no crew. And the silence around her seemed louder than all the girls' combined chatter, causing her to miss them even more.

7

There's no place like a stranger's home

allie was sitting on her bed with Mandy in her arms, and her luggage was still piled on the floor when her cell phone rang. She figured it was one of the girls who had forgotten something. Unfortunately, she was wrong—it was her mother.

"Where are you?" Callie asked, both irritated and expecting the worst all at once.

"No! You promised!" and her voice was angry and sad at the same time. "Tell them you have a prior commitment...because you do." Then she listened for a moment. "So where am I supposed to go?" and she listened to the answer. "You've got to be kidding! They don't even have indoor plumbing. I'm not going and that's FINAL."

Callie's first instinct when she disconnected the line was to throw her cell phone out the window, but her eye's were too blurry with tears. She hugged Mandy tightly and wondered why she never came first with her mother. What she didn't know was that Zoey had tears in her eyes, too.

Callie couldn't decide what was worse—her trip with her mother being delayed or that she had to go to a dairy farm in Wisconsin for the first part of her break. She sniffed and wiped her face.

Zoey was already at JFK International Airport. She had delayed calling Callie until the last possible minute, knowing it wasn't going to be pleasant. Surrounded by an eclectic group of assistants and several equipment cases, she made the call just as the plane began boarding, forcing her to keep it brief.

Her last words to Callie were, "You'll be doing me a favor. I can appease the Osbournes *and* get your grandparents off my back. They've threatened to sue me."

It was news to Callie that her mother had been putting off her grandparents, but she really didn't care. She was just plain mad. She looked around her room at all the things she had—it was a lot more than most! Her mother worked long hours in adverse conditions to give her everything most girls dreamed of—a good school, great clothes, trips to exotic places, and opportunities to meet famous people. Still, she desperately longed for the one thing she didn't have, and that which most girls her age took for granted—an available mother.

Callie had created a support system around herself with her friends, and as much as she was a source of strength for them, they supported her, too. But her friends were gone now, beginning their holidays. And she was alone. There was no one she could talk to who would understand, and no one who cared enough to make her laugh in spite of her disappointment. And where else could she go for the holidays, except to a home full of strangers? Callie realized that she was completely on her own this time. She squeezed Mandy tightly, wishing desperately that the old rag doll could hug her in return.

The trip to the airport started with Callie in a terrible mood. She had nothing to say to the driver. And he had no idea how lucky he actually was because Callie in a bad mood—which wasn't uncommon—was kind of like a tornado on a summer night. One never knew where or when it was going to strike, but it was guaranteed to do some damage.

The flight to Chicago wasn't bad, except that everyone else seemed to be in such good spirits. But at least the rest of her companions in first class seemed to reflect the same segment of society that she was used to. However, once she landed, it was a completely different story.

Callie was directed to a terminal that seemed to be out in the wasteland. And once there, found her fellow passengers to be quite unappealing— couples with small crying children, rather plump elderly women who were squeezed into clothing a size too small and ten years out of date, and a number of older men who she was sure would snore with their mouths open and probably drool, too. And the only teenagers she saw looked as though they hadn't washed their hair in weeks. Nope, there was no one there she wanted to sit next to. But the defining moment was when she saw the propeller-driven plane.

"Where did you get that thing from? A crop dusting business?" she asked the airline attendant who was reviewing her ticket. "On second thought, don't check me in—just tell me where I can find a private car."

The attendant wasn't used to being spoken to like that—let alone from some bratty teenager—but she gave her directions back to the main terminal and to the nearest limousine service.

Callie tossed her ticket at the woman. "Make sure my bags get there."

The limousine driver didn't have it much easier. The service gave him the directions to follow from Mapquest, and once Callie was situated in the back seat, she told him not to disturb her until they reached Deer Creek. Meanwhile, she pulled a bottle of water from the refrigerator and searched the car for an electrical adapter.

What little she cared to see on the drive was as unfamiliar to her as the moon. And once they left Chicago, they also left the highway.

It was still daylight, but there wasn't much to see—just some trees, fields, hills, and an occasional farmhouse. In the city, there was a lot of traffic and noise—but not out here. All Callie heard were the tires moving on the pavement and the wind blowing against the side of the car. She felt like she had landed on an alien planet and only hoped she could find something familiar and civilized.

The countryside appeared strange to her. It was slightly hilly, with large open spaces that were already covered with a couple inches of white powdery snow. And there was only an occasional house or barn and a few stands of trees by creeks to break the terrain. But in the mood Callie was in, it looked like the tundra—frozen and barren.

The air was cold and crisp, and by the time she arrived, the sun was beginning to set. There was a light in the farmyard, but she couldn't see much else of the surrounding area—though she figured there probably wasn't anything of interest anyway.

A big red barn was positioned kind of kitty corner to the house, and behind that were some tall pines, which only reminded her that she should have been arriving in Aspen about then. The farmhouse was a typical white two-story with stairs and railing leading up to the porch. And dim lights glowed through the front windows.

Callie's memory of the farm was so vague that nothing looked familiar except her luggage, which was being unloaded from a delivery van as her car approached. In her eyes, *that* was the only thing that had gone right with this trip. At least all her clothes had made it, not that anyone around here would appreciate them.

Callie wouldn't admit it, but she was nervous about facing a whole group of strangers and a world that seemed light years away from everything else she was used to.

As she stepped out of the limo, she was engulfed in a bear hug from a rather large gray-haired man who called her *schatzie*.

"And who are you?" she asked, miffed at having her grand entrance interrupted, "Santa Claus?" noticing his rather sizable belly.

He was taken aback and let go of her, looking to a short gray-haired woman standing nearby for reassurance and thinking perhaps he had hugged the wrong person.

The woman said quietly, "That is your Opa, Callie—your grandfather. And I am your grandmother. It's been a long time."

"That's an understatement!" Callie retorted, hoping not to get any more hugs.

Johan directed the farmhands to take her luggage upstairs while he observed the strange creature that had arrived in his granddaughter's place.

Elsa merely ignored the tone of Callie's voice and suggested that they move inside where it was warmer.

Callie's grandmother had seen the look of shock on her face when she stepped out of the limousine. This tall, elegant young lady was not the same tomboy that had left years before, at least not on the surface. But Elsa remembered a time—many years before—when a young girl arrived on a farm in Austria, dressed in a traveling suit with a fur collar and cuffs, and carrying a muff. She remembered what it was like to be faced with a world totally different from hers and how she covered her fear with disdain and contempt, so she wasn't totally surprised by Callie's reaction.

She had, however, hoped that her granddaughter had retained some of her memories of her early childhood on the farm. After all, they had nearly raised her until her father died and Zoey moved to the city. But Elsa could see that it was going to take some time for the little girl they knew to resurface. She just prayed that the short visit would be long enough.

Elsa had spent the last few days in a rush of activities—getting holiday baking done, cleaning her already immaculate house, and shopping for groceries and Christmas presents—in addition to her usual duties of chief cook and bottle washer. And for the first time in years, it truly felt like Christmas.

It had been a long day for Callie, and all she wanted was to be shown to her room. She needed to hook up her laptop and recharge her cell phone so she could call the girls and report on her condition.

But apparently, her grandparents had other plans because as she walked through the house, which was warm and comfortably furnished with quality European furniture, they were interrupted by a loud knock at the door. And for the next couple of hours, neighbors and friends arrived in droves—all bearing freshly baked cakes, pies, and cookies decorated with Christmas motifs. Callie knew it was a polite gesture, but they acted like rural *Stepford Wives*, and quite frankly, they gave her the creeps!

Elsa and Johan greeted everyone and made them feel welcome. They were delighted to share their granddaughter's arrival. Callie, on the other hand, was unimpressed, and made minimal effort to be courteous or attentive to any of them. She was tired and hungry, and she didn't want to be there.

Elsa finally suggested that she rest until dinner was ready, and Johan showed her to her room. He knew better than to offer her another hug, but said before he left, "I'll come back and wake you."

She nodded with her back toward him. And as soon as she heard the door close, she dashed to her cell phone and plugged it in to charge. Then she looked for a telephone jack or cable to connect to the internet, but quickly discovered that the only phone in the room was hardwired to the wall. Talk about primitive! She was totally exasperated and flung herself onto the bed, screaming inwardly.

Not long afterwards, Johan knocked on Callie's door. When she didn't answer he opened it to see her lying on the bed with her headphones in place and reading a magazine. She sensed him watching her and looked up—angry that her privacy had been invaded.

"Don't you knock?" she asked, none too politely.

"Ja, but you didn't answer and dinner is ready," he said, as he turned to leave—rebuffed again.

"Hey Grandfather, how come that phone doesn't unplug? I need to connect to the Internet for homework and stuff."

"We never changed the wires. It seemed unnecessary. But we can have it fixed up for you if you like," he answered, more eager to please her than his German heritage would allow him to show. "You know, you used to call me Opa. This *grandfather* sounds so formal—as if you're talking to a stranger."

It was too soon for Callie, and her sarcasm resurfaced. "Oh ja?" She imitated his thick accent. "…well I could call you *Joe-Han* if you prefer?"

His eyes dropped in disappointment. "No, grandfather will do," and he left the room.

Elsa could see the sadness in Johan's face when he came into the kitchen, and she burned her hand with steam—distracted by his pain. He responded to her "ouch" by rushing to her side.

"It's nothing Johan, I'm just nervous." Elsa knew he might not mention his sorrow unless he saw hers first. "It's been so long since I cooked for her, and she has changed so much."

"Ja, she certainly has. Don't worry, liebchen. You're the best cook in the state of Wisconsin and she'll love it just like she used to, and if she doesn't, well…that leaves more for me."

"Ja, like you need more food?" and Elsa laughed softly, poking him gently in the stomach and lightly patting his cheek. "You're a good man, Johan," and she looked at him with total devotion. Little did she know their peaceful loving home was about to be disrupted by a creature from the abyss.

The table was set in the dining room, which was more formal than usual. But this was their granddaughter's homecoming and they wanted to celebrate. Callie, however, was not impressed when she entered.

Johan was sitting at the head of the table with two other place settings to the right and left of him. Elsa came in from the kitchen with the final dish—Brussels sprouts—which she placed in front of the chair she indicated was for Callie.

"I hope you're hungry, I made all your favorites," she said with eager anticipation.

"How do you figure?" Callie answered, sensing a weakness and intending to take full advantage of the situation.

"Well, when you were a little girl…" but Elsa was rudely interrupted.

"In case you haven't noticed, I'm not exactly a little girl anymore. I couldn't possibly eat any of this stuff," she said disdainfully as though the food on the table was somehow spoiled.

"Callie, what in heaven's do you mean? Your grandmother is the best cook in the county." Johan was offended for Elsa who was standing with a puzzled look on her face.

"Let me spell it out for you. First of all, I'm a vegetarian. I don't eat meat, so the chicken is out. And even if I did, I wouldn't eat your chicken because it's fried in vegetable oil."

Callie took a deep breath so she could continue, but Elsa interrupted, "Oh no, schatzie, I use peanut oil." She thought this might be more acceptable. Wrong again.

"Ycch! That's even worse!"

"But there are plenty of vegetables." Johan thought changing the subject from the chicken might be a good idea right about then.

"Yeah, uh huh." Callie shook her head in disgust. "The corn is smothered in a fatty sauce, the potatoes are whipped—probably with butter and cream, the gravy is loaded with carbohydrates, and the cranberries are packed with sugar. This meal is a heart attack just waiting to happen!"

"What about the Brussels sprouts? They used to be your favorite." Elsa hoped one dish might meet with her granddaughter's approval.

"Are they organic?"

"Organic?" Elsa didn't quite understand the question.

"Yeah, that's what I thought," Callie said with indignation.

Johan hoped to break the tension by pointing out that he had been eating Elsa's cooking for over fifty years and was as healthy as a horse. But Callie didn't buy it.

"Sure, if you call obese healthy! Have you looked in a mirror lately? Or don't you have one wide enough?"

"Callie!" her grandmother objected.

She turned her attention to Elsa. "Have you?"

Overwhelmed by her granddaughter's tirade, Elsa left the room. "Excuse me. I have something on the stove."

Callie glared at the table. "Never mind, I wasn't very hungry anyway. Oh, and don't bother waking me in the morning—I'm a late sleeper."

Johan sat there alone for a moment stunned before going into the kitchen to check on his wife. Elsa was standing at the sink, looking out the window, but turned with slightly swollen eyes.

"It's a good thing she isn't a judge at the county fair. I'm afraid I wouldn't have won all those ribbons," Elsa said, laughing off the pain Callie's words had caused.

"Do you think we made a mistake, Elsa?"

"Ja…the day we let her go, but we'll make it better," she said quietly. "Now let's eat dinner before it gets cold."

They moved their plates to the kitchen and ate quietly in its comforting atmosphere. Then together, they put the leftovers away and did the dishes.

Meanwhile, Callie had dug into the bottom of one of her suitcases and hungrily devoured several candy bars she had stashed for late night homework sessions. She was on the phone with her mother, begging for a plane ticket to London.

Zoey was exhausted by the trip and had a full of day ahead of her with an eccentric rock star. Her crew would be starting in about four hours, and she hadn't slept yet, so she cut the conversation short, in no mood for complaints.

"We'll talk tomorrow, baby—it can't be that bad. Besides, we'll be skiing by Sunday." The connection started to fade and the last words Callie could make out were, "Say hello to Andy and Aunt Bee…" before Zoey's phone went dead.

Callie's final appeal was to a disconnected line. "Please Mom, don't leave me here. You're all I have."

Just then, Elsa tapped on the door and entered with a large box. Callie was already upset, but the constant invasion of her privacy was *way* more than she was willing to tolerate. She pulled the blanket up over her head and turned off the lamp rather than converse with her grandmother.

"This box belongs to you," Elsa said. "I've been saving it for years. Sweet dreams, schatzie," and she slipped back out of the room, closing the door quietly behind her.

8

You don't need a farm to have a pig

Callie was jolted awake the next morning by the *clang* of metal on metal. One eye opened and peered at the clock, which displayed six o'clock—just as that god awful sound rang out again. It was followed by a rooster crowing and a very large engine revving just under her bedroom window. And within seconds, she detected the sounds of a cow mooing, chickens clucking, and hammering like some insane symphony with no rhythm. Callie covered her head with the pillow and screamed.

She stumbled downstairs, still in her pajamas and robe. Her hair was tousled and her eyes were half open. The first thing she saw was a smorgasbord—scrambled eggs, ham, bacon, fried potatoes, breads and sweet rolls—and in her starving condition started to rant at her grandmother. "I thought I told you I don't eat this cra…"

Elsa *clanged* a big metal spoon on a large iron skillet hanging by the back door—identifying at least one of the unfamiliar noises. The back door burst open and several men stampeded in, paying absolutely no attention to the fact that she was in the way. They simply pushed her aside, filled their plates, sat at the table, and began eating everything in sight. Callie doubted that locust could clear a field faster than these men stripped the buffet counter.

Elsa turned back from the stove and proudly handed Callie a bowl of disgusting looking gray goop. "It's organic. No added sugar, salt, or animal by-products."

"Excuse me?" Callie asked, dazed by the commotion and presence of the farmhands.

"It's oatmeal, schatzie. Hank delivered it this morning. He usually keeps a box or two around for premature calves, but there's not much demand for it. We're lucky he had some." Elsa was quite pleased with herself for thinking of it.

Meanwhile, the men had finished their food and began reversing the trek they had taken mere moments before. Callie was once again jostled about as they exited, handing their empty plates to Elsa and thanking her politely for the food. But at some point in her rotations, Callie caught a glimpse of herself in the polished silver of the toaster and nearly died. She set her bowl down and dashed upstairs to get dressed.

She emerged from the bathroom about forty-five minutes later with her hair intact and dressed in 7 for all mankind jeans and a cashmere sweater. She returned to the kitchen, which was now a place of perfect tranquility. Elsa had kept her oatmeal warm on the stove while she cleared the last of the dishes and had just refilled the bowl. Callie looked at the mush rather glumly, but ate it anyway.

Once she determined that the milk her grandmother offered was low fat, she poured some over the oatmeal, and when Elsa's back was turned, she added a couple spoonfuls of sugar. It wasn't going to do her any good to eat a healthy diet if she was going to die of starvation while doing it. But it didn't make her feel any better that the smell of bacon still lingered in the air.

OUTSIDE IN THE BARNYARD, there was activity everywhere. Some of the men were hanging up Christmas lights and real garland while others were moving in and out of the barn with buckets.

A familiar face pulled up in a late model Chevy pickup with the company logo *MICHELSOHN & MEYERS DAIRY* prominently displayed on the side. He waved at Johan who immediately came to greet him.

"Casey, so happy to see you," Johan said, as he engulfed him in a bear hug. "How's your dad?" Casey was the son of Johan's business partner, Nick.

"Okay Johan, cut the crap. What's she like?"

"Well…" Johan was at a loss for words.

"That bad, huh?" Casey looked at him more seriously.

"Let's just say she's one-of-a-kind." Johan appeared rather pleased at himself for not exactly insulting his granddaughter.

"It's worse than I thought, isn't it?"

"Much," Johan confessed. "But it's been a long time…she doesn't remember any of this," and he motioned around the farm.

"Always said city girls were a different breed," Casey warned. "I stopped trying to figure them out a long time ago."

They moaned simultaneously and stared into the distance.

"So where did you hide that paint?" he asked, snapping out of his trance.

CALLIE HAD MOVED TO the porch by then and was looking around the farm. It was a chilly day, so she added a suede jacket and matching Armani boots to her low rise flared jeans. Things looked vaguely familiar in the daylight, but smaller than she remembered.

Elsa joined her for a moment and asked if she felt like taking a short walk. "Hank called and said your grandfather's order will be ready for pickup in the morning. Would you mind delivering the message?"

"Sure, why not?" Callie responded. "There's nothing else to do around here."

Elsa motioned to the back of the house. "Use the gate to the left, and one of the farmhands will direct you from there."

Callie forgot her sense of propriety and slid down the porch railing— a bad habit she had as a little girl—then continued on her way. Elsa watched with a smile, realizing that some things just never change.

As Callie turned the corner, a big dog charged toward her from the distance, barking and showing his humungous teeth. In an effort to stay well out of his range, she didn't see that there were two gates and inadvertently took the one to the right.

Once inside the pen, she turned to find an irate goose staring at her. It flapped its wings and began to hiss, pecking at her legs with its beak. In an attempt to escape, she burst through another gate directly in front of her and stopped to catch her breath. She had no idea a farmyard could be so dangerous! Then she felt eyes upon her. When she turned her head, she came nose to beak with an ostrich. She wasn't sure if ostriches were friendly or not, but the dog and the goose hadn't been, so she wasn't going to take any chances. She swung herself over the closest fence and lost her balance in the mud. Firmly planted on her butt, she realized by the smell that this was no ordinary mud and was reluctant to push herself off the ground using her hands. But as she began waving her arms around violently and yelling out her frustration, she heard a loud grunt from behind. Peering cautiously over her shoulder, she observed a huge hog moving in her direction, and he didn't look happy.

Callie forgot all about dirtying her hands when a man yelled, "GET OUT OF THERE!" And she had nearly reached the gate on her own when he forcefully yanked her to safety.

"What kind of an idiot are you?" Roy asked. He was a tall, burly old man with a face weathered from years of working outside.

"I…I was just…and my grandma sent me to…and then that *huge* thing came out of nowhere," Callie rambled, trying to explain her predicament.

Roy just walked away shaking his head at her stupidity. "City folk—think they know everything."

By now, the barn was just ahead of Callie, and she was eager to deliver her message and return to the safety of the house. But when she left the pen area, she narrowly missed a collision with a farmhand turning the corner with a couple of long boards over his shoulder. It whipped her into a tail spin and she was confronted by the sight of an enormous tractor moving toward her at record speeds. Traffic was the last thing she expected and the shock caused her to faint.

She woke up to the sound of voices and a face that could have been in the movies. The image in front of her was celestial and certainly belonged someplace other than in a farmyard. He had sandy blond hair and deep green eyes framed with long black lashes any girl would have died to possess, and beneath his high bone structure, dimples cut small grooves into his cheeks. Casey was gorgeous—even by city girl standards—and the sun was casting a halo affect around his face from Callie's vantage spot on the ground.

"Go get Johan!" she heard, regaining consciousness.

Still dazed and confused, she asked, "Am I in heaven?" thinking that only angels could be that beautiful.

"Yes you are, and I'm St. Peter." Casey played along, giving the gathered crowd an opportunity to laugh.

Callie sat up slowly. She rubbed her eyes to determine if his face was a mirage then realized her hands were covered in muck.

"What happened?" she asked.

"Well either you fainted or you chose a damn stupid place for a nap. My guess is, from the smell of you, that you met Uncle Buck somewhere along the way, too," he replied. "You need to stand up now."

Callie was pleased to think that he was concerned until he added, "You're blocking the tractor." At that point, she pulled her arm away from him and the crowd roared again.

Just then Johan arrived at the scene and the farmhands scattered like mice. They suspected the show was over for now.

"Are you all right, Callie?" Johan asked with more sincerity than she had seen thus far as he guided her to a safe spot out of the tractor's way.

"Oh Grandfather, it was awful," she said, catching her breath. She leaned against the fence, checking to make sure there were no animals around.

"First the dog tried to eat me, then the goose attacked, then…and why do you have an ostrich anyway?…then I fell into a pen with a hog the size of a tank and my arm was yanked out of its socket by a grumpy old man with a real chip on his shoulder, then some guy pushed me into a tractor that nearly ran me over…causing me to faint!" she said in one long rush of words.

She continued before he could speak, "…and now I am battered and bruised and I smell like hog crap! All because of some stupid message from Hank."

Johan's eyes lit up at the news. "Hank called?" he asked with excitement in his voice. The look on Callie's face made him realize that his reaction was inappropriate. "I mean—what an awful experience. That should've never happened."

Casey approached from behind and asked jokingly, "So how's the mud wrestler doing?"

"Fine, no thanks to you—Peter, right?" she retorted sarcastically, disgusted with her appearance and the whole series of events.

Just her luck! The one good looking guy around here and she had to meet him in this condition. His smart assed comment about being St. Peter had not escaped her either, and she had no intention of letting him get away with it. But in her present state she knew he held the advantage and she had to get it back! It was undeclared—but this meant war!

Casey laughed. Her attitude of superiority annoyed the hell out of him and he was delighted to see her off balance. He could tell Callie was a force to be reckoned with and he had no intention of underestimating her. But he also had all the normal reactions of a male his age to a beautiful girl, and even covered in mud and pig crap, she was Paris Hilton hot!

"Oh no, Callie, this is Casey," Johan interjected.

"Yeah, well, I wouldn't want to keep Farm boy from his chores." Her sarcasm was obviously back at work with her consciousness.

"Ouch!" Casey replied, grabbing his chest as if her insult had actually caused him physical pain. "That hurt."

Callie was pleased to note her comment had gotten a reaction, but didn't let it show on her face. She did roll her eyes, however, letting him know that she thought he was reaching with his attempt at drama. Then with her nose high in the air, she began the journey back to the house.

"Tell Elsa I'll be there in a minute," Johan called after her.

"Sorry Gramps, my messenger days are over," and she stormed off with all the dignity she could muster until she heard their reaction from behind. As it turns out, the fence she had leaned up against was wet and her butt was solid white.

Johan lit up. "I see you found the paint," and the two burst out laughing.

Callie looked at their faces first and then at her butt. When she discovered the damage, daggers shot from her eyes.

As she retraced her steps—minus the stops with the goose, ostrich and hog—the dog began its barking. She yelled in her most forceful tone, "Sit down!" and it immediately obeyed, moving to its doghouse with its tail between its legs.

Elsa was waiting for Callie back at the house as if someone had called to warn her. She immediately helped her remove her dirty clothes, leaving her boots on the porch.

In a rage, Callie ordered the outfit to be burned, with only a slight remorse at losing her favorite pair of jeans, and ran upstairs to try to remove the smell of the manure.

After a long, hot shower, she pulled out her cell phone and called Bianca who was trying—in spite of her brothers—to choose her lunch from the buffet set in her family's dining room. *The Three Stooges*, as she liked to refer to them, kept grabbing the serving spoons, stealing food from her plate, and intentionally bumping her around.

Amid the distractions, she heard Callie say, "...and then he had the nerve to call me a mud wrestler..."

"HELL-O...Kaitlin has called you worse than that, and you didn't get this upset. So what does Farm boy look like, anyway?"

"Ew...don't even go there, Barbara Walters. Just the thought of him makes me sick," Callie declared.

"That wasn't my question. I asked what he looked like." Bianca wasn't giving up that easily.

"A big, arrogant jerk!"

"Yeah, I got that part. Does the jerk have a name?" Bianca was still digging for the truth.

"Hmm…Casey, I think is what my grandfather said, but with his accent—who knows?"

"Okay, now we're getting somewhere. So who does Casey look like?" Bianca wanted to put a face on the jerk.

Callie thought for a moment. "Carrot Top!" she whispered, following the sound of a muffled male voice.

And there he was standing in the entry, hanging up his jacket. He was even cuter than she had first thought, and she wondered to herself if there was any angle that was bad for him. Even the male models Zoey photographed couldn't match that.

"Ycch!" was Bianca's reply, still not convinced Callie was telling the truth.

Casey looked up the stairs and caught Callie spying. He flashed a grin, and she immediately dropped her eyes to the floor and ducked around the corner. She had no intention of showing him that she was the least bit interested, and she didn't want him hearing anything she might say—especially about him.

"I've got to go Bianca. I'll talk to you later," and she quickly ended the call, dashing back to her room to get dressed.

Meanwhile, Bianca's brother Michael had been eavesdropping on the conversation. "Ay Callie," he yelled. "Give Farm boy a piece of this!" and he blasted a big fart into the phone.

Completely disgusted, Bianca punched him in the arm. "God Michael, you're such a pig!"

9

Thank God for leftovers

Now it wasn't that Callie didn't have an outfit for every occasion because she did! But the question was, what to wear? It couldn't be too formal—not for this place. That would make her look ridiculous. And the fact that her nails were chipped and needed a fresh coat of polish, only managed to complicate the issue even more. She was hard pressed for a decision, and she didn't have a whole lot of time.

It was three pairs of pants and a pile of tops later before she was finally satisfied with her look. Casey had the upper hand after their last two encounters, making it necessary to pull out all her arsenal. Of course, she refused to admit that he was the reason for her efforts. In her mind, it was a matter of setting the record straight. So once she was convinced that her appearance would get his attention, she perfected a dazzling smile in the mirror and headed downstairs to supper.

Callie entered the dining room with an unusually sweet "hello" and the smile that she had just practiced up in her room. She took her normal seat across from Elsa, and faked her surprise at Casey's presence at the table.

Johan was startled by her transformation. "Callie, you look so pretty."

Casey already thought she was cute when she was covered in mud, but he had no idea just how beautiful she really was. So to throw her off balance, he added, "Yeah—and you don't stink."

"I wish I could say the same for you," she countered, making an obvious reference to some of the barnyard smells that lingered on his clothes.

Elsa had prepared one of her usual family style meals, but entered the room with a vegetarian casserole that she set in front of Callie's plate.

Casey stared at the mass of green matter. "Ycch! What the heck is that?" His usual exclamation was toned down for Elsa's sake.

"Callie is a vegetarian and those vegetables were organically grown," Johan said. "Hank ordered them from a health food store in Madison." He was proud of his granddaughter's commitment to her diet, even if it meant turning up her nose at the foods they liked.

"Why? It looks gross and smells even worse!"

As an athlete, Casey knew as much about the value of nutrition as Callie did. He just happened to believe that food should taste good, and it didn't hurt if it looked like it was fit for human consumption either.

"Not that you would understand," Callie lectured, "but it's a healthier way of living!"

"Yeah right, then how come vegetarians always look so unhealthy?" Casey questioned, asking Johan to pass the roast beef in the same breath.

Callie rolled her eyes and picked at her casserole as she watched the trio dig into the meat, potatoes, and other side dishes Elsa had prepared. Commitment to nutrition was one thing, but the smell of Elsa's cooking was quite another. Callie was used to the food her mother's models ate and the food at Ridgecrest, but she was totally unprepared for the wonderful aromas that were assailing her senses at Elsa's table. Her casserole seemed particularly bland and unappealing in contrast, and she reminded herself—again—that it was better for her. She listened quietly as the subject was changed to a topic they all apparently knew well.

"And how is our Amanda?" Elsa asked. The fact that she cared for this girl was evident in her voice.

"Real good, thanks," Casey answered, pausing to swallow. "She's been invited to speak at the medical school next month."

Elsa looked to Callie. "They call her *The Angel of Deer Creek.*"

Callie flashed a fake smile and pretended to be absorbed in her meal.

"She's been photographed with the President of the United States," Johan added.

"Hmm, nice." She was a little impressed, but her apathetic tone indicated otherwise.

"Amanda does volunteer work at the hospital and still gets straight A's in high school," Elsa said, continuing to sing her praises.

Callie was offended by her grandmother's championing of this stranger. Who was this mysterious girl that commanded all their interest and respect? And why weren't they discussing her—their adored and long lost granddaughter who they made such a big stink about and forced to visit. The whole conversation was starting to get on her nerves!

"Oh and *The Capital Times* is doing another follow up story on her next week, too." Casey kept pausing in between bites to contribute.

"She sounds like a regular celebrity."

Callie *was* slightly curious about this person whom Casey seemed so involved with, but figured anyone interested in his pea brain had to be either completely clueless or desperate, or both!

"You'll have to visit her soon, schatzie," Elsa insisted.

"Do I need an appointment?" She smiled a sugary smile and batted her eyes, mocking the stranger they all admired.

Callie figured Amanda was probably just some small town Mother Theresa who impressed everyone by being a goody two shoes. She was used to being the center of attention in her crowd, and though she hadn't done anything to entice their interest, they could have at least asked about her life—instead of going on and on about some insignificant do-gooder.

Out of the blue, Johan remembered a promise he had made to Callie. He changed the subject—yet again—and requested that Casey update the phone outlet in her room.

"It's about time," he said, and to Callie he added, "I've been telling him for years he needed to upgrade the wiring in this old house."

Callie ignored Casey's remark. "Don't worry about it, Grandfather. I'm sure I'll be long gone before Farm boy, here, figures out the *how to* manual."

"Callie!" Elsa was shocked at her granddaughter's tone. She was used to the language and bantering of the farmhands and frequently overlooked it. But she had no way of knowing exactly what was going on between Callie and Casey. Besides, working on a farm was nothing to insult someone about. It had provided their livelihood for a good many years and a more comfortable future for Callie than she realized.

"No problem. It just so happens I got me a brand new copy of *Wiring for Dummies*. And if you can help me with the big words, I figure I can get you on line in about…hmm…a month or two." Casey was playing along with the role she had set for him.

Elsa and Johan were a little concerned by the animosity at the table and weren't quite sure what to do. Fortunately, Callie's cell phone rang, and the awkward moment of silence was interrupted.

"Speak to me," she answered. "Hey—what's up!"

Callie covered the mouthpiece of her cell phone and whispered to the table, "It's my friend Alex from Los Angeles. She had *her* picture taken with Brad Pitt!"

Callie turned her attention back to Alexia. "No, not at all—I can talk," she insisted, rudely leaving the table without even as much as an *excuse me*.

Her grandparents were mortified at this further breach of etiquette, and in an effort to cover Callie's rudeness, Elsa began urging more food on Johan and Casey who accepted with relish.

Meanwhile, Callie's conversation could be overheard, her voice gradually fading as she moved farther away. "You're never going to believe what happened to me today! I was attacked by wild animals." And after a brief pause, she added, "No really! I swear it's true."

Casey was floored. "Wow, she's something, all right!"

Johan just nodded his head in agreement while Elsa began clearing the table for dessert.

Casey didn't want to say too much—he knew how Johan loved his granddaughter. Johan didn't want to say too much either—he did love her. But this wasn't the same Callie he remembered, and he was at a loss to explain her behavior. So they sat in the comfortable silence that old friends know and devoured every morsel remaining on their plates.

Finally, Johan spoke up, "I'd appreciate it if you could take Callie into town tomorrow."

But Casey was in the middle of drinking his milk, and just the idea caused him to spit it out clear across the table. They were still mopping it up when Elsa returned with the pie.

Callie's conversation with Alexia was starting to get personal, so she closed the door to her room. She was still relating the events of the day with more focus on Casey than she would have admitted. "And then he went on and on about his perfect little girlfriend. I swear it was disgusting! I wanted to barf."

Alexia was sitting at her vanity trying to decide if her eyebrows needed to be waxed in the near future. Her cell phone was conveniently connected to speakers, so she could talk and still have her hands free. But she was so preoccupied with her beauty routine, that she didn't notice the small children hiding under her bed—a few of her many stepbrothers and sisters. They were in the perfect position to reach out with a feather and tickle her foot; and when they did, her freshly pedicured toes moved to scratch the itch.

"I don't know Callie, I think Bianca's right. You've got it bad for this guy!" Alexia said, referencing a conversation she had had with Bianca while Callie was primping for her encounter with Casey.

"Oh great! Barbara Walters can't get the scoop, so she sends in John Stossel. *Give me a break!*" Callie's voice dripped with sarcasm.

"Get over it! We're allowed to be nosy. We're your friends—it's our right." Then Alexia changed the subject to her favorite topic, herself. "Speaking of nosy, do you think I need a nose job?"

"What are you retarded or something?"

"Well no, but I was at the spa today and the woman next to me had the most beautiful nose," she explained.

Callie interrupted her, "I'm so jealous!"

"Of her nose?" Alexia was confused and distracted as she swatted at the feather that tickled her foot.

"No, you idiot—the spa. The only way to get a treatment around here is if you have FLEAS!" she said with disgust.

The children under the bed placed a fake spider next to Alexia's toes and tickled her foot again. They were delighted when she looked down this time, eagerly awaiting her reaction. And they weren't disappointed! She screamed and jumped out of her seat, knocking over all her cosmetics. When she heard their giggles from down under, she yelled, "STAY OUT OF MY ROOM YOU LITTLE JERKS!" and began kicking the bed and throwing everything in sight.

Callie could tell that Alexia had crossed the line into hysteria, so she immediately went into *crisis hotline* mode, talking her friend back into a relative state of calm.

LATER THAT NIGHT, WELL after Elsa and Johan had gone to bed, Callie crept downstairs to the kitchen. With all the stealth of a cat burglar, she moved silently through the house in search of her loot. As it turned out, she was starving, and without the immediate ingestion of real food, she was sure they would find a skeleton in her bed in the morning. In emergency situations such as this, she said "To hell with the diet." Her stomach was crying "Feed me!" and it refused to be ignored. So she reached into the refrigerator and removed a piece of chicken—followed by some leftover mashed potatoes. After heating it quickly in the microwave, she dashed up to her room and devoured it like a contestant on *Survivor*, facing her thirty-first day.

10

Take this bird and shove it!

"I'm too young for this," Callie muttered, as she pulled the covers over her head and tried to fall back asleep. It wouldn't be easy, considering the farmhands were already beginning to arrive and the noises coming from outside were increasing. She peered sleepily at the alarm clock. It was a good thing the numbers were lit up because it was still dark outside, but she cringed when she saw the time.

Eventually, however, she heard the *clang* of metal on the pan and decided not to repeat yesterday's performance. This time, she showered and dressed *before* heading downstairs.

Once again she accepted the oatmeal from Elsa and waited to add sugar until her back was turned—at which time, she also grabbed a piece of bacon that remained on a platter. She figured one of the hands must have missed it somehow.

What Callie didn't realize is that Elsa had noticed the missing piece of chicken from the night before and thought perhaps hunger was getting the best of her.

"Casey is out back with Johan. He said he's ready to leave whenever you are," Elsa informed her.

"Oh great," she thought, "nothing like dealing with Farm boy at the crack of dawn." She didn't need the additional stress—especially when she was already suffering from sleep deprivation. And she certainly wasn't in the mood to shop! But she *did* request this excursion, so she reluctantly went upstairs and chose an appropriate jacket to match her second favorite pair of jeans.

As she climbed into the shotgun seat of Casey's pickup truck, Johan held the door for her and added, "Now don't forget to pickup my order from Hank."

"Why do I think I'm going to regret this?" Callie replied, getting a strange feeling that she didn't have all the facts.

Johan just laughed as he shut her door and watched them pull away.

The stress level was at an all time high inside the truck. Casey was waiting it out, having no intention of starting a conversation just to have Callie stomp it into the ground. And she would have because the first words out of her mouth were *not* intended to be agreeable.

"I can't imagine why anyone would want to live in a desolate place like this." Not getting a response, she continued, "I mean, how do you exist with only five TV channels? Forget cable, hasn't anyone heard of Direct TV? This *is* the twenty-first century, or did someone forget to tell you people?"

Casey continued to let her ramble.

"I don't belong here," Callie said, which was closer to what really bothered her.

Not surprisingly, Casey had reached the same conclusion. "Then why did you come?" he asked, his tone drenched with indifference. He really didn't give a damn what the reason was, he was just irritated that she seemed to want to make her visit unpleasant for everyone she came in contact with.

"I had no choice. My mother bailed on our ski trip. And I'm stuck here because of some stupid obligation to my grandparents."

"You really don't get it, do you?" he asked.

"Get what?"

"How much you mean to them?"

"We have nothing in common."

"You got that right! Your grandparents are two of the nicest people I've ever met. And you...well you're some spoiled, self-centered brat. You don't deserve them." Casey was *not* gentle in his assessment.

Callie was used to being criticized by Kaitlin, but that was a matter of heritage. This was a full frontal personal attack, and no one had ever spoken to her like that before. She was speechless.

"Excuse me?" was all she could manage—her sarcasm being temporarily contained.

"You heard me! You're a disgrace to the Michelsohn name. Here you stand to inherit a fortune from Johan's patents, and instead of taking the time to get to know him, you sit there bitching about TV stations. Hell, if it weren't for his contributions to automation, we'd still be milking cows one at a time. And if he hadn't seen the value in the electric fence, our herds would all just be *Happy Cows from California*!" Casey's voice threatened a long lecture.

But Callie wasn't in the mood to listen. "Money is *not* a substitution for class! And simple minded is not a quality I admire. Now that I know my grandparents choose to live this way, I have even less respect for them." Callie was emphatic in her righteousness. "No wonder my father ran away."

"Yeah, well…your dad was a fool. And so are you if you can't tell the difference between simple minded and living simply."

"You don't know a thing about my dad," Callie snapped. She couldn't go very far with that one since she didn't know very much about him either.

"I know he was their only son and my dad's best friend. And I know Elsa and Johan never got over his death." In reality, Casey probably knew a lot more about Cameron than Callie did.

"Well neither have I. And maybe if my grandparents weren't such country bumpkins he'd still be alive." Callie's voice was full of bitterness.

"And maybe if you weren't so damn stuck up, you'd appreciate what you have before it's too late," were Casey's final words as he came to a stop in front of Hank's General Store. He reached across Callie and opened the door, indicating that she should get out.

"Pick me up at three," she demanded, sliding off the seat.

"No can do, Scarlett. I'm driving Amanda to her treatment, and I have to leave here by one."

"Oh sure, we wouldn't want to disappoint *The Angel of Deer Creek*, now would we?" Sarcasm had returned to Callie's voice.

Casey lost all expression in his face. "I'm leaving here at one—with or without you."

"And I'm telling my grandfather. He'll fire you on the spot!" Callie threatened.

"Frankly my dear, I don't give a damn!" Casey responded, as he slammed the door shut and burned rubber, creating a disturbance.

Callie was left alone on the curb and shouted her comeback, "I've seen *Gone with the Wind*, and you Farm boy, are no Rhett Butler!" Feeling quite smug, she turned to an innocent bystander watching the scene and with perfect dignity added, "It's so hard to find good help these days."

Callie proceeded into Hank's General Store, having her presence announced by a string of bells dangling from the door. This was no modern department store, but rather something straight out of *Mayberry R.F.D.* The floors consisted of old planks—well polished but still showing the patina of age, and wooden signs hung from various locations over shelves, indicating the departments *FEED, CLOTHING, BOOTS, HARDWARE*, etc.

Hank Jolley, the proprietor, came out through a curtain behind the register. He was a portly man, wearing bib overalls and a flannel shirt. Callie cringed when she saw the outfit thinking he would set the fashion industry back at least sixty years.

"Well good morning, Callie!" he said enthusiastically.

"How do you know my name?"

"Well for one, I used to change your diapers. And two, I pretty much know everyone in town," he laughed.

"Excuse me?" Callie was dumbstruck or as close as she had ever come.

"You do remember your old buddy Hank, don't ya?"

Callie shook her head no.

"Damn...oops, excuse me, dang! I just lost another twenty bucks to Arnie on that one." He shook his head in disappointment. "I guess it has been a long time."

Callie had no intention of discussing the last eleven years of her life with Hank, so she got straight to the point. "I'm here to pick up my grandfather's order. Is it ready?"

"Yep, but you're gonna want to grab it just before you leave town," he answered, as he watched her browse the aisles. "Can I help you find something?"

"Just looking for souvenirs."

Hank chuckled. "I don't reckon there's much worth saving from Deer Creek, but you're sure welcome to look around. Let me know if you need any help."

It didn't take long for Callie to locate the only rack of girls' jeans. She held up a pair and asked, "Do you have any other styles?"

"Yep, they come with or without pockets."

It took a moment for Hank's answer to sink in and another moment for Callie to realize he was quite serious. She moved on to a rack of plaid flannel shirts.

"How about these? What are my choices?"

"Blue and red in stock. But I can order just about any color you'd like."

By now Callie was sure that fashion had never arrived in Wisconsin, but an idea was forming in her head.

Hank interrupted her thoughts. "So how did you like that organic stuff from Madison? Never bought lettuce by the leaf before." The look on his face indicated how silly some requests seemed to him.

But Callie's mind was still working on something else. "It was edible," she replied.

"Most folks around here can or freeze their fresh vegetables and fruits. And your grandma does some of the best this part of the country has ever seen. She wins year after year at the county fair. That city stuff is expensive—especially in comparison."

Callie nodded in agreement without really paying attention. An idea had completely formed in her mind, and she grabbed three pairs of jeans and matching shirts in the appropriate sizes and took them to the register.

"Nice choice," Hank said, complimenting her decision.

"Put these on Johan's tab. I hear he can afford it."

It still bothered her to have heard from a total stranger that her grandfather was worth a mint, and it annoyed her even more that she was the last to know. Zoey had always said there was a trust fund set aside for her, but she assumed it would maybe cover college. Her mother led her to believe that she *had* to work all this time so they could live the way they did.

Hank interrupted her thoughts. "Don't you want to try them on?"

"As if!" Callie was insulted that he thought she might really wear clothes like that. "These are gag gifts for my friends. What I need is nail polish…you have any?"

"That'd be at Lucy's drug store—just down the street."

"Oh, and I need them gift wrapped. A pair of jeans and a shirt in each package." She matched the sizes up and shoved them across the counter. "And I need them by twelve forty-five. I've been told I'm on a tight schedule."

She wasn't used to being ordered around and it annoyed her to no end that she had to adjust her shopping to fit Casey's agenda. After all, *she* was the guest of honor and *he* should be catering to her!

Callie turned abruptly and walked out of the store, leaving Hank with a dilemma. One eyebrow rose as he pondered her directive. "Now where the hell am I gonna find wrapping paper?"

Callie paused once she was outside and pulled her jacket a little tighter. It was a sunny day, but the temperature was only about thirty-eight degrees. She had dressed fine for riding in a car or truck, but not for strolling outside.

She looked around Deer Creek. If it had been located on the East Coast it would have been called quaint. Most of the shops were built from brick—at least the ones in the center of town—and there was a building clearly labeled courthouse. The four blocks around it had small shops and an old-fashioned diner.

Callie was used to the city, so the quiet of a small town seemed almost eerie to her. She looked down the street in the direction Hank had indicated for the drug store and located it immediately. None of the businesses looked like they could hold more than twenty people. Of course, that was about as many cars as she saw parked downtown. And when she noticed the street sign at 1st and Main, "Gag me!" was all that came to mind.

It hardly seemed necessary to stop at the light since she hadn't seen any traffic after Casey dropped her off. But knowing her luck, she figured the town sheriff would be watching her, waiting with baited breath to give her a jaywalking ticket just for the fun of it.

"Callie!" an unfamiliar voice called out.

She whipped around to see a scrawny man darting out of the post office. He was dressed in an official uniform and was carrying a U.S. mail bag.

"Hold up! I have some mail for Elsa and Johan. It would save me a trip if you'd take it home with you," he pleaded.

"How in the world does everyone know my name?" she blurted, reluctantly taking the bag. She was surprised by its weight, but not at all surprised that he didn't answer her question.

"What's in this thing anyway—rocks?"

"Naw, just some journals and a few bills by the looks of it. Thanks, honey!"

He was already heading back into the warmth of the post office when she yelled out her terms, "I expect free postage!"

As Callie entered the drug store with the mailbag over her shoulder, a geeky-looking country boy—in dire need of a good dermatologist— hollered, "Mail's here!" He was wearing thick horn rimmed glasses, a red stocker's apron, and a goofy Santa's hat.

Lucy Donovan, the store owner, was a middle-aged woman who was hopefully more capable of filling a prescription than she was of naming her own business. Callie wondered if everyone in the community subscribed to the same marketing plan and made a mental note to look it up online under psychiatric delusions of grandeur. These people obviously didn't think outside the box!

Lucy walked to the front puffing on a cigarette. Her hair looked like it had been bleached to match some of the hay bales Callie had seen in the fields on the way to town, and her eye makeup could have done by Boy George. On second thought, next to this woman, Boy George was tasteful and chic. But Callie didn't know whether to be more grossed out by her looks or by her cigarette.

Lucy smiled. "Callie, what are you doing delivering the mail?"

It was no longer a surprise to find out that everyone in town knew who she was. Callie figured someone must have posted her photo at the post office as a missing or lost child, and she vowed to kill whoever it was as soon as she identified the person.

"You're kidding, right?" She was stumped by the question. "I only have it because your stupid mailman was too lazy to deliver it himself."

"That little weasel! Don't know why we voted Sam Denny into that office! Oh ya I do. No one else wanted the job. But I hate it when he does that. Never know when the mail is going to get here or who is going to bring it."

Lucy's voice dissolved into a bad smoker's hack as she laughed. And when her cough cleared, she took another drag off the cigarette. Callie was thoroughly disgusted.

"So what can I help you with, other than taking some of that mail off your hands?" Lucy asked, as she went through the bag and pulled out several envelopes addressed to her. Callie watched in disbelief. She had been of the opinion that the U.S. mail was under some kind of federal regulations, which didn't include a *help yourself* format.

"Nail polish," she answered, in no mood to chit chat.

"Sure, darling. It's right over there." Lucy pointed to a large rack that contained more shades of pink polish than Callie knew existed.

Jedediah, or Jed to his friends, was staring at Callie in awe. It was quite obvious that he was smitten with the worst case of infatuation that Deer Creek had ever seen.

Lucy scolded him, breaking the spell. "Jed, get back to work!" And Callie added a threatening look that sent chills down his spine.

After reviewing the nail polish selection, she asked, "Uh…do you have any other colors?" And she was hopeful for one brief moment when Lucy reached below the counter and pulled out an unopened box labeled rose, which turned out to be just a darker shade of the pinks already present.

"I'll take the clear," she said, having found two lonely bottles sitting on the shelf toward the bottom of the rack.

"Suit yourself, hon."

Callie felt the necessity to begin one of her lectures. "Did anyone ever mention to you that cigarette smoking is the leading cause of cancer?"

Lucy took another puff and blew the smoke in Callie's direction. "Yep, my doctor—right before he got hit by a train!" Her laugher set off another coughing fit, prompting Callie to reach for her wallet in an attempt to limit her exposure to the second-hand smoke.

"Oh no, sugar. It's a gift!" Lucy placed the polish in a small paper sack and added it to a large bag that she pulled out from under the counter.

"What's this?" Callie asked suspiciously.

"Just some new clothes Elsa ordered. They arrived this morning. You don't mind delivering them, do ya?"

Callie realized that she had been duped yet again and made a mental note to have Bianca come study under these con artists.

Heading back to Hank's via the opposite side of the square, Callie paused in front of Evie's Coiffeur. The sign on the door read *OPEN EVERY SATURDAY & THREE DAYS BEFORE CHRISTMAS*.

Inside, Evie Rider was dyeing an older woman's hair a pale shade of blue. The salon was modest, and from her view outside the window, Callie could tell it hadn't been renovated since the 1970s.

She scoffed at the sight. "Not in this lifetime!"

When Evie noticed Callie's presence, her face lit up. Completely familiar with *the look* by now, Callie moved quickly down the street. But it was too late. By the time she reached 1st and Main again, she was carrying a hat box from Evie's who apparently doubled as the town's milliner.

Callie finally arrived back at Hank's only to discover him missing in action. From the look of things, the shop owners held a convention at noon because most of them displayed signs in their windows that read

CLOSED FOR LUNCH...BACK AT 1:00, though she doubted any of them wore watches. She stood behind two other customers—juggling her purse, the hatbox, the mailbag, and Elsa's package—and warily eyed the clock on the wall that read twelve forty-five. And when she noticed the young female clerk behind the counter moving slower than the five o'clock traffic over the George Washington Bridge, she became increasingly agitated. So she wasn't very pleasant when she reached the front of the line about ten minutes later.

Callie pointed to three white bags with red bows tucked in the corner behind the counter. "I believe those are mine."

"You Johan's granddaughter?" the clerk asked suspiciously.

"Not by choice."

Callie was ready to snap at anyone by now—especially the clerk when she vanished behind the curtain without a word. "Yo! I'm in a hurry!"

"Hold your horses. Johan's got an order back here."

Callie checked her watch. She lifted her eyes just as the clerk returned with a rooster in a cage. "You've got to be kidding!"

Meanwhile, Casey had pulled up in front of the store. He checked his watch, which read one o'clock then looked both ways. Callie was no where to be seen. "She'll learn," he laughed, as he peeled out, revealing a license plate that read *DAR E KNG*.

Callie heard the familiar tire squeal and grabbed the rooster, which squawked out of fear, the three bags with bows, the mail, the hatbox, Elsa's package, and her purse and barreled out the front door.

"Casey, wait! I'm here!" she called out. But he was already making a right turn at the edge of town and was soon out of sight. Callie set down the rooster and the other packages, dug for her cell phone, and tried to make a call. Unfortunately, she had forgotten to charge it and the battery was dead. At wit's end she screamed, "Someone is going to pay dearly for this!" and she gathered up all her cargo and started the five mile trek back to the farm, fuming inwardly.

As time passed she grew tired. The rooster wasn't heavy, but the cage was awkward to carry—especially with the other packages. And it was getting cold.

Once she was outside of town, there were few trees to block the breeze and no buildings. She stopped to check her location, and took Elsa's goofy hat out of the box. With typical German prudence, her grandmother had purchased a straw summer hat at the end of the season when it was on sale. But at least it was warm.

Just then, the rooster decided to *squawk* again as if it had some right to complain. She crouched down with her face nearly pressed up against the cage. "Shut up, bird!"

Callie continued down what she hoped was the right road. She hadn't paid attention to the route on the way to town because she had a chauffeur and there was only one way into Deer Creek. But country roads can be confusing, and she soon discovered that the streets were not lit and the intersections rarely had signs. There weren't many houses either, and no traffic to flag down for directions.

It was starting to get dark and the temperature kept dropping. So one by one, Callie opened the bags she had purchased as gag gifts and slipped the flannel shirts on underneath her coat. She only wished she had thought to grab a pair of gloves as well!

IT WASN'T LONG BEFORE an old beat up pickup truck wobbled into the driveway of the farm. Johan greeted his best friend, Arnie, as the vehicle rolled to a stop. Callie sat riding shotgun—her mouth clenched tightly in anger. She looked like a hillbilly!

"I...HOPE...YOU'RE...HAPPY!" she spewed, barreling past Johan and leaving the rooster on the seat of the truck. She seemed less than grateful for the taxi service Arnie had provided her, and bolted into the house without as much as a *thank you*.

Johan held his laughter until she was safe inside.

"Clara found her wandering by the side of the road," Arnie reported, "...mistook her for a bag lady!" And the old friends shook their heads, pondering both the mysteries of women in general and adolescent girls—Callie, in particular!

11

Accidents are rarely planned

Callie was livid. She burst into the house and flung the ridiculous looking hat at her grandmother who watched in amazement. Elsa was beginning to wonder if her granddaughter always entered with such drama, remembering the scene from the day before when she stormed into the house covered in pig crap.

She was pleased, however, that her hat had finally arrived and exclaimed, "Oh…it's lovely. It looks just like the picture!"

Callie paused mid-tantrum and stared at Elsa as if she were insane. "It's lovely if your name is Daisy Duke or Elly May Clampett!" she interjected with a sneer.

But Elsa had no intention of adding fuel to the fire, and moved to the living room to model it in front of the mirror.

Callie stomped upstairs to her room, not the least bit interested in anything her grandmother had to say. She shoved the door open, peeled off the excess layers of clothing, and threw them over the mystery box Elsa had placed in her room.

She had just started to brush her hair when the fossil on her dresser *rang*. The noise startled her and she jumped. The sound was loud and shrill, and she couldn't figure out if these old-style telephones were designed to be heard a mile away or simply because old people needed hearing aides. Regardless of the reason, Callie found it quite jolting compared to the quiet of the rest of this place.

"Callie," Elsa called up the stairs. "It's your mother!"

Callie rushed to the phone, nearly tripping in the process. "Mom?"

"Hey, baby. Where've you been? I've been calling you all day, but your cell phone kept going into your voicemail." Zoey sounded relieved at finally reaching her daughter.

"Yeah, I forgot to charge it last night… sorry. So where are you?"

"Uh…" she paused before answering, "I'm in Paris."

Callie hesitated before she spoke again. "I thought you said you were in London."

"Well, here's the thing…"

"Oh God, no…please don't say it!"

Zoey was at a chic gathering in Paris, hosted by Johnny Depp. It was nearly midnight her time, and the view behind her was magnificent. The Eiffel Tower glowed in the distance and all of Paris glittered around it.

She was mixing business with pleasure, having just been asked to shoot promo shots for Johnny's upcoming movie. The offer was lucrative, the client was more than charming, and the food and ambiance at the party was to die for. But instead of enjoying herself, she was arguing with her kid half way around the world!

"Wait, just listen. The spread for *Vogue* was expanded and since I'm already in Europe, they asked me to…"

"This can't be happening. You promised."

"Callie, please…it's just for a few more days." Zoey's voice was apologetic, but her daughter wasn't buying it.

"You have no idea what I've just been through!"

"I'm so sorry, baby. I promise I'll make it up to you."

"Don't bother. Your promises mean nothing. You *never* keep them!"

"Please don't say that. I feel guilty enough."

Roxanne placed her hand on Zoey's shoulder in a calming manner as she listened to the one-sided conversation.

"Not guilty enough to keep your promise! I'm just an entry in your Palm Pilot, the one appointment you can break!"

"Stop it Callie. I'm your mother."

"Yeah, don't remind me!"

"Callie!" Zoey whispered firmly, in an attempt to hide the tone of her voice from the people around her. She couldn't afford to lose her composure—especially when her image was at stake. At the same time, she was aching inside, knowing that her baby was hurt. But what could she do? She was thousands of miles away.

Callie was crying by now. She was angry with her mother, and angry with herself for letting it bother her so much. She should have known better than to believe Zoey would actually follow through on a promise. And on top of that, there was no one here she felt comfortable enough to turn to or confide in.

Elsa had left the receiver off the hook and joined Johan in the living room to give Callie more privacy. Unfortunately, they returned to the kitchen just in time to hear the tail end of the conversation.

"I hate this place, and I hate my life, but most of all, Zoey...I HATE YOU!" and she slammed the receiver down and flung herself onto the bed—her tears pouring like rain.

Zoey sighed on her end of the phone and the connection was lost.

Elsa and Johan looked at one another with concern. They hadn't heard enough of the conversation to interject, and decided to wait, hoping that Callie would explain it to them later. But one thing was clear. Their granddaughter was very unhappy, and they had no idea how to help her.

Callie stomped around her room for a few minutes, throwing everything that wouldn't break. Then taking her iPod and *Cosmo Girl*, she stormed out of her room and down the stairs. She grabbed her coat and ran out of the house in a rage.

"This is the *worst* Christmas of my life!" she yelled out in frustration.

Her grandparents looked to each other for guidance. But when Elsa started to follow, Johan held her back. "Let her go—she needs time to think," he spoke quietly.

"That's what you said about Cameron," she replied with a tortured look on her face. He wrapped his arms around her and pulled her close.

Zoey was struggling with her emotions, too. She hated the sound of Callie's tears and hated being the reason for them even more. Roxanne could tell she was agitated, but she kept it well hidden from everyone else. She had overheard Zoey's side of the conversation, and had guessed accurately at Callie's reaction. Having someone there who understood what she was going through meant a lot to Zoey—especially someone who wouldn't judge her.

Her thoughts came back to the present when Roxanne reminded her that Johnny's manager was anxiously waiting to discuss the details of the photo session. And being the true professional that she was, she straightened her shoulders and brightened her smile as she and Roxanne maneuvered through the posh crowd.

THE BARNYARD LOOKED BEAUTIFUL with Christmas lights twinkling brilliantly against the black expanse of sky. But Callie was in no mood to notice. She wanted privacy, and she wanted it now!

Roy was still working, but the other farmhands were preparing to leave. Callie saw the barn door cracked open and moved quietly inside, taking every precaution not to be seen. She climbed an old ladder to the loft and nestled into a pile of loose hay. And after putting on her head phones, she cranked the music and opened her magazine just wanting to escape for a while.

It had been a long day, and she had gotten up earlier than she was used to, walked nearly five miles carrying a load fit for a mule, and experienced an emotionally draining call from her mother, so it wasn't long before she fell asleep—oblivious to the world around her.

When dinnertime came, Elsa and Johan sat at the kitchen table in silence. Callie's place was set, but her chair remained unoccupied. The food was still out, and the elderly couple had only picked at their meals. Every time Elsa heard a noise, she would run to the window over the sink and look out. But the farmyard was empty.

When the clock struck six, it startled them, sending Elsa to the window yet again. She was horrified at what she saw. Big snowflakes were obstructing her view.

"Ach du lieber, Himmel! It's snowing!"

Elsa was alarmed. Callie wasn't used to the country, and in heavy snow a person could easily get lost. Not to mention, she wasn't dressed for freezing temperatures.

"Johan—go find Callie!" Elsa's eyes were afire and this was a direct order.

Johan jumped up from the table and put on his coat and boots. He was carrying a flashlight and calling Callie's name when he met Roy at the animal pens.

"What's all the fuss, boss?"

"Callie's missing, have you seen her?" Johan was more concerned than he had let on to Elsa.

"Can't say I have. What happened?"

"She was upset and ran out of the house…" Johan started to explain.

"Say no more. I didn't see her come back here, but let's have a look."

Roy opened the barn doors and turned on the overhead lights. Johan used his flashlight to check the darkened corners, and they both called out her name.

Callie was in too deep of sleep to notice the lights, and if she were awake, the music would have covered the sound of their voices.

"I can't imagine she'd be hanging out in a smelly old barn—just doesn't seem the type."

"Ja, I know, but where else could she go?" Johan asked. "It's been well over an hour."

They looked at each other contemplating the possibilities, and knowing that it was dangerous to be wandering around in a blizzard—especially for a young girl used to the city.

Roy jumped into gear. "I'll round up the boys."

Johan nodded in appreciation.

The old farmhand turned the lights back off and closed the barn doors, never imagining that Callie was sleeping in the loft.

The warm glow from the outdoor Christmas lights beamed through the cracks in the walls, illuminating Callie's face. And she looked like a sleeping angel, all sweet and innocent.

About half an hour later, the driveway looked like a convention of classic cars and old pickup trucks. And two police vehicles were parked with their lights flashing.

Sheriff Daley was a rugged man in his sixties and a life-long resident of the county. Deputy Wylie was in his twenties, shorter and wiry, but competent. They were coordinating the search party.

Johan, Roy, Arnie, Hank, Sam, Jed and several other farmhands were waiting for instructions. And as Sheriff Daley started delegating assignments, another vehicle was seen heading toward them. It was Casey and his father, Nick.

Nick was a handsome man in his early forties, and after Cameron's death, he and Johan had become very close—almost as if he had taken the place of the son that Johan had lost. They jumped out of Casey's truck and moved to join the group.

"Hank—you and Sam cover Old Mill Road. Go ten miles in either direction. Arnie—you go with Deputy Wylie. Search every property within two miles of here." The Sheriff was firm in his orders.

"Even Old Man Johnson's?" the Deputy questioned.

"Especially Old Man Johnson's. And if that damn dog of his is loose again, pen them both up in the barn while you search." The Sheriff continued, "Roy—you and the boys take that stand of trees," and he circled it on the map. "Make sure you stay within twenty-five feet of one another. That gives the four of you a hundred-foot spread. Grab a pair of searchlights from my trunk. Nick—you take Casey and Johan. Comb the banks of Edermann's Pond—up one side and down the other. And for God's sake stay off it. The thaw we had over the last few days means it's not frozen solid any more."

"What about me, Sheriff?" Jedediah asked, eager to be of assistance.

The sheriff took one look at Jed's glasses and knew he wouldn't be much help in the search. Besides, he knew Jed's mother would skin him alive if anything happened to her precious little boy. "You'd better stick with me Jedediah."

"Oh c'mon Sheriff, I'm eighteen now," Jed was quick to answer.

"I'm going to need some help coordinating the search..." Sheriff Daley said. He realized Jed wasn't buying his story, so he added an incentive. "...and I'll let you control the siren."

"All right!" Jed's eyes lit up, and he readily agreed.

Sheriff Daley folded the map and handed out two-way radios to the men. They piled into their vehicles, and one by one, raced out of the driveway.

Elsa watched from the window as the flashing lights from the patrol cars raced across her worried face. She had been joined by Clara, Arnie's wife, who had come over to comfort her. And when the search party had left, they went to the kitchen where they sat drinking coffee, waiting for news.

Casey pulled his truck over in a clearing between trees, and the men jumped out. They paused in front of the truck's headlights and radioed the sheriff before circling the pond.

"We're here," Nick reported.

"Copy that, Nick. Arnie says the surface of the pond appears frozen, but I doubt it will hold anyone's weight, so stay back from the edge. And be careful!"

"Will do," and Nick hooked the radio onto his belt. "You heard him boys, let's all be careful."

He grabbed Casey in a hug. "Don't be a hero, son. We need you."

Casey looked nearly level into his father's eyes and nodded, reading between the lines. "I know Dad. I'll be careful."

Meanwhile, Callie had awakened to shivers. She was disoriented at first, and then remembered where she was—and why. The barn was dark except for the colorful rays of light from outside, and it was very quiet. She was embarrassed that she had fallen asleep and felt a sense of urgency to get back to the house.

Moving carefully down the rickety old ladder, she peaked outside, looking for witnesses. Relieved that no one was in sight, she attempted to sneak into the house through the kitchen. But Elsa and Clara were at the table and instantly came to life when she opened the door.

"You're alive!" was all Elsa could say, as she grabbed Callie, squeezing her hard and refusing to relinquish her grip.

"Why wouldn't I be?"

"You've been gone for hours, and it started to snow. We were so worried about you. They formed a search party and they're out looking for you right now."

"You've got to be kidding?" Callie replied. No one had ever thought to search for her before.

"Oh no. When your Opa couldn't find you, he called the sheriff."

"THE SHERIFF!" Callie was astounded.

"And Roy, and Hank, and Arnie, and…"

"Okay—I get the point. But I'm here now, so call off the dogs!"

Elsa broke her embrace, thinking she should notify the dispatcher immediately. But Clara was one step ahead of her and already in the process of making the call.

Sheriff Daley was driving down a gravel road at the time, casting a searchlight off to the sides in a one hundred and eighty degree rotation as he slowly crept forward. The dispatcher's voice, female and raspy, broke through the silence. "Sheriff, do you copy?"

"Go ahead Elaine."

"Just heard from Clara. Elsa has the girl. Repeat the chicken has returned to the hen house. So c'mon home!"

"Copy that," the sheriff said—just as Jed grabbed the handset from him.

"Mama, it's me, Jed. Sheriff's letting me work the sirens. Listen to this Mama," and he gave a blast to demonstrate.

Annoyed and ready to strangle the boy, Sheriff Daley grabbed the handset back and told Elaine to notify Roy's group. He changed his frequency to match the radio Nick was carrying. "Nick—Callie's been found and is safe at home. Let's call it a night. I repeat, the search is over. Head on home."

Johan was near the edge of the pond when he heard the static of the radio. It was hard to tell where exactly the shore ended and the ice started because of the falling snow. The flakes were big and white and muffled the sound, so he couldn't hear the message very well.

Living in the country, the men knew the risks of being lost in a blizzard. Not to mention the potential danger of the pond itself. And it took only minutes for a person to freeze to death when immersed in a body of water.

Johan's attention was focused on the radio and he forgot to watch where he placed his foot. As he paused to listen, he heard a *crack* and looked down, thinking he had stepped on a branch. Instead, he saw the ice spreading under his feet and he tried to run. But it was too late. He fell with a splash into the freezing water about eight feet off shore.

The sound *rang* out like an explosion!

12

Denial isn't a river in Egypt

"HELP!" Johan yelled, as his head bobbed above the surface of the water. His body was rapidly growing numb, and while he felt no pain—he knew he was in trouble.

Nick was on the right side of the pond and Casey was on the left. They both heard the splash followed by Johan's cry for help, but Casey was closer. He would have to fight his way through downed branches, trees, thorn bushes, and snow to reach Johan. And on top of that, it was dark.

The woods were dense around the pond with the exception of the deer trail that people normally used for access. But that was not the straightest route to where Johan had fallen in, and they had no time to waste. Casey kept up a steady stream of encouraging dialogue for Johan's sake, using the old man's responses and splashes to pinpoint his exact location.

As he neared, he saw his friend struggling to keep his head above water. The pond was only about fifteen feet deep, but his winter clothes were pulling him down. And every time he got his arm on the ice, it would break. His movements were slowing as Casey arrived on the scene using his flashlight as his guide. Nick, however, was still maneuvering through the brush.

Casey placed the flashlight with its beam projecting upward into the sky, so his father could locate them while he looked around the area for a branch. Not seeing anything strong enough, he took off his coat as his dad approached from behind.

"Be careful, Casey!" Nick warned.

Johan's head slipped beneath the water again, and Casey knew there wasn't any time to waste. He laid down—half on and half off the ice—and instructed his dad to grab a hold of his legs as he tossed his jacket forward. Johan reached for the sleeve, but his fingers were too cold to grasp it.

Nick anchored Casey's legs with one hand and used the other to contact the sheriff. "Call an ambulance!" he yelled, "Johan went through the ice." He was abrupt, and dropped the radio in the snow, securing his son's legs. Casey inched forward until he could grasp Johan's hands firmly. They felt like ice cubes.

"PULL DAD!" he yelled, and Nick pulled with all his strength. The first couple of inches of ice broke beneath Johan's weight as they moved back toward the bank. But they soon hit thicker ice and shallower water, and Casey was able to stand. Together, they lifted Johan out of the pond. And by the time help arrived, they were already at the top of the bank.

ELSA AND CLARA WERE celebrating the fact that no injury had befallen Callie. Both of them had known individuals who were lost in storms, and every winter seemed to bring news of a new tragedy. It was hard to imagine that in modern times, a person could die of hypothermia in a matter of moments. But nature could be cruel as often as it could be kind.

Callie, on the other hand, couldn't believe all the attention she was receiving, but she didn't mind it one bit. Clara was busy explaining that the whole county was out searching for her, and her ego was becoming more inflated by the minute. Elsa was just relieved that her granddaughter was home safe and happy to see her sitting in the kitchen without feeling the urgency to run to her room.

But her sense of relief was short-lived, and she nearly panicked when she answered Elaine's call. Her face quickly changed from happiness to terror, and she lost all color as she relayed the news about Johan.

Clara took immediate action, comforting Elsa first and reassuring her that Johan was strong. She cleverly suggested that they get some food and coffee ready for the men, figuring that movement would keep Elsa sane.

Callie was speechless. She told herself she wasn't responsible, but there was a lingering knowledge that if she hadn't vanished, Johan would never have gone looking for her. She felt uncomfortable and acted defensively.

"No one had to come looking for me! And if they really *had* looked, they would never have left the farm!" She made her voice as indignant as possible, but it wasn't quite convincing.

Elsa and Clara maneuvered around the kitchen anticipating each other's movements. Elsa was preoccupied. Her mind was on Johan. But Clara was finally seeing what everyone else had been saying about Callie, and the look on her face was full of disgust. She turned to concentrate on making sandwiches and shook her head to indicate her disapproval.

Feeling the tension in the room, Callie quietly slipped upstairs. She was worried about her grandfather though her actions and candid remarks seemed to indicate otherwise.

JOHAN'S LIPS WERE BLUE, and he was semi-conscious from the cold or from a possible heart attack—they didn't know which. The men set him in the front seat of the patrol car and wrapped him in blankets until the ambulance arrived.

The paramedics went to work immediately. Johan's heart rate was slow, but he nodded no when they asked if he hurt anywhere. Doc Hermann, their family physician, was on the two-way radio with the ambulance. He ordered the medics to keep Johan warm and take him to the hospital.

But when Johan overheard the instructions, he opened his eyes. And with chattering teeth, he whispered, "No—take me home to Elsa."

The medics were confused and asked the doctor what to do.

"That damn fool," Doc Hermann declared, "but since he's talking take him home. I can get there faster anyway."

The sheriff went on ahead to prepare Elsa for the onslaught of commotion. He anticipated her stress level and wanted to make sure the bedroom was ready for Johan's arrival.

The ambulance was a reconditioned hearse and had an ominous appearance as it pulled up to the front of the house. The rest of the vehicles followed closely behind.

Doc Hermann, a gentle white-haired man in his seventies, arrived moments later and immediately ran up to the bedroom. Johan had been his patient for years, and he had no intention of letting anything more happen to him.

The search party filled the house. And by now, many of them had called their wives, too. Most brought some kind of food, and they served the men who had not eaten. They insisted that Elsa sit down and try to eat as well, but she merely pushed food around on her plate and stared blankly into space. Her mind was in the bedroom with her husband, and if sheer strength of will were needed to keep him on this earth—she had it!

Finally the bedroom door opened, and Doc Hermann called Elsa's name. She pushed herself out of the chair and moved cautiously up the stairs, almost afraid to hear what he had to say.

Johan was lying on the bed, covered to his neck with blankets. His face was ashen. Elsa looked at him first and then at the doctor with fear in her eyes.

"Will he be okay?" she whispered.

"I've given him a strong sedative, and he should sleep through the night. But I'm not going to sugar coat things," he warned. "His body temperature dropped a lot, but the boys did a great job of warming him up. The tests they ran in the ambulance showed no heart irregularities, so the odds of a heart attack happening now are slim." Doc Hermann put his arm around Elsa's shoulder. "He's a strong man, and I really don't think he's ready to check out just yet."

Elsa was relieved, but it still didn't look like her beloved husband. "What can I do to help?" she asked anxiously.

"He needs rest, and you need to keep him warm. We'll let God do the rest. My only concern at this time is pneumonia. He may have swallowed some water, but we'll watch for that." Doc Hermann was much more than their family doctor, he was an old and trusted friend.

Elsa leaned over Johan and smoothed the hair off his forehead. "I love you." Her voice was full of tenderness and concern as she gently kissed him on the cheek. His eyelids flickered and she swore she could see the corner of his lips turn up in response.

The men were finishing up the pie and coffee the ladies had served them, and were discussing the evening's events when Callie came in to get a glass of water. The conversation stopped and all eyes focused on her. She could tell they blamed her for Johan's accident.

Most of the faces were unfamiliar with the exception of Casey. He was the only person she vaguely felt a connection with, and looked to him hoping for some reassurance. But his expression was as blank as everyone else's, and in her mind all she could see was accusation.

"What?" Callie reacted in her own defense. "It's not like I pushed him!" She grabbed her glass and started to retreat to the safety of her room, but bumped into the doctor coming down the stairs. And in her first attempt to do something right, she asked what she could do to help.

Doc Hermann wasn't kind with his rebuff. "I think you've done quite enough, young lady."

Callie took his response as the ultimate dismissal, and dashed up to her room feeling completely confused and out of control.

By the time Elsa got back to the kitchen, the doctor had provided an update on Johan's condition and mentioned that perhaps the family should be allowed to get some sleep after the ordeal. Everyone was tired—both from the exertions of the evening and the emotions that had been spent. But they were relieved that no one was in immediate danger.

The conversations tapered off, and slowly the men got up and said their farewells to Elsa, promising to come around and help during Johan's recovery. Doc Hermann went over a list of instructions and advised her to get some rest, too. He could tell she was exhausted.

When the women finished cleaning the kitchen, they hugged Elsa and gathered their husbands.

She walked them to the door—acknowledging their friendship and good wishes—and watched until the last truck left the drive. Alone for the first time and feeling despair, her true emotions surfaced and she broke down in a flood of tears.

13

Treasures are meant to be found

The house was silent and seemed empty after the frenzied evening—rather like the calm *after* the storm. Elsa stood for a moment looking around the living room where she and Johan had shared so many special moments over the years. She just couldn't imagine life without him.

When she regained her composure, she locked up the house and turned off the lights, following the ritual that was normally Johan's. And with a renewed sense of hope, she went upstairs to join her husband.

Callie came out of the bathroom just as Elsa entered her room. They were used to being alone in the house, so her grandmother didn't think to close the door behind her. From Callie's vantage point in the hall, she had a perfect view through the open doorway to where Johan lay in the bed.

Elsa tip-toed around the room and turned on a small light, so she wouldn't disturb Johan's slumber. Callie watched quietly as her grandmother moved to his bed and neatly arranged the covers. Johan's sleep seemed deeper than usual, which worried her. She picked up his hand and gently touched his wedding band. "Please Johan, come back to me," she pleaded in a voice choked with grief. "You're all I have."

Callie's eyes began to water as she connected with her grandmother for the first time. Hearing those words reminded her of an earlier conversation with her mother, and she suddenly realized that she had more in common with Elsa than she had ever dreamed. Her grandmother's dependency on her grandfather was like hers on her mother. Callie wiped an escaped tear away with the back of her hand and returned to her room.

She wasn't tired, and her mind was spinning with recent revelations. She had taken a nap earlier, and the evening's catastrophe had only served to wind her up even more. Looking around her room, she noticed the box that Elsa had delivered on her first night. It was barely recognizable with all the clothes draped over it, but her curiosity was at its peak.

Layers of tissue paper separated the content, which had obviously been placed in the box with meticulous care. She opened each bundle as carefully as it had been wrapped, and one at a time.

The first package contained an intricately crocheted baby blanket with the initials CM weaved into the pattern. The next one held white baby shoes, which were smaller than the span across her palm. The third package included a tiny silver spoon and cup, engraved with the same initials. And finally, one that was filled with a stack of baby dresses that were lacy and feminine. As time passed and Callie looked at each carefully, she realized these had all been hers, and it wasn't long before piles of tissue paper and keepsakes surrounded her on the floor.

The last item she reached for was a decorative box full of photos, which she quickly rifled through once before looking at each more closely. She saw herself, first as an infant then as a toddler and progressing in age until about five. Callie began to notice a pattern in the pictures. Her face was always lit up with a great big smile and a younger version of Elsa and Johan were always standing by her side.

A *best friends* kind of pose with an unfamiliar little girl caught her attention. They must have been close at the time because their arms were wrapped around each other's waists, and they shared a look of mischief. She set it aside with the intention of asking Elsa about it in the morning.

On the bottom of the photo box was a large manila envelope marked with the letter Z. Inside, were black and white 8X10 photos of the farm—much like the ones that were displayed throughout the farmhouse. The last picture showed a happy young farmhand pausing at his chores.

Callie squinted, trying to identify the face. "Dad?"

She carefully rewrapped the baby items, placing them gently back in the box, and set the photos on top. Then she climbed into bed and attempted to fall sleep.

It was a restless night. She dreamed vividly, woke frequently, and tossed and turned. Her mind refused to slow down. Too much had happened, and she was still processing it as she slept.

Callie awakened well before dawn, and before that obnoxious rooster could play his tricks. She had already showered and was just tying her shoes when she heard his foul wake-up call. That was her signal to grab the box of photos and head downstairs to the kitchen.

Elsa had been up for a while, unable to sleep soundly because of her concern for Johan. She was already in the kitchen, and about to take a batch of blueberry muffins out of the oven when Callie entered. Caught off guard, she bumped her hand against the hot metal and reacted with an "Ouch!" followed by, "Oh schatzie, you scared me."

Callie set the box of photos on the counter and rushed to her grandmother's side. "Grandma, are you okay?"

This was the first time she appeared concerned about anything other than her own welfare. But Elsa didn't want to draw attention to her change in attitude, so she pretended not to notice.

"Ach, it's nothing. It happens all the time." She looked at the clock and said rather frantically, "Your breakfast! It isn't ready yet!" then started rummaging through her pots and pans to find the one she used for oatmeal.

"Those muffins sure smell good. May I have one?"

She heard Callie's request from an upside down position in the cupboard and nearly bumped her head as she stood up in disbelief. "Of course schatzie, you can have anything you want."

Elsa was overwhelmed as Callie lunged at her, hugging her tightly. She was definitely not the same girl from the night before, but rather, more like the little girl who used to greet her every morning with a big hug and a kiss.

"I'm so sorry Grandma. I never meant to hurt anyone," Callie said, as her eyes filled with tears.

"Of course you didn't. It was an accident." Elsa patted her head, reluctant to break contact and yet, uncertain as to how much Callie was ready to accept.

"But if I hadn't run out and fallen asleep…"

"Stop it—you will *not* take the blame for this. It was an accident. It's nobody's fault!"

"And I've been so mean to everyone."

Elsa wiped the tears from Callie's face with the corner of her apron. "You're my granddaughter. I love you no matter what." Then taking Callie's face into the palm of her hands, she said with undeniable sincerity, "You're just like your father, strong-willed and full of life. But also like your mother, beautiful and sensitive. We're so proud of you!"

"Really?" Callie wondered how her grandparents could still care so much about her, but it felt good to hear those words just the same.

"Really. Now eat your muffin."

Callie's face turned from worry to relief as she accepted the plate with eagerness. "You know," she said matter-of-factly, "I used to eat blueberries by the bushel."

"Ja, I know," Elsa replied, as she remembered Callie and her precious face with blue stained lips, stuffing berries into her mouth faster than her little fingers could pick them. She also remembered how Callie used to be her shadow, and how she would help out in the kitchen, unless of course, Johan offered to take her in the truck with him. Then she practically forgot she had a grandmother!

After devouring the muffin, Callie insisted on helping Elsa with Johan's breakfast. And for the first time in years, they worked side by side in the kitchen gathering his favorite foods. It was a perfect partnership. One did all the work while the other got in the way. Every time Elsa reached for something Callie was standing right in front of her, blocking her path. But she was patient and more than happy to show her *little shadow* where things were.

At last, the tray was ready, and just as Elsa was about to pick it up, Callie stopped her. "No Grandma, let me take it."

"Ja, I think he would like that," Elsa admitted. And she watched from the bottom of the stairs as her granddaughter carried it carefully up to the bedroom.

When Johan saw her pushing the door open with her elbow, he started to get up until she ordered him to "lay down!" He immediately obeyed, and Callie grinned inside, enjoying the fact that even a grown man responded to her voice of command. But obedience was not her goal. She was building bridges this morning and wanted the base of this one to be solid. So she modified her voice before continuing.

"I mean, you need to stay in bed," she said in a much gentler tone. Callie set the tray on the nightstand and proceeded to arrange Johan's pillows. "So, what possessed you to go swimming last night?"

Johan cracked a smile. "Maybe I should lose a few pounds."

Callie handed him his tray. "Don't worry, we'll work on that! Right now our job is to get you back on your feet. So enjoy the food while you can. By the way, the muffins taste great!" She flashed a guilty look, and Johan reacted with a raised eyebrow.

"I'm really sorry, Grandfather. I fell asleep in the barn. I didn't mean to cause any trouble—especially not this."

"You had me so scared, Callie. I just couldn't live through another..." and his voice broke with emotion.

"I know Grandfather, me neither." Her hand rested on his shoulder for a moment. Then with a quick little tap, she commanded, "Now eat up!"

The conversation was awkward at first with a lot of small talk. But when Callie pulled up a chair next to Johan's bed and repeated the funny stories Elsa had told her in the kitchen, the tension gradually eased. He, too, remembered the rides she would take with him, and how she used to follow him through the barns, petting each and every one of the cows. And she laughed when he told her she had names for every one of them. She listened to her grandfather's stories until he finished his breakfast. But at the first sign of a yawn, she took the dishes from his lap and tucked him in neatly.

Callie carried the tray down to the kitchen, realizing that there was a lot she had done wrong since arriving in Deer Creek and a lot she could do to set things right. It wasn't her fault that Johan fell through the ice, but it happened because he loved her. And she was beginning to accept just how much that meant to her. She looked outside and saw her grandmother moving toward the henhouse with a basket in her hand and then looked around the kitchen, which was still in a state of disarray.

Deciding it was time to help out a bit, Callie gathered the dishes and filled the sink with soapy water while formulating a plan. Of all the people she had met since arriving in Wisconsin, it was Elsa who had accepted her regardless of her behavior, and she seemed to work the hardest, too, and always for other people's benefit. Washing the dishes was a small gesture. But Callie figured it was the least she could do to make up for the past few days.

THE AIR WAS COLD and crisp outside, but the wind wasn't blowing. Elsa enjoyed mornings like this where the only sounds were those of the animals going about their business. The dog greeted her, nuzzling its nose lovingly into her palm, and she felt at peace as she trekked through the fresh snow.

Roy popped his head into the shack as Elsa gathered fresh eggs. She was humming an old German melody, and he could tell that she wasn't as worried as she had been the night before.

"Good morning, Ma'am," he said respectfully.

"Guten morning," she answered, smiling.

"I take it Johan's doing better?"

"Much—now that Callie is with him," and her smile widened.

"You think that's a good idea? I mean she did cause a whole lot of trouble last night." Roy should have known better than to question any of Elsa's decisions concerning Johan.

"It's a very good idea," she said with complete conviction. "Callie is just the medicine Johan needs."

Roy sensed that he crossed the line and acknowledged it with a polite, "Yes, Ma'am," but he hesitated to leave.

"Is there something else?"

"Well, yeah—Jimmy and Turk are gone for the holidays. And with Johan out of the picture, we're down three men tomorrow. Any suggestions?"

"Call Casey. He'll know what to do."

Johan had trained Casey well, and Elsa had confidence in his abilities to manage the farm for a few days. Besides, she had to take care of the house *and* a patient, and she didn't have time to resolve labor issues. It was evident in her body language that no argument would be accepted, so Roy moved along with his business.

Elsa went in through the back door to put the eggs away and was surprised by what she saw. The kitchen was her domain, and she had never had a gremlin in it before, at least not a helpful one. The men were great at devouring her food and making a mess, but never offered to clean it up. She knew Callie was responsible, and she was grateful for the help—especially considering the source. So after putting away the few odd dishes that remained on the counter, she looked around her gleaming kitchen, proud of the order it displayed, and went to check up on Johan.

Elsa found him fast asleep and snoring loud enough to wake the dead. She rested her hand gently on his forehead and was relieved to find no temperature. Content for the time being, she tucked the blanket up to his chin and went in search of her granddaughter.

Callie was now back in the kitchen, admiring one of the framed black and white photos on the wall. Elsa entered the room with a smile that would have rivaled any Cheshire cat's. Her patient was well, her kitchen was in order, and all was right in her world!

"Is he okay?" Callie asked, having just peeked in on him five minutes earlier.

"He's sleeping like a baby, well…actually, snoring like a bear. But I'm sure you get the picture!" Elsa joked.

Callie turned back to the art on the wall. "Speaking of pictures—I'd like to go through that box with you. I don't recognize all the faces and this photo looks a lot like the black and whites in the envelope."

"It should. It's your mother's. And so are the ones in the envelope."

"Zoey shot this?" Callie had never seen this side of her mother's talents.

"Ja, she's very good," Elsa said with the assurance of someone who knew art.

"I just assumed these were my dad's."

"Oh, no! I could never display Cameron's work. It was much too graphic. He felt he had to show the brutal side of life, but not your mother. She always saw the beauty."

"I guess that explains her *passion for fashion*!" Callie commented, as they moved to the living room to investigate the box of old pictures. They sat next to each other on the sofa, not quite touching, but still feeling the comfortable presence of one another.

"Why aren't my parents in any of these?" Callie asked, before opening the lid to the box.

"They traveled." Elsa's answer was brief.

"Without me?"

"Oh schatzie, it was so dangerous!"

"So I lived here with you?" Callie practically answered her own question.

"Ja, until your father…" Elsa stopped to gather her thoughts. "Until your father died."

"I'm sure that was really hard for you."

Elsa's mind drifted back to the day when she received the devastating news. "Ja, it was very hard." She paused for a moment. "…on all of us." Shaking off the pain, she managed a small smile. "So, let's have a look, shall we?" She grabbed the first picture from the top of the pile. "Ach, I look terrible!"

Callie eyed the photo. "No you don't. Now, who are those people? I don't recognize them."

"That's Johan's cousin Ginny and her husband, Herbert. They were visiting from Munich."

"He sure has big ears."

"You should've seen his brother!"

"And the little girl?"

Elsa was surprised at the question. "Why that's Amanda…and her parents, Sarah and Nick. You don't remember, do you?"

"No—not really."

"Amanda was your best friend. The two of you were inseparable."

"I guess that explains this picture," Callie said, digging out the *best friends* pose.

"Ach, mein Gott! You were so adorable and you still are."

Callie beamed. "And who's the little boy?"

"Why that's Casey."

"Farm boy? What a geek!"

Elsa laughed and explained further. "Actually, that was the day he rescued you from Edermann's Pond."

"What?" Callie was surprised to hear that she and Casey shared a past.

"Oh ja. He was quite the hero that day. You see, you were always climbing trees and scaling rocks. We could hardly keep up with you. So one day, the youngest Willen's boy dared you to walk across a big log in the pond. You made it one way, but you didn't make it back. When you fell in, Casey jumped in after you and pulled you to safety. And from that day on, you called him Rhett Butler and followed him everywhere."

Callie flashed back to Casey calling her Scarlett in the truck and cringed at the thought. "How embarrassing!"

Her grandmother's face became worried as she studied the photo. "She looked so healthy back then."

"What do you mean?"

Elsa looked up with surprise. "You really don't know, do you?"

"Know what?"

"Amanda was diagnosed with leukemia shortly after her mother died."

"Her mother died?"

"Ja, a drunk driver from Madison."

"Grandma, that's so sad!" Callie's voice was completely sincere.

Elsa continued, "So when Amanda got sick, Nick was devastated. First it was his best friend—your father, then his wife, and now his daughter. Thank God for Casey. He takes Amanda to her chemotherapy treatments."

"Why Casey?"

"Well, with their mother gone, Nick really depends on him." Elsa thought she was explaining the obvious, but it was clear now that Callie had no recollection of the Meyers family.

"Oh no, Grandma! I've made a terrible mistake!" She buried her face in shame, suddenly grasping the fact that Amanda and Casey were brother and sister, not boyfriend and girlfriend as she had previously thought. No wonder he hated her. She insulted his little sister who just happened to be terminally ill!

Then, as if divinely inspired, Callie had a great idea. "Grandma, can you teach me how to bake a pie?"

"I'd be happy to, schatzie!" Elsa was delighted at the thought of spending time with her granddaughter in the kitchen.

"So where do you keep your Cuisinart?"

"I don't know this Squeeze-n-Start. But the flour and the sugar are in the pantry and the rolling pin is in the drawer."

"Rolling pin?" Callie gasped. "Where am I—Bedrock?"

14

Assumptions can be misleading

Callie mumbled every ounce of profanity she knew as she struggled with the job at hand. Only a half an hour into the project and she was already drenched in flour, in spite of the apron she wore. Her hair was pulled back into a loose ponytail, and her face was dripping with sweat. She looked puzzled as she pondered the complexity of her task. Never before had she felt so inept and incompetent, and she wondered if it were possible to convert the recipe into a chemistry exercise or an algebraic formula. Only *then* would it make sense!

"How hard can this be?" she thought to herself. "There are only six ingredients." But her first culinary work-in-progress could honestly only be called a catastrophe. The crust, which she had just finished crimping around the edges, looked uneven and was thinner in some spots than others. She eyed the rolling pin distrustfully, suspecting that it was warped and the direct cause of the problem.

The doorbell rang, and Callie looked up from the abomination on the counter. She blew a strand of hair from in front of her eyes and grabbed the nearest towel to wipe off her hands. When the doorbell rang again she yelled out in a forceful voice, "I'm coming!"

Elsa had been upstairs checking on Johan, and managed to reach the door at the same time. She muffled the laugh that threatened to emerge at Callie's flour laden form.

It was Arnie and Clara, checking up on Johan and delivering a perfectly shaped and delicious smelling blueberry pie. They burst into the house, hugging Elsa, but completely ignoring Callie.

Feeling left out, she reached for the pie with the intention of taking it to the kitchen. But Clara reacted rudely and pulled it out of Callie's grasp. "THIS is for Johan!"

Elsa stepped in and graciously accepted the *get well* gift as the elderly couple moved up the stairs. She whispered some advice to Callie, "They're simple people, schatzie. It won't take much to win them back."

Elsa followed her friends upstairs, leaving Callie to ponder the situation. Her immediate concern was to determine if baking her pie would improve its appearance. She doubted it would, but decided to go back to the kitchen and try it anyway.

IT WASN'T LONG BEFORE Johan's bedroom resembled a scene from an old Western movie. Callie's eyes glared with an evil squint. Arnie appeared uncomfortable and shifty. Clara had one eyebrow raised in suspicion. And Johan, decked in flannel pajamas and a fur-lined duck hunting hat, peered over his bifocals, displaying the most obvious signs of guilt. The distrust continued for another round until suddenly, Johan lifted his head and with gleaming eyes, slapped three queens and a sequence of hearts on the bed and yelled "Gin!"

A moan arose from the rest of the group as they tossed all their cards into a pile. But just as Arnie reached to shuffle the deck, Elsa arrived in the doorway. With her hands on her hips, she announced, "Okay everyone. That's enough for today. Johan needs his rest." The look on her face discouraged any debate.

"Thank God!" Arnie spoke emphatically. "I can't take any more of this abuse." He wasn't used to losing every game, and Callie had won the first.

"Don't be a poor sport, Arnie. Johan and Callie beat you fair and square." Clara chastised her husband gently, knowing how he valued his *card shark* reputation.

"That may be, but I demand a rematch!" he said grudgingly.

"Yeah...me, too!" Callie piped. "Do you know what the odds of him pulling that last queen were?"

Arnie smiled at her for her astuteness in tracking the cards and for her positive change in attitude. She responded with a wink.

"Bring it on!" Johan said, reaching for the deck.

"Ja, ja, but not today!" Elsa chimed, taking the cards from Johan. "Arnie can get revenge later. And Roy is waiting for *you* downstairs, young lady!"

After tucking Johan in and saying goodbye to Arnie and Clara, Elsa located Callie in the kitchen. She was staring glumly at the two pies. Clara's was absolutely perfect—and hers, well it was downright pathetic. So when Elsa walked up from behind, she knew what Callie was thinking.

"You should have seen my first try—not even the dog would eat it!" she said, as she took Clara's pie and handed it to Callie, covering it with a clean, dry dishtowel. "And my first loaf of bread? They used it for a brick!" Elsa was not above poking fun at herself to make her granddaughter feel better. "It just takes practice, schatzie. And Clara and I have a lot of that!"

"Thanks Grandma...it was a lot harder than I thought."

"Your welcome," Elsa replied, understanding the importance of a good first impression. "Now you'd better get moving. Roy isn't a patient man!"

Callie had already figured that Roy was going to be a problem. He had witnessed enough of her bad attitude to decide she wasn't worth the effort, and he wasn't the type to readily change his opinion once it was formed. So she stared out the window, not really sure how to bridge the gap. But this wasn't the time to smooth things over. She had something bigger on her mind, and sat quietly, doing nothing to egg him on.

They drove in silence until Roy turned at a big, white wrought iron gate inscribed with *MICHELSOHN & MEYERS DAIRY, since 1982.* The sign caught her attention, and though she didn't know why, there was something familiar about the name.

The paved road was lined with white fencing and large oak trees, which were now bare, and small herds of cows grazed the acres on both sides of the inactive farm. As the driveway bent to the right, a massive estate—festively decorated with garland, wreaths and bows—filled the horizon. Callie's eyes widened with surprise as she broke her silence.

"My grandma said you were taking me to Amanda's house."

The truck came to a full stop. "This *is* Amanda's house."

Callie was intimidated as she looked from the foundation to the chimney. This was no simple farmhouse, it was a mansion!

"Casey lives here?" She already knew the answer and her embarrassment deepened.

"Not bad for a Farm boy, eh?" Roy was gaining pleasure from her apprehension. "I'll be at the main barn," and he pointed to one of several. "Come get me when you're ready to leave."

Callie slid out of the truck then squared her shoulders, marched up the steps, and rang the doorbell with confidence.

Casey opened the door. "What are you doing here?" He obviously wasn't expecting her visit.

"I came to see Amanda," she said, holding her purse and the pie in front of her as if they were a protective shield.

"Why?"

"Because I'm her friend!" Her voice had a certain tone reminiscent of Elsa's authority as she spoke.

Casey just rolled his eyes and laughed.

"I baked a pie," she added, intending it as a peace offering.

"Sure you did," he responded, as he led her into a luxurious, but still earthy family room. "Have a seat." Casey left the room to get Amanda, but returned within seconds to grab the pie. "I'd better take this to the kitchen," he added.

Callie sat patiently for about a minute then got up to snoop. Family photos adorned every spare inch of space, and two attractive display cases filled with awards, trophies, and ribbons commanded her attention. The first was dedicated to the relationship between Johan and Nick—Michelsohn & Meyers Dairy—and it contained agricultural accomplishments in addition to a history of their award-winning dairy herds.

The other case was divided between Casey's impressive academic and football awards, and pictures and articles about Amanda—*The Angel of Deer Creek*—a young leukemia patient who made a habit of volunteering her time helping other terminally ill children.

"Rumor has it you've been stirring up trouble again!" a voice spoke from the doorway.

Startled, Callie spun around. Amanda was standing behind her, holding what appeared to be a scrapbook. She looked thinner and frailer than in the photos, and was dressed in baggy jeans and an oversized sweatshirt. Her big, soft brown eyes were underlined with dark circles, and she wore a pink bandanna to hide her hair loss—a visible sign of her illness.

"Again?" Callie asked.

Amanda hid her excitement and continued with her theatrics. "Well, that was your reputation, you know."

Callie appeared rattled.

Amanda continued her drama. "Folks around here called you *Double-trouble Michelsohn*—the most tenacious five-year-old in the history of Deer Creek!" She couldn't fake it any longer and flashed a big grin at Callie. "Girl, you're a legend! Kids all over these parts aspire to be just like you!"

Callie had already moved to the sofa and was staring up at Amanda. She didn't know how to respond.

"I'm so happy you've come back," Amanda continued. "I can't tell you how many times I've imagined our reunion." She bent down and hugged Callie with one arm as she set the scrapbook on the coffee table in front of her.

"Amanda, I have to be honest. I barely remember my father's funeral. The rest of my childhood is just one big blur," she confessed. "And I've already managed to insult most of the people in this town because I don't remember them!"

"I know. I was numb for years after my mother died, and I was almost ten..." She picked up the scrapbook and handed it to Callie, "...which makes *this* all the more special."

Callie accepted the book with curiosity. The cover read *CALLIE MICHELSON: THE EARLY YEARS* and the first page included the *best friends* picture that she had seen at her grandparent's house.

As Callie leafed through the pages, Amanda extrapolated on the events around which they occurred. Her smile grew broader and broader, and soon the sound of giggles filled the room. She didn't remember their earlier years together, but it seemed as though she belonged there. And gradually, bits and pieces of the past began to awaken her memory.

Casey was in the kitchen—about to slice a piece of Callie's pie—when Nick entered the room with a nervous look on his face.

"So where are they?" he asked, not quite sure he should trust Callie alone with his daughter.

"They were in the living room, but I think they just went upstairs. I was about to look for ear plugs because they were making so much noise," Casey grumbled. But in reality, he was happy to hear his little sister laugh like that again. It had been a long time.

"You want some?"

Nick approached the counter and stared at the pie then looked at Casey. "It looks safe enough. Actually, it looks like Clara's."

Casey licked the knife. "It tastes like Clara's, too."

"Well in that case..."

"You look worried, Dad."

"I don't trust her!" Nick wasn't sure he wanted his precious daughter hanging out with a demon-child like Callie.

"Yeah, me neither. What kind of person would try to pass off another woman's pie as her own?" Casey's voice echoed the suspicion he felt over the authenticity of Callie's gift.

Nick cracked a smile, but his voice was still worried. "I'm serious!"

"Don't worry Dad, I'll keep my eye on her." Casey immediately caught his mistake and covered it well. "Them, I mean...I'll keep my eye on *them*!"

THE GIRLS CHARGED INTO Amanda's beautifully decorated bedroom. It was a warm and inviting nest, and Callie looked around in awe. She spent so little time in her own room at Zoey's apartment that it seemed cold and empty compared to this haven. Amanda's personality filled the room, and her spirit came across like a rainbow after a storm. Callie could only hope that it was a sign of good things to come.

The girls were still finishing a discussion they had started downstairs. "I can't believe I remembered Gunnar Thompson," Callie said. "I always thought he was just a bad nightmare."

"Oh, he was a nightmare all right! That boy would eat anything for attention! Thank God he moved."

Just then Callie spied a hand-crafted rag doll on the bed that looked similar to Mandy. She rushed over and picked it up.

"I have this doll!" she exclaimed, looking to Amanda for an explanation.

"I know. My mother made them for us when she heard you were moving to New York. I named her Callie. And after you left, I would have conversations with her in my bed at night. Casey thought I was nuts!"

"How cute. Mine is named Mandy." She was beginning to catch a thread of thought here.

"That's what you used to call me back then."

Callie studied the doll. "I'm so sorry you lost your mother, Amanda. She was a beautiful woman."

"Yeah, she was." Amanda said with a wistful look. "I used to be really angry with God for taking her away. But when I was diagnosed with leukemia, I realized it would have broken her heart. I don't think she could've handled it." She took a deep breath. "Besides, I know we'll be together again in heaven. That's why I try to make the most of each day on earth."

"Wow, you really are an angel." Callie had never met someone so unfortunate with such a positive outlook.

"Only on my good days," Amanda replied, trying to make an evil face and failing miserably, causing them both to laugh. "So why did you run away last night?"

"I didn't run away. I fell asleep in the barn."

"Are you serious?"

Callie nodded yes. "I was upset because of a phone call from Zoey… my mom, I mean. I ran out of the house with a magazine and my iPod, found a comfy spot in the barn, and accidentally fell asleep. By the time I woke up, everyone was out searching for me. I had no idea my grandparents would freak out like that."

"Well, you were missing for hours!"

"Yeah, I guess, but I'm used to being alone. One time, I sneaked out of my mom's studio in the morning and didn't come back until late that night. Guess what she said when she saw me?"

"Callie, I've been so worried!" Amanda said dramatically.

"Nope, it was *Hand me that lens, baby.*"

Amanda didn't understand.

"I was cruising the streets of New York City for over twelve hours, and my mother didn't even notice I was gone." Callie was pensive as she related the story.

"How sad." Amanda said with sympathy.

"So you can imagine my shock when I heard there was a search party out looking for me. I never meant to hurt anyone. I swear!"

"I believe you, Callie."

The girls continued their conversation, covering just about everything that had happened in the past eleven years. Callie told Amanda all about Alexia, Bianca, and Danielle and explained how Kaitlin's crowd had labeled them *The Alphabet Clique*—a derogatory reference to their first names. Then she went on to describe some of the tricks Bianca had played in retribution.

And by the time Casey made it upstairs, they were being loud and obnoxious again. He could hear their laughter from the hallway and peered through a crack in the door. Callie was applying makeup to Amanda's face, but the conversation was something entirely different.

"Can you imagine driving home in a limo full of mice?"

"Oh my God, Callie! She must have freaked!"

"Yeah, among other things too gross to mention!" The girls cringed at the thought.

"You're lucky to have such good friends."

Callie pulled real meaning from Amanda's words. "You know, you're right. I really am lucky!" then quickly changing the subject, "and *you're* done. Here, check it out."

Amanda took the mirror. "I better not look like a clown."

"See for yourself," Callie said with the utmost confidence.

"Is that me?" Amanda hadn't worn a stitch of makeup in months.

"One hundred percent! Well, ninety anyway," Callie joked while admiring her handiwork.

Casey had heard enough girl stuff. He had checked up on Callie— as promised—and moved on to his bedroom to play video games. His room was filled with state-of-the-art electronics and resembled Circuit City, complete with a flat-screen plasma TV and stereo with surround sound. A programmer's manual was on his desk next to his computer, opened about three quarters of the way through, and everything was neat and orderly. Highly unusual, as everyone knows boys are supposed to be slobs!

He was fully absorbed in *Madden NFL Online* when the girls burst through the door. "Casey, look at me!"

Amanda stood in front of the TV blocking his view, and he immediately took a time out, proving that *some* of his priorities were the same as other teenage boys. He set down his controller and gave her his full attention.

"Wow! What happened to you?"

"Callie."

But Callie was too overwhelmed by the electronics in the room to accept the credit for Amanda's transformation.

"You look great, Mandy." Casey said, knowing his sister had been more upset by her appearance than she had let on.

"Thank you," she replied primly with a slight blush.

"I guess I owe you an apology," Callie said, looking at Casey.

"Oh?" His intention was to make her feel as uncomfortable as he could.

"I just assumed…" her voice trailed off.

"That I was an uneducated hayseed?"

"No. Just that you were behind the times a little."

"Uh huh, well you know what happens when you assume?"

Callie blushed. "I do now. But if your offer still stands, I would love to get online. I'm going to be here longer than I originally planned."

Casey turned his attention back to his game. "I'll check my schedule."

Amanda yanked Callie by the arm. "C'mon Callie—I want to show my dad!"

When the girls cleared his room, Casey leaned back and balanced on the back legs of his chair. "SCORE!" he mouthed, reveling in victory. And he would have patted himself on the back if his arms were long enough. He was feeling extremely confident—that is, until he lost his balance and the chair toppled to the ground!

15

The truth is often hard to accept

N ick was on his knees with his head halfway up the chimney. He had a flashlight in one hand and was attempting to adjust the damper in the fireplace with the other. His back was toward the girls when they entered the room, but it was apparent his frustration was at an all time high.

"Dad," Amanda said apprehensively. "Look what Callie did to me."

Nick bumped his head as he retracted from his contorted position. He had expected the worst, but quickly realized that she was teasing and just wanted his approval and appreciation for Callie's efforts.

"Ouch—Daddy, are you all right?" Amanda asked, sympathizing with his injury as she ran to his aid.

"Damn thing, I can't figure out why it won't close." Nick rubbed the painful lump on the back of his head. "Wow!" he said, amazed by her surprisingly mature appearance. "Aren't you just the prettiest little thing?"

He was delighted with Amanda's makeover, but even more so with the smile on her face. Amanda was popular at school, but once she was diagnosed with leukemia, it seemed like fewer of hers friends would come around. He knew it was partly because of her treatment schedule, and partly because her illness made them a little uncomfortable. So it was good to see her acting more like a teenage girl again.

Both girls had ulterior motives for the visit. Amanda's goal was to prove to Nick that Callie wasn't the terror everyone thought she was, and Callie saw it as an opportunity to finagle information about her father.

"So Nick...Casey mentioned that you and my dad were really good friends." Callie tried hard not to appear overly zealous.

"Yep, that's right," he answered, choosing to remain elusive. He got the feeling she was fishing, but he had no intention of making it easy on her.

"I don't remember him much," she admitted, thinking for sure her statement would trigger a reaction and that he would spill his guts like a stool pigeon facing life imprisonment. But he didn't.

"Yeah, don't suppose you would."

Amanda was impatient with the cat and mouse game the two were playing—Callie, beating around the bush and Nick, taking pleasure in dragging out the inevitable.

"Knock it off, Dad. Just tell her about Cameron." Amanda knew her dad could be a pain in the ass. But this time, he was going too far.

"Cameron, huh? How would I describe him?" Nick chuckled, as his mind drifted back to his best friend. "Intense is the best word I guess. And passionate—about anything he believed in."

"When did you two meet?" Callie asked.

"Meet? Hell, I think we were hatched from the same egg! I don't remember ever meeting him. He was just always there—like a part of my life. We were the best of friends and the worst of competitors."

"What do you mean?"

"Like who could swim the farthest or who could run the fastest. And when we got to high school, it was who would make quarterback or who would be the valedictorian or who would date the best looking girl in class, you know—guy stuff."

Callie's relationship with Bianca instantly came to mind. "And who would win?"

"Well I was quarterback. Cameron could throw farther, but his aim was off. He was my wide receiver, and we took the state championship for two years running. But he got valedictorian—beat me by point one percent, and he never let me forget it."

"Then what?" Callie prompted. She had just learned more about her dad in five minutes than she had in her entire life.

"C'mon Dad, tell her about mom." Amanda got a kick out of hearing how goofy they were when they were young, and it helped to keep her mom alive in her memory. She turned to Callie and explained in a falsetto whisper as if she were sharing juicy gossip. "She grew up with them, too. She was their *other* best friend."

"Really." Callie said with surprise, thinking Elsa had conveniently neglected to mention *that* little tidbit!

Nick took a deep breath. "And then there was Sarah, the most beautiful girl in the world." He stopped and smiled at Amanda. "She looked just like you, Mandy." He paused for a moment and studied his daughter's face. "Everyone loved Sarah. She was like a ray of sunshine that lit up the room around her. Cameron and I were always by her side, showing her off like the winner from *America's Next Top Model*. And the three of us were inseparable—kind of like Tom, Huck, and Becky. There wasn't a boy in the county that didn't envy your dad and me." Nick's devotion to his late wife was apparent in his words and the expression on his face.

Callie was astute for her age and easily read between the lines. "Sounds like you won the grand prize after all."

"I sure did," Nick admitted, directing his comments to Amanda as he confessed. "...But it's a damn good thing your mother was afraid to fly!"

"Yeah right Dad! Mom would have flown through the Bermuda triangle with Amelia Earhart if it meant being next to you." Amanda was adamant in her belief.

Nick grinned.

"I don't get it," Callie said, feeling like the story had suddenly taken a detour and she just missed the exit.

"Well your dad had high ambitions," Nick explained, "and he would always tell us how he was going to travel the world someday. Sarah and I, on the other hand, were quite content with life in Deer Creek. But as much as we loved the country, Cameron loved the city and all its excitement."

Callie and Amanda were at opposite ends of the sofa with their feet up and their arms wrapped around their knees. They watched Nick work and listened to his answers to their questions. It was hard to tell exactly how much progress he was making on the repair because his head kept bobbing in and out of the chimney as he checked to see if his adjustment was working. But for the most part, Amanda was sitting quietly and enjoying her friend and her dad getting to know one another.

"So then when did he leave Deer Creek?" Callie inquired, continuing her quest for details.

"Right after college. He changed his last name from Michelsohn to Michaels and went to work as a photojournalist for *The Chicago Sun*. And he was good. No, that's not right. He was great!" It looked as though Nick had a revelation as he remembered. "That's where he met your mom, you know."

"So you knew my mother, too?" Callie's face became more animated as she realized she might hear about a part of her parents' life that had seemed shrouded in mystery.

"Oh sure. She was quite a lady and Cameron's complete opposite. Sarah used to say that Zoey was the yin to Cameron's yang—the perfect compliment to every side of him."

Callie's head tipped to one side as she tried to reconcile what Nick was saying. "So how did they meet?" Callie asked.

"Well...Zoey started working at the paper a couple of years after Cameron. She was a hotshot art graduate from Columbia University with a scholar's perspective. Everything had to be in writing for her, whereas Cameron operated on sheer instinct. It used to piss him off to no end because they would argue about everything!"

Nick paused for a minute, thinking harder about it. "It's kind of strange—Cameron's work—lots of it was harsh and the subjects were often ugly. But it was art. His technique was incredible, and he could make a camera do anything he wanted. Now don't get me wrong, Zoey's work was beautiful. She was brilliant with landscapes. But her pictures didn't have the raw power that Cameron's did. His stuff would jump off the page at you and make you want to scream or cry."

"Yeah, that's what my grandma said."

Nick continued, "When they first started working together, he'd call and complain about this annoying girl from Chicago who wanted to sugar coat all the stories. Then a promotion came up at the paper, and they both wanted it bad. He ended up getting it, but she put up a hell of a fight. He was so impressed by her competitive nature, though, that he brought her home to meet Elsa and Johan that very next Christmas. And she just loved it here—the scenery, the quiet, and the slow pace. I thought for sure she'd convince him to stay."

"And did she?" Amanda asked, mesmerized by the story.

But Nick was almost done with the fireplace and he was nearing the part of the story that was most painful for him. The rest came abbreviated and in a rush of words.

"No, it was quite the opposite. As soon as they got married, Cameron's career took off. His photographs were making a big impact on the media and he was asked to cover one dangerous assignment after the next— earthquakes, fires, hurricanes..." Nick's eyes turned inward, remembering the scenes Cameron's photos documented. "...war."

"And what about my mom?"

"She went with him."

Callie sensed a change in Nick's attitude as he continued, "And we didn't see much of them after that. A holiday every once in awhile, and of course, the winter they took off for your delivery. But beyond that, they were like long lost cousins who had since forgotten their ties back home."

As much as Callie was making Amanda happy, Nick didn't have any reason to trust anything to do with Zoey or the city. He still blamed her for condoning a lifestyle that ultimately killed his best friend, so he refused to let his guard down so easily.

The girls were quiet and still absorbing everything Nick had said. And as he started to gather up his tools, he asked, "So how is Zoey doing, anyway?"

Caught by surprise, Callie gave the first answer that popped into her head. "Perfect. Couldn't be better!" But it was quite a different story some four thousand miles away.

"DAMN IT! COULD THIS day possibly get any worse?" Zoey yelled, as she quickly covered her equipment from the downpour.

She was in the middle of a night shoot in Paris, which was going anything but smooth. In fact, the only perfect thing about it was that it was a *perfect* example of Murphy's Law. Whatever could go wrong—did!

First Zoey's favorite camera had been misplaced, and then the film was the wrong speed. They fixed those problems, but in spite of all Roxanne's efforts, she still couldn't control the weather. And the shoot, which was supposed to be taken outdoors against the lights of the city, had started with a gentle snowfall. Zoey made the adjustments for that, even thinking she could use it to her advantage when the snow turned into a freezing rain. The crew and models had no choice but to seek shelter in a nearby bistro while they waited for the weather to improve.

"We were so close!" Zoey said, brushing the ice away from her face and wiping her boots off on the entrance carpet. "One more set up and it would've been a wrap." She was frustrated and irritated, and not just about the shoot.

Zoey sat at a table with Roxanne and vented her feelings. "I don't know Roxy…it just seems like I can't do anything right anymore."

"Yeah, you really blew it this time, kiddo! That blizzard was a bad idea," she teased.

"It's all my fault."

"Hello…McFly!" Roxanne pounded her fist on her head. "It's a blizzard, Zoey. Get over it."

"This isn't about the weather, Roxy. It's about my life and my relationship with my daughter." Zoey was staring out the window, hypnotized by the pellets of sleet that were angling through the air like tiny bullets. "I think I'm a bad mother."

Roxanne wasn't prepared for that one. She had been traveling the world with Zoey for years, missing one important event after the next, and never once had Zoey uttered such an insecure statement. Something was up, and Roxanne was going to get to the bottom of it if it killed her!

Just then, one of the younger models—sleek and full of herself—made the mistake of interrupting their conversation. She demanded to know how long they were planning on keeping her and the other girls.

Roxanne immediately jumped into action. She escorted the little princess back to her table and reprimanded the entire group for their impatience. They had a lot to learn about this business. It was Zoey who made them famous, not the other way around.

"Listen up, you little punks! As far as I'm concerned, you're still on the clock. And at six hundred bucks an hour, I suggest you sit your skinny asses down and wait until you're dismissed. That is, if you ever plan on working in this business again."

Having set the matter straight, at least to her satisfaction, Roxanne returned to the table and resumed her conversation with Zoey as if nothing had happened.

"Are the natives getting restless?"

"Oh no," Roxanne replied, "They were just saying what a pleasure it is to be working with you."

Zoey laughed, knowing full well the egos of the models and how unlikely they were to ever make a comment like that. But she didn't care. There were some celebrities she had to cater to, but this was a group of young hopefuls and any of them could be replaced at a moment's notice.

"Now, where were we?" Roxanne asked, remembering *exactly* where they had left off.

Zoey was all too happy to continue with her confession. "I think I made a big mistake—with Callie, I mean. I should've never sent her to Wisconsin.

Roxanne didn't understand. "Why is that such a bad thing?"

"It isn't for her. But it might be for me." Zoey was talking in riddles, and her mind seemed to be drifting in and out of a rational context.

It was against her nature to question her own decisions and to place Callie's feelings above her own.

Roxanne was completely confused by now. "Zoey, you're not making any sense."

"Roxy, there's something I've never told you…about Cameron. Actually, I've never told anyone." Zoey's eyes filled with tears as her face showed the agony she had lived with all these years. "Cameron died in my arms, and I couldn't do anything to save him."

"I don't understand. I thought he was killed in Bosnia." Roxanne was straining to remember the details of Cameron's death as she wiped the tears from Zoey's cheek.

"Yeah, he was on assignment and I was with him. The paper would send him all over the world to capture the essence of humanity, the earthy and often cruel sides. And I went along to bring balance to the ugliness he captured. I wasn't very popular back then. The editors said my work was too soft. But I didn't care, I was just happy to be there with my husband." Zoey drifted to a far off place.

"So—how did it happen?" Roxanne asked with hesitation.

"It was terrible. Shells would land without any warning except a *swoosh* through the air, and all of a sudden a building or a car…or a person would be hit. People would scream in fear or pain, and family members would break down in anguish." Zoey's face contorted as the memories flashed through her mind.

"I wasn't that far from Cameron. I was standing in a doorway while he took some pictures of a NATO jet whose tail had just been hit by ground fire. Another shell came down, not far from him, and the impact threw him into the air. I couldn't find him at first because of the smoke and dust, and I prayed that he had been thrown out of danger. But he was hit by shrapnel, and when I got to him, he had lost a lot of blood. I put pressure on the wound, but the bleeding wouldn't stop. And there was nobody there to help."

"Oh Zoey," Roxanne's eyes opened in shock as if she were seeing the scene in instant replay. "I had no idea."

"I dream about him every night. Some nights I relive the nightmare.

Other nights he gets up and walks away like nothing ever happened. But regardless of which direction the dream takes, he always smiles at me and tells me how much he loves me." Zoey hesitated. "Just like that day."

Roxanne placed her hand over Zoey's, knowing words were of no help right now. "So why are you so worried about Callie being with your in-laws?" she asked, realizing there was still more to this story.

"Callie lived with Elsa and Johan while Cameron and I were chasing atrocities. They were more like parents to her than we ever were. I've never admitted this before, but I was so jealous of Elsa and her relationship with Callie, yet I couldn't bare the thought of being without Cameron." Zoey paused, burdened by the guilt. "Roxy—I'm so ashamed. I chose my husband over my little girl."

Roxanne was beginning to see the big picture. "And you felt like you had to end their relationship, so you could start from scratch?"

"Yeah." Zoey took a deep breath. "I'll never get over Elsa's reaction when I returned home with Cameron's coffin. I could tell she thought I was to blame. Her eyes were closed to me—like I didn't exist. And she hardly said two words about what had happened. But the worst part was when Callie clung to her and refused to let go like she didn't even know who I was. At that point, I had no choice but to take Callie away from Deer Creek and to start a new life that didn't include the Michelsohns."

Roxanne pondered Zoey's dilemma. "So now Callie's back in Deer Creek and you're out gallivanting around the world again." She noticed that the rain had stopped and that billowy snowflakes were floating in the air once again.

Zoey confirmed her theory. "That's the way I see it."

"Well then, I suggest we get our butts in gear, finish this damn job, and go get Callie!" Roxanne stood up like a General about to go to war. "Depp is just going to have to find someone else." And with that, she began barking orders to the girls. "Toothpick! Matchstick! Beanpole!" She eyed the uppity young model. "Chubs! Let's move it. We've got work to do."

THE LOG IN THE fireplace crackled and made a popping sound, startling Callie and Amanda out of their trance. Watching the flames had been hypnotic, and they were feeling relaxed and snug.

Nick was satisfied that the smoke was going up the chimney as it was supposed to and was prepared to make a rapid escape from the room when Amanda spoke up, "Dad, I want to take Callie on a tour. She's never seen a large dairy farm."

Nick was horrified at the suggestion, but modified the expression on his face so Amanda wouldn't see. Her illness put so many limitations on her activities, and he hated to squelch her plans, so he paused before answering slowly.

"I don't think that's a good idea, Mandy. It's about twenty degrees outside," Nick said, thinking the temperature could put her health at risk. Amanda's resistance to disease and her ability to fight infection was greatly reduced by her illness, so his concerns were justified.

"Why do you always have to make me feel so badly, Dad? Amanda replied, embarrassed by the reference to her condition.

"I don't mean to."

Callie quickly interjected a comment to defuse the situation. "Actually, Amanda—I'm kind of hungry, and I baked a blueberry pie for you. Do you want to try it?" Callie knew by now that food seemed to be very therapeutic in these parts, and rather effectively so!

"You baked a pie?" Amanda's attention was immediately diverted. "Now that, I've got to see."

Callie gave Nick a *keep your mouth shut—I just bailed you out* look and Nick happily added, "Oh yeah, and it's quite good."

As they moved from the living room, Nick suggested that Casey could show Callie around the property if she was still interested. Considering the fact that she needed her computer hooked up, and that she really *was* intrigued by her family's enterprise, she agreed. "Sure, that would be nice." The fact that Casey was an Adonis who practically owned the entire county, didn't hurt either. "I'll catch up with him later. Right now though, I'm hungry for pie," and the girls headed off to the kitchen.

❦

AFTER ANNIHILATING HIS CYBER opponent, Casey headed to the barn to meet up with Roy and the boys. They were huddled together, intent upon whatever they were discussing. Their heads were down and their ears didn't detect his footsteps coming up from behind, which could only mean one thing. They were paying up on the day's bets!

"You rolling my boys again, Roy?" Casey asked, as he neared.

"Hey, they're old enough to know better. And I ain't their mamma!" Roy said firmly.

"Hell, no! My mamma ain't nearly as ugly as you," Hurley joked, rousing the men to trade insults back and forth as they compared mothers and birthrights—all in jest, of course.

To a stranger, the farmhands would have looked pretty seedy and definitely dirty. Working outside and in barns all day, didn't make for an elegant appearance. But these men excelled at what they did, and while they were working, looks didn't count. The group continued grumbling as they parted with their cash.

"So how's the big guy doing?" Casey asked, knowing Roy had been over at Elsa and Johan's earlier that day.

"Good enough to beat Arnie in a game of Gin."

"That's my bud!" Casey laughed. He was Johan's biggest fan, and next to Elsa was probably the most relieved by his much-improved condition.

"By the way, Elsa sent me to snag some men. We're short on help this week until Johan is back on his feet—thanks to *you-know-who*.

"Who?" JR asked. He could be a little dense at times. The men all stared at him. "Oh, right—*she* who shall not be named," he said, in a surfer-like voice.

Casey added to the thought, "You know, you could always put *her* to work.

The men burst out laughing, and one after the other, they started imitating Callie's imagined reactions.

"Yeah, I can just see it now. I'm tired. I need a break!" whined Hurley.

"I can't touch that. It's filthy and I might break a nail," was Bud's comment.

Casey added, "I'll tell my grandfather and he'll fire you." His head was turned to the sky with his nose in the air as he spoke.

"I'm hungry—I have to eat," JR added.

The group was silenced.

"No JR, that's *you*!" Roy said with a straight face.

Casey kept going, "You should've heard her whining the other day. It was disgusting!" and he gave a dramatic rendition of her behavior. "Oh grandfather, I was attacked by those…those wild creatures. And now I'm battered and bruised and I smell like hog…!" Suddenly, he realized the men were staring at something behind him and stopped short of completing his sentence. "She's behind me, isn't she?" he whispered.

They nodded in unison and started to scatter. Casey turned to see Callie standing with her arms crossed. He cleared his throat and smiled.

JR checked her out from top to bottom. "S'up?" he flirted, liking what he saw. But Callie wasn't about to let Casey off the hook quite so easily—or for that matter, be distracted by some pervert.

"Disgusting, huh?"

"In the nicest sense of the word," Casey responded, trying desperately to put a positive spin on his last comment.

Callie recalled how mere moments before she would have been willing to ask Casey to give her a guided tour. Not only that, but she had even considered turning on the charm for the jerk in order to get her computer online. It must have been a case of temporary insanity because at this point, he was less appealing than Uncle Buck with a bad case of diarrhea!

"I'll have you know, I can outwork any one of you, any day of the week," Callie responded in a surprisingly calm voice. "I'm smarter, I'm faster, and I'm in much better shape." She said this while staring at Roy's belly, which threatened to burst the buttons on his shirt.

"So what are you saying?" Casey asked, intrigued by her speech.

The men focused all their concentration on what was transpiring. They sensed a bet of major proportions in the making and wanted as much information to weigh the odds carefully—almost as if Bill Gates was about to divulge Microsoft's latest trade secrets.

Callie answered with no expression in her voice or on her face. "I'm saying I'm ready to leave, Roy. I have to work in the morning." And she whipped around with her nose high in the air, leaving the barn with a feminine walk that expressed her confidence and superiority.

"Nice butt." JR commented, as his hormones reacted without regard for propriety.

Roy grabbed his hat and looked to Casey for reassurance. "She's not serious, is she?" He shook his head with concern. "Because if she is, Elsa's gonna kill me."

He barreled out the door behind her, and the rest of the men immediately reached for their wallets and start placing bets. Hurley put up twenty bucks that she wouldn't show—a bet immediately accepted by Bud who pulled out a cell phone the size of a shoe and called Butch to find out if he wanted in. The money was flying and the stakes were growing. This was beginning to look like a bet any bookie would be afraid to cover.

Casey scoffed, "Suckers. Don't you guys know—hell hath no fury like a debutante scorned!

16

It's all in the genes

Beam me up, Scotty! was all that came to mind as Callie approached what appeared to be an alien world. She felt like a voyager on the starship Enterprise about to come face to face with the unknown. And though she would have preferred to beam herself back to Elsa's kitchen, she straightened her shoulders and marched into uncharted territories with her best *take charge* attitude.

The big barn was divided into two areas. The first section had several stalls that were nearly empty with the exception of one, which held a lone cow, staring at her with big eyes. And in the second section, a group of men were congregated in the distance, waiting for their assignments.

"Okay Captain Kirk, put me to work," she demanded, cutting to the front of the line.

Roy was going through a list of chores on his clipboard when Callie arrived wearing the jeans and flannel shirt from Hank's. She had discarded her designer wardrobe in anticipation of manual labor, which indicated that she was actually using her head for more than decoration. Roy took this as a bad omen. He hadn't planned on Callie having the guts to show, but she did. And he wasn't sure if she had any real brains or not, so his ability to predict the day's outcome suddenly took a turn for the worse.

The men watched in silence as Roy studied his list. Then with a wicked grin he said, "Okay, follow me," and he guided Callie to the stall with the cow, grabbing two shiny aluminum buckets on the way. She was unprepared for the sheer mass of the animal—it was gigantic!

Roy set the buckets down on the ground. "Milk her."

"Uh...with what?" she asked, completely clueless. Callie had never really considered just how milk came out of a cow.

"With your hands, stupid," Roy responded, ridiculing her ignorance. He walked away, checking his watch. "Come get me when you're done."

Callie stood there, staring at the cow, which stared affably back at her. She listened as Roy delegated the rest of the work assignments and watched as the men left the barn to do their jobs. After evaluating the situation, she cautiously reached into her pocket for her cell phone. Not sure if cows were known to bite, she decided to seek expert advice from a professional.

Within seconds, Danielle's cell phone rang. She was dressed in riding gear and sat alone eating her breakfast at a grand dining table.

"Dani, HELP!" Callie whispered in a voice indicating panic. "How do I milk a cow?"

"How would I know?"

"Well, you ride horses don't you?"

"Yeah, but I don't milk them. You'd better call someone else."

"Like who? Alex? She wears them. Bianca? She eats them. No Dani, you're my only hope!" By now, Callie was nearly frantic. "Look it up on the Internet and make it quick."

Danielle located the nearest computer. "I can't believe I'm doing this," she grumbled, and within minutes, she found a website and began to relay the information. "You need very clean hands and very clean equipment."

Callie looked at the bucket, which appeared to be brand new, and she knew she had washed her hands after breakfast. Considering that she was surrounded by hay and God knows what else, she wasn't too concerned about sterilization.

"Go on," she said impatiently.

"It is easiest for young people because they are agile and their fingers and joints are supple. Women are believed to be more compassionate than men," Danielle read.

"I think you can skip that section," Callie said sarcastically. "Get to the extraction part."

"Give the cow some food, so she stands patiently and looks forward to the experience."

"She's already chomping on hay, and I don't know what else they eat, so that will have to do," Callie mused in a whisper.

"Put the bucket in front of the udder and sit beside her on a stool, facing her tail."

Callie couldn't see Danielle's look of disgust, but her own face mirrored it. "I have to face her tail? That's just nasty!" And she pulled over the stool. "Now what?"

"Take a hold of two teats," Callie could hear Danielle cringe as she spoke the word, "…gently but firmly, then making a seal, move the milk downward, squeezing your fingers in sequence from the top down. You're supposed to be recreating the sucking motion of the calf's mouth."

"There are four of those things." Callie was reluctant to repeat the word teats. "Does it matter which two I grab first?"

Danielle scanned ahead. "It doesn't say, so I guess not." She read on, "Keep your hands pushed up slightly against the udder. Do not pull! Alternate the squeezing movement with each hand until those two quarters are empty."

"Hey, it works!" Callie said, as milk sprayed against the side of the bucket! "Thanks Dani, you're a lifesaver. I've got to go now," and she broke the connection.

Danielle was left in silence, shaking her head.

Callie worked steadily, remembering the instructions, and until the first two teats appeared empty. Then she moved on to the second two. When she was finished, both buckets were nearly full and awaiting approval. She carried them off to Roy who looked vaguely disappointed at her success, but directed one of the men to use it as a supplement in the mash being fed to an orphaned calf.

After watching the farmhands whisper among themselves and witnessing Roy check his watch again with concern, Callie followed him into the second section of the barn. There, stacked in the center of the room, were fifteen half bales of hay, each about two feet square.

"Move those to the loft," he demanded.

"Where's that?"

"Up there." Roy motioned to the area where Callie had previously fallen asleep. "And use that old ladder," he continued, pointing to something that should have been burned as firewood thirty years ago.

"No problem, boss," she answered, hefting one bale part way off the ground.

Callie cased out her surroundings after Roy left the barn. The half bale must have weighed at least seventy-five pounds and the ladder certainly wasn't sturdy. But that wasn't going to stop her. She might not be as strong as the men, but she could definitely outthink them. As she searched the room, she noticed a hook hanging above her head and a pulley system rigged up off to the right.

"He must think I'm an idiot," she thought, as she released the device by untying the rope. Upon further examination, it became obvious that the pulley was designed for two people. But she figured that if she tied another rope to the bale, she could swing it up and onto the loft.

The task was physically challenging and she didn't have gloves, but she made steady progress once she found her rhythm. And by the time she was finished, blisters had formed on her fingers—another first for her! But she figured she deserved some kind of payback for her earlier behavior.

Callie was exhausted when she decided to take a break. She spied an old basketball hoop hanging crookedly over the barn entrance then searched the room for something resembling a ball. Locating a mini bale of hay that looked like a remnant from a Thanksgiving decoration, she grabbed it and took aim. The bale swooped through the hoop just as Roy entered the barn. Bits of hay landed everywhere, including the top of his head!

"Oops—missed one," Callie said, as she gathered the remnants from the floor and dashed up the ladder. She had already tied the hook back into position, so there was no indication of how she managed to accomplish the job. Roy looked around the barn in disbelief. He suspected foul play, but had no way of proving it.

Word spread like wildfire. And within minutes, the farmhands gathered, adding money to their pool.

By this time, Callie had a pretty good idea of what was going on. She had seen the boys in action the day before and figured that her ability to complete the chores within a given time was the wager of the day. It was clear they didn't like her, and she really couldn't blame them. But it was up to her to prove them wrong, and if she had to shovel some cow poop to do it then so be it! After all, she was a Michelsohn!

Elsa was suspicious when she saw Callie leave early that morning, and decided to monitor the situation closely. She had years of experience with the farmhands and the tricks they played on one another. So she watched their activities from a distance, ready to intervene if necessary. She found nothing wrong with a sense of humor, but wanted to make sure the guys were following the loose set of rules she had set over the years. Besides, she knew Callie's capabilities and wanted to make sure that her granddaughter wasn't making fools of them!

Elsa had a sense of humor, too, and hated it when the men underestimated her. Her tendency was to lie in wait and catch them when they least expected it, and her goal this morning was to scare the bajeebies out of them. But they were so intent on divvying up their money that they didn't even notice when she tiptoed up from behind.

"Don't you boys have some work to do?" she said, in a threatening tone, having removed the smile from her face for added effect.

They looked up, startled—like kids caught with their hands in the cookie jar.

"Morning ma'am, been there long?" Hurley asked, quickly blocking JR who was safe-guarding the cash.

"Long enough," Elsa declared, as she pushed him aside and stripped JR of the money. "I'd say it's time to get back to work, wouldn't you?"

"Yes, um..." was all Elsa heard as the men dispersed in every direction.

Roy and Callie approached just in time to overhear the tail end of her directive. But rather than joining Elsa, Roy took a sudden detour to his truck, abandoning his protégé.

"Hey, what about me?" Callie called out, as he revved the engine. "Weren't you going to show me how to slop the pigs or something?" She had witnessed Elsa's masterful theatrics and decided to complement it with a similar performance.

Roy lowered the window as he gave the truck some gas. "Naw, we'll do it later."

As he sped out of the driveway, Elsa yelled behind him, "You should know better than to bet against a Michelsohn!" She knew Johan would get a kick out of the story—especially the part where she caught the men in the act and confiscated the money.

"Damn that felt good!" Callie admitted, as she threw boxer-like jabs into the air and did a victory dance in the gravel.

"Ach, they're not so bad—just little boys that never grew up," Elsa said with maternal affection. "And look what they put together for the children." She pulled out the wad of cash and handed it to Callie. "I think you should deliver it tomorrow when you go to the hospital with Amanda."

Callie fanned the money for a moment before putting it safely into her coat pocket. She was impressed. Working a farm was no picnic, and she was just beginning to appreciate the effort required to complete many of the tasks. Even if the jobs she did weren't considered normal chores, her blisters bore witness to how labor intense farm work could be.

Callie realized there was more to this operation than met the eye, and she was curious. So she asked Elsa for a quick tour. In the process, she concluded that *farm* was much too simplified a word for the business her grandparents had developed. The property included the farmhouse and the barn in which she had just milked the cow. The latter served as their central hub. It was big and old with thick timbers and large planks, and had a sweet smell from the hay. It was one of the few remnants of the original farm, and was still painted rustic red in the old barn style.

Against the recent snow, the structure stood out crisply and somehow warm and welcoming. Beyond it were tall pine trees, and beyond those were fields. The trees had been planted for a wind break years before and were the only green on the landscape.

Elsa explained the business briefly and incompletely as they went through the building. "We feed our cows with the grain we grow in the fields surrounding us. Right now we have about six hundred cows, which we milk, not by hand as Roy had you do, but with machines. The milking barns and the majority of the cows are at the Meyers' farm. The law requires very strict procedures, so all the equipment must be cleansed after each milking. From here, a certain amount goes directly to a dairy and is shipped mostly to the Chicago area. Another portion goes to our cheese factory in town. We make specialty cheeses that are shipped throughout the country and even overseas." Elsa spoke modestly, but proudly. "And your Opa holds the patents on some of the smaller pieces that make the milking machines work."

Callie was amazed. The old barn had hidden the fields from her view, so she had thought this was just a sleepy little farm in the middle of nowhere. But now it seemed to have worldwide connections. Thousands of questions were churning through her head, but she figured Johan would know the technical details, and it would give them something to talk about later. Now that her interest was piqued, she wanted to know everything!

"I have to get back to the kitchen. It's nearly suppertime," Elsa said, watching Callie's reaction to the tour. She noticed the blisters on her fingers, adding, "And I think I should take a look at your hands. Those boys don't know how to treat a lady, though I have to admit I was proud of the way you beat them at their own game." And the two Michelsohn women celebrated their victory as they headed back to the house.

The kitchen was warm and smelled delicious—as usual—when they entered. "You'd better take that money up to your room," Elsa instructed, amazed by the difference a day could make. Up until now, it was all she could do to keep her granddaughter out of her room.

Callie moved up the stairs slowly. Her muscles weren't used to physical labor and she felt stiff. Plopping down on her bed, she pulled out the wad of bills from her pocket and started counting it. She liked spending time with her grandmother and the feeling of camaraderie they shared in working together against the boys—especially when they walked away with the cash! She was beginning to feel like a part of this family and more secure than she could ever remember. That is, until she heard an ominous scraping noise on the floor by her desk.

She knew Elsa was in the kitchen and that Johan was still tucked in his bed—she had just peeked in on him. And it was too loud for a mouse, unless it took steroids and trained with the Green Bay Packers! Her heart started to pound in her chest when she realized there was something, or someone, uninvited in her room! Visions of Freddy Krueger and Jason were running through her mind as she tried to imagine what could be causing the noise.

Callie's thoughts were racing as fast as her heart, and her eyes darted around the room searching for the best possible escape. She slowly and quietly reached for her cell phone with the intention of calling 911, but quickly determined that doing so would only alert the intruder—duh! And she couldn't scream—that would place Johan and Elsa at risk. But whatever was under her desk was breathing harder as if it were watching her and preparing to attack.

17

Royalty rules...even at Ridgecrest

"You've been terminated!" a threatening voice announced, causing Callie to scream like a banshee. Casey popped up from under her desk with a look of fright in his eyes and an old-fashioned telephone connector in his hand.

"Casey, you scared me!" She wasn't used to having her privacy invaded. "Why are you in my room?" she demanded to know, still clenching her rapidly pounding heart.

Casey lifted the old wires above his head. "You asked me to fix this—remember?"

Callie immediately realized her mistake. "You're right, I'm so sorry. Please continue!"

"Forget it."

"But I said I'm sorry. I need my computer. Please Casey, PUHLEEZE!" she implored, adding her best *sad puppy* look for good measure.

"Okay, enough," he said with his back toward her. "Stop groveling and flip the switch!" He whipped around with a big grin on his face.

Callie's voice turned cold as she realized how she had just been played. "You mean it's ready?" Her first urge was to ring his neck and she would have if he hadn't saved himself in the nick of time.

Casey nodded yes as Callie's anger emerged. "What an ass..." Then he pressed the keypad himself and a *ding* was heard, followed by music as her computer opened to the Windows screen. She stopped mid-sentence as if possessed by the sound. "...SET, you're a real asset, Casey! I owe you."

Casey gathered his tools and headed for the door as she finished her slightly adjusted sentence.

"Yeah, that's what I thought. Just be on time tomorrow." His tone was decidedly cranky. Here he had gone out of his way to be helpful, and this was the thanks he got!

"I have a big donation from the farmhands," Callie said proudly, pointing to the money on the bed. She was eager to get to her computer, but not eager to see him leave.

"I know. I contributed to the fund."

Callie was mad at herself for always appearing so bitchy around Casey. Why couldn't she ever get her timing right? She wasn't used to being treated with such indifference, but she wasn't used to being this attracted to anybody either. Butterflies tickled her stomach, and she felt tongue-tied and awkward. So she followed him to the door and flashed her most beguiling smile in an attempt to make up for her earlier reaction. "I really do appreciate what you did, Casey. Thank you."

"Your welcome," he replied, mesmerized by her beautiful eyes and her soft, pouting lips.

Callie annoyed the hell out of him with her stuck up attitude, but damn she was beautiful—especially when she dropped the chip from her shoulder and acted like a human being. He couldn't help but wonder what it would be like to kiss her. But before he did something he knew he would regret, he turned and headed toward the stairs, breaking her enchanting spell. What was he thinking? A kiss from Callie would probably be like the kiss of death from a black widow spider!

Callie watched until Casey cleared the hallway then ran to her computer and banished all thoughts of him, or at least tried to. She checked her email and found *way* too many messages waiting for a reply. And not having the energy to sort through the spam, she figured an hour or two more wouldn't make any difference. So she closed her email program and headed downstairs to be with her grandparents.

When they sat down to eat, Elsa was surprised to see Callie add meat and potatoes to her plate. "I guess the work made me hungry," she admitted with a quirky smile.

"That's what I've been saying all these years," Johan agreed, patting his belly.

Elsa kissed her husband on top of his head as she stopped him from overloading his plate. "No—I think it's all those extra large helpings that did that," she laughed.

"Or all the samplings of your cheeses," Johan admitted sheepishly.

Elsa rubbed his shoulder in appreciation, but didn't offer any further explanation.

"That's right. Grandma mentioned you have a little cheese company. What is it? Two little old ladies working in the back of Hank's with a butter churn or something? I can just picture Lucy's mother sitting with a corncob pipe and churning away."

The picture Callie painted was clearly intended to be funny, and Elsa and Johan laughed at the imagery she created.

"It could've been, if Johan hadn't taken over the marketing," Elsa said, proud of her husband's entrepreneurial skills. "It was his mastermind that led to the company's success. That, and of course, a strict adherence to Wolfgang's theory."

"Wolfgang?" Callie hadn't heard that name before.

"You know, Wolfgang Puck—the Austrian chef that makes gourmet pizzas," Elsa continued.

"Oh *that* Wolfgang!"

"You see, Johan figured that we could carve a niche in the specialty cheese industry if we added a few extra ingredients, spruced up the packaging, and labeled it *gourmet*. And he was right. The company was an overnight success—especially in New York.

"Wait...a...minute," Callie pondered, as she recalled the beautifully wrapped cheese Uncle Vito had given Bianca that day at Patsy's Pizzeria. "I think I've tasted that cheese! My friend received a big basket of it last month. It's to die for!"

"So we've been told." Johan said, pleased with their reputation. He had a file drawer full of letters praising their products, but he never got tired of hearing how delicious they were.

"So you're Michelsohn & Meyers Gourmet Cheese?" Callie was

stunned as her brain slowly processed the words that were coming from her mouth. "No wonder I recognized the sign above Amanda's gate. I've been peeling your labels and eating that stuff for weeks." Callie stopped mid-thought. "But wait—what does Wolfgang Puck have to do with your cheese?"

"Humph!" Elsa scoffed with a look of...did Callie sense jealousy?

"I knew his family," Johan admitted.

"His family?" Elsa's voice changed pitch.

"Okay, his mother...Maria."

"Don't tell me you dated Wolfgang Puck's mother," Callie said jokingly, but quickly realized she was the only one laughing. "You dated Wolfgang Puck's mother?"

"It's not what you think. We were just friends. I met her when I studied in Austria. She was training to be a chef at the time and needed someone to sample her foods. She liked to cook and I liked to eat. That was the extent of the relationship. Though I have to admit, she was very good and her talents were indisputably passed on to her son, Wolfgang. It was very interesting to watch him follow in her footsteps, and we've kept in touch through the years, mostly over business."

"Wow," Callie exclaimed. "This is *way* better than being on any stupid DAR list!"

"What is this list?" Elsa asked, curious about her granddaughter's life.

"Oh, it's just some snotty group of rebellious daughters that have to pass a test of lineage or something. I'm really not sure. I just know I'm not on it!"

"Well, if it's a question of ancestry, your grandmother has quite an impressive bloodline." Johan and Elsa never bothered to brag about her pedigree, but it was older and far more illustrious than Mrs. Hamilton's and Mrs. Marriott's combined.

"Your grandmother is a descendant of King Frederick Augustus II of Saxony!" he boasted.

"Ja, my family was prominent in Dresden in the mid 1800s until my great uncle lost our title and castle in a game of cards! It was a blow to the family, but we were able to keep the artwork, a copy of the coat of arms, and the family tree!" She looked fondly at Johan and Callie. "But it's of no use to us here."

"So I'm related to a king?" Callie's head was spinning with the infinite possibilities this had, primarily in her rank within the social structure of Ridgecrest. Even with Kaitlin and her group of goons, royalty ruled. Not that Kaitlin's opinion mattered—because it didn't! But Princess Callie sure did have a nice ring to it! "Do you think I could get a copy of that coat of arms?"

"Of course, schatzie. It's your birthright." Elsa replied.

"Okay, now back it up to that uncle part. Did you say he lost MY castle in a game of cards?" Information was coming in too fast for Callie to process it all.

"Ja." Elsa was embarrassed by *that* fact.

"What an idiot!" Callie declared. "It's a good thing he's dead or I'd have killed him myself!"

Elsa laughed at her granddaughter's reaction. "Funny, that's exactly what I said when I heard the story."

Callie felt like the box with her dreams had finally been opened and held riches beyond anything she could possibly have conceived. Not only did she have a family, and a heritage older than anyone in her snobby school—technically, *she* was a princess! Now all she needed was a prince and her world would be perfect!

"So tell me all about the cheese company. I don't even know how it's made." Callie was suddenly aware that she was the *Queen of Cheese*— well, she would be once she started relating the story to her friends, and she needed to know exactly what her kingdom consisted of.

Johan briefly explained the procedures involved, from milking to using a starter culture, then a coagulant, then removing the whey, and finally adding salt and the other ingredients. Once those stages were completed, the cheese was molded or pressed, bandaged, and then cured. It was a lot more complicated than Callie had imagined.

"That's wicked awesome," she said, as Johan finished his explanation.

Callie's grandparents were delighted to see her interest in their lives.

Her questions and animated responses were exactly what they had hoped for. This was their first real conversation with their granddaughter since her arrival, and it made them feel like their family was intact again.

Callie was still buzzing with excitement over the gourmet cheese company and her lineage when she offered to help with the dishes. But Elsa was too concerned about the blisters on her fingers and insisted that she relax a bit. Considering the events of the day, Callie didn't put up much of an argument, but instead, politely excused herself and headed upstairs to email the good news to her friends.

This time, however, she turned on the light before entering her room and listened for suspicious noises before walking in. Then she peeked under the bed, the desk, and even behind the door and curtains just to make sure there were no unexpected guests. She was relieved to find an empty room—well, she was kind of relieved.

Callie turned on her computer and went directly to her emails. Her friends had been busy, and she was too tired to read all their letters closely.

Bianca's messages were full of complaints about her brothers and her work as a hostess. The men in her family were driving her up a wall, and she wanted to know if she could send them to Wisconsin to work on the farm. Callie replied with, "one more obnoxious male on the farm, and I'm joining a convent." This was an obvious sign to Bianca that at least one of the males was attractive, but that Callie wasn't having any luck snagging him. She also informed Bianca that she was now connected to the company that made their favorite cheeses with no explanation as to how it happened.

Danielle had been busy fulfilling the social schedule her parents had set, most of which revolved around her older siblings who were home for the holidays. She did report that Kaitlin's hair was not growing back very quickly, having seen her at a recent party. Callie's reply was "it must have been nice to see someone from school," leaving Danielle gasping for air and ready to call the paramedics.

Alexia reported major shopping sprees. But Callie didn't even bother to respond to that statement, which was written especially to get attention and usually worked pretty well. Alexia also wondered if maybe her father had opened an orphanage, as the number of children around seemed to have tripled since last year. Callie's normal response would have been to offer to ship a case of duct tape, but no mention was made of this in her reply.

Each of their letters contained one identical paragraph. Callie had cut and pasted it to save time because her eyes were getting heavy. It read...

"Since I've been here, I've been a mail person, a missing person, and a delivery person. Mom bailed on me again (like that's a surprise); my grandfather fell into a frozen pond (now that WAS a surprise); I baked a pie (it was a culinary disaster); and I only JUST got the Internet today (they're a little behind around here)."

Her sentences were vague and rambling—especially for Callie who was usually so direct. But the clincher was the final sentence... *"I milked a cow in the same barn where I slept."*

Callie's eyes felt like lead by now, and instead of proofreading, she clicked *send* on all the emails. She looked at her pillow longingly and decided to curl up on her bed and close her eyes for just a few minutes. But when her grandparents turned in for the night, they discovered her fast asleep. Elsa pulled up the blankets over her shoulders and gently kissed her forehead. And when she smoothed the hair away from Callie's face, she was rewarded with a small smile as if the touch had passed through into her granddaughter's dreams.

THE NEXT MORNING, BEFORE heading downstairs for breakfast, Callie did some research. She figured she still had a lot to learn about dairy farms, and she wanted to show her grandparents that she was truly interested in their business. She also needed to learn more about leukemia and what exactly Amanda was facing. Callie knew very little about the disease—mostly that it was a form of cancer and that many patients experienced hair loss. She realized that it was a serious condition, and she had no intention of hurting anyone's feelings out of ignorance.

She was rushed for time because Casey was coming to pick her up, and she knew from past experience that he had absolutely no tolerance for being late. So she bookmarked several sites including the University of Wisconsin's Cancer Treatment Center and Michelsohn & Meyers Dairy, adding them to her favorites. By now, she wasn't surprised to find her grandparents' business listed on Google.com, but she was going to have to wait until later to investigate all of it properly.

She shut down her computer, grabbed her purse and the envelope with the money, and bounced downstairs. The farmhands were still finishing their breakfasts as she grabbed a plate from the buffet and carefully chose some of the healthier options. She kissed Elsa on the cheek before taking an empty seat at the table between Roy and JR who was nearly delirious from the smell of her perfume.

"I'm sorry I can't help you guys today, but I have to deliver your donation to the hospital."

Roy winced at the conclusion of yesterday's events. It was a very unprofitable day for him. Not only did he have to cover all the bets he lost, but he also had to forfeit the money he should have won.

"Ja, I'm sure the children will be very grateful!" Elsa added, tightening the screws just a little bit more.

Roy sat there stewing and thinking that two Michelsohn women were more than any man should have to take. It was bad enough when Callie thought she was smarter than everyone, but it was even worse when she proved that she was right. He felt like a lamb being lead to slaughter, and was visibly relieved when Johan walked in carrying his coat and jacket, having eaten breakfast earlier.

"And where do you think you're going?" Elsa asked with a stern look.

"There's work to be done, woman!" Johan answered in his best authoritarian voice.

"Ja, but not by you!" she responded, her hands moving to her hips in a *don't mess with me* position.

"But liebchen," he said, hoping to wheedle permission out of her.

"Talk to the hand because the ears aren't listening!" Elsa recited, as she lifted her arm and bent her palm into a stop position.

"All right, Grandma!" Callie responded, thinking that in spite of the gray hairs on her head, her grandmother was pretty cool.

"I've seen *Beautician and the Beast*," she said with a wink. "Now hang up the coat or it's back to bed with you. The men can handle things for another day or so. Can't you boys?"

Seeing the stance she had taken, the men agreed in spite of the fact that they wanted nothing more than to rescue Johan. But rather than risk Elsa's wrath, they escaped one-by-one.

Callie had finished her breakfast by then and was giggling to herself as she studied how her grandmother maneuvered her grandfather. It was perfectly clear that Johan wasn't going to get away with anything.

Elsa informed him that Arnie was coming over later that day to play cards, but that she would cancel the visit if he dared to cross her. She had arranged the entertainment in an effort to keep his activities under control. But just as Johan was about to argue his point, Casey honked the horn of his truck.

Callie quickly kissed her grandparents goodbye then grabbed her jacket, purse, and the envelope and dashed outside. Johan put his hand to his cheek and stood there amazed for a moment. Then, in a gesture very similar to Callie's of the waiter back in New York—perhaps it was genetic—Elsa slapped him in the stomach with a kitchen towel and ordered him to dry the dishes.

Amanda was waiting in the pickup truck with Casey, and after their initial greeting, the girls started yapping and giggling to the extent that Casey thought his ears were going to burst. But he loved seeing his sister so animated. Her illness had zapped a great deal of her energy, and this was a return to her old self. So the drive to Madison didn't take nearly as long as usual, or at least that's how it seemed.

Casey dropped the girls at the entrance to the medical center, which was huge and sprawling. He parked the truck while they entered, informing Amanda he would meet them upstairs.

The hospital lobby was big and quiet, almost like a library. People spoke in hushed tones for the most part as if someone were sleeping right next to them. It was immaculate and nicely decorated with silk flowers and paintings on the walls.

Callie had never been in a hospital before and was relieved when she didn't see any obvious signs of illness. She was amazed at how many people acknowledged Amanda as they made their way to the elevators. Their faces would brighten the moment they saw her, and she seemed to know all the staff and a lot of the visitors by name.

"Wow, you really are a celebrity," Callie said, impressed by all the accolade.

"Well I spend a lot of time here, and the volunteer work with the kids always gets my face in the papers." Amanda made a celebrity pose then broke into laughter.

They were delayed enough by all the greetings that Casey caught up to them at the elevator. "What's taking you so long, Mandy? Signing autographs again?" He teased her gently, but if the truth were known as many people had acknowledged him as Amanda.

The trio made their way to the nurses' station of the Pediatric Oncology Unit where the Head Nurse greeted them with a big smile.

Amanda made the introductions. "This is Winnie, the coolest nurse in the whole, wide world!"

Winnie, a black woman in her mid-fifties, was wearing brightly colored tie-dyed surgical scrubs, and the stethoscope and ID card around her neck were the only indication of her position of authority.

"Sweetie, you are too kind. I just do my job," she responded modestly then looked to Callie. "And who's this?" It wasn't unusual for Amanda to drag in volunteers.

"This is my very good friend, Callie. She's visiting from New York."

Callie extended her hand to Winnie. "Nice to meet you," she said, as Amanda further explained their history.

"Likewise," Winnie responded. "Any friend of Amanda's, is a friend of mine. Welcome to the ward."

Callie pulled out the white envelope from her purse and presented it to Winnie. "The men on my grandparents' farm put a collection together for the kids. They asked that I deliver it to you."

Winnie's eyes widened as she rifled through the bills. The expression on her face indicated relief as she explained the situation. "Our Christmas party for the kids this year was in jeopardy due to hospital budget cuts. We really needed this money. Please tell the men how appreciative we are and how happy they've made our kids."

"I will." Callie said, thinking back to how she obtained the cash in the first place.

Then Winnie turned to Amanda. "They're waiting for you, honey."

"I'd like to introduce Callie to the girls first. She'll keep them entertained while I get my treatment." Amanda seemed in no hurry to start her chemotherapy.

"That's a great idea, sweetie. Just buzz me when you're ready."

Casey gave Amanda's hand a squeeze then left to get a wheelchair. She knew he would be back well before she was done with all the introductions. Not wanting to waste any more time, she looped her arm through Callie's and escorted her to a sign that read *PLAYROOM*.

"This is where I get my strength," she said, turning the handle and walking through the door.

Seven little girls were playing quietly until they saw Amanda enter. They were small, frail, and bald, and had the same dark circles under their eyes as she did. Their faces lit up, and they mobbed her with hugs. Amanda kneeled down to receive their affections as they chanted her name and demanded attention.

Through their chatter, she managed to introduce all the girls to Callie—Becky, Shannon, Rachel, Joy, Courtney, Kristin, and Dixie, ages four through ten.

"Hello, ladies."

Callie was shocked by their appearance, but touched by their concern for Amanda and their pleasure at seeing her. She wasn't used to children, let alone sick ones, but these kids, although kind of quiet, didn't act any different.

"Callie is going to stay and play with you while I get my treatment. Is that okay?" Amanda asked.

They all gave rapid assent, and Callie added, "Don't worry, we'll be just fine!"

By that time, Casey had arrived with the wheelchair, and the little girls—familiar with the drill—wished Amanda good luck as he wheeled her out of the room.

It was an old routine. Casey would steer Amanda down the hallway—veering and speeding—and she would hang on tight and squeal like it was the front seat of a roller coaster. The staff and visitors new to the scene would frown with disapproval. But the ones used to this ward, understood that the kids needed to laugh and have fun as often as they could.

The pair had grown closer than most siblings when their mother died, and as her big brother, Casey felt it was his duty to protect his little sister. He just had to be careful not to be *too* obvious because that would really make her mad.

They both cherished the moments they had together, knowing their time could be limited. So Amanda used the opportunity to pry into her brother's business. She had noticed Casey watching Callie when he thought no one was looking and she knew her brother *very* well.

"Callie sure is pretty, isn't she?" Amanda probed, slowly working into the topic she was investigating.

"I guess so, if you're into that high maintenance thing." Casey answered, pretending to be disinterested.

"Real smart, too."

"A smart *ass* is more like it."

"It's not like you made it easy on her!"

"She's a spoiled brat! What do you expect?"

"That maybe somebody would've noticed that she was out of her element," Amanda snapped back. She paused for a moment, realizing that criticism was counter productive then quickly changed her tactics. "It sure was nice of you to hook up her computer. She really misses her friends."

"Yeah, well I did it for Johan."

"She said you scared the hell out of her when you popped out from under the desk."

"Is there anything that she didn't tell you?"

Amanda laughed. "I don't know. Is there?"

Casey blushed remembering how he had thought about kissing Callie as he left her room, and Amanda caught his reaction, but didn't acknowledge it out loud. She had all the evidence she needed.

"Well, I'm glad she's back," she smiled happily—her suspicions having just been confirmed. "She makes me laugh. And she definitely brought excitement to Deer Creek!"

Casey looked at his sister, replaying the events of the last few days in his mind. "Now how can you argue with that!" were his final words as the oncology nurse took over the helm of Amanda's wheelchair.

18

True beauty lies beneath the skin

The room fell silent, and seven little faces peered up at Callie, waiting for the show to begin. "So—what would you like to do?" she asked.

The girls continued to stare in a quandary. Any decent entertainment director should have known what to do, so they expected her to develop a plan, and that didn't include standing around asking stupid questions!

Callie searched the room for inspiration. "Do you want to play a game?" she asked, eyeing a stack of board games along the wall. They all shook their heads no.

"How about a story? I could read to you." Still nothing. "Or not." she said, nearly out of ideas."

Finally, Dixie spoke up. She was the youngest and the most outspoken. "Is that your real hair?"

"Of course it is, silly! Why wouldn't it…" Callie stopped short. She noticed that hair was at a minimum in this room, which gave her an idea.

"Hey, I just happen to have my makeup bag with me. Does anyone want to play beauty salon?"

The girls immediately sprang to life and began clamoring, "I do! I do!"

Callie designated a table to be used for the salon treatments and lined up all her makeup as if it were rare and precious. The girls watched and listened with anticipation as she explained what each product was for and how to use it. Then she allowed them to practice on one another, using eye liner, shadow, and blush. Their makeovers were less than professional, but within a short period of time they were admiring each other's work.

Frequently, a nurse would come in and prick someone's finger for blood or administer someone's medication. The girls tolerated all the interruptions without complaint, although Dixie did flinch when the nurse checked her IV. Callie didn't say anything at the time, but she was really beginning to admire these brave little souls.

It was hours before Nurse Winnie held the door open for Casey who wheeled a very tired looking Amanda into the room.

Callie was sitting on the floor with a decidedly wacky new hairstyle and reading a story to the group. Dixie was curled up in her lap, and the other girls surrounded her in a half circle. Excited by Amanda's arrival, they jumped up and offered their support with gentle touches and soft kisses.

Becky couldn't wait to relay the good news. "Amanda, Amanda! Callie let us play with her hair just like you used to do!"

"And what a great job you did!" Amanda spoke cheerfully, but Callie could see a look of sadness in her eyes.

"Will you bring her back?" Courtney asked, and all the girls starting pleading and begging.

Amanda looked to her friend for an answer, and Callie immediately agreed. She had enjoyed her time with the children—especially little Dixie who really touched her heart.

"Of course," Amanda answered, watching the girls bounce with excitement. "But we have to go now. It's a long drive home."

After their farewells, Winnie pulled Amanda's wheelchair out of the playroom and wheeled her down the hallway. Callie started to follow, but was rudely yanked aside by Casey.

"Ouch! What's your problem?" she asked, rubbing her arm.

"You shouldn't make promises you don't intend to keep," he hissed in a whisper.

"And *you*, shouldn't *ass*ume you know my intentions," she replied with indignation then ran to catch up with Amanda at the elevators.

The drive home was peaceful. It had been a long day and they were all exhausted. Amanda rested her head on Callie's shoulder and dozed in and out of consciousness while listening to the latest Coldplay CD. And when they arrived at the Meyers' farm, Callie escorted Amanda inside and upstairs to her room.

Amanda crawled into bed feeling tired and weak. The chemotherapy would keep her alive, but it took its toll on her health. She would feel sick for days. Kind of like a bad flu. But she loved having Callie by her side. It seemed to make things better.

Callie fluffed Amanda's pillow and pulled up a chair along side her bed. In spite of the research she had done on leukemia, there was still a lot she didn't know. Amanda started talking quietly about what it was like—the chemo, the illness, and the fear of dying. And she exposed Callie to a whole new vocabulary of medical terms as she explained the details of each girl's case.

Callie learned that cancer was not selective and that it affected children of every age and gender, without discrimination. And she was crushed when Amanda told her that many of the children in the ward would not survive.

"How is that possible?" she asked. "They're so full of life!"

"I know. It's their optimism that keeps me going."

"And Dixie?" Callie had developed a special fondness for the littlest member of the group.

"She's on a transplant list, but no luck so far."

"There just has to be a match somewhere!" Callie was adamant in her belief, having just read about bone marrow transplants and the process of locating a compatible donor.

"Oh, there is. It's just a matter of finding one in time."

The girls were silent for a moment as they considered the alternative. It was getting late and Amanda was tiring. Her head was on her pillow and her usual energy was missing. Callie was about ready to leave when Nick gently knocked on the door and peered into the room.

"Amanda, you need your rest."

"I know Daddy, just give us one more minute, please?"

"Amanda," he said more sternly.

"Please?"

"One minute. I'm timing you!"

"I have a Christmas present for you, Callie. It's on the shelf in the closet."

Callie walked over and located a wrapped box high above an overflowing and disorganized ledge. "But I don't have one for you."

"Are you serious?" Amanda asked. "*You* are my gift!"

Whoa! Callie didn't know how to respond. She ripped off the wrapping paper and lifted the lid to the box. A crocheted beanie, scarf, and mitten set were nestled inside.

Callie's face lit up. "Sweet. Thanks, Mandy!"

"I made them myself," she announced proudly.

"Dude, you're so Martha Stewart!"

"I started a matching sweater, but I've been so tired lately. I just didn't have the energy to finish it in time for Christmas."

"Are you kidding? This is *way* cool, and besides, there's always my birthday."

Amanda cracked a smile. "I wanted you to have something to remember me by," she said, implying that her condition was uncertain.

Callie held back her emotions. "You inspire me to be a better person."

Amanda was trying hard to keep her eyes open, but was drifting in and out of consciousness. Callie stood up and adjusted the down comforter, knowing that Nick was lurking around the corner ready to throw her out.

"Sweet dreams, angel," she whispered, before turning off the light and tiptoeing out of the room.

Callie was lost in thought and barely said a word to Casey during the ride back to her grandparents' farm. She couldn't stop thinking about the girls, and the hospital, and Amanda. This was serious stuff! So before opening the door to get out, she paused to ask Casey the question that was foremost in her mind.

"What are her chances?"

"Pretty good so far. She's managed to maintain her white blood cell count," he replied. "But she still has another year to go."

Callie backed out of the truck, reading between the lines.

Casey continued, "Sorry, for acting like a jerk today. I'm just overly protective of my sister."

"You should be. She's worth it." Then realizing she had forgotten her manners, she added, "Oh—and thanks for the ride."

Casey smiled, acknowledging her sincerity. Damn he hated when Amanda was right. Just when he was convinced Callie was a stuck up brat, she switches to Miss Congeniality—gorgeous, smart, with a *take charge* attitude and a heart! She was a ten by any definition, and he couldn't take his eyes off her from the moment she got out of the truck to the moment she entered the house.

Callie went directly to her room and carefully placed the hat, scarf, and mittens on the nightstand. She thought about her life at Ridgecrest and compared it to Amanda's. All the things she and her friends considered important seemed so petty compared to having leukemia. And yet, it didn't stop Amanda from helping others. Callie had never witnessed such altruism.

She was quiet at dinner, but it was a serious kind of quiet and her grandparents didn't want to intrude into her thoughts. They figured she was still processing the visit to the hospital and that she would talk about it when she was good and ready. And they were right.

So when Johan found Callie in her room later that evening, staring intensely at her computer screen, he stuck his head through the opened door and finally asked, "Are you okay?"

"Yeah, I'm fine. Hey, aren't you supposed to be in bed?"

"Ja, but the warden let me out for a while since I helped with the dishes. Not to mention, I'm bored and I can't sleep. Do you want to play a game of cards?" he asked hopefully.

"No, not tonight. I have a lot of research to do."

Johan turned away. "All right then, goodnight."

Callie could hear the disappointment in her grandfather's voice. "Opa?" she called.

At first he thought his ears had failed him then he realized she had just called him Opa—grandpa in German. His tone perked up as he answered. "Ja?"

"Have you ever surfed the net?" she asked.

"No, but Arnie says he plays Hearts with people from around the world," Johan replied with definite interest in his voice.

"That figures," she remarked. "Like he can't find enough suckers around here! So are you ready to join the twenty-first century?"

"Sure," he said, like an eager teenager with the keys to the car for the first time.

"You'd be amazed at what I can do with a mouse and a FedEx truck!"

"What does a rat have to do with a computer?" Johan asked, thinking he might need to set a trap in Callie's room.

"No. The controller…it's called a mouse," and she realized she would have to start from scratch.

Johan moved a chair next to hers and focused his attention onto the computer screen. He watched closely as Callie typed in *leukemia* and clicked her mouse on the word *search*.

"I need to learn everything about this disease," she declared, as the computer processed millions of bytes of information.

"Ja, I understand."

Callie further explained the basics of a computer as the next window opened. And they continued to research information well through the night until Elsa tracked them down.

She stood in the doorway for a moment, listening to their chatter. Much of what they said was too technical for her, but she was delighted to see they were rekindling their bonds.

Elsa hated to interrupt, but she was the warden and it was her job. "Okay you two. It's time to take my prisoner back to his cell!" she said, laughing.

Callie and Johan looked up with guilt in their eyes as if they had been planning a jailbreak.

"Doc Hermann says you still need a lot of rest," Elsa insisted.

Johan was tired, although he never would have admitted it. He had cherished this time alone with his granddaughter and was delighted to find out she had a very good understanding of both scientific and technical matters.

Callie, on the other hand, had been amazed at just how much Johan seemed to know about nearly everything; and he was a quick study on the computer, too. She was certain he would be a pro in no time!

After her grandparents left the room, Callie briefly visited the FedEx website before checking her emails and shutting down the computer. Her mailbox was full of notes from the girls and she promised herself that she would answer them in the morning. But for now, she had a date with her pillow!

19

Remdemption is a mouse click away

"Hey Grandma, how do I get an appointment with Evie?" Callie asked, as she bounced into the kitchen fully dressed and ready for the day.

"Well, it is Saturday. And I'm sure she'd love to see you again. Her number is in my address book. Just give her a call."

Callie grabbed the book off the counter and went into the living room to use the phone. After her initial greeting and a squeal of excitement, Elsa heard nothing but whispers until Callie said, "Thanks, Evie—I'll see you then!"

"Grandma?" Callie asked in a sugarcoated voice. "Do you think Opa could drive me into town this morning? It's really important, and I promise to take extra good care of him."

"Hmm." Elsa took a moment to think. "It has been a week now, and he's getting awfully restless. I suppose it would be okay…*if* you make sure he takes it easy."

Johan was hiding around the corner and entered the kitchen just as Callie responded with a "YES!" She gave him a high five to celebrate. "You've been paroled, Opa! And you know what that means, don't you?"

Johan shook his head no. Freedom was beckoning and he didn't care what the terms of the deal were. Anything to get out of that house!

"You owe me. And I never forgive a debt."

Johan acknowledged the favor with a wink then vanished like a ghost before Elsa had a chance to add conditions to the deal—or worse yet, change her mind.

Callie made one more call before running upstairs and grabbing Amanda's gift from her nightstand. She stopped in front of the mirror to stuff her hair up into her new beanie and wrap the scarf around her neck. There was a sparkle in her eye, and she wasn't sure who was more excited about the trip!

Arnie was waiting for them outside of Hank's. He was sleeping in the cab of his pickup truck, snoring loudly under his fishing hat. Callie woke him with a violent bang to the glass. She had no tolerance for slackers and he was officially on her time.

When he rolled down the window, she covertly slipped him a deck of cards and instructed him to meet them at the local diner. He was to keep her grandfather occupied until she finished her business. Card playing was one of the activities Elsa had listed as approved for Johan; and Callie was afraid that if her grandfather was allowed to wander freely, he might get stuck delivering the mail, which was not approved.

Once the men were settled, it was time for the next step of her plan. She marched through the front door of Evie's Coiffeur and plopped into an available chair. The old hairdresser was happy to see her and anxious to get started.

Callie pulled a page from a magazine out of her purse. She explained exactly what she wanted and how she wanted it done. Anyone watching would have thought she requested the most intricate hairstyle yet designed, which was not the case, even though her mission did require compliance to *very* specific instructions.

When the job was done, she reached for her wallet, but Evie refused compensation. "I'm just glad to help."

"Aw, come on, Evie," Callie urged. "I interrupted your whole schedule."

But Evie stood firm in her decision, prompting Callie to think a little harder.

"Hey—what if I do free makeovers for your customers, let's say on Christmas Eve? I can give them a fresh new look for the holidays!"

Evie's face brightened, "Now that, I'll agree to," and she gave Callie a hug to seal the deal.

Mission accomplished! Callie was happy that Evie would be repaid, and Evie felt good about her contribution to the master plan. They watched together from the window as the FedEx truck pulled away from the shop. Callie thanked Evie again and swore her to secrecy then put on her beanie and scarf and went in search of her grandfather.

Not surprisingly, she found Johan exactly where she had left him and about $5.25 richer. She telephoned Elsa and told her that they would be having lunch in town then proceeded to mop the floor with the old men in a game of Texas Hold'em. And within an hour, she had taken them both for about twenty bucks a piece. Arnie was beginning to suspect the curriculum at Ridgecrest included advanced strategies in Poker.

Callie stashed the money into her purse and gathered her deck of cards. She was anxious to get home for a couple of reasons. One, she had a ton of work to do. And two, she knew Elsa was likely to come looking for Johan since he missed his scheduled nap.

The rest of her day she spent immersed in her computer. She couldn't stop thinking about the kids at the hospital and the lack of funding for their holiday party. It was bad enough being sick at Christmas, let alone terminally ill, but to have their annual celebration affected by a hospital budget crisis was just too much to bear. The farmhands' donation would help, but a few hundred dollars wouldn't go that far. Callie figured it was time to test the limits of her credit cards and make this a Christmas to remember!

"So what do you think?" she asked, hoping Amanda would like her plan.

"I think it's one of the nicest things I've ever heard," she replied from the other end of the telephone. Her voice sounded tired and lacked its normal enthusiasm. "I just wish I could help you more."

"Are you kidding? The entertainment is critical. I wouldn't have a clue how to keep thirty kids occupied for two minutes let alone two hours." Callie knew Amanda's participation would be limited, but it was great to have someone in her corner, giving her encouragement and appreciating her efforts.

"How about an art project?" Amanda suggested. "The kids could make tree ornaments and give them to their parents as gifts."

"It would keep them busy, too. That's a great idea!" Callie said, having just solved one more of her problems. "I'll add tissue paper and ribbon to my shopping list."

"And I'll go through my craft books," Amanda declared, feeling a little more useful. But before she hung up the phone, she added one more piece of information that would make things much easier for Callie—the direct number to the pediatric unit.

One quick call and Nurse Winnie joined the team! She was designated as the hospital contact, and all questions and authorizations were to go through her. They decided that Tuesday would be the day, and there was a lot to accomplish before that time—presents, food, decorations, and above all else, acquiring a real Santa Claus!

Callie drafted a thorough outline of all her ideas then immediately went to work. Winnie had given her a list of children who would be attending the party, so her first stop was to ToysRus.com. She ordered specific gifts for the girls she had met, and age-appropriate gifts for the kids she hadn't. And by the time she proceeded to the checkout, the playroom was completely restocked with the latest games and educational toys.

From there, she contacted a caterer in Madison and arranged for the delivery of a buffet, complete with servers, table linens, and silver chaffing dishes. She carefully selected a menu designed to entice the appetites of underage epicureans. The dessert section alone was designed to break any diet in the world. Cakes and cookies, petit fours, Godiva chocolate—for the grownups present—and a self-serve ice cream station were all on the menu. This was no ordinary buffet. It was a feast! And she continued to bounce in and out of websites with the blink of an eye, evaluating and making decisions quickly.

Her next stop was to one of her favorite online shops, Hollywood-costumes.com. Her mission was to order the perfect Santa's suit. She chose the deluxe red velvet ensemble for the yet unidentified Santa and the best wig and beard she could find. She ordered Santa hats for the staff—some with blinking lights, reindeer ears for the kids, and a special little elf costume for Dixie. And of course, the cutest Miss Santa outfit they had for herself!

Callie knew she would look hot in a red miniskirt and black fur-rimmed boots, and she knew that Casey would be there to see it. She was determined to get his attention—even if she had to go to all the way to the North Pole to do it.

Elsa and Johan couldn't believe how generous their granddaughter was. She had given more of herself in one day than most people give in a lifetime. Callie's mind was racing with details of the party and she was mentally going over her checklist as she explained what had been accomplished up to that point.

"The only thing I don't have yet is someone to play Santa," she said, looking at her grandfather's belly with speculation. "I ordered an extra large costume."

Johan looked hopeful at the thought of escaping all the way to Madison for a day.

"NEIN!" Elsa's veto—spoken in German—was a definite end to that plan.

"Any other suggestions, Grandma?" Callie was disappointed, but not discouraged. "He has to be kind of, well…plump, and about Opa's height. Oh, and he has to be jolly!"

"Ja, I think I know just the man." Elsa's eyes had a mischievous glint. "You tell me where and when, and I'll make sure he's there."

Callie felt confident in her grandmother's guarantee. "All right! Another item checked off the list!"

After helping with the dinner dishes, Callie borrowed Johan for her next round of shopping, placing him in charge of the keyboard and mouse. She directed him from over his shoulder as he successfully navigated to BedBathandBeyond.com.

She had pretty specific ideas about how to make her grandmother's life simpler and she wielded her credit card like a sword slicing through layers of red tape. Johan knew Elsa's tastes and Callie used his feedback in her final selections. Short of completely gutting the kitchen and starting over—which she didn't have the time to do—she would have to settle for ordering nearly every modern small appliance known to man.

Johan was in awe. He immediately recognized how the speed, variety, and ease of shopping online could easily replace small business owners like Hank; and at the same time, expand the business of other companies like their own cheese factory.

I'm buying stock in FedEx," he announced. "It might be the only way to get your money back from all this shipping!"

Callie laughed. "Money is meant to spent, Opa. And if you're lucky enough in life to have it, it's your duty to share it." She paused then added, "Within reason, of course."

"Ja, of course," he agreed. This granddaughter of his was smart! Not only did she understand business, but she also had compassion to match—two very admirable qualities.

Callie noticed that Johan was beginning to look fatigued and she was getting tired herself. Besides, the next stop on her shopping spree involved *his* present. So in spite of the fact that she was on a roll, she called it a night. There were still two days left to play Santa.

IN THE MORNING, CALLIE barricaded herself in her room after giving Elsa strict orders to keep Johan out of the vicinity. She wanted him totally surprised when he found his new computer set up on his desk Christmas morning. It wasn't easy finding someone to put a system together on such short notice, but she sweet talked and bribed until she found a store in Madison with a technician who was willing to work a few extra hours of overtime.

Callie was good at buying computers for herself, but Johan's needs would be more specific, so she sought input from someone who knew him well. One call to Amanda and Casey was on the line within minutes.

"I need your help," Callie admitted reluctantly.

"Again?"

"It's for Johan, but if you're too busy, I can ask JR," she said, knowing her statement would be an effective ruse.

"JR barely knows which end of a cow to milk," Casey laughed. The thought of JR giving Callie advice about computers was like Courtney Love giving fashion tips to Ralph Lauren. Not to mention, he was the second best looking guy in town and Casey's only real competition. No way, no how was JR going to step into his turf.

"Go ahead, I'm listening."

Callie explained the hardware she had in mind but wasn't sure which software to order. Casey immediately started listing names of applications, amounts of memory, and connection speeds at a pace too fast for her to remember.

"Stop!" she finally blurted. "I can't keep up with you. I found a store in Madison that agreed to put the system together. Will you please call them for me? Just order everything you think he needs!"

"It's going to be expensive," Casey warned.

"That's okay, they already have my credit card information."

She gave Casey the store telephone number then called the manager to authorize his involvement. And while she had him on the line, she ordered a few extra electronics to be shipped at the same time. Her final business call of the day was to FedEx where she made arrangements to have everything picked up on the 23rd and delivered on Christmas Eve.

As Callie shut down her computer, she overheard a voice coming from downstairs. It was Doc Hermann in the living room, giving Johan a checkup. He was pleased with the exam and about to lessen his restrictions when Callie enter the room with additional concerns.

"What about his cholesterol, Doc? And his um…well, weight?" Callie asked.

The doctor peered over the top of his glasses, trying to determine if the sudden interest was sincere. It seemed as though it was, so he answered, "I can't get the man into the office long enough to check his cholesterol count, and quite frankly…yeah, he's a little overweight."

Johan pointed to Elsa. "It's all her fault!"

"No one forces you to eat, Opa!" Callie responded, not about to let Johan pass the buck.

She continued with a detailed discussion of dietary issues that had her grandparents reeling. The doctor listened carefully as she proposed a plan that included taking them grocery shopping and teaching them how to make healthier choices. And he was so impressed with her knowledge of nutrition that he gladly approved her request to act as the family dietician.

"But schatzie, I'm too old to learn how to cook all over again." Elsa looked dismayed at the thought.

"It won't be that bad, Grandma. I just need to show you some alternatives."

Elsa didn't appear convinced.

"Don't be scared Elsa, there are a lot of substitutions that won't affect the quality or taste of your dishes, and it appears that Callie has a good grasp of what you can change." Doc Hermann turned his attention to his new associate. "But remember young lady, your grandmother's cooking has been winning prizes for years, and if you ruin it, you'll be risking a mutiny around here!"

"Yes sir!" Callie said with a smile. She had the distinct impression that the doctor was beginning to respect her. "I won't let you down."

Just then a FedEx truck pulled up in front of the house. "Right on time," Callie said, looking at her watch. "I should get Roy to bet against him!" she exclaimed with a grin. "I'd clean up."

The farmhands were beginning to enjoy the now frequent appearances of the FedEx man and were laying odds on what was being delivered this time. But none of them were prepared for the quantity of boxes that came out of the truck and they watched in awe as Callie inventoried every one of them.

After the thirty-plus packages were organized into stacks, she directed the men to take them into the house. Some of them were to be delivered to her bedroom, and some of them were to be stored in the utility room. But the majority of the boxes were to be placed in the kitchen.

Callie asked Johan to slice the tape and instructed Elsa to remove the contents. Each package contained a culinary appliance that would make her life much easier, and it wasn't long before the counters were cluttered with a food processor, a juice maker, a bread maker, a yogurt maker, a coffee grinder, and a newer version of just about every tool she already had in her kitchen.

"The dishwasher will be delivered tomorrow," Callie announced. "Merry Christmas, Grandma. You work so hard for everyone!"

Elsa was overwhelmed. "Thank you, schatzie. You'll have to teach me how to use all of these," and she laughed when she saw the name on the Cuisinart. "Ach—so *this* is the Squeeze and Start."

Callie grinned. "Yep, that's it. I'll show you how to use it tomorrow. And you can show me how to cook." She wrinkled her nose. "I think my baking skills need some improvement!"

20

The best gifts are from the heart

Callie arrived at Amanda's house earlier than expected Tuesday morning—delivered by Roy, her designated slave for the day. She was wearing the hat, the scarf, and the mittens that Amanda had made for her and carrying a beautifully wrapped box.

"You're early," Casey moaned, as he opened the door with a big yawn. His hair was messy and his eyes were less than focused. "Amanda's still sleeping and we're not leaving for another hour!"

Callie dashed past him and called back over her shoulder, "That's okay! I'll wake her," and she was up the stairs before he could gather his wits, or for that matter, try to stop her.

She burst through the door of Amanda's room without knocking. "Rise and shine, lazy butt!"

Amanda sat up slowly and yawned. "Hey, I've missed you!"

Callie flipped on the lights and ran to open the drapes. "It's only been a couple of days. And you know how much stuff I had to do."

"Three days to be exact! And you could have done the majority of it from here." Amanda slowly climbed out of bed and grabbed her robe.

"Oh, stop your whining! I promised it would be worth it!"

"You know, you're the only person who treats me normal. I really like that."

"Blah, blah, blah. Now get over here," Callie ordered. "I have your Christmas present!"

Amanda wiped her eyes clear of sleep and blew into her cupped palm. "My breath stinks. Can't I brush my teeth first?"

"No! I promise *not* to get too close. Now open this box or I'll take it back!"

Amanda happily obeyed, slowly peeling off the wrapping paper and folding it neatly.

"AMANDA!"

"Okay, okay," she squealed, then wildly ripped the rest of the paper off the box and lifted the lid. As she riffled through the tissue, she discovered a beautiful brown wig made from real hair!

It took her a minute to realize what it was, "oh my God...oh my GOD...oh MY GOD! Is this what I think it is?" and she danced around the room, swinging it high above her head.

"Not if you think it's a dance partner!" Callie replied.

Amanda ran to the mirror and slipped on the hairpiece. She was surprised by the style. "How did you..."

Callie cut her off. "Evie."

As Amanda fidgeted with the skull cap, she caught Callie's reflection through the mirror. "Damn girl, you don't miss a thing."

Callie's face lit up. "It's real, you know."

Suddenly a light went on in Amanda's head. Callie hadn't removed her hat. The excitement drained from her face as she reached for the beanie—slowly pulling it off her friend's head and exposing a short, spiky hairstyle.

"So, what do you think?" Callie asked. "Fierce, huh?"

Amanda's voice quivered as she realized the extent of Callie's sacrifice. "What did you do?"

"I was getting tired of long hair. And I can't think of anyone else I would rather see wearing it than you. Besides, it's just a temporary fix until your custom-fitted hairpiece arrives."

Now that her secret was out, Callie was free to reveal all the details of her findings. "Did you know that it takes ten to twelve ponytails to make just one wig?"

Amanda was still in shock and shook her head no.

"I know. Who'd have thought? Well anyway, I found this really cool non-profit org that offered to help us with the process. As a matter of fact, they're sending a rep over to the hospital today to measure all the kids."

"But most of their families are lower income."

"It doesn't matter because the hairpieces are free."

Callie had researched the organization's guidelines thoroughly, and made certain that everyone would qualify for the program before scheduling the appointment.

"You've made this the *best* Christmas of my life," Amanda proclaimed, hugging Callie with all her strength.

"Uh Amanda, you were right about your breath!"

Amanda burst into laughter then covered her mouth and dashed into her bathroom to brush her teeth. She left the door open, so they could chat while she showered. And when she came out, Callie had her cosmetics lined up on the dressing table, waiting to be applied.

The girls took a little more time than expected, and Casey was beginning to get impatient. He grabbed a large duffel bag and yelled upstairs in a forceful tone, "C'mon Amanda, we're going to be late!"

"Casey, get dad for me!" she responded.

"Why?"

"Never mind why—just get him!"

"DAD!" Casey yelled, not sure what the emergency was about.

Nick burst through the front door in a panic. "WHAT?"

"I don't know. Amanda wants you."

"Okay you guys...close your eyes," she called down from the top of the stairs.

"We don't have time for games, Mandy." Casey insisted.

"Close them!" Amanda was unusually forceful and waited until she was sure they had complied with her request before descending the stairs. She stood in front of them for a moment, adjusting her stance. "Okay, you can look now."

Nick and Casey opened their eyes to a stunning sight. Amanda didn't look like the little girl they were accustomed to, nor did her face mirror her illness. She was a beauty and she had a glow to her that they hadn't seen in years.

"Well, say something!" she insisted.

"You look like your mother!" Nick answered, and that was the biggest compliment her father could pay anyone.

"Awesome, Mandy…really awesome!" Casey was fascinated by her womanly appearance.

"It's my Christmas present from Callie."

He sat the duffel bag down and reached for Amanda's hair. "It looks real."

"I know, isn't that cool!" Amanda couldn't suppress her excitement any longer.

By now, Casey had noticed Callie watching from the stairs. It was obvious what she had done and he was more impressed than ever. "Well, stunning as you *both* are, we really do have to go."

"Okay, okay—did you remember to pack my art supplies?"

"Yep, they're in the backseat," Casey said, as he ushered Amanda out the front door. Callie started to follow, but was held back by Nick.

"I was wrong about you," his voice was choked with emotion. "Your father would've been proud."

"Thank you, I appreciate that."

Nick's words meant a lot to Callie, but she began to feel awkward when his eyes lost all expression. His mind was clearly in the past. She figured he needed some space, so she casually slipped through the front door and joined the chaos outside.

"My glue gun! It was in the garage!" Amanda panicked, as she went over her list of supplies.

"I've got it!" Casey insisted. "Now for the last time, get back in the truck!"

21

Sometimes the end justifies the means

"Step on it!" Amanda ordered once they were situated. "We can't be late!"

"Oh sure, now you're in a hurry," Casey remarked.

"We have to make a stop on the way," she added, smiling sweetly.

"Oh, we do, do we? And what exactly are we stopping for?"

"Decorations."

"They already have a tree, Amanda. Do you really think they need more?" Casey was a little bewildered. He didn't think he was ever going to understand girls.

"Yes, as a matter of fact we do," Callie interjected.

"Oh Casey, it's for the kids' Christmas party. Callie set it up and everything is going to be delivered and…" Amanda's words came out in a rush, but Casey got the gist of what she was saying.

"Okay! Okay! Remind me to hire her for my graduation party," he said, looking at Callie. "You sure don't cut any corners, do you?"

"Not when my reputation is at stake!" she replied. "So if you don't mind…can we get moving?"

Casey didn't need to be told again. He stepped on the accelerator like a jet on a runway and they flew down the drive!

Callie didn't know much about Madison other than it was a lot smaller than New York City. It was a pretty little town with a simple charm and most of the businesses were decorated for the holiday season. There were a lot of cars and more available parking than she was used to seeing. But as interested as she was in sightseeing, she kept one eye opened for a particular store.

Amanda spotted it first and started yelling, "Turn...there it is... TURN!"

Casey was pretty sure he would never hear out of that ear again, and as soon as he came to a complete stop, the girls bailed out of the truck and ran into the hardware store. He found them minutes later in front of a humongous blowup Santa, sleigh, and reindeer.

"I want this one," Callie announced.

"Don't you think that's a little too big?" Amanda questioned.

"It's for kids...it can never be too big," Callie replied optimistically.

"Sure if it's being delivered to Trump Tower," Casey teased, "...but the playroom? I don't think so. And besides, how would we fit all this into the truck? I drive a pickup, not a semi." But the girls were already in motion and Casey's opinion fell on deaf ears.

Callie and Amanda located a sales clerk who tried to convince them that the Santa and reindeer were only displays and not intended for resale.

"That's bogus!" Callie exclaimed. "Everything in a store is for sale. That's why they call it a store...duh."

Callie wasn't about to take *no* for an answer and demanded to speak to the clerk's supervisor. Amanda just stood there smiling, admiring her friend's tenacity. But when the store manager heard Callie's offer, his eyes lit up with dollar signs and the deal was quickly consummated.

"You do take VISA, don't you?" Callie said, as she removed a platinum credit card from her wallet.

The manager's face brightened even more. "Absolutely," he said with a grin as big as Lambeau Field.

"I can't believe you did that." Casey protested. "This is Madison, Wisconsin, not Tijuana, Mexico!"

"Hey, I learned a long time ago that everything is for sale. It's just a matter of how bad you want it," Callie stated, exuding wisdom beyond her years. "Now all we have to do is figure out how to get it loaded into the truck!"

Casey folded his arms in protest, threatening a strike. "So then...

what's the transportation worth?"

"Knock it off, Casey," Amanda demanded, as she grabbed the sleigh. "You take Santa, Callie can carry the reindeer, and we'll use those bungee cords of yours to hold them in place," and she was out the door before he could argue his case.

"You heard her, Dairy King," Callie teased, referring to the license plate on his truck. "We'd better get a move on or Amanda is going to leave without us."

On the way to the hospital, the girls spent most of the time peering out the back window to make sure Santa and his reindeer didn't fly away. But the journey was a success, and they arrived with all their cargo in place.

Casey pulled up to the circular entrance at the front of the medical center and Callie and Amanda piled out. They had the bungee cords loosened before he even had the engine turned off. The reindeer came out first, then the sleigh, and then Santa to the amusement of all the people watching.

Casey couldn't believe the stupid things his sister made him do. "Wait here while I park the truck," he instructed.

"Aye Aye, Captain." Amanda saluted, as he pulled away from the curb.

The girls couldn't do much until Casey returned. They were too busy trying to control the oversized inflatables while dodging the traffic coming in and out of the hospital. No matter where they stood they seemed to be a nuisance, but just the sight of them made people laugh.

Casey wasn't interested in performing in some impromptu comedy club. He didn't mind taking Amanda to her treatments; however, being a part of Callie's ridiculous antics was just too much! But as he approached, the scene looked so stupid that even he couldn't help but crack a smile.

"Okay, let's get the *flock* out of here!" he said, looking at the reindeer and the girls with the same look of disbelief. "And if I forget…please remind me how much you owe me for this one."

The girls were laughing so hard by the time they reached the entrance that Callie could barely walk. Amanda kept saying, "Go left…go right," for no apparent reason, other than to mess with their minds. So the path to the revolving door had become more like a zigzag than a straight line.

When they finally reached the front, a couple of strangers who had been watching their progress from across the parking lot, held the door in place and kept it from spinning as they loaded their cargo.

"Thank you and have a Merry Christmas!" the trio chimed.

Casey's sense of humor had returned once he reached the safety of the building, figuring they were pretty much home free by then. Boy was he was wrong! The comedy of errors was just beginning.

Santa made it in—only slightly squishing Callie against the glass. Amanda, however, wasn't so lucky. She got stuck with the sleigh and continued going around and around until Casey finally stopped the door from the outside and yelled, "HELP HER!" to Callie through the glass.

Both Amanda and the sleigh popped out and spilled to the ground like a tire exploding under pressure.

"Are you okay?" a portly security guard asked, helping her to her feet.

"I'm fine," she said through her laughter.

Casey stood outside shaking his head at the reindeer and the doors, which had taken on an evil character of their own. He was afraid to ask for help!

Finally, Callie spotted an orderly. "Would you please hold Santa for me?"

He gladly obliged and took control of the oversized figure as she opened the handicapped entrance and helped Casey with the reindeer. They retrieved Santa from the hospital worker and marched off to the elevator under the escort of the security guard who was convinced they were the most suspicious looking trio he had seen all year.

As the elevator doors opened, Casey took charge of the operation, having learned his lesson at the entrance. He instructed Amanda to get in and move to the back and Callie to get in and hold open the door. Then he loaded Santa, the sleigh and the reindeer before squeezing in himself. The elevator was completely full and they were wedged against the sides by their massive cargo.

"Amanda," he yelled, even though she was only about five feet away.

"I'm right here, Casey!" she laughed—her voice rising from somewhere on the other side of the sleigh.

"Callie?" he called out, as if he was taking roll call.

"Present!" she replied.

"Press that button and get us upstairs," he ordered.

"Yes sir!"

When the elevator doors opened to the pediatric ward, Casey and the reindeer emerged first. Amanda followed next—her cheeks still pink from laughing—then Callie, peeking out around the corner.

"Are we there?" she asked, making Amanda giggle again.

Nurse Winnie was standing at the edge of the nurses' station with her hands on her hips and a big smile on her face. "There you are—I was getting worried!" she said, staring in astonishment at the so-called decorations they were carrying.

She stopped mid-thought at the sight of Amanda. "Goodness gracious, child!" she exclaimed. "Amanda, is that you?"

"In the flesh, Winnie!"

"Well I'll be damned." She took a long, hard look. "Girl, you're gorgeous!"

Winnie was like a surrogate mother to Amanda, and having her approval meant a lot.

A big smile stretched across Amanda's face. "Thanks, Winnie. I have to admit, it feels pretty good."

Winnie pulled her close, hugging her with all her strength. "I know, honey," she said, patting her head. "I know." And for a brief moment, Amanda felt like her mother had reached out to her from the heavens.

After an unusually long and heartfelt embrace, Winnie released her hold and got back to business. "Now I'm pretty sure everything has arrived or at least I thought it had. But the kids are getting antsy, so you'd better get those things into the playroom right away!" She shook her head in disbelief. "Though I am not quite sure where you're gonna put them. The caterer is setting up the buffet and the playroom is already filled with packages."

"Don't worry," Callie said with a smile, "I'm German!"

As the group made their way to the playroom, Winnie pulled Callie off to the side and whispered, "There's a grumpy old man roaming the ward with a dolly full of luggage. He says he's with you."

"Oh yeah," Callie made the connection. "I'm donating some play clothes to the kids. I'll have him set it up in one of the corners."

"But which corner?" Winnie demanded to know. "There are only four to the room!"

Once the decorations were in place, Amanda immediately went to work on the craft table, Callie unloaded the boxes of gifts, placing them neatly under the tree, and Casey went in search of an appropriate chair for Santa.

After combing the pediatric ward to no avail, he remembered seeing furniture in some of the offices on the lobby level. And sure enough, there it was—the perfect winged back chair positioned right behind the hospital administrator's grand old walnut desk! It wasn't going to be easy, but Casey figured the lunch hour would provide a window of opportunity for the heist. So he borrowed a dolly from the maintenance closet, loaded the chair, and bolted down the hall! There were plenty of witnesses, but they cheered him on as he made off with the loot.

"Hey Roy!" Callie called. "It's show time!" and she pointed to a special box.

Roy—the mysterious grumpy old man—had already assembled the racks and was unloading the clothing from Callie's luggage. He looked at her with disdain in his eyes. "Yeah, I'll get right on it."

Finally, everything was in place, and the kids and their parents were on their way. Callie looked great in her outfit—just as she had planned, Dixie was adorable as an elf, and every square inch of the room was covered with decorations, packages, and seating for the guests.

The children's eyes widened when they entered the room—their delight was unmistakable. The plan was to make ornaments, play dress up, and eat before opening presents from Santa. And they didn't waste any time. Amanda supervised the crafts and Callie helped with the play clothes while the caterer served the food and Casey stuffed his face.

The room was filled with a joyous buzz until a "Ho, Ho, Ho" was heard from the hall. The children stood frozen in their place as they turned their attention to the robust man in the doorway.

Dixie's eyes grew *so* large that Callie thought they were going to pop out of her head!

"SANTA!" she screamed, dashing across the room and firmly attaching herself to his leg.

The older kids nodded at one another, determined to let her keep her belief. And within minutes, Santa was passing out gifts to everyone! The children received toys and their parents and the staff received gift certificates. Nobody was left out. There was even a stash of gift baskets from Starbucks Coffee available for emergencies, such as when the hospital administrator came looking for his chair!

"How did you know about him?" Casey whispered into Callie's ear.

"I didn't," she confessed. "I just know there's always a big party pooper lurking around every corner, and they're normally caffeine addicted morons!

"Damn," Casey thought. "Is there anything this girl didn't think of?" He watched in amazement as Callie bounced from guest to guest—her skirt in constant motion, revealing glimpses of her long, shapely legs. She achieved her goal—the outfit was a hit!

Amanda had been taken away for a brief treatment after the buffet was served and returned just as Santa was finishing up with the gifts.

"Perfect timing!" Callie said with a smile. "Santa could never forget his favorite little angel!"

"Open it, Amanda....open it!" the kids yelled, more excited for her then they had been for themselves.

Amanda pulled out a Precious Moments angel figurine from a gold metallic gift bag with a card that read...

You bring out the best in us. Hugs, kisses and Christmas wishes! Love Santa

The party was nearing its end, but Nurse Winnie had a final announcement to make. "Earlier today, a really nice lady came and took some measurements of all the children's heads, and I know you were all curious as to what that was about. Our new friend Callie, made a phone call to an organization called Locks of Love. They've offered to make custom hairpieces for all of you that will look just like your real hair until yours grows back."

Squeals of delight echoed throughout the room, accompanied by a burst of applause. A couple of the older girls reached their hands to their heads like they had just won the grand prize—they were the ones that felt the most out of place at school, and the parents were so overwhelmed that many of them broke into tears.

Callie was instantly bombarded with "thank yous" and hugs of appreciation, almost to the point of embarrassment. "It was nothing really," she said. "You have the bravest, sweetest group of kids, and they've taught me so much. All I did was make a phone call."

"I'd hate to pay your telephone bill," she heard Casey whisper from behind. He had a pretty good idea of just how many calls were required to pull the whole thing together.

"Don't worry, I have unlimited minutes," she whispered back, grinning. Then noticing Amanda's condition, she added, "I think we need to get someone home."

"I think you're right!" he agreed. "She's had a long day."

On the way out, Amanda stopped next to Santa who was still sitting with Dixie on his lap. She whispered into his ear, "I didn't think you had it in you," recognizing that it was Roy hiding behind the beard.

"I don't," he said quietly enough for Dixie not to hear. "Trust me, there's going to be hell to pay for this one!"

When they got back to the truck, Amanda leaned her head against Callie's shoulder and closed her eyes. She was asleep before they hit the highway.

Casey turned on the radio and they listened to Christmas carols in comfortable silence.

It was later than usual, and Nick was waiting for them out front. He knew about the party and figured Amanda would be exhausted. She was in a deep sleep when they arrived, so Callie gently slid off the seat while

Nick picked up his daughter and carried her to her bedroom.

Callie climbed back into the truck with Casey. She remained quiet during the ride home, replaying the day's events in her mind. The smiles on the kids' faces made all her efforts completely worthwhile; and for the first time in her life, she felt a genuine sense of accomplishment.

When they arrived at the farmhouse, Casey got out of the truck to open the door for her. He paused for a moment as he reached for her hand and stared into her eyes. "Ya did good, Scarlett!"

As she climbed down the step, his face was within inches of hers and his lips looked positively scrumptious. It took every bit of willpower she had to keep herself from jumping into his arms and permanently attaching her lips to his.

"Why thank you, Rhett," she said, praying that her voice wouldn't crack. Her palms were sweating, her heart was racing, and there were butterflies swarming in her stomach. She wanted to scream, "Kiss me you fool!" but before she totally embarrassed herself, she released his hand and walked to the porch.

Callie waved as he drove away. She waited to go inside until she was sure her heartbeat was back to normal and her face wasn't flushed with excitement. There was so much to tell her grandparents, yet the only thing she could think about was how close she had come to planting a big, fat *wet one* on Casey's gorgeous face!

She didn't know it then, but Casey was feeling the same way. No girl had ever affected him like this. Adrenalin pumped through his veins every time he was around her, and she was more exciting to him than running for the winning touchdown.

He watched her through his rear view mirror. "This is either extreme attraction," he thought to himself, "or a really bad case of the flu!"

22

It takes a snipe to catch a snipe

"Ew!" Callie proclaimed, as she entered the kitchen. The sight of Roy's butt sticking out from under the counter accosted her eyes. "That's enough to scar me for life!"

Realizing what she was referring to, Roy attempted to pull his shirt down and his jeans up from his awkward position on the floor.

The kitchen was in shambles and Elsa was hovering nervously as Roy and Johan connected her new dishwasher. It was nearly dinnertime and she could barely maneuver around the room.

"Schatzie," she said with excitement. "Look—it arrived!"

Callie stepped over tools and piping to get to her grandmother's side. She peered at the men's progress. "Make sure you get it right!" she hollered to Roy who glared up at her from his contorted position.

Elsa continued singing her praises. "I can't believe all the new features. It does everything but load the dishes! I just love it. Thank you so much."

"Your welcome, Grandma—you deserve it," she said with sincerity as she accepted the heartfelt hug Elsa had extended.

Callie felt a hostility emerging from Roy and figured he had something devious planned for her after having to dress up as Santa. She had learned the basics of retribution from Bianca and knew when to anticipate trouble. So when Roy's voice changed from vinegar to honey, Callie figured he was up to no good.

"Hey, Cal!" he chimed. His voice slightly muffled by his work area and his face hidden from view. "Some of us guys are going snipe hunting tomorrow evening up at Four Corners. Do you want to come?"

Callie was suspicious of Roy's invitation and wasn't quite sure how to respond.

"There's nothing better for Christmas dinner than fresh snipe," he insisted.

She looked to Johan for some kind of clue, but her grandfather merely smiled. What he couldn't explain was that snipe hunting was a trick country folk played on city folk—a form of harmless initiation, and going along with it meant instant acceptance. This was an offer to let bygones be bygones, and Callie got the impression she was expected to be a willing participant.

No one in these parts had ever really seen a snipe. But the idea was to give the intended victim of the prank an old burlap potato sack and a couple of sticks, and put them out in the middle of nowhere in the dark. They were supposed to hit the sticks together and call out "Here snipe" and then snag one—supposedly, in the potato sack. But in reality, they made fools of themselves while the pranksters sat behind nearby trees laughing at them.

"What's a snipe?" she asked innocently.

"Uh—it's a game bird. Not common in most of the states, but we have a big flock of them around here," Roy answered.

"Do I shoot it?"

Roy looked alarmed at the thought of Callie with a gun. "No! You catch 'em in a bag."

"Damn!" she exclaimed, playing city girl to the hilt, "because I've always wanted to shoot a gun."

Callie thought Roy was going to choke—his reaction was so extreme. "You better take care of that cough, Roy," she added.

Johan spoke up just as he and Roy had rehearsed, and said with apparent concern, "Are you sure it's safe to go snipe hunting this year? You know…with all the werewolf sightings."

"Werewolf?" Callie interjected with fear. Actually she didn't really believe much in werewolves or ghosts.

"Now you hush, Johan. You're gonna scare her. You know that thing was spotted over twenty miles from here!"

"Yeah, but nobody knows for sure how far they range." Johan spoke with complete sincerity.

Callie made a mental note to nominate her grandfather for an acting award as she continued to play along. "Wait a minute, that kind of changes things. Has anyone ever been attacked?"

"Naw—just some small animals it kind of mauled up and left on the road," Roy replied.

"Well that's reassuring…NOT!" Callie continued to act nervous about the whole thing.

"Don't worry, we'll all be out there. And Elsa would kill us if anything happened to you."

"That's true," and she reluctantly—or so it seemed—gave her assent. "But I'm looking into that werewolf story and if there've been any recent sightings, we're having turkey instead!

Callie didn't waste any time. She had the words *snipe hunt* typed into Google before Roy even knew she had left the room.

She discovered that *snipe*—although real birds—were not native to that part of Wisconsin. And that *snipe hunt* was code for *prank, commonly played by locals*.

"Oh, Roy," she thought, "you're such a fool."

An idea flashed through Callie's mind, and within minutes, she had a local wildlife conservationist on the phone. After a lengthy discussion, a plethora of charm, and an offer of a hefty donation to his program, she persuaded him to join her cause and deliver the required ammunition by morning.

And just for the heck of it—because she knew Roy would like nothing more than to see her eaten by a werewolf—she checked up on that story, too. It turned out there had been reported sightings of what some people described as a werewolf in the southeastern region of Wisconsin. But like he said, the only things known to have been eaten were small animals. So Callie decided to add a can of mace to her supplies for the evening, just in case! Now all she needed was a bit of assistance from her main ally against the men—her grandmother!

At dinner, Callie fell into the routine Elsa and Johan had in place. She discussed the day's events in detail, minus the attraction she felt for Casey.

"I hope you got a picture of Roy in that Santa suit," Elsa chuckled. "He really was a good sport—not that I gave him much of a choice in the matter."

"Actually Grandma, he did a great job and the kids loved him. I might even have to give him a Christmas present!"

Elsa began to reminisce, "When I was a little girl schatzie, we decorated the tree on Christmas Eve, and there were no presents put out until the children had all gone to bed. In the morning, we would go to the living room and the tree would be glowing with real candles and strings of popcorn and cranberries."

Johan nodded his head in agreement then added a few memories of his own.

Callie was fascinated with their stories and could have listened for hours. But she was planning on doing some research for the science fair that evening and wanted to get her grandfather's input. Reluctantly, she changed the topic and started explaining her project's parameters. She was amazed at how much her grandfather knew about conservation as he illustrated how even simple farmers had an impact on the environment.

"We have three major responsibilities, Callie," he explained. "One is soil conservation. Over the years, we learned that if we left the ground bare during the winter months, we lost measurable amounts of topsoil. The soil here is rich and dark, and we'd like to keep it here. So take a moment the next time you are out, and you will see that we leave the stubble from the crops in the fields until springtime when we plant again."

Johan took a sip from his glass of milk before continuing.

"The second concern is run off from fertilizers into the water supply. It's not so much an issue on our farms because we use mostly manure. But some farmers use chemicals, and they disturb the balance in our streams. Many have been linked to fish kills and contaminated water in some areas just like manufacturers."

Callie listened carefully since she had to address the water supply issue in her project. She knew from previous research about the potential hazards of manufacturing plants, but didn't realize that farmers took the issues so seriously as well.

Johan continued, "And finally, we have to dispose of the animal waste or manure. As I've already mentioned, we use ours as fertilizer. So the milk and dairy products we produce are pretty much—as you say, organic."

Callie had a number of questions for Johan and was surprised when he knew the answers, some of them quite technically. "Come upstairs with me Opa, and I'll show you what I have so far." She was eager to get his input.

Johan looked at Elsa who nodded her approval, and they headed to Callie's room. As they climbed the stairs, he suggested a number of topics for her to explore online.

"Nope—you're doing the research, Opa. You need to get used to using a computer," she insisted.

Johan sat in front of the screen and pulled up site after site, adding them to Callie's favorites as she directed. Their conversation turned to his patents, and he explained modestly how he developed the ideas.

"Remember Callie, I grew up in Germany. And we had some of the finest engineers in the world back then. Most of them had to work on the war efforts, but many of us chose not to utilize our abilities for that."

Callie would have asked him more about his youth, but recognized a reticence in his face and opted to change the topic. "Pull up MichelsohnandMeyersDairy.com, Opa."

"You mean Goggle has us, too? I knew Casey was developing a website, but I've never seen it!" Johan's interest spiked.

The website was both impressive and comprehensive. It included pictures of both farms, information about all their products, and an extensive history of their business. There was even an e-store with a shopping cart for the cheeses.

"Casey designed this?" Callie asked, impressed with his artistic presentation.

"Ja, I like it," Johan said, pleased with what he saw. "Casey is a very bright young man and understands technical matters just like you." Johan didn't want to say too much. He knew there had been some tension between them and figured it was best if they became friends on their own.

Callie spoke more to herself than to Johan. "Hmm...not bad."

Johan merely smiled at the screen and they continued surfing the net until Elsa—the warden—came to retrieve her prisoner. She was allowing her husband to return to his normal routine a little at a time, but still insisted that he get plenty of sleep.

Before saying goodnight, Callie requested that they wake her up earlier than usual. She wanted to help with the morning chores—the real ones, this time!

"Okay," Johan said with a smile. "You can help me." And again, he looked to Elsa for approval.

"Better you than Roy," she winked, acknowledging Callie as her co-conspirator. "You never know what he's got up his sleeve!"

Callie sighed happily as they left her room. She was exhausted and really wanted nothing more than to sleep. But she still needed to look at her much neglected emails. The girls were likely to send out a search party if they didn't hear from her soon. She had already been through one of those, so she checked her mailbox. And just as she expected, most of her mail was from her friends who were sounding concerned over the absence of return phone calls and reply messages.

The last communication from Bianca read...

Hello out there! Are you still alive? Have you been captured by Indians, or worse yet...Farm boys? Have you found any signs of intelligent life? Do you need rescuing? Why haven't I heard from you? WRITE ME OR ELSE! Love ya, Bianca

Callie figured she had better write them all before they called the FBI or the mob, whichever they thought of first. Her response was...

Hello from the Heartland! I'm going on a snipe hunt tomorrow, but I expect to survive (that is, if I don't get eaten by a werewolf). I threw a party for the bravest kids on the planet, and made the meanest old man

play Santa (rumor has it, he's plotting revenge). My grandpa has been a great help on our science project (we're sure to win) and I've taken Grandma's kitchen from "rolling pin" to "squeeze and start" in just over a week. Oh, and maybe, just maybe, Farm boy isn't totally hopeless (actually, he's pretty good with a mouse). Well got to go for now; they're making me do chores in the morning (tell your Dad, Bianca...it will make his day!) and I'm dying of sleep deprivation. Love you, miss you...
Callie

She figured that was enough to keep them busy for now, and realized she would have a lot of explaining to do later.

23

Even old dogs can learn new tricks

Morning came *way* too soon. And it seemed as though Callie had just fallen asleep when she felt the gentle nudging of her grandfather who was fully dressed and seemingly wide awake.

"Callie, it's time to get up," Johan whispered.

"Alrrriggghhht," she answered, regretting the offer she had made mere hours before.

Johan flipped on the light switch, which triggered Callie's eyes to immediately close as they adjusted. Boy that felt good! And that dream she had been having about Casey—what was up with that? She sighed to herself as she shook off the temptation to hide under the covers then sat up in bed and rubbed her eyes.

"Hey Opa, does Grandma have some warm clothes I can borrow? I'm kind of running out of things to wear," she asked, just as Johan reached the door.

Not having the right outfit was completely against Callie's nature since her motto was *always pack more than you need*. But she was aware of the work she was about to do, and cow poop just didn't go well with designer labels!

"I'm sure she has something. I'll let her know."

"Thanks, Opa," Callie said with a yawn. She stretched and pushed the covers to the foot of her bed just as the rooster crowed. "Ah ha!" she gloated. "I beat you again!"

The room was chilly, so she threw on her robe and dashed to the bathroom to take a quick shower. And just in case Dairy King was in the vicinity, she spent an extra couple of minutes applying makeup.

It was still dark outside when she headed downstairs. Elsa was already busy in the kitchen mixing batter for pancakes when Callie entered the room. She stopped to kiss her grandmother good morning then reached for a cup of coffee.

"Nothing like getting half the day's work done before sunrise, Grandma," Callie commented, appearing more energetic than she actually felt.

"Guten morning," Elsa said with a smile. "I put some clothes out for you on my bed. You can get them as dirty as you like."

"Yippee," Callie replied with her usual tact. "I see you're not taking advantage of your new appliances yet. How come?"

"I'm sorry, schatzie. I'm kind of set in my ways. But I promise I'll start using them soon."

"You're a woman with strong convictions, Grandma, and I admire how you do everything by hand. That's a skill, not a handicap! But you'll be amazed at the amount of time you'll save."

"And just what would I do with all that extra time?"

"I don't know," Callie answered, "but we'll think of something. Now, what can I do to help?

"Hmm," Elsa thought carefully. "You can either start frying the bacon or gather the eggs for me."

"Uh, I'll do the egg thing." Callie had no clue what frying bacon entailed, only that it sounded extremely messy. And the way the men around here ate, she envisioned a whole pig in the frying pan. At least she knew where to find the henhouse.

"Wunderbar!" Elsa said, realizing that Callie still had limitations, and that certain jobs were well beyond her comfort zone. "You'll find the basket in the pantry."

"That's it?" Callie asked. "So do the chickens just hand over their eggs to me or do I have to smack'em around a bit?"

She had already determined that some of the simplest chores on the farm were a lot harder than imagined, and while she figured she could outthink a chicken, any advice to simplify the task would be greatly appreciated. Besides, she liked making her grandma laugh.

"Don't be ridiculous," Elsa chuckled. "There's no trick to it. If the hen is sitting on the nest just slip your hand underneath and grab the eggs. Most of the time they move right away, but sometimes they're too lazy too get up. And they don't have teeth, so they can't bite you!"

Callie downed her coffee, grabbed her jacket, and headed for the henhouse with the basket wrapped around her arm. She couldn't help but think about Alfred Hitchcock's classic, *The Birds*, and was certain the chickens were watching her—just waiting to attack! But when she was convinced they hadn't seen the movie, she gathered the eggs in record time and rejoined her grandmother in the kitchen.

"Now that you've collected them," Elsa instructed, "go ahead and break them!"

The feat looked pretty simple, having just watched her grandmother the day before. But Callie hadn't thought much about it before gently tapping the first one against the side of the bowl. Nothing happened. She looked over at Elsa, then down at the egg and chided herself, "Okay, this isn't rocket science!" Holding it a little more firmly, she cracked it hard against the edge and watched as the shell broke loose. The yolk landed half into the bowl and half onto the counter.

"Uh, Grandma, can we make scrambled eggs this morning?" she asked, attempting to justify her method.

Elsa looked up and winked. "I think the boys would like that."

By the time Callie had cracked open two dozen eggs, she had the hang of it pretty well. Elsa was very organized in the kitchen and staggered all the jobs so that everything was ready just before the hands came in and sat down. As usual, they flocked to the kitchen at the sound of Elsa's *clang* and immediately began to fill their plates.

"I made those," Callie announced, just as Roy was about to swallow his first bite. The rest of the hands acknowledged her efforts by bobbing their heads in approval—their mouths too full to speak.

Roy, on the other hand, wasn't sure what to think.

"You sure you want to eat that?" Callie warned. Her look was *way* too innocent for Roy to trust, and nothing made him more suspicious than Callie being concerned for his welfare.

He was already regretting his first bite—even though it tasted okay—and sat for a moment pushing the rest of his meal around on his plate.

Elsa finally had enough. "Oh for God's sake Roy! She's just kidding!"

He continued to eat tentatively until he saw Callie take food from the same platter and eat it with gusto. But for some reason, she had a satisfied smirk on her face, which irritated the hell out of him!

After breakfast, Callie went upstairs to change into the clothes Elsa had set out for her. She found old blue jeans, long underwear, a flannel shirt, and an oversized sweatshirt lying neatly on the bed. She checked the size of the jeans and was surprised to find they were only a 7/8. These either belonged to someone else or they were the oldest pair of Levi's she had ever seen! But they were warm and fit perfectly, and with the welcomed addition of the rubber boots in the utility room, she felt *armed and ready* for battle.

Callie was amazed by the organization of her grandfather's farm as she watched everyone move like clockwork. Johan took her under his wing, and by nine o'clock, she was already measuring the grain for the cow in the barn and tending to a cut on Uncle Buck's hindquarters. Their next job was to feed the goose and the ostrich, which were quite pleasant when they wanted to be fed.

The other farmhands were involved in their own assignments like mucking out stalls and changing the bedding for the animals. Two of them were fixing a tire on a tractor, and another was replacing a belt on a John Deere combine. Apparently this massive machinery—it was bigger than some houses—was designed to harvest, separate grain from unnecessary product, and place it in a wagon all in one fell swoop. Pretty cool! And it was air conditioned, too.

For their final chore of the day, Johan took the opportunity to demonstrate his *expert* cow-milking skills. Callie had done it quite well for a rookie, but her grandfather made it look like a piece of cake and she watched in amazement.

Frequently, the men would come to Johan with questions about settings for some piece of equipment or other, and he always had the answer.

"How'd you get so smart, Opa?" Callie probed, impressed with the diversity of his knowledge.

"A solid education and years of practice."

"That's right—you mentioned you went to school in Austria. Which one?" Callie's mind flashed to the story Johan had told her about his friendship with Maria Puck.

"The Vienna University of Technology. I was studying civil engineering. I wanted to design cities and improve public works."

"So you weren't a farmer?"

"Heavens no! We laugh about it now, but it was actually your grandmother with all the farm experience. I had to learn everything from scratch."

"Hey…you told me she was related to a king and that I was a princess!" Callie protested, suddenly feeling robbed of her birthright.

"Even princesses fall on hard times, Callie. Elsa's parents sent her to live with her Austrian cousins when the war started. They wanted to keep her as far away from politics as they could. She was a little girl at the time, a *spoiled* little girl mind you, but a little girl just the same. Suddenly, she was reduced from aristocracy to working-class and it was either sink or swim."

"Why does this story sound so familiar?" Callie commented, immediately catching the similarities in the situation between Elsa and herself just as Johan had intended.

Her grandfather laughed. "I thought you'd pick up on that."

"So how did you two meet, anyway?"

"Vienna…1948, at an art exhibition. Elsa had just turned sixteen." Johan was smiling as he made the comment. He could still see her face in his mind, unlined and untouched by all the years. It was the way he would always think of her.

"I'm turning sixteen in February," Callie announced.

"Ja, and you are very much like her."

"So who was the artist?"

"The artist?" Johan had assumed that Callie knew more about her heritage.

"Yeah, the artist who had the exhibition?"

"Why…that was your grandmother! And it was more like a sidewalk sale than an actual art auction." Johan laughed at the image of Elsa peddling her paintings on his campus. "She was so beautiful! And she had a practical side that most young women her age seemed to lack."

"Grandma painted? Canvases?" Callie was blown away. Apparently artistic ability wasn't just a trait of her parents.

"Oh ja—her family was actually known for their extensive art collection. And she would've had a brilliant career if the bombings hadn't destroyed Dresden's museums and fine art galleries."

"Wow, that's harsh," Callie observed. "But why didn't she continue painting?"

"A lack of money at first, then a lack of time. And as soon as we bought this farm, Elsa was pregnant with your father. I don't think she's ever had a moment of extra time since."

"Funny, we were just discussing that this morning." But Johan's answer gave Callie an idea, and she set it aside in her mind for later.

Their conversation had kept them busy while they completed their chores and it was time to call it quits. They put everything away and headed back to the house where they found Elsa trying out her new appliances—all of them at once it would appear!

Eggs were being hard-boiled in the Oster Egg Cooker; coffee was being made in the Braun automatic coffee maker—having just been freshly ground in the new Hamilton Beach grinder. Cookie dough was being mixed in the Cuisinart; chickens were being roasted in the George Foreman rotisserie; and the new Maytag dishwasher was churning like ocean waves on a stormy day.

Elsa looked up from her Presto Salad Shooter like a mad scientist— crazed by his latest invention. "Bitch'n!" she exclaimed.

"Grandma!" Callie's voice indicated her surprise at Elsa's choice of words. "Where did you hear that?"

"JR," Elsa confessed, as she added carrots to her favorite new toy. "He says it all the time."

"I should've known," she said, shaking her head.

Johan looked vaguely alarmed. "You know, liebchen, this old house may not have the wiring capacity to handle everything at once! We'll need to upgrade."

Callie laughed at her grandfather's use of computer lingo then headed upstairs to shower off the mud and splatter that decorated her *not-so-designer* outfit.

"I'm proud of you, Grandma!" she yelled over her shoulder. "Keep up the good work!"

Johan began tinkering with Elsa's new appliances, checking out the control settings and peaking under the lid of the Cuisinart. She slapped his hand and exclaimed, "Paws off, mister!"

"But liebchen, I just wanted to taste it and make sure it doesn't change your recipe."

"Ja, right! And eat a half pound of cookie dough before they reach the oven. I know how you are!" And once again, she snapped the dishtowel at his belly.

"Elsa! Put that away—it's a lethal weapon." Johan covered his stomach as he attempted to grab the towel away from her.

"Back off, Herr Michelsohn!" she threatened, as he took a step toward her. But the grin on her face denied the threat she issued.

"Ach, I know when I've been beaten."

"And so you should!" Elsa exclaimed victoriously.

Johan was still full of questions about the rest of the appliances, and she proudly gave him a guided tour, explaining everything she had learned up to that point. It was a toss up as to who was going to enjoy them more.

Callie was anticipating the first leisurely break of the day, but no sooner did she step out of the shower when a light bulb went on in her brain. "How could they have forgotten?" she thought. And in a near panic, she rushed back downstairs to the kitchen.

"Hey Grandma—aren't we going to put up a Christmas tree?" she asked.

"Of course, schatzie. We always get it on the 23ʳᵈ," Elsa answered, as she pulled a batch of cookies from the oven.

"That's today, Grandma."

"Ach mein Gott! I lost track of time." She looked to Johan for a suggestion.

"I'll go right now," he said, reaching for his coat and hat.

"Sit down! You're still under doctor's orders. Roy can get it." Elsa had suddenly become the warden again, and she wouldn't accept any arguments on this one.

"But Elsa, it's a family tradition," Johan exclaimed.

"Ach! Tradition—schmission!" Elsa stood firm on her decision.

"I'll get it, Grandma. I'm good at picking trees."

"Picking? You mean chopping," Johan declared.

"Chopping? You mean shopping—right?" Callie was totally confused by now.

Johan shook his head. "Oh boy, I'd better call Casey."

BY THIS TIME, BIANCA, Alexia, and Danielle had all received Callie's last email and were very concerned with her message. They had envisioned a number of scenarios, all of them disastrous—kidnapping, ransom requests, and worst of all, the Schwartzeneggar muscles she would have gained from all the chores they suspected she was being forced to do.

Danielle was the most bored and was in desperate need of Callie's guidance. So she placed the conference call, linking them together as they discussed what to do.

"Hello?" Danielle asked anxiously, hearing the ring tone end. "Is anyone there?"

"Hi Dani," Bianca replied, her voice coming across loud and clear.

"I'm here, too!" Alexia announced.

"I'm worried sick about Callie. She sent me a really weird email last night!" Danielle skipped all the small talk and went straight to the point.

"I got it, too—something about werewolves and snipes! And what the hell is a snipe? Do you think she meant sniper?" Bianca envisioned Callie being held against her will by terrorists.

"Werewolves don't really exist, do they?" Danielle asked.

Bianca moaned. "Dani, you watch *way* too much TV!"

"Where is Wisconsin anyway?" Alexia asked. "It's a state, right?"

"Yeah, it's a state, Alex—it borders Illinois. And Deer Creek is about two hours from Chicago. It must be out in the boondocks though." Bianca knew that much for sure.

Just then her brother rushed past her and snatched her purse. "Hey, give that back!" she screamed. "All my money is in there! Mom!" she called out. "Michael took my purse again!"

"Can't we call the police and report her missing or something? I mean she is a citizen of New York and we can't reach her!" Alexia's voice sounded funny—like her head was in a fish bowl.

"Alex, are you okay?" Danielle asked with concern.

"Totally—I'm in the middle of a massage and my head is crammed into a towel…continue."

"New York is not a separate country, Alex, and we don't know for sure that she's been kidnapped." Bianca made a mental note to send Alexia an atlas and a study guide, or better yet, a private geography tutor!

"Maybe that Casey guy has her hypnotized and is forcing her into submission!" Danielle suggested, adding a general sense of hysteria to the conversation.

"Svengali himself couldn't hypnotize Callie if she didn't want to be," Bianca replied. But something's definitely up, and I don't like being kept out of the loop."

"So what do we do now?" Alexia asked. "*The Academy Awards* are coming up and I need her to pick out my clothes!"

Danielle chimed in, "And my mother is talking about sending me to Europe for the summer again. Callie always comes up with best excuses not to go!"

"Okay, we have to think this through! We can't call the police until we know for a fact that she's being held against her will. I'll try her cell phone one more time then I'll call Zoey's assistant. I have her phone number for emergencies. If I don't get anywhere with that we'll have to regroup." Bianca sounded decisive. "But right now, I have to locate Michael's new Sony PSP because blackmail is the only language he speaks! I'll catch up with you guys later." And she disconnected the line.

Danielle was having trouble understanding Alexia with her muffled voice and the occasional yelps of pain she made when the masseuse hit a tender spot. So they weren't making much progress. And when Alexia became agitated with Danielle's constant request for her to repeat herself, she quickly put an end to the conversation. "I'll talk to you soon, Dani. And don't worry, Bianca will come up with a plan!"

When she hung up the phone, Danielle's imagination went into overdrive. She envisioned the three of them dressed in black leather jumpsuits surrounding a farmhouse like *Charlie's Angels* going to the rescue!

24

Some things are just inevitable

"W hat took you so long?" Callie scolded, as she ran to Casey's truck with an ax in her hand. It had only been about fifteen minutes since Johan's call, and she was already pacing the porch.

"I'm fine thank you, how are you?" he responded, calling attention to her lack of manners.

"Sorry," she said, jumping into the passenger seat and realizing that she was acting like a brat again. "Thanks for coming?"

"That's better," he said with a smug look on his face.

"Now come on, you're wasting time. I've got a tree to chop." Callie's personality switched from humble to bossy within seconds.

"You? Chop? Now this, I've got to see," Casey laughed, visualizing Callie in a designer dress and high heels assaulting a tree.

"Why? You don't think I can do it?"

"Hey—I stopped betting *against* you a few days ago.

Callie was happy to hear that at least some people in Deer Creek learned from their mistakes. Roy, on the other hand, just wasn't that smart! She figured Casey probably knew about his little prank though, and started to probe.

"Roy invited me on a snipe hunt tonight." She realized she had to be careful about what she said and how she said it, so as not to send up any red flags.

"Yeah, I heard."

"Do you have any advice for me?" she asked, sensing he knew more than he was willing to reveal.

"Dress warm?" was all that came to mind as he desperately tried to keep a straight face.

That's all he needed to say! Casey was definitely involved. Callie continued with her line of questioning. "Are you coming along?"

"Naw…Roy invited me, but I already had plans." He turned his head slightly, so she couldn't see the guilt in his eyes.

"Yeah right, plans…" Callie thought to herself, "…plans to make me look like an idiot!"

Just then, Casey's truck pulled into a shaded clearing. The area was circled by a stand of blue spruce trees with long needles. The smell of pine filled the air and a few inches of snow remained on the ground. There was something very familiar about this place and Callie had the feeling she had been there before.

"Where are we?" she asked.

"About a hundred feet off Edermann's Pond," Casey answered. "It's just over there behind that stand of pines."

"I'm not in any danger, am I?"

"Not unless you want a twenty-five footer. The trees around the pond are too tall, but you should be able to find something you like around here." And no sooner had he spoken, Callie spotted a group of trees that were picture perfect.

She climbed out of the truck and pulled the heavy ax from behind her seat. Dragging it through the crunchy snow, she located a tree with the ideal height and shape.

"Can I help you with that?" Casey asked politely, wondering how she was planning on swinging something she could barely lift.

"No thanks," Callie responded. "I've got it under control."

After a quick analysis to determine the proper height for the cut, she took her first swing. Callie heaved the ax up over her shoulder and planted her feet squarely, but she underestimated the weight of the ax and the momentum threw her backwards. She landed firmly on her butt.

Casey managed to suppress his laughter. "You know, I could make that a lot easier for you."

But Callie scrambled to her feet and dusted off the snow. "I said I've got it under control."

Casey figured she must have learned that line from Johan and replied, "Okay, suit yourself." He leaned back against his truck and continued watching her. Damn, she was hot! Even those bulky winter clothes she was wearing couldn't hide her long legs and that perfectly shaped butt. And her face—it just didn't get any cuter than that. He studied her intently, admiring her every shape and curve. But she was *way* too engrossed in her work to notice his infatuation.

Callie set down the ax and tried to wriggle the tree loose. It didn't budge. So she picked it up again, modified her swing, and continued to chop.

Time passed and she began to look fatigued. Having already worked half a day with Johan, she was wearing down and getting winded. Casey calmly waited in the background as Callie checked her progress. But the largest indentation was only half an inch when she stopped to catch her breath.

"How long does it normally take to chop down a tree?" she asked hopefully, thinking perhaps it was just harder than she anticipated and that she was really making about average progress.

"Depends on who's doing the job," Casey answered, not really telling her much.

"Like you could do it faster?"

"Much."

"Okay, smart ass. Put your money where your mouth is." Callie was more tired than ever and the break was a welcomed relief. "I bet you fifty bucks you can't bring this tree down in less than an hour."

"Make it a hundred and you're on," Casey challenged, upping the anti.

"Deal!" she agreed, figuring she had found another sucker. She knew she wasn't *that* bad with an ax, nor was she used to losing her bets.

Callie held out the ax, but Casey declined and instead, walked past her to the back of his truck. Taking out a gas powered chain saw, he pulled the starter cord and held down the choke. The saw came to life with a roar! He set the teeth against the cut she had started, and within seconds, the tree was down.

"You jerk!" she protested.

"Hey I offered to help you, but you said no. Now pay up," he insisted.

"Oh I'll pay up, all right!" she said, as she reached down to the snow, forming a snowball and hurling it into Casey's head. He immediately retaliated and a snowball fight ensued.

Callie's aim was a good testament to her tomboy childhood and her basketball skills. She was deadly and fast, too! She pelted him with two, and managed to dodge the first few he sent her way until the fourth caught her directly on her butt when she stopped to reload.

"You're dead!" she yelled out, desperately searching for more ammo.

The snow wasn't that deep in the clearing, and within minutes they had run out of solid patches. Callie turned to gather another handful and was gently tackled to the ground by Casey from behind. She squirmed to get free as he tickled her sides, but only managed to twist her body enough to face him. He had her trapped.

"I should've never turned my back on the enemy," she said, staring into his deep green eyes, which were only inches away from hers.

Suddenly, they found themselves in a compromising position. Casey was directly on top of her—his muscular body pinning her to the ground. She swore she could feel his heart pound against her chest. Or was that hers, echoing like some primal drum beat from within?

Callie let her defenses slip away and yielded to the power of Casey's magnetism. He sensed her lack of resistance, in both her muscles and her spirit, and took advantage of her complete vulnerability. They both knew—in that split second—that their attraction was undeniable.

Casey broke the silence. "I want to kiss you."

"Okay," she whispered, closing her eyes and slowly pressing her lips up to his.

Callie had been kissed before, but nothing like this. Casey's lips seemed to mold to hers as if they were attached. And when he brought his hand up to her cheek and gently pulled away, she felt a part of her was suddenly missing.

He rolled off to her side and gazed at her for a moment with a smile. Then standing up, he reached out his arms and pulled her close to his body. "I have a confession to make," Casey said, wrapping his arms around her and staring deeply into her eyes. "I've never felt this way about anyone."

Callie lifted her hands to Casey's face and ran her fingers up through his hair. Taking control, she gently pulled his head down towards her. "Me neither," she whispered in his ear. And they kissed again, only this time, it was with an intensity and passion that neither one had ever experienced.

Suddenly, Callie's cell phone rang, and they both jumped as if they had just been caught making out on the couch by their parents. She paused before answering, making sure Casey's arms were secured tightly around her waist. She had no intentions of letting him go!

It was Bianca at her family's Christmas party, and the connection was weak. "Callie, is that you?" Her voice was faint.

"Hey B, I can hardly hear you." Callie was happy to receive Bianca's call, but her timing was reprehensible. She turned away from Casey as he brushed the remaining snow off her back, cupped her hand over the phone, and strained to hear her friend.

"Where've you been?" Bianca questioned, her voice filled with anxiety. "It's like you dropped off the face of the earth or something. Are you okay?" It was completely unlike Callie to be out of touch with the girls.

"Yeah, I'm great." Callie said, looking back at Casey with a sparkle in her eye and a fire in her heart.

Just then Michael passed behind Bianca. He saw the cell phone glued to her ear and made an assumption. "Ay, is that Callie?"

Bianca was not in the mood to be messed with. She had already spent her entire vacation taking abuse from her brothers. "Shut up, Michael. I can hardly hear."

But Michael wasn't done yet. He grabbed the phone from his sister.

"Ay Callie, ya make out wit Farm boy yet?" His voice carried traces of that distinctive New York accent.

Bianca jumped on his back, fighting to gain possession of the phone as he made loud kissing noises into the receiver. Throwing a series of random punches, she screamed, "Give me back my phone, Dweeb!"

The connection was weak, and Callie had other things on her mind, so she blamed the poor reception as she ended the call. "Bianca, I'm losing you. I'll talk to you later." And she turned off her cell phone to prevent any further disturbances.

Not sure if Casey had overheard Michael's comment, she added, "New Yorkers—you gotta love 'em!" then tossed her phone into the snow and wrapped her arms around his neck. "Now, where were we?" she asked in her most seductive voice.

"Right here," he answered, and they picked up exactly where they had left off. It was quite a bit later before either one of them had anything else to say.

The sun was starting to lower and the temperature was dropping quickly. Casey felt tiny shivers traveling through Callie's shoulders. "You're cold," he said with concern. "We'd better get that tree loaded and head on back." He was reluctant to let her go, and gave her one last squeeze followed by a light kiss to her temple.

"Thank you, Casey."

"For what?" he replied.

"For giving me a second chance. I know I didn't make it easy."

"Yeah, well…I probably should've noticed that you were *out of your element*," Casey answered, quoting his wise little sister. "Besides, country living isn't for everyone."

"Country living?" Callie laughed. "I don't know, Dairy King—I'm not so sure you even know the meaning of those words."

Casey squinted his eyes. "Just grab the back of that tree, would ya?"

"Aye, Aye, Captain!" she responded, making a conscious effort to squelch her normal sarcastic comeback.

Casey decided to take the scenic route home, so he could spend more time getting to know Callie. But without all the jibes they were used to poking at one another, both were amazed at just how much they had in common. They compared schools and favorite subjects and discussed their friends and hobbies. And when Callie told him she read Einstein for pleasure and understood the theories of Brian Greene, he figured she was the only girl he had ever met who didn't think *string theory* was a reference to flying a kite.

"You think that's bad," Callie admitted. "My favorite TV show is *Nova* on PBS!"

"No way, dude!" he replied. "I love that show."

Callie quickly realized that she could talk to Casey about stuff that would have instantly labeled her a *geek* at school. It was obvious that he was impressed by her intelligence as she was with his. And her notion that jocks had bigger muscles than brains—well, maybe that wasn't always the case.

"So what are your plans when you graduate?" she asked.

"I don't know. I really like computers, but our business needs a staff veterinarian. So I guess it will all depend on my SAT scores. What about you?"

"I'm not sure," Callie admitted. "I just know I want to use my brains and not my beauty. I grew up around the fashion industry, and it's a tough business. There's a huge gap between the top and the bottom, and very few people land in the middle."

"Well don't forget, you're part of the dairy business now," Casey reminded her as he pulled off to the side of the road and turned off his engine.

"That's right!" she exclaimed. "I forgot, I'm the *Queen of Cheese!*"

The truck was warm and Callie had established her new position next to Casey, comfortably tucked under his arm. Her head rested on his shoulder as they listened to Bing Crosby's *White Christmas* on the radio.

The view ahead of them was like something from an old-fashioned Christmas card. The fields were empty of crops, but neatly surrounded by white fencing and covered with a thin blanket of snow. There were trees scattered here and there, most of them barren of leaves, except for the pines. And smoke could be seen coming from the chimney of a distant house just over the hill.

"What a beautiful view," Callie observed. "Where are we?"

"The backside of our property. That's my house in the distance. I come here when things get too intense."

Casey didn't have to explain his last statement. Callie knew what he had been through with the loss of his mother and Amanda's illness, so it made perfect sense that he would need a place to regroup every now and then.

"You're a good person, Casey Meyers. Amanda just adores you."

"Yeah well, she's pretty special herself." He fluffed the bottom of Callie's short hair. "I still can't believe you cut your hair for her."

"It's not that big of a deal."

"To you maybe. But to Amanda? It's everything. My dad and I will always be grateful to you for that."

Oh my God! Could this guy be any more perfect? Callie couldn't restrain herself any longer. She turned her head and gently kissed him on the lips. "You're just too cute," she confessed.

"What can I say?" Casey replied, shrugging his shoulders. "I aim to please." He wrapped Callie's arms around his neck and pulled her across his lap. They began to kiss again—lightly at first then more passionately as the moments passed.

"Oh no!" Callie said in a panic, noticing the twilight. "What time is it?"

Casey checked his watch. "Quarter past four."

"Crap!" she exclaimed. "I've got that snipe hunt tonight."

Callie looked away from Casey for a moment then lifted her eyes back up to his. They spoke at the exact same time—their voices sounding slightly embarrassed with just a tinge of guilt.

"There's something I have to tell you," they blurted in unison.

"You first," Callie said, her mind churning with details.

"No you first," Casey replied. "I insist."

Reluctantly, Callie explained how she researched *snipe hunt* on the Internet and discovered she was being set up. She told Casey about the conservationist, and how he agreed to lend her his pet skunk in exchange for a donation to his program. Casey just shook his head and laughed.

"So how are you going to get the skunk into the bag without Roy knowing?" he questioned.

"My grandma—she's hiding it behind a tree for me at Four Corners," Callie divulged. "Then I planned on transferring it from its cage to the sack once the guys ditched me."

"Elsa," he laughed. "I should've known!"

"Now you," Callie insisted. "TELL ME!"

Casey took a deep breath. "Remember how I said I had plans this evening?"

"Yeah."

"Well...Roy asked me to dress up like a werewolf and jump out at you." He buried his head in Callie's chest to avoid her wrath.

"That jerk!" she declared. Then she pulled Casey's head up by the front of his hairline. "I thought you said you didn't bet against me."

"I didn't," he replied, "my bet was *for* you!"

But it didn't take long for the pair to figure out a new plan. Casey had an idea that included his BB gun—without the BBs of course, Callie's iPod, a gunshot sound effect, and a simple electronic trigger that would activate a speaker. They didn't have much time to pull it together, but Casey's house was close, and Callie could use her laptop to transfer the sound effect into the iPod.

"Let the games begin," she announced, planting a big sloppy kiss on Casey's lips. "I hope you had a lot of money on me!" she said, squeezing his cheeks. And they buckled up and hit the road.

Casey and Callie paused briefly to say hello to Nick and Amanda as they burst through the front door holding hands. Then they charged up to Casey's room like a couple of lovers, not wanting to be detained.

Nick yelled up after them, "Hey! Don't forget the rule about girls in your room!"

"Don't worry Dad," Casey yelled down from the top of the stairs. "All I need is five minutes!"

Meanwhile, Amanda was grinning from ear to ear and laughed when

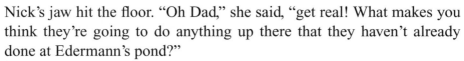

Nick's jaw hit the floor. "Oh Dad," she said, "get real! What makes you think they're going to do anything up there that they haven't already done at Edermann's pond?"

Nick stood frozen as he digested Amanda's words. He wasn't sure now if he should be more concerned with his son or with his daughter!

25

All is fair in love and war

Four Corners, as its name implied, was a place where four gravel roads met. The area was heavily timbered with bushes and briars and the visibility between the trees was only about three feet. It was a perfect place for the devious intents of pranksters and the ideal location for a snipe hunt.

"I shouldn't be doing this," Johan protested, as he gently placed the skunk cage behind the trees designated by Elsa.

"Well if you weren't so damn nosy, you wouldn't be!" she replied, checking the skunk's water supply then covering the cage with a burlap cloth. "You're worse than the dog now, poking your nose around every time a delivery van pulls into the drive."

Johan was perturbed, and he waved her off like a swarm of gnats. It went against his sense of loyalty to aid and abet the women in this plan, but the doctor hadn't quite lifted all his restrictions and Elsa was still in command. So he was forced to cooperate, whether he liked it or not!

Meanwhile, Casey and Callie had finished gathering their supplies and were heading back to the Michelsohn farm. They agreed it would be more convincing if they maintained their adversarial relationship and decided to cause a scene the moment they arrived.

"Make yourself useful, would ya?" Casey ordered, as he lowered the tailgate of his pickup. "Grab hold of the tree's trunk."

Roy overheard Casey's demands from a nearby vantage point. He was keeping a close eye on JR in case he blurted out something by mistake. And it was a good thing he did because JR was standing by the pens looking moonstruck at Callie.

"Do it yourself, Farm boy," Callie replied, as she climbed the porch stairs and held open the front door. "You're lucky I'm helping at all."

The grin on Roy's face widened as he listened to the squabble. Yep, the boy was definitely on *his* side! He rushed to Casey's aid, helping him unload the tree while Callie stood in the doorway tapping her foot impatiently.

"Come on guys," she nagged, "the light's not getting any greener!"

Casey acted as if he was going to ram Callie with the tree, but Roy wanted her in one piece for the snipe hunt, so he began a wrestling match, which ended up looking like a bad dance routine. He finally got close enough to Casey to whisper, "Knock it off. You're going to ruin everything."

Meanwhile, Callie continued with her tirade. "I'm waiting…"

Roy held his tongue, but secretly wished he could boot her in the butt! As Casey passed, Callie tipped her head and looked up the stairs, indicating he should meet her there as soon as possible. He winked, acknowledging her gesture.

Once the tree cleared the entry, Callie slammed the door. "Don't bother thanking me!" she exclaimed and stormed up to her room.

Roy helped set the tree in the stand then went in search of Johan. With the coast clear, Casey dashed up the stairs to rendezvous with his new accomplice.

Callie had been listening for his footsteps and was hiding behind the door. She leaped out at him as he entered the room, and somehow wound up in his arms again. They mixed laughter with kisses then moved on to business. She had already replaced the batteries in her iPod and was about to download the gunshot sound effect. All that remained was to connect a small, wireless transmitter to the headphone jack and review their plan.

"There's a seven-second delay before the gunshot," Casey stated. "That should give you enough time to press the play button and take aim at my heart."

"Then what?" Callie asked.

"Freak out, and let me do the rest. Just don't be too shocked if it gets a little gory," he said with a devilish gleam in his eye. "I really get into special effects."

Feeling confident in their plan, Casey gave Callie another quick kiss then dashed back downstairs and out to his truck where Roy and Johan were plotting.

"Hey guys, what's up?" he said with an unassuming look.

"Just going over the work schedule for tomorrow," Roy answered with a wink followed by a whisper, "and finalizing things for tonight." Roy was patting himself on the back, thinking he was a genius. And Johan was consoling himself with the thought that at least the werewolf stunt was still in tact.

"Okay then…" Casey said with a grin. "I'll see you in about…an hour?"

Johan nodded, thinking the less he said the better.

Elsa found Callie spying on the men from the upstairs window. They watched Casey get into his truck and head down the drive while Roy and Johan huddled together configuring logistics.

Roy decided that Callie would ride with them, he didn't trust JR. The rest of the men could ride with Hurley. And Casey would obviously have to get there on his own. To Roy's satisfaction, everything was in place. This was going to be the best snipe hunt ever—and the most profitable!

Callie filled her grandmother in on the werewolf scam and the slight adjustment she and Casey had made to the plan. Elsa clapped her hands with delight then looked alarmed. "I'd better let the sheriff in on this. The first thing those boys will do is notify him!" and she rushed off to make the call while Johan was still outside.

Dinner was somewhat hurried that night. There were so many secrets and alliances that it was hard to keep track of who knew what. They felt like actors in a play, trying hard to remember their lines. So rather than blurting out something by mistake, each of them decided it was better to remain quiet. Callie helped clear the table then headed to the door. Johan went out first and didn't see the *thumbs up* she gave Elsa, nor did he hear the whispered promise to fill her in on everything later.

The time had come, and the men were itching to go. The group climbed into their assigned trucks as Elsa stood on the porch waving goodbye. Her only regret was that she wouldn't see the drama unfold!

On the way to Four Corners, Roy explained to Callie how to make a snipe call. According to him, it was rather like a turkey call, and she played along practicing as they drove. She was to do this while banging two sticks together. "For some odd reason," Roy said, shrugging his shoulders, "they're attracted to the sound." And Johan found it harder and harder to keep a straight face the deeper Roy buried himself.

The men positioned Callie in front of a tree, not too far from where the snipe were supposedly hiding. They gave her a sack and two sticks, and because the moon was full, they insisted she didn't need a flashlight—that would only scare the birds. The plan was for them to drive down the road a bit then walk back through the woods, flushing out the snipe. She was instructed to catch one in the bag as they ran past her.

Callie played her role to the hilt, making a comment about the strange noise that she kept hearing—even city girls recognize the sound of an owl. And she asked stupid questions like if she needed to be aware of lions or tigers or bears. To the men, she looked like a perfect victim!

But before they took off, Roy told her that if she heard a wolf howling—and he did a good imitation—she should scream for help, and they would come to her rescue.

Callie widened her eyes with fear, and when she took the sticks from him, she made sure her hands were trembling. "Okay, but I brought *this* just in case," she said, showing Roy a clove of garlic she borrowed from Elsa's kitchen.

"Great idea!" He turned to JR. "Why didn't we think of that?"

The men climbed back into their trucks and headed out. "Poor little thing!" Roy said, looking at Johan. "She's going down!" And his smile was as wide as the Texas sky.

Callie remained in place for a moment until she heard the truck doors slam in the distance.

She began making the snipe call and knocking her sticks together as she searched the area. The cage was precisely where Elsa said it would be and she quickly transferred its resident.

The farmhands were moving toward her through the brush, so her time was limited. She set the open edge of the sack under her foot and continued banging and calling until they were just out of sight. As the men got a little closer, she called out, "Hey guys...is that you? Hello?" And the more she said, the more muffled chuckles she heard in the distance. Apparently they thought she was deaf as well as dumb and blind!

Deciding the time was right, she yelled out, "I caught one! I caught one!"

At first, there was a sudden hush in the distance then the men came running toward her with their flashlights.

Callie stood there beaming proudly as something moved in the sack she was holding. "Look! I did it!" she exclaimed, offering the evidence to Roy.

He gave his flashlight to Hurley then peered into the bag and jumped back! "It's a skunk! RUN!" he screamed, taking off like a zebra with a lion on its tail. Hurley dropped his flashlight on the ground and took off after Roy. Callie followed right behind, and in the process, witnessed Roy trip over a fallen branch, hitting the ground in a perfect spread eagle.

The other men began their retreat until they heard her laughing hysterically. "You big brave men aren't afraid of an itty bitty pet skunk are you?" she said, as she coddled the little creature in her arms.

They looked at one another foolishly and started to laugh along with her.

"You must think I'm a real idiot," she said, as she retrieved the hidden cage from behind a tree, gently placing the skunk back inside.

"Damn it, girl! You cost me a fortune!" Roy grumbled. Callie was still laughing as JR helped him to his feet. He dusted himself off and glared at her.

"Didn't Grandma tell you not to bet against a Michelsohn?" Callie reminded him. "I suggest you learn how to research your odds."

"OWooo," a wolf howled in the distance. "OW...OW...Owooo."

Callie reacted by grabbing Roy's arm and squeezing tightly. Her eyes widened and her voice quivered. "What's that?"

Roy was relieved that at least one thing was going according to plan—or so he thought. "Well I'll be damned. It must be that werewolf! Quick, everyone back to the trucks," Roy ordered, pulling his arm away from Callie. She stood frozen in terror just as he had hoped.

The howling grew louder and movement could be seen just inside the timber. Roy slowly backed away to watch the rest of the show. He saw Callie reach into her coat pockets and pull out what looked like… a gun? Suddenly a blackened form burst through the trees and lunged toward her. The beast was tall and hairy, and though the light was dim, it appeared to have the body of a man and the face of a wolf.

"Run for your lives!" she yelled. "It's a werewolf!" Callie raised the pistol out in front of her and pointed it directly at the creature. Her stance was good, but her hands were shaking badly.

The men saw the gun and screamed out in unison, "Noooooo!"

But it was too late. A gunshot echoed through the trees! The werewolf grabbed its chest and dropped to the ground as blood oozed from between his hairy fingers like ketchup being squeezed from a bottle.

Callie screamed as she relinquished the weapon. "Oh my God, I think I've killed it!"

The group of men rushed to the scene with urgency. Johan pulled the mask off Casey who was still holding his hand to his heart and moaning loudly.

"Call the sheriff!" Roy yelled, kneeling by his side. "He's been hit!"

Bud immediately jumped into action and pulled out his cell phone. He had Deputy Wiley on the line within seconds. "They're on their way," he said to Roy who was now covered in Casey's blood.

"Casey, hang in there buddy," Roy said, on the verge of cardiac arrest.

Johan turned to his granddaughter with pain in his eyes. "Callie, what have you done?"

"Me?!" she replied. "This was your stupid game—I just played it better!"

She pushed the men aside, knelt down by Casey, and poked at his ribs. "Okay Dairy King, the show is over. They're about to kill me." And miraculously, he opened his eyes. His lips turned up in a grin and he burst out laughing.

The men were shocked. They had just been betrayed by one of their own.

"Pay up!" he said, bending his body to an upright position.

Callie offered Casey her hand and helped him to his feet. She grabbed the skunk cage and turned back to the men. "Elsa has coffee and dessert ready. You're all invited to the house. She can't wait to hear how many *snipe* I caught." That being said, her straight face gave way to a dazzling grin. No winner of an Olympic gold ever looked happier.

As Casey passed to collect his speakers, Roy muttered under his breath, "Traitor!"

"No," he said, without the slightest bit of remorse. "I just secured my bet!"

The men looked at one another—mentally totaling their losses—and realized once and for all that it *was* a bad idea to bet against a Michelsohn. They dreaded having to face Elsa, but they figured the tasty dessert awaiting them would be well worth the lecture.

26

"Who's wants warm eggnog?" Elsa asked, as she entered the room with a tray of mugs. The farmhands had already gone home for the night, and everything had settled down except for an occasional wisecrack from Callie or Amanda, as bits and pieces of the day flashed through their minds. Roy and his motley crew of second-rate pranksters were completely humiliated at being duped by a teenage girl. Nonetheless, they had accepted full stomachs in exchange for their dignity, which had been left somewhere back in the snow at Four Corners.

Elsa set the tray down on the coffee table. "Help yourselves," she insisted.

Nick and Johan relaxed in front of the fire as the girls decorated the tree. And Casey sat nearby, handing them ornaments as directed. They sipped eggnog and nibbled on holiday cookies while the fire crackled and the tiny lights from the tree twinkled like small stars. The room was cozy, and there was a general feeling of harmony that spread like the scent of the pine tree.

"I don't think I've ever had a more action-packed day," Callie declared with a look of satisfaction. "I chopped a tree…well kind of, caught a snipe…actually, quite a few of them, and shot a werewolf!"

"And you thought life in the city was exciting," Amanda replied, her voice indicating her pleasure in the way the events had played out.

Callie was finally seeing how much fun country life could be, and why Amanda was so proud of her community.

The tree was positioned in the center of double windows at the front of the house and provided a perfect vantage for Callie to see the headlights of an approaching vehicle. She suspected it was Roy coming back to apologize, yet again, now that he knew what a formidable opponent she was!

So when a knock was heard, Callie said, "Relax Grandma, I'll get it. It's probably just one of the boys delivering another slice of humble pie."

But when she opened the door, her face lit up.

"MOM!" she exclaimed. Callie had completely given up hope that her mother would show and had actually forgotten that she was supposed to.

"Hi, baby," Zoey said, not at all sure what kind of response to expect. And she wasn't sure whether to feel guilty over her much delayed arrival or ecstatic over her much anticipated reunion.

Callie threw her arms around her mother's neck and squeezed tightly. Zoey was both relieved and pleasantly surprised at the same time and reciprocated with a nurturing hug. Then she held Callie at arms length and studied her face. "I hope I'm not disturbing anything," Zoey said, hearing voices in the living room and seeing Callie's head turn in that direction.

"Don't be silly—you're family."

But Zoey didn't feel like family. The family she had spent time with in this house had included Cameron, and without him, it seemed strange.

Elsa recognized the voice. Her eyes widened and she was torn between her desire to welcome Zoey home and her fear that she would take Callie away. She nudged Johan. "Pay attention!"

"What did you do to your hair?" Zoey asked, running her fingers through Callie's freshly cropped style. There was something different about her daughter and it wasn't just her hair. Callie hadn't made one sarcastic comment since opening the door, and yet she seemed as in charge as ever.

"I gave it to Amanda," she said with a smile that was too innocent to indicate anything but mischief.

"You did what?"

Zoey didn't understand her daughter's answer, but before she could ask her to explain, Callie dragged her through the doorway and into the living room.

"Look who's here!" she announced.

Elsa was standing behind Johan's chair as he stood to greet Zoey, almost as if he would protect her from the bad news she expected to hear. He offered his hand. "It's so good to see you again, Zoey."

Elsa was still quiet and hovered nervously behind the chair. "What a wonderful surprise," she said with trepidation.

Friendly "hellos" radiated from the Meyers as Callie refreshed her mother's memories with introductions. "Mom, you remember Nick, don't you?"

"Of course I do. Hello, Nick," Zoey said with a smile.

There was a sadness in Nick's eyes and she could tell that life had taken its toll on him. His body was still lean and fit, evidencing the physical work he did. And he was still nice-looking—in a mature kind of way.

"It's been awhile," he said, as he stood to greet her.

"And these are his kids, Casey and Amanda," Callie continued, figuring her mother probably had no clue who either one was.

"It's a pleasure, Ma'am," Casey said, as he offered Zoey his hand. His memories of her were even vaguer than Callie's were of Wisconsin.

"Hello," Amanda added, peering from around the tree.

Zoey stared at Amanda. "My God, you look just like Sarah." She noticed that Amanda's face had the same beautiful bone structure as her mother's and that her eyes and hair were the same color, too.

Amanda beamed with pride. She loved when people saw a resemblance between her and her mom. It made it seem as if Sarah was still alive and a part of her life.

Elsa *finally* remembered her manners and recovered her composure. "Zoey, go sit down. I'll bring you a cup of eggnog," she said, heading to the kitchen to get another mug. Zoey felt uncomfortable in the living room and followed Elsa—grateful for the opportunity to escape what she was sure were judgmental eyes. Callie was still attached to her side, but the mood was about to change for the worse.

As they crossed the entry, Zoey broke the news. "Well actually…my driver is waiting to take us to the airport. We're catching the red-eye out of Madison in a few hours.

Callie pulled away from her mother as if a bomb had exploded between them. This was the very last thing she expected to hear! "You're kidding, right?"

"Well, no. We're going to Aspen, remember?"

"Yeah, I remember. But that was before you *blew me off* for the Osbournes." Callie's mood suddenly changed and the chip on her shoulder reappeared with a vengeance. All the hurt and frustration she felt toward her mother's career was suddenly exposed and within earshot of strangers.

"I didn't blow you off. I had to work."

"Yeah—whatever." Callie's anger was apparent. The nerve of her mother! First she ruined their ski trip. Now she wants to drag her away just when things were getting interesting. Could she be any more selfish?

But Zoey stood her ground, asserting her parental authority. "That's enough, Callie. I jeopardized an account to get here in time for Christmas, so I demand a little respect. Now go gather your things."

Angry voices from the kitchen caused a tension in the living room, forcing Nick to bridge the silence. He brought up the first thing that came to mind—the anticipated calving results for spring and the last vet's report on the number of pregnant cows. It was all just *busy* talk, meant to add a sense of normalcy to a tense situation. But Amanda and Casey were too concerned about Callie to hear a word he said. Johan, on the other hand, had learned to multitask long before computers made *that* word common, and was quite capable of listening to several things at once.

"But I…" Callie objected.

"Now!" her mother insisted.

Humiliated at being treated like a child, Callie darted out of the kitchen and up the stairs, leaving her mother alone with Elsa.

"I'm so sorry," Zoey said, embarrassed by her daughter's behavior. "I'm sure she's been quite a handful."

The Meyers' were concerned for Callie and also for Elsa and Johan who were enjoying her visit. Casey and Amanda obviously had their own reasons for not wanting Callie to leave, but they figured this was a private matter and it wasn't their place to interfere. So they sat quietly, keeping their opinions to themselves as their ears strained to hear more of Zoey's conversation.

"Let me make you a cup of hot tea," Elsa insisted. "I'm sure Callie will be a few minutes. She has a lot to pack."

When Callie entered her room, she began violently shoving her clothing into her suitcases. She was furious with her mother, and her mind was racing like water in rapids, churning with no sense of order. Just when she began to feel at home in Deer Creek, and rekindle her friendship with Amanda, and develop a relationship with Casey—her mother shows up and decides to change things without any regard for her feelings!

As she crossed the room to disassemble her computer, she caught a glimpse of her short hair in the mirror.

NO…NOT THIS TIME!

ZOEY WAS SITTING AT the kitchen table confessing her feelings of inadequacy to Elsa. All the strain of the trip seemed to hit her at once and her face sagged with exhaustion. Her normal confidence was gone, leaving her exposed and vulnerable.

Elsa sat beside her and patted her hand in consolation. "No—you're not a bad mother. It's not easy raising a child on your own."

"Then why do I always feel so guilty?" Zoey asked.

Elsa answered based on her years of experience. "Because you want the best for her. And it's not always easy to know what that is."

"I've made a lot of mistakes, Elsa." Zoey admitted.

"Ja...me, too, but who hasn't. There isn't a day that goes by that I don't regret letting you and Callie slip away from us. But I was so consumed with my own grief that I didn't pay enough attention to yours...until it was too late." Elsa realized that this was her one chance to reconnect with her daughter-in-law and rebuild her family. She was prepared to wear her heart on her sleeve and admit to Zoey that she, too, shared the same sense of loss and pain.

"I never told you how sorry I was that you lost your son, Elsa."

"And I never told you how sorry I was that he put you in such danger."

"All these years, I thought you blamed me." Zoey took a deep breath. "I thought Callie would, too."

Until that moment, she had never discussed Cameron's death with Elsa. And it was so out of character for her to expose her inner feelings like this. In her mind, she was taking a big chance and leaving herself wide open for the guilt she expected Elsa to lay on her.

"Cameron chose his profession, Zoey. He died doing what he loved the most. I could never blame you."

A sense of relief filled her heart. Elsa didn't blame her—she empathized with her!

Zoey had quick flashes of what the last few years could have been like if Elsa and Johan had helped to raise Callie. How could she have been so insecure?

The combination of jet lag, sleep deprivation, and grief therapy overwhelmed her all at once and she began to cry. All the emotions and pain she had suppressed for so long seemed to disappear as if the weight of the world had just been lifted off her shoulders!

Callie entered the kitchen without her luggage, causing Zoey alarm. "Where are your bags?" she asked, wiping the tears from her face.

Callie had a decision to make. If she left with her mother now, she would risk hurting her grandparents and Amanda and Casey—and that's the last thing she wanted to do. On the other hand, she really missed her mom, and was looking forward to spending Christmas with her, too. There was only one solution to this problem.

"I'm not going," Callie said with firmness.

Zoey was caught off guard. "What do you mean you're not going?"

"I'm not going…and neither are you," she continued.

"But it's Christmas. You wanted to be in Aspen." Zoey replied, completely confused.

"No Mom…I wanted to be with my family, and my *family* is right here."

Zoey tried to view the situation through Callie's eyes. She saw a mom who was gone too often and a pretty cool kid who needed some family bonds. And here she was, surrounded by loving grandparents in a wholesome environment. Even *she* was hard pressed to find a problem with that. So she voiced her last remaining concern. "But I didn't shop for you."

"That's okay because I didn't shop for you either." Callie fibbed to make her mom feel better. But if there was one thing she had learned from Amanda, it was that possessions didn't matter nearly as much as people. No present could compare to having the family and friends she loved together for Christmas.

Zoey turned to Elsa. "What do you think?"

Elsa didn't like being put in the middle, but knew that Zoey needed a nudge in the right direction. She worded her answer carefully, knowing it could sway Zoey's decision. "She's right—you belong with us."

Zoey took a deep breath and succumbed to the pressure. "Then I guess it's settled."

"Yes!" Callie squealed, rushing to deliver the good news to the living room. She popped her head back in within seconds and added, "By the way, you're doing glamour shots tomorrow at the local hair salon."

"Glamour shots?"

Elsa confirmed the plans. "You remember Evie, don't you?"

Zoey shook her head and laughed. "Some things just never change," she thought, as she headed outside to get her luggage and release her driver.

When she returned, the scene in the living room was so serene it touched her heart. Elsa was sitting on the arm of Johan's chair, Callie was next to Casey on the couch looking as if she belonged there, and Amanda was lying on the loveseat with her head in Nick's lap—half dozing and looking like a sleeping angel.

The fire was blazing, and the room was scented with pine and spices. The tree had been given a final layer of tinsel and shimmered in the dim light, and stockings were neatly hung on the fireplace.

Callie and Casey moved over, making room for Zoey then resumed their conversation as if she had been there the whole time. And it wasn't long before she truly felt a part of the group.

Zoey listened for a bit before joining in as the kids talked about life in Deer Creek since Callie's arrival. They described some of the funny predicaments like the confrontation with Uncle Buck, the missing person escapade, and the Christmas party. And by the time they got to the snipe hunt, the room echoed with laughter. It was obvious that Callie had made quite an impression!

It didn't take long, however, for Zoey to notice the special attention Casey and Callie were showing one another and she looked to Elsa with a raised eyebrow.

"Don't worry," Elsa whispered with a wink and a nod. "It's all good!"

But Zoey didn't share her enthusiasm. "Oh yeah?" she said to herself. "For who?"

27

No news is good news...or is it?

Callie waited until the last moment before heading upstairs to wake her mother. "Mom!" she nudged, "it's time to get up." Zoey slowly opened her eyes and moaned, "Do I have to?" just as the rooster crowed. "That damn thing!" she mumbled from under her pillow. "You'd think he'd be dead by now."

"Wake up, Mom—I really need your help today!" Callie said, pulling the pillow away from Zoey's grasp. "I brought you some coffee. Now get up and get dressed, PLEASE!" she begged, yanking off her mother's covers and exposing her to the chilly air.

In a way, Zoey was happy to see her daughter's normal, slightly overbearing personality return. And if the goose bumps on her arms were any indication, Callie meant business. It was either head for the shower or freeze and Zoey opted for the warmth of the shower, taking her coffee with her. The last words she uttered before closing the bathroom door were, "You're a tyrant!"

"Not when you think about it!" Callie called out, her voice fading as she bounced downstairs, carrying a duffel bag filled with cosmetics and other supplies.

But it wasn't long before Zoey joined Callie and Elsa in the kitchen, looking radiant as usual. "Good morning," she said, as she reached for the coffeepot to refill her mug. "Okay I'm here...and I'm almost awake. So what's up?"

Callie's demeanor switched from commander to charm school graduate. "I promised Evie that I would do holiday makeovers for all her regular customers in exchange for cutting my hair. All you have to do is take the before and after shots. You know—like the ones you get from those family portrait studios in the mall."

"For how many?" Zoey's mind conjured up images of crying babies and agitated mothers waiting in line during the height of the Christmas rush.

"Not many," Callie replied. "Six or seven the last time I spoke to Evie."

Zoey breathed a sigh of relief. "Hmm…that's not too bad."

Elsa, on the other hand, turned away with a look of panic. "No use in stirring the pot," she thought to herself, as she considered the consequences of her recent actions.

"Come on, Mom. It *is* Christmas. And according to Alex, women would just die to have their picture taken by the famous Zoey Michaels." Callie widened her grin to the max then dropped an itty-bitty bomb. "Besides, I used your name when I ordered the hair color from L'Oreal," she confessed. "I told them it was for you."

"You did what?" Zoey's voice rose slightly and indicated concern at mixing personal favors with her business relationships—especially without her knowledge.

"Chill out," Callie insisted. "When I explained what we were doing, they were more than happy to donate a couple of cases of their latest colors. I figured the samples should last Evie at least a couple of months, and now that you're really here, I can keep my promise.

"What promise?"

"Publicity photos…in exchange for the dye. Corporate just loved the whole community outreach thing!"

"Oh great, you're starting to sound like my publicist. Even when I'm not working—I'm working."

Callie took that as a yes and rewarded her mother with a hug that nearly sent her coffee cup flying. "Forget all the bad things I've ever said about you!" she teased then headed to the utility room to locate the boxes of dye.

Now up until recently, Elsa's utility room was immaculate. She used it as a *catch all* for supplies such as laundry detergent, light bulbs, and seasonal things like canning jars and holiday decorations. But with the recent surge of deliveries, the room was completely unrecognizable. Boxes were piled from floor to ceiling, and it looked more like a Midwestern substation for FedEx than the neatly organized room to which Elsa was accustomed.

Callie crossed her fingers, hoping the L'Oreal boxes were on top. But that wasn't the case! The ensuing search turned out to be more like a *Where's Waldo* challenge than anything else. Her battle cries could be heard in the kitchen, making it difficult for Zoey and Elsa to keep a straight face. It wasn't clear who was winning the fight, but if it got any louder, Zoey would be forced to get up and find out. So instead, she diverted her attention to Elsa who was pretending to be busier than she actually was.

"Are you coming, too, Elsa?" Zoey asked.

"I wasn't planning on it," she replied without hesitation.

"We'll be fine, Mom." Callie yelled out from the distance. "Amanda is meeting us there to help with the makeup."

"All-righty then," Zoey conceded. "It sounds like you've got it *all* under control!"

But toppling cartons, followed by a *shriek* in the utility room, sent Zoey to her daughter's immediate rescue. The room wasn't that big, maybe ten or twelve feet square, but it was crammed with fallen boxes and difficult to maneuver through.

"Callie, where are you?" Zoey called.

A muffled voice answered from the center of the room, "Help…need help now!"

Zoey's alarm level lessened as she pulled a box off her daughter's head, revealing a slightly dazed and cross-eyed young woman.

"Found them!" Callie announced optimistically, as she lifted one of the L'Oreal boxes up to her mother. "Farthest corner, bottom left… couldn't have buried it better myself."

"If this is any indication of how many makeovers we have to do today—count me out!" Zoey said, reading the product content from the labeling on the box.

"Relax, Mom. It's a small town. How bad can it be?"

Elsa's face took on a renewed look of alarm with Callie's last sentence. "On second thought," she called out, "I'm going with you just in case you need an extra hand."

Elsa sent Johan for the car while she and Callie brought the supplies to the porch and Zoey ran a final check on all her camera equipment. But Callie was surprised when her grandfather pulled up in a late model Lincoln Navigator because it seemed so unlike him.

"I didn't know you had an SUV, Grandma."

"Yeah, your grandfather bought it last year for my birthday. We store it in the garage and drive it on special occasions."

"Nice gift."

"Yeah, that's what I used to say."

"Why, what's wrong with it?"

"Well I don't know—I couldn't tell you because I NEVER GET TO DRIVE IT!" she said loudly enough to make sure the message reached Johan through the closed window.

Johan pretended not to hear Elsa's last comment as he stepped out of the vehicle. He had a grin on his face and looked almost smug as he started loading the boxes into the back.

"Then maybe you ought to learn how to drive," he mumbled under his breath.

"I heard that," Elsa exclaimed. "I may be blind as a bat, but I'm not deaf!"

"Yet," he added.

When the vehicle was loaded, they all piled into the truck. With the preparations completed—digging, sorting, and repacking—everything was under control. Or so Callie thought until they pulled into town!

"What the hell?" she said, completely unprepared for the chaos awaiting them.

A small mob of women had gathered in front of Evie's, and the scene looked like a Macy's lingerie sale—women pushing and shoving and grabbing like sharks in a school of minnows. It was no place for the faint of heart.

And poor Evie—she resembled a prison guard during a riot, hiding behind the bars and cautiously peering out at the unruly crowd. She wasn't about to unlock the front door until help arrived!

"Uh oh," Elsa blurted, covering her mouth with her hand.

Callie caught the blunder. "Grandma, when was the last time you spoke to Evie?" she asked, remembering how quickly news spread in Deer Creek.

"Last night."

"And what did you tell her?"

"Just that Zoey was in town."

Elsa paused for a brief moment then decided to come clean. "And that she might be taking pictures today."

"Might be?"

"Okay...that she was!" Elsa quickly defended her actions. "But I told her it was a secret and to keep her damn mouth shut."

"And did she?"

"No. She told Elaine and Lucy."

"And?"

"And Elaine announced it over the sheriff's radio and Lucy called every one of her clients."

"Anyone else?"

"Clara, and of course Johan and the boys." Elsa took a deep breath. "Every one of them."

"Well then," Callie surmised, "I guess that explains the three ring circus. Do you think you could have mentioned that back at the house?"

Elsa's face acknowledged her responsibility for the fiasco unfolding in front of them. "Sorry?" was all she could come up with.

I've never seen so many feather boas and tiaras in my life!" Zoey observed, gazing in amazement at all the commotion. She stopped mid-thought as her eyes threatened to pop out of her head. "What an ugly dog!"

"That's not a dog, Mom. That's a pot bellied pig!"

"Ew," Zoey replied, realizing the women were actually serious and expected to have their pictures taken with those, those...*things*! She was used to adverse conditions, but this was like working in outer space with no lifeline to the mother ship! And her confidence was fading quickly.

Callie took the only path available to her and reacted with humor. "Just think of it as a really bad reality TV show," she laughed, noticing her mother's sudden change in attitude. "Why *Nip/Tuck* when you can simply *Snip/Pluck*?"

Any other time, Zoey would have had an equally lame comeback. But she was still trying to figure out how to make a pot bellied pig appear glamorous and for some reason nothing was coming to mind.

Johan pulled into a reserved spot in front of Evie's door and removed the orange cone Deputy Wiley had thoughtfully placed there for him. He instructed the gathered crowd to clear the area with all the authority his voice could carry and effectively created some room for his passengers. As they emerged from the vehicle and began unloading their supplies, Evie felt salvation was at hand and rushed to the front.

Callie realized that she had grossly underestimated the potential pitfalls of the project, but she wasn't about to let it affect her. Instead, she kicked into overdrive. She dispatched Zoey across the street to the diner and Elsa into Evie's. She demanded the clusters of women stand against the wall and directed the men to follow Johan to the restaurant. "I suggest you order a lot of food," she announced, "you're going to be there awhile. Oh, and be sure to tip well!"

Over twenty women were waiting to be glamorized, and Callie had a feeling more would be arriving as the morning progressed. There was no time to waste. She glanced inside and saw that Amanda had the makeup station ready and that Evie had recruited an assistant stylist for the event. At least some things were going according to plan!

Callie gathered the women into a circular formation and gave them a brief description of what to expect. She reassured them that the reward would be well worth the wait then escorted them over to the diner to register and to have their Polaroid pictures taken.

The women entered the restaurant slowly, looking cautiously about like children on the first day of school. Casey was sitting at the counter as they shuffled in. His eyes widened and his lips threatened to break into a grin, if not hysterical laughter. He had never seen a rattier bunch!

Every size and shape of woman was represented. There were old and young, and a few somewhere in the middle. Hair colors ranged from black and white to every shade in between and some of them appeared to have wrinkles deeper than the Grand Canyon. But one thing was certain—they were all ugly!

As he continued his mental evaluation, one in particular caught his attention as potential wagering material—an older woman that resembled a gray-haired poodle buried beneath a mop of overly processed hair. What color were her eyes? That is, assuming she had eyes. Casey was amazed by one fact in particular. He had lived in Deer Creek his entire life and he still didn't recognize any of these women without their caked-on makeup.

Callie noticed his reaction and blocked his face from the women. "Hey—zip it!"

No way did she want them to see his expression! She handed him a stack of index cards and a can of pencils. "Assign a number to each lady, attach it to her Polaroid, then have her wait for her number to be called. I'll take one through five first, then I'll send for the rest as space becomes available."

"And what's in it for me?"

"You get to…" Callie moved in close to his ear as if to make a seductive proposition, "…have the inside track on all the betting! Remember, you're connected."

"Ah, sweet," Casey said, the grin on his face widening as he *mastered the possibilities*!

Callie's face moved softly against his cheek then paused at his lips, touching but not kissing. She whispered, "But I get half."

Casey felt like he had just sealed a deal with the devil as he kissed Callie, setting her into motion. And it wasn't until she left the building that he realized she had just conned him out of half his profits.

"Whoa," he thought to himself, "it's a good thing she's on my side!"

28

ecessity is the mother of invention

The door to the hair salon burst open with a *whack*!

"Okay, ladies—pay attention!" Callie ordered, entering the shop like a drill sergeant on the first day of basic training.

All eyes were focused on her as Evie, her assistant Marjorie, Amanda, and Elsa carefully listened to the plan.

"First they'll come to me for a consultation and a style recommendation, then they'll go to Evie and Marjorie for processing, then to Amanda's makeup station, and finally to Grandma for matching fingernails."

"Why do I have to do the polish?" Elsa questioned in protest.

"Because *you* got us into this mess. How about that?" Callie snapped, refusing to let her off the hook that easily. "And besides, you need to brush up on your painting skills."

"My what?" she answered, completely puzzled by her granddaughter's last remark.

Elsa didn't have time to ponder Callie's statement with all the commotion coming from the front door. At first, she didn't recognize any of the colorless faces entering the salon, but then she noticed the poodle-like hairstyle of her dear friend, Mrs. Daley.

"Georgia, is that you?"

"Yeah…it's me, Elsa," she replied.

"Well I'll be darned. Come on over here and have a seat," she insisted. "You can be our first patient."

"CLIENT, Grandma. Our first client."

"Ja, that."

The *makeshift crew* flocked around Callie with curiosity as she clipped Mrs. Daley's hair away from her face and compared her complexion to a skin-toned color chart.

"Definitely a summer," she assessed. "We'll want to keep you in soft pastels and neutrals."

"Oh no," Mrs. Daley replied. "I was told I'm a winter."

"Well you were *told* wrong!"

Mrs. Daley's instinct was to make a mad dash for the front door at this point, but Callie was blocking her path. "But I have pale, white skin," she insisted as emphatically as she could, considering she was trapped.

"And you also have light blue eyes. I bet you were a natural blond before you turned gray. Am I right?"

"Well actually—yes."

"See…that's your problem!" Callie boasted. "Here—let me show you something." She searched her bag for a navy blue scarf then wrapped it around Mrs. Daley's neck and shoulders. "Notice how this color makes your wrinkles stand out?"

The women in the salon were horrified by the insult, but Mrs. Daley's humiliation was immediately alleviated by Callie's next move.

"Now check this out." She selected a pastel blue and placed it under the elderly woman's jaw line. "Viola! Instant facelift!"

"Oh my," Elsa remarked.

"Amazing!" Marjorie exclaimed.

"You sure have pretty eyes, Mrs. Daley." Amanda added, trying to relax her with a compliment. She was the peacemaker in any argument and capable of seeing something good in just about anything.

"Well I'll be…" she declared. "I guess I'm a summer after all."

With Callie's first success in the bag, the women were feeling much more confident and were actually looking forward to their own consultations.

"And now for your hair…" She released the clips holding back Mrs. Daley's frizzy bangs then peered over at Evie. "What's with the Weird Al look? Haven't you heard—tight perms went out in the eighties!"

Evie had a wicked sense of humor when it was turned loose, and with Callie playing the bad guy, she was free to be herself. "Haven't you heard? This is *The Land that Time Forgot*...the eighties *are* progressive for Deer Creek."

Callie thumbed through several pages of hairstyles before finding one that would emphasize Mrs. Daley's eyes and bone structure. Then she chose the perfect color of silver that would blend the grays without looking tinny.

"And we're going to need something extra strong for damaged hair," Callie ordered, as she examined Mrs. Daley's split ends. "Whatcha got, Evie?"

"Conditioner," she replied, not sure whether or not it was a trick question.

"I know that, silly. I meant, what brands do you carry?"

Evie opened a cabinet and pulled out an oversized bottle labeled conditioner. Callie gasped at the sight, making her repugnance known.

"I buy in bulk," Evie admitted. "It keeps my overhead down."

Amanda thought for a moment then offered an alternative. "I'm pretty sure Lucy carries Paul Mitchell. Maybe she could send Jed over with a few bottles."

"I love that stuff!" Callie chimed. "I'll take everything she has."

"I'm on it, Dawg!" Amanda replied, complete with urban-like head bob and hand motions.

After writing a list of instructions for Mrs. Daley, Callie congratulated her then called her next victim. Evie, on the other hand, immediately went to work snipping, thinning, straightening, and coloring. Everyone watched in fascinated awe as the transformation began.

The scene at the diner was equally chaotic. The kitchen staff was overwhelmed with breakfast orders, and the waitresses were sorry they hadn't requested the day off. Business like this was rare and only happened during the annual Fourth of July celebration or during summer sidewalk sales when everyone in the county came to town looking for a bargain.

The manager placed Zoey in the back alcove and gave her a full pot of coffee, which she sipped while snapping and labeling Polaroid shots. She wasn't quite sure how to achieve a glamorous look against a wall that included a deer head and a spittoon, but then she remembered that Hank's General Store carried fabric and hardware, and if she wasn't mistaken, *that* was Hank sitting across the way having breakfast with his friends. Zoey took inspiration from Roxanne—a master of manipulation—and searched the room for an ally.

She discarded the idea of asking Johan or Arnie because they were too busy trying to find some easy marks for a card game. Casey, on the other hand, was a likely candidate.

"Casey," she called out, waving him over. "I need your help."

Casey thought her statement sounded extremely familiar. "Like mother, like daughter," flashed through his brain. "You remind me of someone," Casey replied, remembering all the times Callie used that exact phrase. He was beginning to think attitude was hereditary and that mother and daughter shared it as well as certain physical characteristics like body shape and beauty.

But Zoey was in her zone now and just as Callie would do, she ignored him, moving directly into what she needed accomplished. "I have to transform this area into a studio, so I can adjust lighting. And I have to disguise the fact that I'm shooting on the outer wall of a restroom. Do you know anyone who would be willing to donate their time and efforts in exchange for a couple photos sent to the local paper?" Zoey—much like her daughter—was willing to barter one favor for another.

"Well, considering we have an electrician and the owner of a lumberyard in this room, I'd say your chances are pretty good," Casey replied in his most entrepreneurial voice.

"Like I always say…it's not what you know, but who you know," Zoey quoted with a beguiling smile, and proving once again that the apple doesn't fall far from the cart!

Casey moved to the front of the room, made a simple announcement to the audience, and within seconds Zoey had an entire volunteer work force at her command.

Across the street, the salon was in full swing. Evie had never been so busy! From consult, shampoo and processing, to makeup and nails, her clients moved from one chair to the next like pieces on an assembly line. And by the time Mrs. Daley reached Elsa's table, another five women were lined up behind her. It was like a factory and Callie was the inspector general!

The women all worked as quickly as they could, but it still took nearly an hour to get Mrs. Daley to Elsa, and that long for Jed to arrive with the supplies. The very sight of him caused a light bulb to go on in Callie's mind and nearly blow out. Jed was the perfect candidate for an *Extreme Makeover*!

Amanda tapped Callie's arm. "You thinking what I'm thinking?"

"Oh yeah!" Callie replied, her expression like that of a deer hunter, having just spotted the perfect five point buck. "You want to take him… or should I?"

"You better do it," Amanda suggested. "He stopped listening to me a few years ago when I talked him into buying my last four boxes of Girl Scout cookies." She hesitated for a moment. "How was I supposed to know he was allergic to chocolate and that he'd blow up like a balloon? His mother was furious with me. She had to take him to the ER, and he hasn't talked to me ever since!"

The sound of hammering emanated from the restaurant, prompting Callie to look at her watch. She was already running behind and couldn't afford any more distractions if she was going to coordinate the makeovers with their photo sessions.

Zoey's corner was well on its way to looking like a professional studio with all the resources from Hank's store and the collective experience of the men in the diner. And before long, the frame was built, the lights were positioned, and a bolt of dark green cloth was installed to her liking.

The rest of the men were far too fascinated by the construction project—and the odds that were developing—to concentrate on the card game Arnie and Johan were promoting. And when Casey announced that Jed was being cornered by Callie in the beauty shop, all eyes hit the window and watched in horror as he fought to retain possession of his coat. Interest was suddenly renewed in the betting, and Casey took it upon himself to keep track of all the wagers in his notebook.

"If she gives him a boa, I'm running for the hills," Arnie insisted.

Granted, Jed wasn't the most masculine guy in town, but he was still a kid—and one of them. So they were just as concerned for his dignity as they were for his safety.

Casey was already playing a combination of traffic cop, registrar, and all-around gofer in a restaurant with a maximum capacity of seventy-eight. But with the change in the décor, came a change in his demeanor. He was about to add Casino Host to his list of titles.

His plan was to escort the women through the restaurant and parade them in front of the betting pool, showing off their makeovers. Then shift to bookie mode, after delivering them around the corner to Zoey. He figured he was perfect for the job with his charming personality and trustworthy face. And he knew he could get the inside scoop on each transformation well before the men had an inkling of what was going on. Now that Callie was his partner, he didn't think twice about exploiting the situation. After all, if you can't use your friends, who can you use?

So while Casey worked the diner, Callie worked the salon, analyzing skin tones and giving beauty tips. Each client was a challenge in her own right, and for some strange reason, insisted on questioning her judgment. So the last thing she wanted to do was deal with another prima donna.

"Aw, I don't know." Jed said, staring down at his feet.

"What do you mean you don't know? When have you *ever* had an offer like this?" Callie demanded to know.

"It's not that I don't want it," Jed whined. "Hell, any guy would be crazy not to want *you* touching him."

The old ladies got a kick out of watching Callie manipulate Jed and listened in silence to a conversation that showed the possibility of turning risqué. They waited eagerly to hear the drama unfold.

"So then what's the problem, Romeo?"

"This is girly stuff and I'm *not* a girl," Jed proclaimed. "And I don't want to be one just in case you were wondering."

"Girly stuff?" Callie was shocked at Jed's chauvinistic attitude. "Do you honestly think looking good is exclusive to women?"

"Well, no…I…I just think…"

"Haven't you heard the term *metro sexual*?"

To her surprise, Jed nodded yes. "Lucy sells GQ. Sometimes I read it when I'm bored."

"Now *that's* what I'm talking about. So you can appreciate the value of my offer!"

Callie noticed Jed looking nervously across the street. Men in this town went to the barber for a crew cut and a shave, not the beauty shop! He knew they would be watching, and he knew they *wouldn't* approve. It was a tough choice—the respect of an ugly man or the fondling of a gorgeous woman!

She quickly sealed the blinds. "There," she said, isolating the salon from the prying eyes across the street. "Now it's just you and me!"

"So are going to let her do you or what?" Amanda blurted, demanding an immediate decision.

"DO IT…DO IT…DO IT," the women in the shop chanted, pounding their fists in the air like fans at the Super Bowl, demanding their team move in for the kill!

With his public humiliation now under wraps, Jed bowed to the pressure. The women burst into whistles, cheers, and applause, causing even more intrigue at the restaurant. With no visible sign of life from Jed and the unexplained noises from Evie's, the men's alarm grew to a fever pitch.

"Don't worry, guys. I promise she won't hurt him." Casey paused for dramatic effect. "Much!"

29

The bigger they are...the harder they fall

Zoey was quite pleased with her makeshift studio! Lights were strategically placed to create shadows, and milk crates were stacked and covered in fabric to add depth and variation. It was elegant and it was glamorous. And even Roxanne would have been pleased with the final result. Now all she needed was a subject, and it just so happened the first one was crossing the street and moving tentatively in her direction.

Stares rapidly turned into whistles and applause as the mystery woman approached the diner entrance. That is, until the sheriff glared at them and got up to hold the door open for his wife!

Casey announced Mrs. Daley and guided her around the room, showing her off like a prize heifer at the county fair. He delivered her to Zoey then quickly got to work.

"By the way, boys—her eyes are a striking blue!" he divulged.

All attention was redirected to the odds sheet in the center of the table to see who had guessed correctly. A few men cried out in victory, but most moaned in disappointment as Casey tallied who owed what.

"Thank you!" he said, snagging the bills from each man's hand and marking them *paid* in his ledger.

Now it was time for Zoey to do *her* job. She climbed a ladder and called down instructions to her model. The commands came faster than Mrs. Daley could move, "head up...tilt it left...a little more...perfect," and the men couldn't decide who was more interesting—their wives or the sexy photographer!

One by one, the women progressed through the system. And it was almost like clockwork until Old Man Johnson's wife, Helga, walked through the door with her pot-bellied pig, Rosebud. Helga was huge. No other word would do her remarkable stature justice, which made for very tight quarters in an already small area. But by the time Helga was situated, Rosebud got loose and had to be chased to the front of the restaurant. And when Zoey returned, holding the squealing pig, Helga had moved from her spot.

"You're not very organized, are you?" Helga asked in rapid fire. "Don't you have an assistant? What if I need my makeup touched up?"

Zoey was still out of breath from crawling under the table to rescue Rosebud and had little patience left for a critic. "It's not every day the famous Zoey Michaels works in Deer Creek," she replied in a self-confident voice.

Helga didn't take her comment the right way and reacted vehemently, "You mean this isn't *Glamour Shots*! I was told my picture would be taken by a professional!"

Zoey quickly realized that she wasn't a celebrity here, but rather a standard garden-variety photographer. She paused for a moment, humbled and slightly insulted then continued the shoot as professionally as she could.

The men were so consumed with the pig chase and rescue, not to mention their fear of being targeted by Helga's rather wicked tongue that they nearly forgot about their buddy, Jed. So when he entered the diner, they almost didn't recognize him.

He was no longer the gawky geek they had all come to tolerate, but rather a decent looking young man with styled and highlighted hair, new clothes, and a great smile. As a temporary fix for his bad complexion, Callie used a mellow yellow blemish concealer combined with a special translucent powder to cover the acne that plagued him. She also advised him to check out a specific prescription acne medication for a permanent solution. After all, a teenager's life is hard enough without having to walk around with a face full of pimples.

Zoey was positively thrilled to see Helga leave and Jed take her place because she knew there wasn't a teenage boy on the planet that she couldn't handle. And with her confidence firmly intact once again, she removed his glasses for the picture and discovered his soft brown eyes.

"Honey, you should wear contact lenses," she commented. "You have beautiful eyes." A young waitress peeked around the corner and Jed was rewarded by her smile—flirtatious and friendly.

The staff at Evie's finished first, and after cleaning the shop, they moved to the restaurant to watch the final shoot. Jed had become quite a ham in front of the camera with a confidence no one suspected him of having.

"Hey, Zoolander!" Callie heckled.

Amanda made a noise somewhere between a sneeze and a goose honking, as she tried to stifle the laughter that threatened to erupt. "Ooh…baby, baby!" she added, mocking Jed, as he strutted and posed for Zoey.

The girls continued to watch as Zoey moved from one angle to another and directed the lights to be shifted for different looks. Jed pouted, lowered his eyelids, and widened his smile just as she directed.

"You know, he's really not that bad if you look hard enough," Callie whispered. "His eyes *are* kind of pretty."

Amanda squinted and reflected for a moment. "I guess," she admitted, drawing out her words, "…in a repulsive kind of way."

Amanda liked boys and they had always liked her, too. And though her illness cut into her dating activities, it didn't slow down her interest. Because of Jed's obvious flaws, she had never really considered him as a possible candidate for her affections. But now he showed definite possibilities and her interest built as they continued to watch.

When Jed was finished, Zoey's recruits began tearing down the backdrop and returning the restaurant to its former state. The morning had passed quickly and the day was edging well into the afternoon. The pockets of the servers were bulging with tips as they cleaned mounds of used coffee mugs off the tables and refilled the condiments. Everyone was moving slowly—tired by the day's efforts—but there was a sense of accomplishment in the air.

Zoey couldn't remember a more exhausting shoot, or for that matter, a more insulting client! Most of the women were friendly and pleasant and so delighted with their new looks. But then there was Helga who made Zoey appreciate the rest of them all the more. Even Rosebud, who was inappropriately named, had better manners than her mistress!

Zoey had visions of a relaxing bubble bath and a nap for the near future, and assumed—incorrectly, as it turned out—that the rest of the day would be spent recovering from the makeovers. But Callie was far from being done with her day. She still had a lot of work to do, and the job required Amanda and Casey's help back at the house.

She also needed Johan out of the way, so she asked Arnie to keep him occupied for a couple of hours. And without much difficulty, Johan agreed to join the boys in a game of Gin Rummy. With their immediate problem solved, they loaded up the SUV and headed home, giving Elsa the perfect opportunity to *finally* drive the Lincoln!

Back at the house, the group moved with the same urgency and speed as a S.W.A.T. team about to confront a hostage situation. Grabbing the stacks of boxes from the utility room, they bolted to Johan's study where Elsa had already cleared his desk.

Instead of taking the nap she so desperately needed, Zoey opted to join Callie and her friends. The idea of hanging out with them was irresistible to her. It was an opportunity to see her daughter in a whole new situation—relaxed and not performing for anyone. Besides, good parents should get to know their children's friends, and Zoey was no exception to that rule.

Casey was put in charge of assembling the computer. And the girls, while trying to be helpful, acted more like court jesters, tossing him different peripherals and fetching tools, drinks, and snacks as needed.

Callie assigned her mother to wrapping detail, knowing she would use her artistic abilities to make each package a work of art. And she positioned her on the floor in the middle of the room surrounded by holiday paper, ribbons, scissors, and tape.

"Wow, these are really nice gifts," Zoey exclaimed.

"I'm glad you like them because *you* paid for them," Callie replied.

"Come again?"

"Yep! All this and a whole lot more!" she said, posing with one of the gifts and describing it in great detail like a game show hostess from the *Price is Right*.

Amanda and Casey looked at one another with concern. They had a pretty good idea of how much money Callie spent and weren't quite sure how Zoey was going to take it.

"By the way, how high is my American Express limit?" Callie asked, intentionally pushing her mother's buttons.

"Why?" Zoey asked—her parental defenses going on high alert!

"Because I kept charging and charging, and it kept approving and approving. I spent so much money this past week that I'm actually *burned out* on shopping!" Callie admitted, knowing her indifference had to be killing her mother.

Zoey wasn't exactly frugal, but she wasn't a philanthropist either. She knew that Callie was the ultimate shopper and could go neck in neck with anyone—anytime! She considered the potential damages before she asked, "So what are we talking here, five...ten thousand?"

"For the computer," Casey blurted, swallowing his laugh then trying to cover it with a fake cough.

"Don't worry Mom, it's not that bad."

"...said the spider to the fly," Zoey quipped.

"For the record, you would've spent a lot more on *me* in Aspen."

"If it makes you feel better, Zoey," Amanda interjected, "your money made a lot of sick children really happy this Christmas."

"Well when you put it like that." Zoey's heart was melted by Amanda's statement and she was now beginning to understand some of her daughter's new and improved attitude, which was apparently going to cost her a fortune!

"Besides, now you really *do* have to work, Mom!" It was obvious Callie's attitude hadn't undergone a full adjustment.

"Ha, Ha, Ha!" Zoey mocked, indicating her lack of appreciation for the comment.

"No, that's Ho, Ho, Ho to you!" Callie teased. "Now keep wrapping, there's another stack behind you."

Within an hour everything was connected, and Casey was tweaking the operating system and loading the numerous applications he had selected for Johan. And by the time he was done, the computer was nearly self sufficient and would require minimal maintenance.

The marathon wrapping session eventually came to an end as well, and Zoey excused herself to take that much delayed and needed nap. She felt comfortable leaving Callie with Casey and Amanda. They were good kids that influenced her daughter in a positive way, as her compassion and generosity levels were at an all time high and her biting responses to adults were minimized. She was even beginning to develop some tact! It was either something in the local water or her little girl was growing up. In either case, Zoey definitely approved!

Callie gathered the wrapping supplies and escorted her mom upstairs. When she returned to Casey and Amanda, she was brandishing a big roll of yellow plastic tape—the type used by police officers when barricading a crime scene. They attached it liberally to the door at first, then to each other, as they initiated a three-way wrestling match.

Their laughter drew Elsa from the kitchen, and before freeing them with the scissors, she pulled out the camera and got it on film. "Now that's a crime scene if I've ever seen one!"

30

To err is human...to forgive is divine

It was Christmas morning and a light snowfall blanketed the scenery like powdered sugar on a cake. The weather outside was cold, but not frigid. And the animals were warm inside the barn, waiting to be fed. The cow was lowing softly, and Uncle Buck snorted upon hearing the door slide open. The goose even flapped its wings as if to say good morning when Roy, Bud, Hurley, and JR walked in. They had to work—even if it was Christmas—because on a farm, the animals have to be fed and certain chores just have to be done, regardless of the date.

It was still dark outside but there was a festive mood in the air. The snow helped with that. And when Johan turned on the Christmas lights, the barnyard sparkled like it was lit by hundreds of tiny stars.

The men were eagerly anticipating Elsa's holiday breakfast. Year after year she went overboard on Christmas, making waffles and strudels, baked apples with fresh cream, and homemade cinnamon rolls. Callie may have convinced her to reduce fats and cholesterol in her daily cooking but this was Christmas and there was no way to impose dietary restrictions on *this* feast.

Elsa was singing O' Tannenbaum when Callie stumbled downstairs. It was earlier than usual, but the house smelled *so* delicious that she woke from a deep sleep. Following the aroma to the kitchen, she found her grandmother wrestling with the world's largest turkey. Elsa was trying to get it to swallow the last spoonful of stuffing before she set it in the oven.

"Merry Christmas, Grandma," Callie said, giving her a kiss on the cheek. "Merry Christmas, schatzie."

Callie filled a mug with coffee, stifling the urge to drool over the heavenly scents assaulting her. She reminded herself that she was just passing through as she grabbed her drink. "Stay out of the living room for a while, Grandma—it's a surprise."

Within moments, Zoey appeared in her robe, looking half-awake. And just as Callie had done, she inhaled the aromas for a moment, wished Elsa a Merry Christmas, then made a mad dash for the coffeepot.

"Callie is in the living room and I am not allowed in!" Elsa reported with mock indignation.

"GET OVER IT!" Callie bellowed from the distance then added, "Hurry up Mom, I need you."

Zoey looked to Elsa then raised her mug high in the air. "I'll be back."

The living room floor surrounding the tree was now covered with an abundance of wrapped packages. Zoey spotted Callie assembling an easel in the far corner and had to gingerly step through all the boxes to reach her.

"Perfect timing!" she observed. "I need you to hold this together while I tighten the bolts."

The pair made a great team, enough alike to think similarly and yet different to compensate for any lacks the other might have. Zoey's hands seemed to anticipate Callie's next move and the task progressed quickly. They finished the job by arranging paints, brushes, canvases, and a palette—all to be clearly visible when Elsa entered the room. Callie couldn't wait to see her grandmother's reaction, and she could only hope that the painting supplies would fulfill one of her deepest desires.

Elsa's heart was full, almost to overflowing. This was the Christmas she had dreamed about ever since Callie had left for New York. The emptiness she had felt by not having a child in the house was relieved by her granddaughter's presence, and it was almost as though Cameron were there in spirit, watching his family share the holiday.

It wasn't long before Callie rejoined her grandmother in the kitchen, and Zoey went upstairs to get dressed. As a surprise, Elsa had arranged a special breakfast call for the men. She directed Callie to flip a switch by the back door and suddenly the refrain to *Jingle Bells* was heard through out the barnyard. The rooster, which was just beginning to flap his wings in preparation to crow, jumped with a start at the noise.

Johan grinned and announced, "Breakfast is served."

The men's boots left imprints in the new snow as they trekked toward the house. The door opened with a blast of cold air, which was immediately absorbed by the heat emanating from the kitchen. They wiped their feet in the utility room and said "Merry Christmas" to Elsa and Callie before heading to the table in a leisurely stroll. Since all their chores were done for the day, they could relax and enjoy their breakfast in peace.

As they devoured the food, Callie slipped away to the living room. When she returned, she had a stack of wrapped presents in her arms and a cutesy Santa's hat on her head. She set the gifts to the side, and grabbed a spoon and a glass. Tapping the two together, she captured the men's attention.

"I have an announcement," she said.

The room fell silent and all eyes focused in her direction.

"I know you didn't like me much at first," she began, playing the role of guest speaker, "and you did everything you could to make me look like a fool." She handed a gift to each man. "But you underestimated me and assumed that I was an easy mark. Big mistake! Because as you know, it backfired and now you have to eat crow for the rest of your lives," she gloated, shaking her head in sympathy.

The men didn't know what to think. A flood of mixed emotions passed through them and the fear of revenge took foremost place in their minds. They became skeptical of their packages, and for a brief moment, let their vivid imaginations take over.

"I'm just kidding!" Callie said with a sudden burst of energy. "Geez— you're so gullible!" She flashed her biggest smile. "Merry Christmas, guys."

The farmhands were hesitant and sat for a moment looking bewildered.

"Go ahead…open them," she insisted.

JR did as he was told and had the wrapping paper halfway off his gift by the time the other men could see the humor in Callie's speech. He yelped with delight when he discovered an iPod—complete with a prepaid account to iTunes.

"Turn it on," she said. "I've already loaded it with some of my favorite music."

"Bitch'n," he exclaimed. "Thanks, Callie!"

Roy scoffed, "Like he needs another distraction!"

"Maybe he does, Roy—if it prevents him from listening to anymore of your lame-brained ideas," Callie snapped back in JR's defense.

"Touché," was all that Roy could think to say as Bud and Hurley eagerly ripped into their packages.

One by one, the men found equally impressive and meaningful gifts in each box. Roy received a Sony laptop with several downloaded PFDs on practical jokes. Obviously, Callie thought the ones he was using needed some updating.

Bud pulled out a compact cell phone with all his buddies preprogrammed into the auto-dial, and he looked at Callie suspiciously when he realized she could contact *his* contacts.

And Hurley received a portable DVD player with two DVD's: *Rat Race* and *Vegas Vacation*—intended to reinforce the pitfalls of gambling. Like that was really going work! The men were astounded at Callie's generosity and thanked her profusely.

Just then, Roy got an idea and stood up as spokesman for the hands. "We have a present for you, too, Callie."

"We do?" JR blurted, confusing the situation.

Roy mouthed the word *idiot* at JR and would have smacked him in the head if he had been any closer. As it was, he had to be satisfied with a glare that squelched any further comments.

"Well…kind of. But you have to be at Edermann's Pond at one o'clock. Have Casey pick you up at twelve-thirty, and don't be late!"

Knowing that Roy probably hadn't given up on getting revenge, Callie would have preferred to decline the trip, even if it meant losing the gift.

But the thought of time alone with Casey was extremely appealing, and she wasn't about to pass up an offer like that!

The men were stuffed to the gills, and it was time to let the Michelsohn family celebrate their Christmas in privacy. They gathered their gifts and headed outside into the cool, crisp air. The sky was a bright blue and there was a hint of clouds in the far distance. It truly *was* a glorious day.

"Now don't forget about this afternoon," Roy exclaimed, reminding her once again about her present.

"I'll be there...one o'clock...Edermann's Pond," was what she said. "Making out...with Casey...in his truck," was what she thought!

For the most part, Zoey was quiet during breakfast—this was Callie's show. She had watched the events around the table with amusement and knew it was just the forerunner to what Callie had planned in the living room. As the men departed, she waited in the kitchen and helped Elsa load the last of the dishes into the dishwasher.

Johan hovered around Elsa impatiently, though he wasn't quite sure why. He had been banned from his study, and no amount of bribing or threatening could get Casey to spill the beans. Finally, Elsa pronounced the kitchen respectable and they all headed to the living room.

Callie demanded that Elsa close her eyes as she guided her one step at a time, stopping at a point where her grandmother could get the full effect. Johan trailed behind, but he could easily see over the tops of their heads.

"Don't peak," she instructed, moving to the tree and turning on the lights. "Okay, now open!"

Elsa's eyes widened as she viewed the wrapped presents flooding the carpet. She stopped in her tracks when she saw the easel and equipment strategically placed in front of the window. Moving carefully across the room, she picked up the card nestled within a big bow. It read...

To Grandma, It's never too late. Love, Callie.

Her face filled with emotion as she fingered the easel like a priceless treasure. "Oh schatzie," she said, turning to Callie. "How did you...?"

"Opa." Callie revealed, already anticipating her grandmother's question.

Elsa had never mentioned her passion for painting to anyone in Deer Creek. She hadn't even mentioned it to Johan in years. It was as if she suddenly saw all her dreams within her grasp, and she was speechless and overwhelmed by emotion. But when she threatened to break into tears, Johan handed her one of the smaller gifts for Callie just to distract her.

And it worked! Elsa looked at the tag on the first package, smiled and passed it over to her granddaughter. There were gifts there from just about everyone she had met. Clara gave her a cookbook with handwritten recipes. Evie gave her fancy accessories for her new hairstyle. And Lucy gave her an array of nail polishes, none of which even remotely resembled a shade of pink. Callie was surprised that everyone had taken the time to remember her.

Even Zoey pulled out some little trinkets she had gathered on her shoots around the world—all carefully chosen from exotic locations with her daughter in mind. It wasn't her style to show up empty handed, so she always carried a ready supply of Swiss chocolates, a tie or belt from a designer's most recent show, and some costume jewelry from one of the couture houses she visited regularly. These items were often given to her as *perks* and she saved them for situations like this. Elsa loved her scarf and brooch from Dior, and chocolate was one of Johan's favorite foods. So the gifts were a hit!

"I have something for you, too, Mom," Callie admitted. "I kind of fibbed when I said I hadn't shopped." She moved to the mantle of the fireplace and retrieved a box from Tiffany's. Even from the couch, Zoey recognized their distinctive wrapping.

Opening the package carefully, she discovered a silver filigree frame, heart shaped with Callie's face beaming out at her. The frame itself was a work of art, but to Zoey the true treasure was her daughter's precious face. She reached for Callie and hugged her. "I love you, baby," she said with a squeeze.

"Okay, enough mush!" Callie said, as she escaped her mother's arms, which threatened to crush her.

"It's time for Opa's big present—to the study!" Callie pointed, expecting everyone to immediately jump up and follow her lead.

But to her surprise, Johan stood up and spoke, "Not so fast, young lady. We have one more present for you." He nodded at Elsa who pulled a box from behind the tree. It was medium-sized and flat with some heft to it.

Callie acknowledged the weight of the package as Elsa handed it to her. She unwrapped the box slowly and lifted the tissue off the contents. It was a three-sided folding picture frame, obviously a finely crafted antique. The center frame displayed a mounted coat of arms with the family name beneath. And the right and left frames contained photos documenting the lives of Elsa, Johan, and Cameron. Some of the pictures were black and white and dated back to the nineteenth century. Others were more recent and in color. It was like a pictorial history of her family tree. Elsa and Johan had given Callie her heritage—more than just a name, a place in time.

"Thank you," she said, speechless as she had ever been. "This means so much," she added in a softened tone. Callie gazed at the pictures, finding family resemblances in some of them and trying to identify the faces she saw in others.

"Now turn it over," Johan instructed.

"There's more?" She was surprised to discover an envelope taped to the back containing a grant deed. The document read...

Johan and Elsa Michelsohn, on this 25th day of December, hereby transfer...

Callie looked up in shock.

"What does it say?" Zoey asked. She had no clue what Elsa and Johan were up to.

Callie was still speechless as she handed the papers to her mother and got up to hug her grandparents.

"Wow! I guess you really are the *Queen of Cheese*!" Zoey exclaimed, reading the certificate. "What a generous gift!"

Callie carefully took back the papers from her mother and set the framed photos in a safe place behind the tree. "Now it's your turn Opa. Come with me."

She was excited about her grandfather's gift. Aside from everything else, it would provide a link that would keep them closer—especially while she was at school. She led him by the hand to his study and assisted him in removing the large amount of yellow tape denying entry to the room. He swung open the door and swiftly moved to his desk, which was the home to his brand new computer! It was already booted and humming quietly.

"This is state-of-the-art stuff, Opa," Callie boasted. "You're officially cutting edge!"

Elsa cracked a smile and shook her head. "Oh dear, we're in trouble now!"

31

Who said bigger isn't better?

As the morning waned, Zoey found herself alone in the living room for the first time since her arrival. Elsa hadn't redecorated much after Cameron's death and the memories were bittersweet. But once she had gotten past her feelings of guilt, she was at ease with her in-laws. They had always treated her like she was part of their family and continued to show their devotion by displaying her landscapes on the walls and her wedding picture on their mantle. She sighed as she studied the photo, missing her late husband even more. If only he were there, everything would be perfect.

Callie entered the room with a limp. She felt cross-eyed, and her butt ached from working with Johan at his computer. She read the look on Zoey's face and approached with caution, not wanting to interrupt her mother's thoughts.

"Mom?" she asked tentatively, waiting for a response. She knew it had to be painful dealing with the flood of memories, but she really needed help. "Can I get your advice about something?"

Zoey was startled by the question. Callie's independent spirit rarely allowed her to solicit outside opinions. "Sure," she answered, listening carefully.

"I want to give Casey a Christmas present, but I don't know what to give him."

Zoey's mind flashed back to her first gift from Cameron. She remembered how carefully he had chosen it, and how pleased he was that she liked it. But at Callie's age, the *perfect gift* could be hard to choose—especially when you were head over heels for someone.

"How about the heart-shaped frame that you gave me?" Zoey suggested. "I'm sure he would love the picture."

Callie's face lit up. "And you wouldn't mind?"

"Not if you promise to replace it when we get home," Zoey answered with a smile.

"Deal!" Callie hugged her mother once again. "You're so cool."

"Yeah right! I'll be sure to remind you of that the next time you're mad at me," she replied. "Now you'd better get going. You don't have much time."

Callie checked her watch. Her mother was right! She had less than an hour to get ready and completely repackage the frame. It was important to her that Casey appreciated the sentiment and not the Tiffany packaging, so she grabbed a substitute box from under the tree along with the gift and dashed up to her room.

She set out her makeup, selected the perfect outfit, and wrapped the present in record time, shifting from one task to another with not a moment to spare.

When she was finished, she checked and rechecked her outfit in the mirror, fiddled with one lock of hair that refused to behave, and paced like a caged lion while waiting for Casey. Zoey watched with amusement as Callie kept peeking out the window. And she was relieved—for her daughter's sake—when he arrived.

"Casey's here!" Callie yelled to the household, grabbing her coat and hat off the rack. She was eager to spend as much time with him as she could.

"Don't be gone too long, schatzie," Elsa hollered from the kitchen. "Dinner is at three."

Callie mentally calculated her window of opportunity then waved goodbye to Zoey and darted out of the house, joining Casey in his pickup. He draped his arm over her shoulder and pulled her close as if it were the most natural thing in the world. They immediately started chatting like best friends and exchanged details about their Christmas gifts. He teased her about being the official *Queen of Cheese* and even threatened to order personalized license plates to match his for her 16th birthday.

"*Queen* has a very different meaning in New York," Callie laughed. But secretly, she was just thrilled that he was thinking that far ahead!

They arrived at the pond with about fifteen minutes to spare. Casey had allowed for the roads being slippery from the snow, and Roy had been very specific about the schedule. Besides, the more time he had alone with Callie, the better.

The area was isolated, and their tire tracks were the first ones down the road. The world around them was solid white and perfectly quiet—except for the sound of birds chirping and the breeze rustling through the branches of the trees.

It was a romantic setting, and they were the only two people in sight. But all Callie could think about was giving Casey his gift. She was nervous, and hoped he wouldn't think she was being too forward. They watched in silence as a squirrel searched for his stash of nuts and Callie searched for the right words.

Fortunately, Casey spoke first, "I have a Christmas present for you."

"Really?" she questioned. What a relief! Callie was hoping for an indication that Casey cared about her, too.

"But you can't see it until we get back to the house."

Her confidence level immediately skyrocketed as she pushed for more information. "What is it?"

He continued to toy with her. "Nothing you'd expect."

"TELL ME!" she insisted, squeezing his knee. And her eyes narrowed as if she were going into attack mode.

"Are you sure you want to ruin the surprise?"

"Positive—Now tell me or I'll be forced to hurt you."

Casey grinned for a moment as he considered how she would attempt to get him to submit, but then he caved and started explaining the personal website he was building for her. It was password protected and viewable by invitation only. And he designed it like an interactive diary with live audio and video, allowing her to share events in her life with her family and friends as they occurred. Some areas would be permanent, and other areas would need regular maintenance. All she had to do was pick up the phone, which just so happened to be the intention behind the idea. Of course, Casey was hoping she would want to anyway, but it made for the perfect excuse.

"So let me get this straight. I send you pictures, personal information, and my complete schedule on a weekly basis?

"Or daily, if you'd like."

"And you add it to my website?"

"Yep."

Callie thought for a moment. "It's kind of like a gift that keeps on giving."

"Exactly!"

"That's *way* cool." She briefly considered the fact that he would be publishing her private life and added, "A little stalker-like, but cool."

It pleased her that Casey wanted to be a part of her life, and she was thrilled that he would put so much time and effort into her gift. But the best part was that he promised to continue doing so. She thanked him with a barrage of kisses then declared, "I have something for you, too."

"Oh?"

Reaching into her pocket, Callie pulled out the box with the frame. She moved over just a little on the seat, so he could use both hands to unwrap it. She watched his reaction as his eyes carefully scanned the folded slip of paper she had enclosed. It read...

So you don't forget me, Love, Scarlett.

He smiled while examining the picture, trying to decide which adjective best described her, beautiful, gorgeous, sexy—or maybe a combination of all three. He knew one thing though, and he answered her message out loud, "I could never forget you!" Pulling her close, he added, "It's awesome...thank you."

Just then Casey recognized the sound of a small plane engine approaching from the distance. "It's time!" he exclaimed. "We have to get out!" And he pulled Callie from his side of the truck, directing her attention to the sky.

Suddenly the aircraft dove towards the ground as if it had caught fire. Callie was about to call 911 when it started an uphill climb and the white smoke began to take shape in the air. There, across the sky, in big, bold letters was the farmhands' concession, *YOU WIN, CALLIE!*

The men had hired a skywriter to proclaim her superiority to the entire county. It was the perfect gift from them, and Callie laughed in appreciation. The plane dipped a wing in their direction and headed back toward the hanger.

She felt great and spun around in circles, spreading her arms wide with delight. "Isn't this just the perfect day?" she asked.

"I think so," Casey agreed. "Oh before I forget, there's one more thing!"

"More?" Callie stopped dead in her spin and looked at him. She couldn't imagine what else might be waiting, but she was all eagerness trying to find out. "What, where?" and she started checking his pockets.

"You won't find it in there," he warned with laughter. "You'll have to follow me."

Casey took Callie by the hand and guided her through a maze of trees and up to an old oak. "First let me explain. For generations now, Edermann's Pond has been a place where people come to make their feelings public. They use the trees as billboards and carve messages in the bark, for all eternity, and for everyone else to see."

"Like graffiti?"

"No, more like history."

Callie looked at the older trees in the grove and noticed little messages everywhere around their trunks. She spotted a "C+Z forever", which immediately caught her attention. She looked to Casey for confirmation.

"Is that my mom and dad?"

"Yep, and mine are over there," he said, pointing to a heart that framed "Nick loves Sarah."

Callie continued reading the carvings as her fingers reached out and traced the letters. They were so romantic. She moved from tree to tree, caught up in the names and feelings they shared with her until she reached the letters "C+C" and the current date. Once again, she looked to Casey for the answer. He was standing over her shoulder, waiting patiently for her to find his inscription.

"Is that us?" she asked.

"Yep. It's official," he said with a smile, turning her around and wrapping his arms around her waist. "Merry Christmas."

Callie's heart was pounding and her pulse was racing. She lifted her lips to his. "Merry Christmas, Casey."

At that point, an earthquake could have hit, and Callie wouldn't have noticed. It had only been two days since their first kiss, and yet she felt so comfortable. It seemed as if they were born to be together. But in spite of how hard it was to break away, it was chilly outside and eventually the cold air started to insulate the cocoon that seemed to have wrapped around them.

Casey's common sense finally replaced his desire for Callie and he reluctantly broke the kiss. He knew their time together was limited and that they needed to make the most of each moment. But it was warm in the truck and they could be together there, too. They slowly walked back, their arms clinging to each other like castaways clinging to a raft.

Callie spoke first. "You know I'm leaving tomorrow."

"Yeah, Amanda told me." Casey was torn between his macho image and revealing how badly he actually felt. In reality, he was hopelessly in love, and he was finding it hard to maintain his poker face.

"It'll be strange seeing my friends again," Callie said. "So much has happened in the past two weeks."

"Like us?"

"Yeah, like us."

Casey stopped at the side of his truck. He pinned Callie against the door with his body, holding her close as he continued talking, "Did Amanda tell you I'm taking her to her chemo treatment tomorrow morning?"

"Yeah, she mentioned that."

"So I can't be there to say goodbye."

Callie was used to Zoey's departures. And though it made her mad sometimes, it didn't hurt like this one. She now knew where the term *broken heart* came from because there was a physical pain associated with the separation.

"That's okay. I get enough of those from my mom. Besides, it's not goodbye, it's until next time. Right?"

"Right."

Callie had things she wanted to say, but she knew it was too soon. Her attraction to Casey was serious, but she was young and not ready to commit her whole future just yet. Casey seemed to be tentative with the situation as well and chose not to disclose his true feelings either.

It was the first time they felt awkward together, and Callie searched for something to change the mood. It wasn't very creative, but it broke the tension when she looked at her watch and stated, "Okay—enough depression. We still have an hour to kill. So what's there to see around here, anyway?"

Casey smiled, welcoming the obvious icebreaker. "Right this way, Miss," he said, helping her into the truck. "Your tour is about to begin."

He showed her a herd of deer feeding in a field and a bald eagle that flew overhead—a rare sight in recent years. He pointed out some of the homes belonging to the various people she had met and all the local *make out* spots—known only to teenagers. The gravel roads that linked the community were like a maze, and Callie was astonished at how Casey found his way with no map or street signs to guide him.

They pulled into the drive just behind Nick and Amanda, having timed their outing perfectly.

"Quite an air show today!" Amanda blurted, even before hugging Callie hello. "It doesn't get much bigger than that."

As soon as she let go, Amanda pulled presents out of the back seat and placed them in Callie's arms while Nick did the same thing to Casey on his side of the truck. There were so many packages to carry that they had to use their chins to keep them from toppling over.

Callie couldn't wait to tell Amanda about the carving Casey had done for her, but she wanted to share the news in private. And Casey was sure starvation was imminent, so they didn't waste any time.

Elsa and Johan welcomed them at the door, taking their coats and packages.

The house was warm and cozy, and a heavenly aroma wafted through the air. The dining room table was set with Rosenthal china and Baccarat crystal, which sparkled brilliantly under the small chandelier. It was a combination of pure elegance and down home country charm, perfectly blended by Elsa's artistic eye.

The centerpiece was made of pine boughs, cones, and candles, which were lit. And the table linens were in traditional Christmas colors, red and green, with napkin rings made from strips of ribbon. Elsa had considered even the smallest of details in the arrangement.

The fire was roaring in the fireplace, and the tree was shimmering under the lights and tinsel. It looked like a scene from the December issue of *Better Homes and Gardens*, depicting the perfect Christmas.

As soon as everyone had settled in, they moved to the table and Johan carried in the freshly carved turkey. Elsa followed with the gravy, fresh off the stove. She indicated they should all sit as Johan stood at the head of the table. Everyone followed Elsa's lead and bowed their heads.

Johan led the informal prayer. "Dear Father in heaven, we give thanks for the bountiful gifts of food here on our table. And for our family and friends who have gathered here today to share it. Amen."

"And thank you, Lord, for bringing our family together again," Elsa added, before passing around the dishes. There was turkey and stuffing, baked ham, mashed potatoes and gravy, candied yams, scalloped corn, honey carrots, Brussels sprouts, red cabbage, homemade rolls, cranberries, and plenty of desserts waiting in the kitchen for later.

The first few minutes passed quietly as they sampled all the foods and complimented Elsa who beamed in response. But gradually, as their hunger subsided, they began discussing the gift from the farmhands. Everyone had seen the message written to Callie in the sky, and they knew it would be the talk of the town for quite some time—especially if Elsa had anything to do with it!

After dinner, Casey invited everyone into the study to show off the website he had designed for Callie. She was delighted at the detail he had gone to, and the rest were impressed at how professional it looked. From there, they moved to the living room where they sat like overstuffed chairs.

Johan dozed in his recliner and nearly missed the call for dessert. His snores were so loud that they almost drowned out the ongoing conversation, and the usual nudges and calls didn't begin to make a dent in his sleep. Even waving a piece of pumpkin pie under his nose was unsuccessful, though he did wiggle and scratch in response. They were fascinated by his resistance to their efforts and surrounded him like Indians around a wagon train. Their laughter intensified with each attempt and finally succeeded in jolting him awake. His eyes opened with a start and saw their faces peering down at him.

"I was just resting my eyes," he muttered.

"Yeah right, Opa. And that was just a freight train rumbling through the living room," Callie said, as she offered him her hand and tugged him out of his chair.

The group laughed again as they moved back to the dining table for the delicacies that Elsa had prepared. Her presentation of desserts was magnificent, and even Casey's teenage appetite was satisfied. But Christmas had to end. There were travel plans for most of them, which couldn't be put off, and it was getting late.

Nick stood up and addressed his kids, "We'd better get going. We have an early morning."

Amanda made a mock frown at the thought as she sadly went for her coat. She lightened up though when they said their farewells, joking about the makeovers and hoping there wouldn't be any serious regressions while Callie was gone. She agreed to provide periodic updates on Dixie and the other girls, and they double checked to make sure they had each other's email and cell phone numbers. The bond that was formed in their childhood had intensified into a deep and lasting friendship, and they promised to stay in very close contact this time.

Casey had his own truck there and wanted to say goodbye to Callie without his dad around. He told Nick and Amanda to go ahead and that he would see them at home.

"Don't be too long, son," Nick said firmly. "You need your rest."

Casey knew his dad meant well, but he didn't appreciate being treated like a kid in front of Callie! But he curbed his instinct to talk back and calmly answered, "I'm right behind you."

Finally, Nick and Amanda drove off, leaving them alone on the porch. Casey waited until his dad was completely out of sight before wrapping his arms around Callie. She pressed her lips up to his and they kissed softly. Then she laid her head on his chest and listened to his heartbeat. They held each other in silence, wishing time could stop. Casey kissed her one last time then reluctantly pulled away and headed for his truck. He couldn't believe how she made him feel and how hard it was to leave.

Callie remained on the porch, watching him with a smile on her face and the strangest ache in her heart. She waved until his truck was almost out of sight, suppressing the urge to scream, "Don't go!" But she knew *that* would only prolong the inevitable. She felt sick inside and wiped away a tear that escaped her eye.

He had just left and she already missed him!

32

Home is where the heart is

"Beautiful, isn't it?" Callie's footsteps made crunching sounds in the snow as she came up behind her mom. Zoey turned and faced her daughter. She was amazed at how different she appeared. Instead of the high maintenance debutante who wouldn't be caught dead in anything other than designer labels, Callie looked more like the girl next door, relaxed and comfortable in her Levi's and plaid flannel shirt. She hadn't even bothered to put on makeup!

"I can't believe I gave this up," Zoey said, swinging the camera toward her daughter who immediately went into a model pose out of habit.

"Smile," she instructed, snapping the shot.

Zoey was doing what she did best—taking pictures and making everything she saw somehow come to life even more. It was another crisp, clear day and the snow from the night before covered the ground like a blanket. She positioned herself about halfway between the barn and the house where she could get a view of both the farm and the scenery around it just by moving a step or too in either direction.

The men were bustling about doing their normal chores, and without their knowledge, had been included in a couple of Zoey's shots. One of her specialties was catching people being themselves with no pretense like when they weren't paying attention or when they were preoccupied with their work.

"What are you doing up so early?" Callie asked. She knew her mother's habits and they didn't include getting up before noon if she didn't have to—especially after an overseas trip.

"I slept through the night."

Zoey seemed surprised at her own behavior. Sleep was something that frequently eluded her. "And I didn't dream." She stopped shooting for a moment and brushed the hair from her face. "I can't remember the last time that happened."

Since Cameron's death, Zoey had been haunted by the same recurring nightmare. It was so vivid and real that it jolted her awake and made falling back asleep difficult, if not impossible.

Callie was aware of her mother's disorder, but assumed it was a direct result of her fast-paced lifestyle. It wasn't easy keeping up with the rich and famous! However, as much as she sympathized with Zoey's plight, her mind was on thoughts of Amanda and Casey, not her mother's less-than-impressive achievement.

Callie checked her watch. "Amanda should be starting her chemo right about now. I wish I was with her."

"You are…in spirit," Zoey said, turning her attention back to the landscape. She lifted the camera in front of her face, in part to disguise how she felt. It wasn't easy for her to reveal her emotions, even to Callie. "I've been meaning to tell you how proud I am of you."

"For what?"

"For cutting your hair. That was a heroic thing to do."

"It's only hair, Mom. It grows back. Amanda's the hero…not me."

Zoey turned to Callie and evaluated her mature perspective. Looking at her without the bias of a mother, she saw a beautiful, compassionate young woman. "Wow, you really have grown up. I guess it's my turn."

"You won't get any arguments from me!"

Zoey laughed. Okay, so there was still a little smart ass kid in her daughter after all. She grinned even more when she saw a familiar vehicle coming down the drive, knowing the nature of its business.

Callie was facing the opposite direction and didn't turn around until she was startled by the *honk* of a limousine's horn. She couldn't have been more bowled over!

Bianca, Alexia, and Danielle screamed and waved through the

sunroof like prom queens in a homecoming parade. They barely waited for the limo to come to a complete stop before they cracked the doors. Callie looked back at her mother who merely shrugged her shoulders and shook her head.

"They've been driving me crazy all week."

She ran to greet her friends as they tumbled out of the car.

Bianca held Callie at arm's length, inspecting her for obvious damage. "Looks to me like you're in one piece!" she finally announced.

"Callie, what did you do to your hair?" Danielle asked.

Alexia continued the cross examination. "And those clothes. Are you making a statement?"

Their rapid fire questions left no time for answers, and Zoey couldn't tell who was talking to whom as they asked about her Christmas presents, her clothing or lack thereof, the availability of boys, and even about the science project. Callie's head was turning from one to the other as she attempted to blurt out the answers. And Zoey was getting dizzy just watching the inquisition.

Bianca put one hand flat over the other, in the universal signal for time out, indicating the girls should take a break from their nonstop probing. Alexia and Danielle had grown used to her acting as second in command and immediately hushed, ending the chaos. Of course she only shushed them so she could get a word in, too!

"Hey, leave the girl alone," she ordered, then quickly took over as lead prosecutor. "So where's Farm boy?"

"He's...," Callie started to explain but was interrupted by a familiar voice.

"Right here," Casey said, approaching from behind. He had come in the back way, wanting to surprise Callie and had watched in amusement as her friends conducted their interrogation. He wasn't at all intimidated by girls, but this bevy of beauties was something new. And if they had even half the attitude of his girlfriend, Deer Creek was in for a rude awakening!

Callie spun around totally elated. Casey's was the last voice she had expected to hear, and the one she really wanted to hear the most! He had her full attention now, and in her excitement, she forgot about her friends.

"Casey!" she screamed, running to greet him. She jumped into his arms, and he swung her around and kissed her. She was oblivious to everything around her, focusing her full attention on him. Then she remembered where he was supposed to be and her thoughts turned to worry.

"Why aren't you in Madison? Is Amanda okay?"

"Yeah, she's fine. My dad is with her. I just couldn't let you leave without saying goodbye...again."

Callie was instantly relieved about Amanda, and her delight at Casey's presence continued to intensify as she realized how little time they had left. She hated leaving Deer Creek, but if this was what *goodbyes* were like around here—well then, bring 'em on!

The girls watched in silence and were more than just a little jealous. Callie had forgotten to explain how totally, utterly, and completely gorgeous Casey was. And if drooling had been an acceptable public behavior, there would have been puddles in the snow.

Bianca finally cleared her throat, trying to get Callie to make the introductions they were all dying to receive.

"I'm sorry," she blushed, realizing they were watching, listening, and probably taking notes. "These are my friends Bianca, Alexia, and Danielle. Girls, this is Casey."

Casey figured he would be under the microscope and gave his best grin. The one that was famous for knocking girls off their feet.

"Hi."

Mesmerized by his exceptional good looks, they responded with giddy "hellos." Danielle nudged Bianca then whispered, "He's so hot!" But Bianca was too busy staring to do more than just nod her head in agreement.

Alexia, on the other hand, was doing a thorough mental survey and found everything in perfect order. She had a tendency to take things too literally and had missed the hints that Callie had been putting out about Casey. Her forehead puckered in a puzzled look as she made her confusion known. "Who said he looked like Carrot Top?"

Callie didn't want to explain that one to Casey and quickly diverted the conversation by responding with a question. "So why are you guys here, anyway?" she asked, knowing how difficult it would have been for them to escape the eyes of their parents—especially this far off the beaten path.

Danielle spilled the beans, seeing that Callie was in no apparent danger. "We came to rescue you."

"Too late!" Bianca commented.

"And we thought we'd bring you home in style," Alexia added, evaluating Callie's humble attire. "Not that you're into that anymore."

Bianca had planned their rescue carefully. It was easiest for Alexia, since she was spending the second half of her vacation with her mother who wasn't even home. And once her father put her safely on the plane, he wouldn't bother checking on her until at least spring break.

Mrs. Hamilton, likewise, had been so distracted by her upcoming New Year's Eve party that she agreed to let Danielle enjoy a day of shopping in the city with Bianca just to get her out of her hair.

And Bianca, who was scheduled to work the lunch shift, contrived a story about how Danielle was having *female* problems that required a visit to a local gynecologist. As she started a very graphic explanation intended to embarrass her father, he insisted she take the day off and accompany her girlfriend to the doctor, claiming the subject matter was completely over his head.

When Danielle arrived at the restaurant, she performed her best dying act, walking in slowly and buckling over in pain for dramatic effect. And it worked! Feeling extremely uncomfortable, Mr. Bertoli went outside and flagged down a cab himself. Not only that, but he gave Danielle his arm to lean on. And just before he closed the taxi door, he pulled out his money clip and handed over a couple of C notes, suggesting they have lunch on him! Bianca congratulated herself. She would have to remember to use that one again in the future.

The girls waited until Mr. Bertoli was out of sight before redirecting the driver to La Guardia Airport where they were scheduled to rendezvous with Alexia and catch a flight to Madison.

Once again, Bianca's creative thought process had achieved the desired results as they managed their getaways without being detected. The only parent who knew about the scheme was Zoey. And they hadn't asked her permission, but rather informed her of how and when they would be arriving. Everything was perfectly timed and Bianca was determined to pull off this caper with her usual finesse.

"So, chop chop!" she ordered, clapping her hands. "The meter's running and I can't go over budget."

Callie stared into Casey's eyes. "Well actually, I was about to help my Grandma serve brunch to the boys and we already have a ride to the airport." She was searching for some excuse, any excuse to delay her departure. Then with a spark of brilliance, an idea flashed through her mind. "Besides, it's Saturday—there's someone very special I want you to meet."

The girls were hoping the mystery person was a Casey look-a-like and agreed to Callie's plan. But what she neglected to mention was that the term *boys* in these parts referred to a group of ordinary farmhands. It was an intentional oversight on her part, needing every ploy available to string them along for a while.

By now, Zoey's camera had switched focus and was aimed at the girls who seemed just as relaxed as Callie. They pulled Casey into the center of their group and surrounded him like dancers in a music video. They leaned on him, fell into him, and wrapped themselves around him, imitating actions they had seen on VH1.

Casey was definitely *the man* and Zoey captured it all! And by the time she ran out of film, he had three shades of lipstick on his face and was beginning to look a little too comfortable.

"There's one for the yearbook!" she commented, snapping the last shot. Zoey motioned to Callie. "Take the girls inside and introduce them to your grandparents. I'll release their driver."

Casey wiped the lipstick off his face in a hurry—before any of the hands could see it—and trailed along behind the girls trying to clear his head. He watched as Johan and Elsa became visibly dizzy trying to keep up with Callie's lengthy introductions. And while her grandparents were still figuring out who was who, she ran to the living room to make a phone call.

Casey stuck to her side like glue, prompting Bianca to ask if they were attached at the hip. Callie just laughed at the question and remarked, "You wouldn't let him go either!"

"Hmm, true!" Bianca's answer was definite as she continued her thought. "So Casey, I don't suppose you have a twin brother do you?"

But before he could answer, the room was invaded by a swarm of hungry farmhands. The kitchen became crowded and noisy, and Elsa was in seventh heaven! Brunch included leftovers from Christmas dinner, in addition to the normal breakfast buffet, so there was more than enough to go around. With twice as many choices as their normal meal, the only difficulty was in deciding what would fit on their plates. Some of the men had never tasted Elsa's holiday spread and would be in danger of bursting at the seams if they ate everything they wanted to try.

Bianca was starving, and if she had known that Callie was eating like this all along, she might have shown up sooner. She took full advantage of the situation and ate to her heart's content, knowing that life was likely to return back to normal at school.

JR immediately spotted Alexia and struck up a conversation, even before loading his plate. His tenacity amused her, and strangely enough, he kind of reminded her of the surfers and skateboarders she knew in California. He wasn't GQ like Casey but he was a little older, and if the truth be known, she had a real weakness for the beach-bum type. Besides, she enjoyed the attention.

When brunch was finished, Callie ordered the girls to grab their coats. She apologized to Elsa for not helping with the dishes but said, "Evie is expecting us!"

Zoey and Elsa were surprised to hear the destination Callie had chosen, but understood the secret code when she ran her fingers through her hair. Alexia bid a reluctant farewell to JR as Callie herded them outside. And Elsa watched from the doorway, laughing as the girl's crammed into the extended cab of Casey's pickup—all of them trying to fit through the doorway at once!

On the way to town, Callie gave her most persuasive speech ever. She told her friends about Amanda and the reason for cutting her hair. The girls were amazed at her motivation and quieted as she explained how sick the children in the hospital really were. None of them had experience with leukemia, or for that matter, knew anyone that had. She continued explaining how much good came from her actions and they were all very impressed until she got to the point.

"I want you to cut yours, too!" Callie blurted.

They looked at one another as if she had lost her mind. It wasn't that they were against doing something nice for someone in need, it was just that their hair was such an important part of their image. And at Ridgecrest, image was everything next to pedigree.

Bianca had no fear of looking different, and Danielle would go along with just about anything Callie suggested—especially if it would somehow aggravate her mother. But Alexia, in spite of her slightly bizarre taste in clothing, was the most reluctant. That is, until Callie mentioned starting a new trend at school—the ultimate incentive! Finally, Callie was giving them permission to standout, and maybe, just maybe, even her parents would notice her, too!

Alexia reluctantly gave her consent. And with her entire crew on board, Callie pressed the speed dial on her cell phone and scheduled an afternoon pickup with FedEx.

Evie was still recovering from Christmas Eve, but was more than happy to accommodate Callie and her friends. "More victims, huh?" she said, as they descended upon her shop.

"Yep, just the basics," Callie responded. She could see the look of concern in the girls' eyes as they scrutinized the salon. "I don't think they need a full makeover!"

Danielle was grinning from ear to ear. She knew her mother would object, so she offered to go first!

Alexia and Bianca's fear grew as Evie pulled Danielle's hair into a tight braid. She wrapped an elastic band at both ends of the thirteen-inch pony tail then took a deep breath—totally for effect—before approaching with the scissors. Her precision measurements and motions resembled a ritual sacrifice, without the blood, of course! But what they didn't know was that the *ritual* was for a specific purpose. Locks of Love had strict guidelines, and Evie was merely following the rules.

Fortunately, Danielle's face was enhanced by the short, pixie-like *do* that emerged after her hair was styled, gradually lessening Bianca's and Alexia's concerns. The girls immediately began envisioning themselves with a short cut as they pulled their own hair back and away from their faces, checking to see how it looked.

Alexia kept chanting the word *trendsetter* as if it were a mantra while she stared intensely at her reflection in the mirror. It was obvious she was trying to psych herself out!

Casey did his part, too, telling them stories about Callie's victories against the farmhands in an effort to take their minds off the threatening sound of Evie's scissors.

Alexia went next, finding her inner strength at an all time high. So much of her ego was tied to her beauty that even the smallest change could trigger a panic attack. The first snip of the scissors still made her wince, however, and she couldn't stomach watching the procedure as Evie chopped away. It was a painful process, but in the end, she agreed that her bone structure appeared more striking and her eyes were suddenly the focal point of her face, more noticeable now then they ever were.

Whew! Two down, one to go! Callie was on a roll, and it was Bianca's turn at bat.

"Just give me a standard issue buzz cut," Bianca instructed, as she plopped into Evie's chair. "You know, like the one Demi Moore did on herself in *G.I. Jane.*"

Alexia gasped out loud, Danielle was horrified, and Evie looked to Callie for direction. She had no clue that Bianca was teasing, and in her mind shearing that thick, wavy Italian hair would be a sin. But Callie knew Bianca would never do such a foolish thing without being paid a fortune. Besides, her hair was one of her best features and there was no way in the world she would part with it all!

"Hmm, how about a Mohawk instead," Callie suggested, feeding the frenzy. "You could spike it up and color it to match your clothes!"

"Callie!" Alexia burst out, convinced that she and Bianca had both lost their minds.

"No!" Danielle wailed, as if she was watching a Wes Craven horror flick and the victim was about to unlock the door for the serial killer.

"Um…not a bad idea," Bianca answered, paying close attention to the expressions on her friends' faces. But as Evie moved closer with the scissors in hand and a psycho look in her eyes, Bianca caved and blurted out, "You know I'm just kidding, don't you?" She turned to Callie with urgency. "TELL her I'm kidding!"

"Oh all right," Callie laughed. She winked at Evie. "Leave at least an inch!"

The girls were still in shock when they passed the FedEx truck on their way back to the farm, but Callie kept reminding them it was for a good cause in an attempt to soften the blow.

When they pulled into the driveway, Roy was already loading the last of Callie's luggage into the bed of his monster truck. The girls skulked into the farmhouse, realizing just how devastating it must be for kids with permanent hair loss. They knew they were going to be teased by the girls at school until *the look* caught on, and none of them wanted to face Kaitlin or any of her followers without the support of the others. By themselves, they were targets—in a group they were a force of nature!

Callie ran upstairs to change her clothes. And for the first time in days, she actually had to think about what to wear. She couldn't decide whether to combine the Gucci with the Prada or the Versace with the Manolos. The stress of the decision was beginning to get to her and she briefly considered traveling in her Levi's and flannel shirt before realizing the girls would make her ride in the baggage compartment if she did! So after selecting the perfect outfit, she carefully folded and tucked her *fashion by Hank* into a chest of drawers, preserving them for her next visit. And with one last look around the room—in addition to a mental checklist of her appearance in front of the mirror—it was time to say goodbye. She packed a few stray articles of makeup into her cosmetic bag and moved downstairs without her customary bounce.

Elsa and Johan were waiting for her in the living room, chatting with Casey and the girls. Callie paused in the doorway for a moment, checking out the action and making sure that Casey noticed her more stylish appearance. When his eyes lit up, she moved to the arm of Johan's chair and leaned in toward him, resting her head upon his shoulder. "It's time, Opa," she said with sadness in her voice.

The girls were more than ready to leave and jumped to their feet without hesitation. Elsa and Johan, on the other hand, would have given anything to delay the departure. They reluctantly stood and walked toward the door where Callie handed Elsa yet another slip of paper that contained her cell phone number, her dormitory number, and her email address. She grabbed her purse and cosmetic bag and promised to call later that evening to let them know that she had arrived safely.

Everything truly important to Elsa and Johan rested with their granddaughter, in both their business and their family name. Callie was all they had and it wasn't easy letting her go, even for a brief time. Elsa wiped a tear from her eye as Johan stood with his arm around her waist. They knew that Callie would be back, but oh, how they were going to miss being a part of her everyday life.

Alexia, Bianca, and Danielle waited until Elsa and Johan were occupied with Callie before they walked past the family. They mumbled quick goodbyes as they passed, not really caring if their sentiments were acknowledged or not.

The girls were still uncomfortable with their newly cropped hairstyles and preferred not to be noticed until consulting their own stylists back in the city. They were able to maintain some semblance of dignity while not looking anyone straight in the face as they grabbed their belongings. In their eyes, Callie's version of *Utopia ala Wisconsin* had definite drawbacks.

Roy was chosen as their designated driver and he didn't appear to like the assignment. But then again, Roy didn't appear to like anything—especially if it had to do with Callie. That made it easier for the girls to get past him without any pretense of politeness or a second look. They were just thankful no one at school could see them...not just yet.

Callie ignored her friends, knowing that they would eventually adapt and even manage to use the situation to their advantage. She had the entire trip home to stroke their egos. And besides, Zoey would be there to distract them with stories of her latest photo shoot.

She watched, as the girls skulked outside, then turned back to her grandparents for what seemed like the umpteenth hug and kiss. Their emotion was starting to get to her, and before it became too overwhelming, she turned her attention to Casey.

In an effort to ease the tension, she shifted the topic away from herself. "Take care of her for me."

"I will," he answered, needing no explanation as to who she meant.

"And be sure to give her a hard time. She likes that, you know." Callie wasn't quite done giving orders.

"Yeah, I know."

"And don't..."

Casey placed his finger against her lips and stared into her eyes. "You're breaking my heart, City girl."

A tingling sensation raced through Callie's body. She smiled and took a deep breath. "Then I guess I'll just have to come back."

"Is that a threat?" Casey asked with mock alarm in his voice.

"Oh no, Farm boy, that's a promise!"

And as the truck pulled away from the farmhouse, Callie was consumed in thought. She stared back at the figures standing on the porch and was amazed at how much they had come to mean to her. She loved Deer Creek—her roots were there. And even though it was worlds apart from what she was used to, she finally had a sense of family and a real place to call home!

About the Author

Sylvia Hysen, an Associate Producer, screenplay writer and first-time novelist wrote *A Very Dairy Christmas*, the novel, as an adaptation of her award-winning screenplay of the same title. Born in Frankfurt, Germany and raised in Las Vegas, Nevada, she graduated with a film degree from California State University, Northridge and has worked in the entertainment industry since the late 1980's.

Sylvia resides in Southern California with her husband of twenty-one years, her two teenaged children, and her menagerie of pets.

Acknowledgements

I couldn't have written a story about family relationships without drawing from my own experiences, so I have to thank my entire family, immediate and extended, for being the main source of inspiration, not too mention, a constant source of amusement! Mark, my Knight in Shining Armor, you're my nomination for Father of the Millennium! I'm so lucky to have found you, and I'm grateful for all the years we've shared. Britt, my little trendsetter, without your constant scrutiny and knowledge of pop culture, I could have easily fallen into the category of "Magoo". Fortunately, you didn't allow that to happen, and for that, I will forever be in your debt. Jeremy, my up and coming Arliss, you defy the notion of unattainable, and it is through your tenacity and perseverance that I have learned the true meaning of the phrase "the squeaky wheel". There is nothing wrong with setting goals and achieving them! Don't let anyone tell you differently. To my new friend Marie, I humbly thank you. Your suggestions were invaluable and your patience, a virtue. You're a credit to single mothers everywhere and an inspiration to women starting over again! Stay the course. And finally, to my mother, thank you for sharing the stories of our ancestry, for without them, this story would have never been possible.

Help spread the word...

I first heard of Locks of Love many years ago traveling home from a business meeting in a torrential rain. It was night time and my windshield wipers could barely keep up with the downpour. I'll never forget that evening. I was listening to a story on the radio about a little girl with cancer that had lost her hair due to extensive chemotherapy treatments. Now normally, this would have been a depressing report; however, the news suddenly took a turn for the better. You see, the child had just received a prosthetic hair piece from a newly formed charitable organization that recycled donated ponytails. The story touched my heart, and as most writers do, I kept it in the back of my mind for future reference. So when I outlined the plot to *A Very Dairy Christmas*, I found incorporating the idea simply irresistible. Imagine the good that could come from exposing young adults to the concept of selfless giving! Eighty percent of all donated ponytails are from those under the age of eighteen. But it wasn't until I met with Locks of Love founder, Madonna Coffman, back in 2003 that I was made aware of her plight. That is, informing the 2 million financially disadvantaged children suffering from temporary and permanent medical hair loss that her program exists and is ready to help.

Unfortunately, the media only gravitates to the donation side of the process and does little to spread the word about the true goals of the organization. Now, it takes six to ten ponytails, 10-12" long, to make just one hair piece, so obviously, donations are a critical element in the process.

However, to date, 1,000 prosthetic wigs have been produced since the organization's inception back in 1997. But this number represents only a handful of the children suffering from alopecia areata (an autoimmune disorder), treatments from cancer, burns, injury, trichotillomania and several other genetic disorders. What's worse, is that the small percentage of beneficiaries isn't due to a lack of funding or lack of hair donations. It's because the process of locating disadvantaged children isn't nearly as good for the ratings as witnessing the excruciating act of someone cutting years of hair growth!

Therefore, I appeal to you as parents, community leaders, educators, and students to help bring back a sense of normalcy to those children who are desperate to regain their dignity and self-confidence. The resources are there. They just need to be tapped! You can help by simply *spreading the word*.

Respectfully,

Sylvia Hysen

Please direct all communications, prospective candidates, and donations to:

Locks of Love
2925 10th Avenue North
Suite 102
Lake Worth, FL 33461
Phone: (561) 963-1677
Toll Free: (888) 896-1588
www.locksoflove.org

C'mon back for
A Very Dairy Summer
coming soon!